SPY THY NEIGHBOR

The Story of Hunter Kane

SHANDI BOYES

ALSO BY SHANDI BOYES

Denotes Standalone Books

Perception Series

Saving Noah *

Fighting Jacob *

Taming Nick *

Redeeming Slater *

Saving Emily

Wrapped Up with Rise Up

Protecting Nicole *

Enigma

Enigma

Unraveling an Enigma

Enigma The Mystery Unmasked

Enigma: The Final Chapter

Beneath The Secrets

Beneath The Sheets

Spy Thy Neighbor *

The Opposite Effect *

I Married a Mob Boss *

Second Shot *

The Way We Are

The Way We Were

Sugar and Spice *

Lady In Waiting

Man in Queue

Couple on Hold

Enigma: The Wedding

Silent Vigilante

Hushed Guardian

Quiet Protector

Enigma: An Isaac Retelling

Twisted Lies *

Bound Series

Chains

Links

Bound

Restrain

The Misfits *

Nanny Dispute *

Russian Mob Chronicles

Nikolai: A Mafia Prince Romance

Nikolai: Taking Back What's Mine

Nikolai: What's Left of Me

Nikolai: Mine to Protect

Asher: My Russian Revenge *

Nikolai: Through the Devil's Eyes

<u>Trey</u> *

<u>The Italian Cartel</u>

Dimitri

Roxanne

Reign

Mafia Ties (Novella)

Maddox

Demi

Ox

Rocco *

Clover *

Smith *

<u>RomCom Standalones</u>

Just Playin' *

<u>Ain't Happenin'</u> *

<u>The Drop Zone</u> *

Very Unlikely *

False Start *

<u>Short Stories - Newsletter Downloads</u>

Christmas Trio *

Falling For A Stranger *

<u>One Night Only Series</u>

Hotshot Boss *

Hotshot Neighbor *

<u>The Bobrov Bratva Series</u>

Wicked Intentions *

Sinful Intentions *

Devious Intentions *

Deadly Intentions *

DEDICATION

My mum!
Thanks for all your help!
Shandi xx

CHAPTER ONE

"*Holy* mackerel! Is she an Olympic gymnast?" I mumble to myself while chewing on the end of my pencil with teeth marks gnawed along the edge. "Now that just looks painful."

I wasn't aware you could bend like that without distorting at least one muscle in your body. I wonder if she's a contortionist because that's not natural. No woman should be able to bend like that.

I certainly can't bend like that.

After straying my eyes away from the sweat-producing visual in front of me, I add a few key pointers on the brunette's back-breaking position to my extensively documented notepad.

My neighbor, whom I've nicknamed Archer, has been entertaining his most recent guest for the past hour and a half. By entertaining, I mean he's undertaken sheet-clenching, core-clustering, screaming-at-the-top-of-her-lungs sexual activities.

This type of entertaining is nothing new for Archer. He has a new bed companion a minimum of three to four times a week. He doesn't seem to have a preference for his bed-hopping friends.

Blonde, brunette, Asian, African American, Caucasian, it doesn't matter to him. The only preference he seems to have is 'the louder they scream, the better.'

Although the women I've seen him with are undoubtedly gorgeous, they don't have an intellectual bone in their entire body.

Well, that's my personal assumption.

Considering I've never met my mysterious neighbor or his bevy of bed companions, I can't give a fair opinion on the capacity of their brain power. So, instead, I'm callously judging a book by its cover because even with me knowing every precise detail of Archer's well-formed physique, we are perfect strangers.

But even being a stranger, I still know Archer very well. It's not just the rigid panels of his stomach that carve into his formidable V muscle, the way the veins in his arms pulse during exertive activities, or how his sixth ab muscle is slightly larger than the other five that I can divulge to you. I can also tell you what his face looks like in the middle of ecstasy, how he always gets a smear of peanut butter on his top lip every time he eats three pieces of toast for breakfast, and that he doesn't drink coffee or tea.

How do I know this if we've never met?

I've been stalking him relentlessly over the past six weeks.

My mysterious bearded neighbor lives in a glass house perched on the edge of Bronte's Peak. With his bathroom the only room finished with sturdy walls, every detail of his life is on display for all to see. Like one big performance for the prying eyes of strangers— for people like me.

I was desperate, on the verge of a nervous breakdown, and incredibly close to missing an important deadline when I spotted Archer for the first time.

Ever since that night, my life changed...

I've been staring at the screen of my Mac Notebook for three hours straight. The incessant blink of the cursor on a blank white page has my nerves rattled and my conundrum intensifying. I have a deadline. A very strict deadline. Three months are all that remain for me to pen a three hundred and sixty-five-page document.

With fingers that type at the speed of lightning and more free time on my hands than I've ever had, you'd assume the deadline will be an easy feat. It isn't. I'm suffering from the worst case of writer's block I've ever experienced. Not just writer's block. Writer's. Block. *I haven't penned a single word in over a month. Not even something as simple as a grocery list. But I have no choice. I must finish my novel.*

Writing is my bread and butter. It is my sole source of income. Without it, I'll soon be a pauper who can't afford the luxury of flying over to the other side of the country to a beachside cottage for a writing vacation. If I don't pen my latest creation, I'll lose contracts well into the six figures and royalty payments even more lucrative than that. So, no matter how much my heart is decimated into tiny shreds, and I want to live in the shadow of a dark cloud, I must write a bestselling romance novel. It isn't an option. It is a requirement.

I'm so desperate, I'll happily accept a bad rendition of the manuscript I wrote as a senior in high school. Heck, I will even accept the childish novel I penned on my fascination with Joseph Gordon-Levitt, star of 3rd Rock from the Sun. *It might be rubbish, but it was something, and I have nothing. My brain is blank.*

"Words? What are words?" are the only phrases flowing through my overworked brain.

Once another hour ticks by, my usually calm composure cracks. With a grunt, I push away from my makeshift desk, stand from my old leather chair, and start pacing.

Pacing is never a good thing. If you ever see me pacing, I suggest you run far far away from me. I only pace when I'm on the verge of snapping or sitting dangerously on the edge of normality.

And that is precisely where I am tonight.

I've reached breaking point.

With a hard yank on my laptop, I pull its charging cord out of the power plug and bolt down the wooden steps. My heart thrashes faster with every thump of my feet on the rickety old stairwell. I trudge through the impec-

cably clean kitchen and living area. It's spotlessly clean since I have the obsessive habit of scrubbing surfaces until they sparkle when I'm seeking writing inspiration.

I grasp my laptop for near death, strangling it as it has done to my creativity. A blast of humid, sticky air momentarily distracts my pursuit of introducing my laptop to the cruel, wordless world I am a part of. The smell of a fall night filters through my nose, lightening my senses as the refreshing scent of salt and sand from the beautiful, blue-watered beach below calms some of the rage boiling my blood.

I raise my arm into the air, ready to send my laptop and its annoying blinking cursor into the pitch-dark ocean. My throw suspends mid-air when a ragged scream shrills through my ears.

The glass-shattering squeal is so ear-piercingly loud, it rattles through my hand, loosening my death-tight grip on the laptop. I fumble, curse, then fumble some more when my much-loved electronic device slips from my hold and plummets to the ground.

My teeth grit when my laptop crashes onto the stained wooden deck with an almighty thud.

While bending down to survey the damage inflicted on my beloved Mac, an even more riveting sight enters my peripheral vision. My throat becomes scratchy, and a surge of excitement dashes through me when my eyes lock in on a couple in a lust-filled lovemaking session.

Heat inflames my cheeks as I snap my gaze to the ground, beyond mortified that my temper tantrum has interrupted their intimate gathering.

With my wide gaze locked on the wooden floorboards, I gather up the broken pieces of my laptop with the hope I can salvage some of the unpublished manuscripts from the hard drive.

My pulse quickens when the female's cries of ecstasy intensify partway through my scavenger hunt. Although I can't see the woman's face, her ear-piercing screams tell me she's close to climax.

I'm not proud to admit this, but it's been a while since I've heard anything remotely like the pleasurable groans seeping from her lips.

Actually, I don't ever recall hearing those noises come from my mouth.

While vainly endeavoring to keep my focus on the black night sky with *its sprinkling of stars peeking out from the darkness of storm clouds. I step back until my sweater-covered torso connects with the outer wall of my bungalow. My heart is wildly racing, and my body is covered in a dense layer of sweat. It is reacting the same way it did when my research for erotic novels found me visiting websites much steamier than the sweet young-adult romance I am accustomed to writing.*

I turn my torso and sneakily slip through the glass sliding door I'd only exited mere seconds ago. I'm almost in the clear, then my quick steps halt when I catch the quickest glimpse of a perfectly round, muscular, booty-luscious, drool-over-for-months male ass.

I'm not lying when I say it is the most spectacular male ass I've ever seen.

My eyes bulge as the moisture accumulating on my skin moves to a much lower region of my body.

I should look away.

I should respect my neighbor's privacy.

But I'm in such awe of the fluidity of his movements I can't force my eyes away.

I've never witnessed anything so primal, raw, and awe-inspiring...

I used to watch Archer for a few minutes each night. Then, as the days crept on, my stalker obsession grew. If I'm not watching Archer, he invades my thoughts—always—even while I'm sleeping.

This will make me sound like the character Glenn Close played in *Fatal Attraction*, but I assure you I am not a psychopath. I'm perfectly sane.

Well, I was until I traveled to the other side of the country and started a slight obsession with my tattoo-covered neighbor. But my fascination isn't what you think. I'm not some crazy stalker who wants to sink my claws into Archer and never let go. I don't wish ill harm to his female companions, nor am I secretly plotting their demise.

I stalk him as if he's my savior.

My inspiration.

My Yoko Ono of the book-writing world.

He's my current series alpha male book boyfriend.

Without him and his busty bevy of companions, I'd still be staring at the blinking cursor on the blank screen of my monitor, praying for a string of words to magically appear. I would have never penned half of my latest, no doubt, *New York Times* best-selling novel.

The way Archer moves his hips with such fluidity and ease, how every muscle in his body ensures his female companions' cries of ecstasy are heard over the crashing of waves in the distance, and the way his perfect Adonis ass constricts and releases with each precise thrust has inspired magic.

Pure book alpha male magic that's flowing onto the pages more quickly than I can write them.

My editor is in love with the first one hundred pages of edits she has completed. My agent is using snippets of my newly created masterpiece to secure book spotlights on major television programs for the three months following my scheduled release, and my publisher and I are in negotiations about a new three-book deal on the intriguing life of Archer Boyd—my mystery neighbor's pseudonym I created.

A grin curls on my lips when I lock my eyes back on Archer. His nickname is highly fitting, considering how well he's had his latest companion arched over his couch the last twenty minutes. His moves should defy physics, but somehow, he makes it look easy.

I stop taking dot points of his impressive technique when my cell phone dings with an incoming text. After drifting my eyes back to Archer and his companion and taking note that their romp has moved from the couch to the fur rug in front of the roaring fire in the living room, I set down my pencil and pad onto the side table, then move into the kitchen to grab my phone.

A grin curls on my lips when I spot who the message is from.

PEPPER:

Did you get the package?

I chuckle so loud, I snort.

ME:

Yep! I'm using it right now.

That's a lie. I opened her package the instant it arrived, but it's been sitting on the wooden bench near the entryway door for the past three days.

After quickly checking Archer's status, I devote my attention back to my phone.

PEPPER:

Are you shitting me? Does it work? Hook a girl up with some army man porn!

ME:

Army porn??

PEPPER:

Yeah, army porn. Any images you take with the night vision lens will be green, but from what you've been describing, I'll happily accept Archer in any color I can get him.

I giggle even louder than earlier. Pepper is my best friend. We've been friends since preschool. Her real name is Quinn, but everyone calls her Pepper after her disastrous karaoke rendition of the Salt-N-Pepa song "Shoop" at my twenty-first birthday party four years ago. Ever since that drunken night, Pepper's nickname has stuck.

ME:

No images. It's against the law to photograph people without their consent. Isn't it?

PEPPER:

And stalking them for the past several weeks is entirely legal?

I grimace.

ME:

True…

My breath hitches when I raise my eyes back to Archer and discover he's vanished from the large living room at the back of his residence.

ME:

BRB. My target has slipped the net.

PEPPER:

Go get him, Tiger!

ME:

Roar!!

Laughing, I place my phone onto the kitchen counter then tiptoe closer to the window. I have the shades open, but all the lights in the three-bedroom rented wooden bungalow are switched off. I'd hate for Archer to catch me spying on him before I've finished penning the first draft.

When I fail to locate Archer within his house, I head for the back deck. I've noticed over the past few weeks that he has a slight fascination with outdoor activities.

The coolness of a late fall night blasts my face when I step onto the patio's wooden deck, but my temperature rises instead of plummeting. The hunch I was running with is accurate. Archer and his companion have taken their lusty twist to a more scenic location. Although, I have no clue why. Neither of them are looking at the spectacular scenery.

Even in the darkness of the night, I can recall the marvelous views that distracted me from my writing goals for the first four days after I arrived here. Crystal blue waters, pristine white beaches, and little pockets of caves hidden throughout like treasured gems make Bronte's Peak a spectacular destination.

It's so beautiful that millions of tourists invade its pristine beaches at all times of the year. Luckily for me, the beach below is for the private residents who live in this elite gated community.

That reason alone was why I chose to rent this bungalow. I wanted seclusion and privacy. My plan had been to hide away from the world. No social media, no television, and no mobile devices to distract me as I finish my fourth book in a five-book series.

My well-thought plan lasted a total of three hours.

Thank God I stumbled upon Archer. Otherwise, I have no clue where I'd be right now.

The night I first spotted him, I sat down and scribbled relentlessly on an old notepad I found in the kitchen drawer. I'd always been an electronics girl when it came to writing, even jotting down book ideas on my iPhone while standing in the line at the bank, but with words flowing from my brain faster than my hands could write them, I couldn't risk the chance of losing my inspiration since my Mac was broken.

I had to get every word down while they were fresh, and thus began the fictional story of Archer Boyd—an alpha male billionaire who lives in a crystal house.

Although I've been using my backup laptop for the past five weeks, my notes and sketches on Archer have continued as they did the first night I spied on him. Such as now, when Archer curls his female companion's torso over the glass railing of his back patio, I sketch their position in my trusty notepad.

Surprisingly, his companion's cries of pleasure are only just heard over the scribbling of pencil to paper. Usually, I can't hear my pulse over the volume of his date's squeals.

A smile tugs at my lips when I finish my rendition of Archer and his companion's lust-filled pose. To call this piece 'art' would be a grave injustice to the art community. It's horrific. Many people class writing as an artistic craft, but you can be safely assured it's the *only* creative bone I have in my body. My sketch looks more like two dogs having fun at the local dog park than the romance novel cover I was aiming for.

My immature giggle dampens when a disappointed moan jingles through my ears. I've not once heard that type of response from one of Archer's companions. Even with him kicking them out immediately after the deed has been done, displeasure has never been voiced.

When I raise my eyes from my notepad, I discover the cause of the brunette's devastated cry. Archer is no longer tangled in a mind-hazing adult-only game of *Twister*. He's angrily storming down the glass stairs and stomping across the small patch of sand that divides our patios.

Oh crap!

I plaster my back to the outer wall of my cabin, cowardly trying to hide. I don't know why I bother. From the expression crossing Archer's face and the white-hot glare beaming from his eyes, I have no doubt he has spotted me spying on him.

If I were smart, I'd scurry into my cabin, lock the doors, and book the first flight home. Unfortunately, my brain has never been able to think on the spot. So instead of scurrying, I remain glued to the glass door, watching Archer's quickly advancing form span the distance between us.

The veins in my neck pulsate when I catch sight of his... umm... package that's generally hidden from view in numerous female crevices. Even though I've been watching him for weeks, I've never seen him this up-close and personal. The hardness of his cock is as firm as his fists are clenched, and it's an even more spectacular view than I've witnessed from a distance.

My throat dries when Archer stops in front of me. His hasty movements stir up an intoxicating smell of salt and sweat-slicked skin, accelerating my pulse. I'm taken aback when my eyes float up from the hairless ridges of his tattooed torso to his face. I've always imagined his eyes were light brown, so I'm somewhat surprised by their unique dark-blue coloring.

His heavy-hooded gaze roams over my face, absorbing the blush blooming on my cheeks before locking in on my wide grayish-blue eyes. "Are you only a voyeur, or do you also participate?" he asks with his lusty eyes burning into mine.

Even in the intense circumstances of our meeting, a dash of euphoria pumps through my veins from the husky roughness of his voice. It reminds me of Tom Hiddleston—rough and gritty but as smooth as chocolate.

Archer stares at me with his brow bowed high, reminding me that I've failed to answer him.

"Am I a what?" The shakiness of my voice makes it more seductive than normal.

My already wildly beating heart hastens even more when a smirk tugs on Archer's lips. "Are you a voyeur?" he repeats.

I shrug, truly unsure. "I don't know what that is." My voice is as weak as my reply.

My body temperature rises as the battle to keep my eyes on Archer's face moves into dangerous territory. Even standing in the briskness of a fall night, wearing nothing but a cocky grin, the thickness of his cock hasn't subsided a bit. If anything, it's become firmer.

He is primed and ready to go.

I snap my eyes up from his impressively large cock to his face when he advises, "A voyeur is a person who gets sexual satisfaction from watching others have sex." He's not the slightest bit embarrassed he's explaining a sexual term to a virtual stranger. "Do you only watch people have sex, or do you enjoy participating as well?"

You'd think his question would have me blushing like a naïve virgin, but it doesn't. I've watched him enough the past six weeks that he's more like a close acquaintance than a stranger. Second only to Pepper, he's one of my dearest friends—even without me knowing his real name.

Okay, Paige, I think it's time to seek professional help.

When Archer continues staring, I swallow to relieve my parched throat before saying, "I participate too."

Holy crab cakes, I can't believe I openly admitted I've been watching him.

Any concern about him calling the police to report me for stalking fades when a brash grin etches on his kiss-swollen mouth. He has an outrageously gorgeous smile. It is almost as breathtaking as his cock—which is ripped from my vision when he pivots on his heels and stalks back down the stairs without another word seeping from his lips.

When he reaches the bottom step, he cranks his neck and stares me straight in the eyes. "Are you *coming?*" His tone couldn't be laced with more sexual innuendo if he tried.

I remain frozen like a statue, more confused than ever. "Coming where exactly?"

Now I'm blushing like an idiot.

My heart thrashes against my ribs when Archer replies with a salacious grin, "To join us." He nudges his head to the brunette splayed over the patio railing, patiently awaiting his return during the 'us' part of his reply.

My eyes pop out of my head as my throat works hard to swallow, then I shake my head. Although I've been extremely deviant the past six weeks watching him in a range of lust-driven exchanges, I'm not adventurous enough to participate in a threesome.

No way in hell.

Archer's blazing eyes scorch my skin when he rakes them up my body. He drags them from my French-tipped toenails, past the frilled edges of my mid-thigh denim shorts, to the white knitted one-shoulder sweater. When his heavy-lidded eyes lock with mine, my breath hitches. This is the first time in six weeks I've spotted disappointment in his candid eyes. "If you change your mind, you know where to find me."

After a brazen wink, he continues his journey.

CHAPTER TWO

The instant Archer steps foot on his glass and steel patio, I slip into the bungalow. As my heart hammers my ribs, I keep my eyes glued to my bare feet scuttling across the wood floors. The shake of my hand runs up my arm when I yank on the blinds covering the large window spanning the living room. When my harsh pull on the cord causes the mechanism to lock into place, a quiet squeal emits from my lips.

I can't hide my shameful face from the world if I can't get the damn blind to slot into place.

After a few inaudible swear words and a couple of gentle tugs, the blind finally lowers into position, concealing Archer and the busty brunette from my view.

After dashing into the kitchen, I snatch my phone off the counter, then scurry into the makeshift writing cave I created in a room in the upstairs attic. While taking the stairs two steps at a time, I log into Skype and connect to Pepper's account.

"Wow, that's an all-time low for Archer. I don't think you've ever called me within half an hour before," Pepper says down the line, not bothering to issue a greeting.

"He busted me spying on him," I confess with a grimace.

Pepper's pupils enlarge to the size of dinner plates as her mouth gapes. "During..." She stops speaking, allowing the shocked expression on her face to ask the question her mouth is failing to produce.

"Yep! Right in the middle of the deed," I respond while entering the darkness of my writing cave. The trembling of my heart is apparent in my tone.

After flicking on an overhead light, I stroll to my old, cracked leather chair stored behind an even more outdated desk.

"Are you sure he saw you? Maybe he was just *peering* in your direction?" Pepper asks, her tone laced with humor.

A massive creak bounces around the small, dingy space when I slump into my old writing chair. "I'm certain he busted me." I spin my office chair around to look at the extensive collection of notes and sketches I have of Archer taped around my office space. "He didn't just bust me, Pepper, he walked over and invited me to join him."

My attention turns from the inaccurate description of Archer's eyes I have in his profile to my phone's screen when Pepper's loud chuckle thunders down the line. She's laughing so hard her face is nothing but a blur as she rolls around on her bed in her apartment.

I huff at her absurdity before standing from my chair and heading to the storyboard on my right. "He asked if I was a voyeur," I inform her while scrubbing out the light brown coloring of his eyes and switching it to a murky blue.

When Pepper's laughter settles, she wipes under her hazel eyes, removing her cackling-induced tearstains. "Technically, you *are* a voyeur, Paige."

My eyes narrow into thin slits.

"You've been watching a man sleep with a range of women over a six-week period. If that isn't voyeurism, then I'm Mother Teresa," she argues, her words brittle with laughter. When I roll my eyes, she inches closer to the screen. "Did you just roll your eyes at me?" Her tone switches from playful to a deep, commanding voice. "If you roll your eyes at me one more time, young lady, I'll take you over my knee and spank you until you beg me to stop."

My laugh bounces off the sea-scented walls. "You've been reading my manuscript."

I sent Pepper the first half of my draft two days ago, hoping she'd beta read it for me to ensure the storyline was heading in the right direction. I'm surprised she's already begun reading it. Normally, she does anything in her power to avoid perusing my rough drafts. Once, she even faked having pancreatitis—hospital stay and all—just to get out of reading my months of hard work.

It isn't that she doesn't enjoy reading, she just prefers smut and erotic novels, not clean young- adult-only reads.

Pepper waggles her brows and nods. "Damn, Paige, when you said you were switching your genre from young adult to steamy romance, I didn't think you'd pull it off."

I stick out my tongue and roll my eyes again.

Pepper cocks her brow high into her rich, chocolate-brown locks. "Come on. The hotness scale of your last three novels was pathetic. I've seen kindergarten kids get more action than your characters did."

Even though my ego is stung by her catty remark, a smile pulls at my lips. I'll be the first to admit I've never felt comfortable adding sex scenes to my storyline.

Don't take my admission the wrong way. I lost my V card only a few weeks after my eighteenth birthday. Unfortunately, it was with the same guy who stabbed my heart with a spear gun twelve weeks ago. The same guy who was the cause of my decision to fly to the other side of the country.

Trying to ignore the twisted mess of confusion in my heart, I flop onto my office chair and spin around to face my outdated laptop screen. Stream upon stream of beautiful words reflect back at me. Although Riley tore my heart out of my chest, I'm still grateful he was a part of my life. If it weren't for him, I would have never stumbled upon Archer.

I have no doubt the words displayed in front of me are pure brilliance, an absolute best seller. That would have *never* happened without Riley, my first high school boyfriend, my one and only sexual conquest, and, until three months ago, my fiancé.

My focus returns to my phone screen when Pepper taps her finger on her iPad speaker, dragging me from my dreary thoughts with a loud doink. "Oh, you're still there. You went all stiff and robotic. I wasn't sure if it was a glitch or if you let that *asshole* invade your thoughts again."

Other than huffing softly, I remain quiet. I can't argue with Pepper. She knows me well enough to know where my mind strayed. We've been friends since the day we started preschool, and at times, I swear, she knows me better than I know myself.

Pepper adjusts her position, folding her legs under her bottom before lifting her mischief-filled eyes to me. "Why are you spending your Thursday night thinking about he-whose-name-will-never-be-spoken-of-again when Mr. I'm-going-to-spank-your-ass-until-you-beg-for-mercy offered you a chance to join him for a night of crazy monkey sex? I know what opportunity I'd be taking, and it most certainly wouldn't be recalling memories that aren't worth rehashing."

"It isn't that simple, Quinn." I sink deeper into my chair. "Riley and I were together for nearly seven years. I can't just simply forget him and jump into bed with a random stranger."

"Uh, yeah, you can," she responds with a brisk nod. "And don't think pulling out my real name will change the facts. Riley is an *asshole*. You deserve ten times better than he could ever give you. I can see it. Everyone in our hometown can see it. The only person who doesn't see it is you, Paige." She leans in closer to the monitor so her head engulfs the entire screen. "I love you, Sweet Pea, but it's time for this momma bear to bring out the big guns."

A grin curls on my lips, loving her use of our favorable nicknames.

"You need to get your skinny derriere off that hideous writing chair you dragged across the country, march your pasty white butt over to the Adonis-assed male specimen living next door, and climb aboard his sex train for the ride of your life. You're well overdue to cash in your earth-shattering climax ticket." Any pain festering in my heart eases from the playfulness in her tone. Pepper can always bring me back from the ledge.

"I love you, Pepper." My tone relays the truth of my statement.

"I know you do. But right now, I only want to see your back end walking away from me."

I screw up my nose. "I can't. Even if I wanted to ride Archer's sex train all the way to climax station, he isn't alone. His brunette friend has been happily keeping the neighborhood awake the past two hours."

"And? What's wrong with that?" Pepper interrupts with her brow arched high.

My heart beats triple time. "I could never do... *that*."

"It's called a threesome, Paige. Look it up the next time you're googling research for your *steamy* romance novel."

A set of heavy lines groove into my forehead. "Whatever," I scowl. "I'm writing steamy contemporary romance, not ménage. My readers don't want to read about my heroines doing the deed with other people. They want a loving, heartfelt connection crammed with the warm and fuzzies."

Pepper gags. "No, they don't. They want mind-hazing, multi-climaxing, sheet-clawing, can't-walk-straight-for-days sex! Trust me, if you're going to dip your toes into this genre, you need to go in deep. Hard-cock-thrusting-to-the-brim deep."

I roll my eyes and shake my head. Pepper's arched brow becomes lost in her dead-straight hair as she stares at me, daring me to negate her claim. Everything she's saying is true. Steamy contemporary romance readers want steam—it's the whole reason they pick that genre. But I don't necessarily believe I have to practice what I preach. I've never stepped foot in an ice hockey rink, but I penned a very sweet hockey romance two years ago that's still selling well today.

My eyes drift between the numerous notes pinned to the wall about Archer. "Even without having a bucketload of sexual experience, I have enough encounters between Archer and his female companions to pen *at least* ten steamy novels."

"It's not the same," argues Pepper with a brisk shake of her head. "Not even close."

"I thought you liked the first half of my draft?"

"I didn't like it," she replies, still shaking her head.

My heart slithers into my gut.

"I f'ing *loved* it! Why? Because you haven't reached the sex scenes yet. You're at the crazy flirty stage every reader loves devouring." Her lips quirk. "But I will admit, you have me hooked. I'm dying to know who will bring Archer to his knees."

I giggle, loving the eagerness in her voice. "I'm still working on the final scene. I'm not exactly sure how it will end for Archer just yet."

Normally, I plot the entire storyline before I commence writing the first chapter, but even with more notes than I've ever compiled for a novel, the second half of Archer's story is void of an ending.

"Maybe you could go through my notes and help me choose an ending?"

"I don't need to see your notes. Archer falls head over heels in love with a novelist named Paige, and they have numerous Kindle-melting sex scenes. He then uses his endless bank balance to pay for Paige's wannabe-actress best friend to star in her own movie. Then they all live happily ever after in a lust-driven relationship filled with multiple orgasms and sheet-clawing sex. The end."

My eyes bug. "We all live happily ever after *together?*"

"No," Pepper interrupts dramatically. "Archer and Paige live happily ever after. Pepper becomes famous and has sex with cabana boys while holidaying in the Caribbean six months out of the year."

I giggle. "I'm glad to hear your cabana-boy infatuation won't end when you become famous."

"There's no possibility my cabana-boy fascination will *ever* end. Have you seen the cabana boys at some of the resorts? My god!"

I laugh even louder, but it isn't strong enough to miss gravel crunching under tires. "Archer is on the move. I'll call you back," I say into the screen.

"No," Pepper squeals before I have the chance to disconnect the call. "Just the quickest glimpse. Please," she shamefully begs. "Then I can make sure you're describing him right."

I run my teeth over my bottom lip while I contemplate her suggestion. She's been begging me relentlessly for the past six weeks to snap a sneaky picture of Archer. I've denied every one of her requests. I don't know why, but photographing Archer seems like it would be crossing the line I drew in the sand to ensure my stalker fixation with him didn't become manic.

Like stalking someone is sane to begin with.

After a beat, I say, "Okay, but I don't have much zoom power on my iPhone."

"It's fine. I'll grab my glasses," Pepper retorts, giggling.

While she searches her bedroom for her glasses, I tiptoe to the only window in my writing cave. The beat of my heart kicks up the closer I get to the small arched opening. I've never considered writing suspense novels, but the range of emotions I've been experiencing the past six weeks while stalking Archer has me contemplating penning something suspenseful and mysterious.

When I reach the window, I pull back the lace curtain and peer down at the driveway in front of Archer's house. His brunette companion is dressed back in her tight black pencil skirt and fire-red satin blouse, and her arms are flung around Archer's shoulders. An odd feeling hits me hard and fast when I notice she's nuzzling his neck. Considering what they were doing only moments ago, I shouldn't find a goodbye cuddle so upsetting.

"Perhaps red week is closer than I thought." After shrugging off my comment, I return my focus to Archer. The further the yellow and black taxi rolls down the driveway, the tighter the woman's grip on Archer's shoulders becomes. My jaw gains a spasm when she encloses her red-painted lips over his lipstick-smeared mouth to kiss him farewell.

From the excitement on her face and the length of her embrace, she has no clue this will be her one and only encounter with Archer. I've seen him with a range of women the last six weeks, but not once has he slept with the same woman twice.

My heart leaps out of my chest when Pepper reappears on my phone's screen, loudly declaring she's back. After apologizing for giving me my first gray hair, she requests I turn my phone's camera to Archer. When I do, we watch the unnamed brunette naïvely blow a kiss to Archer as she slips into the back seat of the taxi. Archer remains standing on the front porch, barefoot and in a pair of jeans and plaid shirt rolled up at the elbows—his attire of choice.

"Wow, your description is pretty accurate, Paige. Although he's wearing a little more clothing than I've imagined the past week." Pepper's voice is barely a whisper. It seems as if she's afraid Archer might hear her.

I giggle, shocked she's rattled. Usually, nothing lowers the volume of her voice, not even my father.

My laughter dissipates when Archer cranks his neck to the side and peers straight at the window I'm gawking at him from.

"Move, move, move!" Pepper barks out like a TI drill sergeant breaking in a bunch of rookie recruits.

"He can't see us," I assure her while maintaining my original position. "It's a mirrored window. I can see out, but no one can see in."

"Are you sure?" Pepper's usually smooth voice shakes with unease. "Because he looks like he's staring right at you."

"I'm sure." The weakness of my tone dampens my certainty. "The same thing has happened a few times over the past week. I swear he's staring straight at me, but he can't see me. I've checked. *Numerous* times."

Several heart-thrashing seconds pass with Archer peering at my window before he scrubs his hand across his beard then enters his house, switching off every light on his way.

CHAPTER THREE

The crispness of a late fall afternoon causes goosebumps to form on the nape of my neck. While adjusting my position, I pray for the sun to emerge from the cloud it snuck behind. I've spent most of the last hour lazing on the pristine beach of Bronte's Peak, relishing in the unusually warm conditions for late fall.

When the glare reflecting off the white pages of the novel I'm reading becomes too much for me to bear, I bookmark my current page, set the book down on my towel, then roll over. My lips purse when the sting of a sunburn tingles my shoulders from my abrupt movements.

With it being fall, I stupidly forwent my sunscreen. From the warmth spreading across my shoulder blades and down my back, I can tell my complacency will cost me dearly. It's fair to say I have pasty white skin. It takes mere minutes for the sun's rays to have my skin switching from Alaska snow white to pastel pink. Within an hour, I'm almost as red as a lobster.

Although I flew across the country solely to finish my novel, after being busted by Archer last night, my desire to write is waning. I've never penned a single sentence when my mood is woeful. Last night was no exception. I figure if I bask in the sun for a few hours and enjoy the splendor of the scenery surrounding me, my mood will improve, closely followed by my word count.

A dog's bark echoing in the silence gains my attention. After shifting onto my backside, I peer over the sand dunes to the flat beach below. A gorgeous golden retriever is charging along the water's edge. His coat becomes saturated when he dives into the waves barreling onto the shore.

My eyes dart in all directions when he vanishes under the no doubt frigid water. The beat of my heart increases when he fails to emerge from the pounding waves. After snapping up from my sandy seat, I rush to the dune's edge. With a hand covering my eyes from the rapidly setting afternoon sun, I scan the ocean's horizon, seeking any signs of the dog in the dark blue waters.

I release the breath I'm holding in when the golden retriever emerges from the sea with a large stick dangling from his mouth.

That darn dog nearly gave me a heart attack.

While clutching my erratically beating chest, I slump back down onto my towel and watch the drenched dog race across the sand. He's not the slightest bit concerned he had me on the verge of heart failure.

My chances of falling into a coronary attack amplify when I discover who the golden retriever runs back to.

Archer.

What is he doing here? He's rarely home during the day, and if he is, he's not once stepped foot onto the sand beyond his back patio in the six weeks I've been watching him.

After slumping low into the dunes to conceal myself, I drink in every inch of him. Unlike the other times I've seen him dressed, his legs aren't covered by designer jeans and a plaid shirt. He's once again barefoot and wearing black knee-length board shorts with a plain white t-shirt. His long dirty blond hair is pulled off his face, exposing more of his scruffy beard, defined cheekbones, and piercing eyes. He looks incredibly delicious.

If I squint, he reminds me a lot of Jax from *Sons of Anarchy*. Although he's more built than Charlie Hunnam, and he has a much more extensive tattoo collection, they do have a lot of similarities.

My pupils balloon as my heart freezes.

Archer couldn't be Charlie Hunnam, could he? He does live in an extremely elegant-looking glass house in an exclusive neighborhood. I've also noted numerous flashy cars in his four-car garage at the side of his driveway.

Shit! Imagine how much trouble I'd be in if I were caught spying on a celebrity?

Stalking is a big no-no in general, but I'd be ridiculed for life if I was found to be spying on someone famous. The press would have a field day.

Through shaky hands, I snag my iPhone out of my Nordstrom beach bag, open the Safari app, and type 'Charlie Hunnam' into the search app. I sigh loudly when the first bit of information I stumble over is Charlie's eye color. His eyes are hazel. After staring into Archer's heavy-lidded gaze last night, I can recall with the utmost certainty that his eyes are as blue as the ocean when the sun sets over it.

Thank goodness.

After gathering my belongings, I contemplate trudging through the dunes back to my rented bungalow. Although I've reached my quota of sun for the day, I don't want to risk Archer spotting me sitting here. If he thinks I'm spying on him during the day, it might be the final push he needs to switch me from a nosy neighbor to verified stalker.

My attempts at a quick getaway are foiled when a cold wetness runs down my bare thigh. I spring into the air, my heart leaping out of my chest as quickly as my legs leave the sand. A giggle escapes my lips when I realize what caused my third heart stutter of the day. It's the gorgeous golden retriever who was also the cause of my earlier panic. My laughter bubbles in my chest when his bumpy tongue tickles the skin between my fingers as he licks off the sticky remnants of the Boston bun I devoured for afternoon tea.

After running my hand through the gloriously smooth fur on the top of his head, I dig the leftover bun from the paper bag at my side and hand it to him. I swear he swallows the entire half without chewing. Although grateful he enjoyed the sugary treat as much as me, my heart constricts when I catch sight of the name engraved on the bone-shaped pendant dangling from his leather collar.

Charlie.

"Please tell me your name is Charlie?" I gaze into his big adorable brown eyes pleading into mine, no doubt begging for more bun. "Because I know people create fake identities all the time. Hair color, eye color, none of that matters if you have the right amount of money. Trust me. I wear contact lenses all the time."

I've *definitely* reached my quota of sun for one day. I'm talking to a dog for crying out loud, and if that isn't bad enough, I'm waiting for him to reply.

My pulse speeds up when a chocolatey smooth voice rumbles over the padded cell, quietness swamping me from all sides. "Charlie, come on, boy," calls out the male voice I usually only hear during sexual activities. "Come on, Charlie, it's time to head home."

Charlie's head cranks to the side when he hears Archer calling him.

"Go on, boy," I say, encouraging him to leave before he blows my cover. "Go to Archer."

Charlie peers at me with his tongue dangling out of his mouth. Even being a dog, I can't miss the confusion on his adorable face.

"Do you not like the name Archer? I thought it was very fitting." I lean in close and whisper, "You've obviously missed the number of times he *arches* women over his couch."

My blubbering ends when the top of Archer's head pops over the sand dunes. I inwardly squeal before flopping to the ground. My crouched position finally alerts me to Charlie's interest. The stick he lugged from the bottom of the ocean is resting against my beach bag.

Charlie's eyes dance between me and his beloved stick when I stretch out to grab it. The instant my hand wraps around the slobber-covered branch, he jumps up from his seated position, ready to play fetch. He wags his tail excitedly, spraying me with splatters of salty water from his wet coat.

"Here you go..." I grunt while throwing the stick as far as I can from my hidden position.

When Charlie takes off for the stick, I get hammered by the sand his eager sprint kicks up. My mouth, nose, and unfortunately, my eyes are invaded by the grittiness of fine white particles.

I'm still rubbing the sand from my eyes when a cold wetness brushes my thigh for the second time. It is closely followed by a drool-covered stick.

After furrowing my brows together, I glare into Charlie's big brown eyes. "You're meant to take the stick back to Archer." Although my words are meant to come out as threatening, neither Charlie nor myself are buying my attempt at sternness. How could I be angry at a dog as beautiful as him?

I freeze like a statue when "Who's Archer?" comes from a voice at the side.

A voice I immediately recognize.

A voice I only hear in the middle of ecstasy.

I snarl at Charlie for blowing my cover before shifting my eyes to the side. Archer is standing to my right. His heavily tattooed arms are braced in front of his well-formed chest, and his unamused eyes are firmly fixated on me.

"Charlie's owner." My voice is as unconvincing as my perplexed expression. Can you blame me? This is the second time I've been caught snooping on him in not even twenty-four hours.

Archer's murky blue eyes glare straight into mine as he asks, "You know Charlie's owner?"

I purse my lips, feigning ignorance before briefly shaking my head. "No. I just like naming strangers."

If he doesn't call the looney hospital after that line, I might consider calling them myself.

Shockingly, Archer finds my attempt at humor more entertaining than my woeful shot at anger. But even more shocking than that is the stir of emotions that twists in my stomach when awarded his deep, throaty laugh. I didn't think anything could sound as provocative as the carnal moans he grunts during sexual activity, but his laugh has made a quick liar out of me.

Once Archer's chuckles ease, he uncrosses his arms then offers me his hand to shake. "Hunter," he introduces while grinning a smile that does stupid things to my insides.

"Paige," I reply while endeavoring to keep surprise out of my introduction.

Although his name isn't exactly Archer, I was pretty darn close.

After standing from the ground and wiping the sand from my hand, I accept his handshake. His eyes rake my barely covered body as he displays his beard isn't the only manly part about him. His shake is very masculine as well. Thankfully, I'm wearing a gorgeous gold and black sequined O-ring side-tie monokini I purchased on a shopping spree last summer. Unfortunately, my chest doesn't resemble *any* of the busty ladies I've seen Hunter with the past six weeks. That whole more-than-a-handful-is-a-waste platitude is one I regularly use when describing my less-than-stellar female attributes.

When Hunter's eyes return to my face, I smile, appreciating the glint of lust in them. "Enjoying the last few rays of sun?"

I nod. "I like taking advantage of anything I'm offered."

He tries to conceal it, but I don't miss the corners of his lips tugging into a wry grin. "Then why didn't you take me up on my offer last night?"

As I blubber out the first response that pops into my head, my cheeks turn the color of my sun-kissed shoulders. "Brunettes aren't really my thing."

When my comment comes out both witty and intelligent, I bite the inside of my cheek, fighting to keep my smile at bay.

I've never been overly good at flirting, but I seem to be a quick learner.

My attempt to hide my smile is worthless when a broad grin stretches across Archer's face.

Shit! I meant to say Hunter.

"I'll keep that in mind for next time." He clips a lead onto Charlie's collar before guiding him back toward the beach. "I'll see you around, Paige?"

Since his statement sounds more like a question than a declaration, I nod.

Once he's halfway down the dunes, it dawns on me what he said. I cup my hands around my mouth to ensure my girlie voice projects down the dunes, then shout, "Sexually cavorting with women isn't really my thing either." My reply is as embarrassing as it comes, but I need him to understand my objection had nothing to do with his female friend being a brunette.

I cringe when my loud voice echoes in the quiet of the late afternoon, then my face turns a shade of crimson when a group of teenage boys at the water's edge respond to my declaration.

"You don't know what you're missing out on."

"Give it a go. You may just like it."

"Don't knock it till you've tried it."

I wave my hand in the air, silently thanking them for their recommendations, but even with their snickers bellowing into my ears, I don't miss Hunter's hearty chuckle.

While grimacing at my stupidity, I gather my bag and towel from the sandy ground then head back to my bungalow.

"If you learn to laugh at yourself, life will become a whole lot funnier," I mumble to myself.

That was one of my mom's favorite quotes, and I've lived by it as often as possible in the past twelve weeks.

CHAPTER FOUR

"*No!*" I glare at the blank screen of my laptop, certain I'm not seeing what I think I'm seeing. "Don't you dare, you son of a bitch." I shake the monitor, begging for the words I just finished typing to magically reappear. "No! Oh god, you can't do this to me now."

I push away from the desk then start pacing in the small confines of my writing cave. Hours upon hours of hard work just vanished in an instant. I don't know what happened. I was eagerly typing away, then the screen glitched before it plunged into blackness.

After roughly yanking on my hair, I snatch my phone from my desk and FaceTime Pepper.

"Jake, I'm taking a quick break," she shouts to someone in the distance before switching her focus back to me. "Hey, Sweet Pea. Any sand-stuck-in-crevices stories to share today?"

A broad grin stretches across her face when she weaves through the coffee bean chain store she works at.

"I broke my laptop." My voice is high as devastation dangles on my vocal cords. "Not a little broken. The screen is black! I-lost-everything broken."

Pepper's flawless face gets a new wrinkle when she screws up her nose. "Show me."

As I twist my phone to show her my blank laptop monitor, my hand trembles.

"Did you try a hard reset?"

Even though she can't see me, I nod. "Yes. I've turned it off at the wall, begged to the writing gods, and I even promised not to write smut on it if it would turn back on. Nothing has worked." Groaning, I flop onto the writing chair I salvaged from a dump site over three years ago. It is hideously ugly, but it's my good luck charm. I penned my very first best-selling novel on it. "Hours of hard work, gone. I'll never get the entire first draft rewritten before my deadline." I burrow my head into my shaking hands before stammering out, "God, Pepper, what am I going to do?"

"First, you need to take a deep breath."

I suck in a deep, nerve-cleansing gulp of air.

"Second, you need to remember you've never missed a deadline. Not once in three years."

"This is different. I didn't have a computer malfunction weeks before my final draft is due." The crackling of my voice displays I'm on the verge of crying.

"That's where step three comes in." Pepper moves in close to the screen. "Grab that piece-of-shit computer I told you to get rid of years ago and get your tushie to the local IT shop. Upon entering, fall to your knees, cry like you're a baby who had its binky stolen, and beg for them to save the hard drive."

"Save the what?" Although my mood is dire, it seems nowhere near as bad just from talking to Pepper. She has a way of bringing me off the ledge.

"Just because the outside of the laptop has gone kaput doesn't mean the inside is worthless. But if you don't get your backside out of that revolting chair and to the computer store, you'll never know what data can be saved." I jump from my chair like my ass is on fire when Pepper screams, "Move, Paige! Move, move, move." Her demanding voice bellows down the line like it did four nights ago when she thought Hunter had spotted us spying on him.

I yank my laptop off the desk then charge down the stairs. "I love you, Pepper."

"I know you do, Sweet Pea."

After air-kissing her goodbye, I disconnect FaceTime and call an Uber.

By the time I make it to Ravenshoe, I'm sweating like a pig. Unfortunately, perspiring is one of the many side effects I endure when nervous. I'm not normally a bumbling idiot, but when something stands between me and a deadline, all my normal traits vanish, and a naïve, fumbling imbecile takes over my body.

"Thank you," I mumble before slipping out of an SUV in front of an IT shop called *Mr. Fix It*.

Once I've gathered my belongings, I scan the unfamiliar street. Ravenshoe is busier than I was expecting. The sidewalks are packed with residents, and the roads are clogged with traffic that's nearly thicker than the sweat slicking my body.

After shrugging off my surprise that Ravenshoe is a bustling hive of activity compared to the serenity of the private beach at Bronte's Peak, I saunter through the single glass door of the computer shop. A bell above the entryway chimes when I pull open the heavily weighted door.

I scrunch my nose when burning wires and *toast* stream through my nostril cavities. Upon spotting a gentleman in his mid-fifties with a rounded stomach and a comb-over, I adjust my bag before making a beeline for him.

My brisk pace slows when the quickest glimpse of a profile

freezes my heart. Hunter is darting through the moderately-sized store, grabbing a selection of computer parts and accessories. A grin curls on my lips when I discover his outfit has returned to his much-loved combination that consists of a pair of designer jeans and a plaid shirt.

After watching him in silence for a few minutes, mentally taking note of his finer quirks I could use for Archer, I continue with my original pursuit.

"Hi," I greet the computer repairman with a large smile. I'm hoping my over-the-top friendliness will have my laptop pushed to the front of the line.

The gentleman sets down a weird-looking green and silver contraption before joining me at the counter. It's a hard-fought battle to maintain my smile when his sullied eyes rake my body, not once, not twice, but three times. His depraved stare is so inappropriate, it's downright unprofessional.

"What can I do for you, honey?" he asks, his voice as slimy as his greasy hair.

I place my laptop on the glass counter, which houses small camera devices and a collection of pens. "I've broken my laptop."

He shifts his dark brown eyes from my not-that-impressive bosoms to my laptop. "Hardware malfunction or malware issue?"

I shrug. "Ah... you tell me?"

The grooves indenting my head amplify when he cranks open the laptop screen and pushes the power button. I look a little ridiculous sweating in the coolness of a November day, but I'm not a complete idiot. I know how to turn on a laptop.

After a short deliberation, he grunts out, "Fixing an old girl like this is pointless. You're better off purchasing a new device." He tosses my laptop to the side like trash before moseying to a shelf full of fancy laptops.

"Oh no, I don't want a new laptop. I need the documents stored inside this one." My voice squeaks as panic sets in. "Very important documents are hidden somewhere in this laptop. Very *very* important documents."

The repairman's lips quirk into a cunning smile as he strolls back to me. "That important, hey?"

I eagerly nod, willing to do anything to get him on my side.

Well, almost anything.

Sweat forms on the top of his shiny head as his eyes scan my laptop for the second time. "I'm sure I can get your *important* documents off this device for you."

"Really?" My excitement is as high as my voice.

"Sure, the hardware in this old girl would survive a house fire. Even if you've fried the motherboard, I'll still be able to retrieve some data." He lifts his dark eyes to mine. "It will cost you, though."

"That's fine. Charge any amount you want." *I'm sure it won't be as high as the advance I'll lose if I don't get this draft handed in by the end of the year.*

"Alright, leave it with me, and I'll have it back to you in around eight weeks."

My heart slithers into my gut. "Eight weeks?" I squeak out.

"It's only six weeks until Christmas, honey. My schedule is fully booked."

Tears prick my eyes as a sweat mustache forms on my top lip.

"Oh, don't go crying on me. I can't stand seeing a girl cry." He yanks two tissues out of a box on his left and hands them to me. "Maybe we can make a deal. I could have it back to you by the end of the week."

My tears dry from the sheer relief scorching through my veins.

The blessing doesn't last long.

"For the right incentive, of course," he adds after pushing his protective glasses up his blackhead-covered nose.

My suspicious eyes dance between his. Even though his covetous gaze is already horrifyingly displaying his true intentions, I want him to spell it all out, as clear as day, so I *fully* understand the agreement he wants me to sign up for.

When my arched brow doesn't give him the hint, I ask, "What's the condition?"

Without pause for consideration, he blurts out, "You have to go out with me."

While awaiting my reply, he peers at me like Hannibal Lecter stared at Clarice in *Silence of The Lambs* when they first met. All he needs is a slithering tongue, and the scene would be set.

"On just a date?" I clarify with a suspicious stare. "No *extracurricular* activities required?"

My stomach churns when the corners of his mouth tug into a sly smirk.

I grit my teeth before snarling through a tight jaw. "No deal. I'll take my laptop to another computer shop."

After snatching my laptop off the counter, I charge for the door. My brutal pace slows when the computer repairman shouts, "I'm the only repair shop within a hundred miles of Ravenshoe!"

"Then I'll stop by the local high school," I snap back after spinning around to face him. "I'm sure any teen there will have better computer skills than you and your hideous comb-over." A blast of cool air hits me in the face when I yank open the door, but before I merge into foot traffic on the sidewalk, I crank my neck back and give the repairman one final serve. "And just for the record, *buddy*, I wouldn't care if the map for Pablo Gaviria's buried billions in Columbia was on this computer. I'd rather go poor than slap skins with a man like you."

My sassy attitude dampens when a deep, rumbling laugh barrels through my ears. I'm taken aback when I switch my narrowed eyes from the slack-jawed computer repairman to my right. Hunter is responsible for the laughter booming around the repair shop, and my angry face only makes him chuckle harder.

After hitting him with the same stink-eye I gave the repairman,

I spin on my heels and charge out onto the sidewalk. Halfway down the block, I'm still rambling incoherently under my breath. Even if it forces me to walk straight into a shitstorm without an umbrella, I'd rather miss my deadline than be a random guy's side platter for the night.

I also despise when men use a woman's desperation as a way in. If they were smart, they'd realize most women would pick the helpful geeky, glasses-wearing guy over a Calvin Klein underwear model any day. Because at the end of the day, looks vanish. Brains don't.

My fast strides down the bustling sidewalk slow when I hear my name being called over the hum of activity. When I spin on my heels, my heart beats double time. Hunter is weaving his way through the throng of people mingling on the sidewalk. My lungs struggle to secure a full breath just from the way the muscles in his thighs stretch and expand as he endeavors to bridge the distance between us.

"Hey," he greets me, still smirking the same smile he wore in the computer store.

"Hey." My breathlessness makes my single word come out as a long pant. "Sorry about that." I nudge my head in the direction he just came from. Even though I was irate, he didn't deserve my knee-shaking stink eye.

Hunter's smile enlarges. "It's all good. Bosco deserved it."

I don't refute his claim. Bosco should be glad his nuts are still attached to his body.

As his shrewd eyes bore into mine, Hunter scrubs his hand along the edge of his scruffy beard. I return his stare with just as much vigor, loving the chance to study a side of him I can't access from a distance.

When I commenced writing about Archer, I placed him in his mid-thirties. But from the youthfulness of his eyes and the fact his face is void of any wrinkles, I need to lower his age range to late twenties, making him closer to my twenty-five years. He has a straight, defined and pierced nose, sharp cheekbones partially hidden by a maintained but full beard, and intelligent eyes.

He's handsome in a unique, masculine way.

After Hunter finishes his assessment of my body and face, he announces, "I can fix your laptop for you."

I curve my brow before giving him the same dubious stare I gave Bosco. "At what cost?"

His chuckles gain him the attention of a handful of residents walking by. Upon noticing we've acquired unwanted eyes, he places his hand on my elbow and guides me into a small bakery at our side. His simplest touch causes a surge of awareness to prickle my skin.

Thankfully, the loud grumble of my stomach distracts Hunter from my body's reaction to his closeness. The yummy smell of freshly baked goodies and pastries slams into me when he moves us to the corner of the bakery. Peering down at my watch, I note it's a little after two. No wonder I'm hungry. I haven't eaten since breakfast. I have a terrible habit of forgetting to eat when I am writing.

Hunter draws my attention away from the delicious goodies on display in the glass cabinets when he says, "It won't cost you anything." I stare at him, confused by his offer. It's only once he continues speaking does it dawn on me what he's talking about. "It will make up for the rudeness of my... *approach* the other night."

My brows become lost in my hair. *I* was busted watching *him* during a sexual encounter, yet he's worried about his rudeness.

"It will only take around an hour. Easy work," he assures me after spotting my angst-ridden face.

I peer into his wholesome eyes. "Are you sure you don't mind?" Although I hate asking for help, especially from a stranger, I'm in a real pickle.

"Certain," Hunter responds without a snip of hesitation, easing my guilt about taking up his valuable time.

"Alright. That will be great. When can you do it?"

I send a silent prayer to the writing gods that he says sometime within the next week.

My prayers are answered when he replies with a grin. "Now."

My eyes bulge, but I play it cool. "Okay, great," I stumble out through the tumbleweeds in my throat. "Let me grab us a couple of treats first, then we'll get this show on the road."

a tittle-
w, there
d chaffin
ll waterf
did nothi
I an
for d
rever
esides
a knot
poor Rar
eded
cam
e s

CHAPTER FIVE

*M*y dropped jaw gains leverage the more Hunter's Hellcat rolls down the driveway of his residence. Although most of my time the past six weeks has been spent spying on him, I never paid much attention to the splendor of his home. Let me tell you, I've been missing out. This place is enormous. Panel upon panel of multi-hued glass, meticulously joined with thick steel beams painted the color of the ocean backdrop creates an awe-inspiring architectural delight.

When Hunter parks his car in front of a four-car garage, I toss open my door. The gravel crunching under my feet matches the rhythm of my thumping heart when I follow him up a small flight of stairs to a set of double glass doors. I don't know who this guy is, but he's obviously stinking rich. His residence screams of wealth. I'm not talking Ivanka Trump asked daddy for a loan. I'm talking about Eric Berry signing his deal with the Kansas City Chiefs rich.

I rub my hands together like a kid in a candy store when an electronic face fills the computer panel once it notices our approach.

"Are you shitting me?" My voice is equally eccentric and high. "You have a computerized security system?"

Hunter smirks at my giddiness but remains quiet. My eyes bulge even more when a female voice booms out of the speakers. "Welcome home, Mr. Kane... and *guest*."

My eyes rocket to Hunter as my mouth falls open. "Is that a computer program, or is a real-life person watching us?" I'm putting bets on it being a real-life person because I swear she sneered when she said, "Guest."

"She is a computer." Hunter turns his eyes to the panel on his right. "Patricia, this is Paige. Add her face to your database for future recognition."

"Yes, Mr. Kane," the computer program replies.

Even though Hunter has declared Patricia is a computer, I stand by my original statement. There's no doubt she's sneering.

Ignoring my bug-eyed expression, Hunter pushes open the thick glass door and enters the opulent foyer of his home before offering to take my jacket. His house has a cold, sterilized feel with stark white cabinets and marbled floors, but it's surprisingly warm.

After shrugging out of my red bomber jacket, I hand it to Hunter. While he hangs our coats in the coatroom at the side of the foyer, I step deeper into the space. I inwardly chuckle when my eyes absorb the nude paintings adorning his pristine walls. They're a similar color to the ocean backdrop, but unlike the disastrous pieces I've sketched of Hunter and his companions over the last six weeks, these resemble humans.

With my laptop slung under his arm, Hunter gallops down the three stairs to the living area at the back of his residence. As my eyes categorize every inch of his home, I closely shadow him. A ten-seater dining table sits on my right, an expansive and adeptly decorated white marble kitchen is on my left, and a vast living area is directly in front of me.

From this vantage point, there are uninterrupted views of the pristine beaches below. It's nearly as spectacular as the scenery I've witnessed in this space numerous times over the past six weeks.

My eyes stray from the beautiful vista when tinkering sounds through my ears. Spinning around, I spot Hunter seated on a glass barstool at the breakfast bar where he eats his three slices of toast every morning. The back of my laptop is removed, and he's fiddling with stuff inside my computer that is way over my technical knowledge.

Curious, I step closer to him. "Do you work with computers?"

The corners of his lips crimp before he shakes his head. "It's more a hobby I stumbled into."

My brows stitch. "But you know what you're doing, right? Because I wasn't joking when I said *very* important documents are stored in that laptop."

Every crude joke I've ever heard filters through my brain when Hunter throws back his head and laughs. I'll dish out more one-liners than Chris Rock at the Comedy Cellar if it guarantees he'll laugh like that again.

When his chuckles settle down, his glistening eyes lock with mine. "I've got you covered, Paige." After a lengthy stare, he returns to tinkering with my laptop. "I work for a telemarketing company in New Delhi."

My brows stitch together. "As in you own the company? Or..." My words trail off when I can't think of a plausible reason why a guy who works in telemarketing would live in a house worth well into the millions.

When he chooses not to answer my question, I head for a small selection of photo frames on the fireplace mantel. The photographs cross a broad span of years in Hunter's life from a young teen to a college graduate.

"Have you always had the beard?" I pick up a photo of him I'd guess was taken four or five years ago. Although his beard isn't quite the thickness it is now, it still covers most of his jawline.

I hear Hunter's nod more than I see it. "Yeah... pretty much since I could grow one."

My lips twist before I return the photo to its rightful spot. I've never really been a fan of beards, but Hunter's has grown on me. When I first began writing about Archer—the fictional character based on Hunter—I initially removed the detail of his beard. But after a few paragraphs, something felt off in the story. It was only after I added his beard back in did the storyline progress with a natural flow.

Archer is the very first character I've penned with a full beard.

"Is this your mom?" I ask after taking in an image of a lady with sandy blonde hair and blue eyes. She is grinning broadly, and her arm is wrapped around Hunter's waist. She's quite short, the top of her head only just reaching Hunter's shoulder.

Hunter's eyes drift from my laptop to the photo I am holding. "Yeah, that's my mom and my little sister," he informs me, his tone gruff and reserved.

"Your sister is very young," I respond, my voice high in surprise.

The girl in the photo appears to be around the age of four or five, so I didn't consider that she'd have some type of family connection to Hunter.

"She was five in that photo," Hunter announces. "She's ten now."

I place the picture frame back on the mantelpiece before moseying closer to him. "How old were *you* in that picture?"

He cocks a brow and eyes me curiously. "Are you trying to find out how old I am?"

Smiling, I nod.

My smile slips when he mutters, "Then why don't you just ask how old I am?" Although his tone has an edge of annoyance associated with it, the twinkle in his eyes doesn't relay any anger.

I prop my elbows on the counter and gaze into his dark blue eyes before asking, "How old are you, Hunter?"

His almost hidden smirk really has a way of doing stupid things to my insides, especially when it follows his gravelly voice that's full of mischief. "Old enough to know from the sparkle in your eyes, it wouldn't matter if I were twenty-five or fifty-five, you'd still want to jump my bones."

My mouth gapes open. Nothing against Hunter, he has the body of an Adonis and many other impressive attributes, but he's the opposite of the men I've dated. I like my men clean-shaven and smooth. Hunter is rough and a little too edgy for my liking.

He couldn't be more opposite of Riley if he tried.

Riley is as stiff as the overly starched ties he wears every day behind his crisp, perfectly laundered suit. The only time I saw him out of a suit was when he was returning from a soccer match. He shaves his face every morning at precisely seven and polishes his shoes every Thursday night while sitting on our bed watching *Scandal*.

Unlike Riley, I've not once seen Hunter in a suit. He favors designer jeans and a range of plaid shirts over stiff, restricting mate-rial. Most of his handsome face is covered by a thick beard, and his hair is a little too long for my liking.

If you saw Hunter and Riley standing side by side, it would be like comparing night and day. Riley looks like a cut-throat business-man, whereas Hunter looks set to cut down a tree.

I stop smiling about my comparison portfolio when Hunter announces, "I'm twenty-eight." His rough tone demands my atten-tion. "I'm a Capricorn, don't like long walks on the beach, am allergic to shellfish, and have one sibling." His lips perk as his brows furrow. "I think that about covers it. Unless you have any other questions you'd like me to answer?"

Now his eyes are sparked with annoyance.

Obviously, he isn't a fan of being interrogated... *or holding a conversation*.

I plop onto the stool next to him. "Nope, we're good."

Several minutes pass in silence. It's awkward and highly uncom-fortable. If my laptop weren't in a million pieces across his kitchen counter, I would have snatched it from his grasp and went and hid, only emerging when the devil-horn-wearing Hunter disappeared.

It sucks to admit this, but I prefer the fictional Hunter I've created on paper to the one sitting next to me.

After cursing under his breath, Hunter sets down a small screwdriver and scrubs his hand along his scruff-covered jaw. "I'm sorry. I'm not used to... *this*." He gestures his hand to me.

"*This?*" I ask through arched brows.

He rakes his teeth over his lower lip before muttering, "Interacting with girls."

I bow my brows even higher while glaring into his eyes. That's a blatant lie. I've seen him *interact* with plenty of women over the past six weeks. Other than sleeping, that appears to be the only thing he does in his pretty glass house.

"Interacting with them while they are stilled clothed," he adds when he notices my contemptuous face.

"Oh, well, in that case..." I stand from my chair while fumbling with the buttons on my crushed linen shirt. When he fails to acknowledge my attempt at humor, I flop back onto the barstool then cross my arms in front of my chest. "I'm not getting naked just for you to feel comfortable."

His murky blue eyes lock with mine. They're sparked with amusement. "Oh... was that for my benefit? I thought it was part payment for fixing your laptop."

My mouth forms an 'O.' "Part payment? Believe me, *buddy*, if I were going to strip naked for services rendered, you'd be stamping the invoice paid in full."

Hunter chuckles a full-hearted laugh.

It once again does stupid things to my insides.

After several long, tedious minutes, he snaps his mouth shut and mutters, "I like you, Paige." He sounds surprised by his admission, but not as much as I am stunned about my pleasure from his compliment. Anyone would swear he told me I'm beautiful.

Another length of silence passes between us. This time, it's void of the earlier awkwardness. Hunter continues dismantling my laptop into hundreds of tiny pieces, making it look like a giant jigsaw puzzle I'd never have the chance of putting together while I watch him in awe.

After a beat, he raises his eyes to mine and asks, "What do you do for a living, Paige?"

I won't lie. I like the way he says my name. He adds a tinge of huskiness to it, giving it a sexy feel.

"I'm a... *writer*?" I half-inform, half-question.

I don't know why, but even with fourteen books penned under my name, I still feel like a fraud when I tell people I 'write' for a living. I've never had any other occupation. I started writing short stories for the high school newsletter when I was a junior, then I went to college to study my craft.

With the ease of self-publishing, my first novel was listed for download the month I started college. And as they say, the rest is history.

Now don't read my admission the wrong way. It's often quoted that being a writer is hard work. It is. To gain traction in this industry, you must see it as a marathon, not a sprint. It took a good two years to upgrade my dinner selections from ramen noodles to microwave meals. Only once my 'work' was put into the right hands did I see substantial readership growth.

But if I don't continue producing new novels every couple of months, I'll lose my vivacious audience, which, in turn, means I'll lose revenue. Since I don't want to go back to eating peanut butter sandwiches for lunch and ramen noodles for dinner, I must hand in my draft by the end of next month.

When the smell of burning skin streams through my nose, I shift my eyes to the side. Hunter's face is lined with anger. His nostrils are flaring, and his ferocious gaze is burning a hole in the side of my head.

His voice is vicious when he snarls out, "You're a reporter?"

You'd think the panic I felt when he stormed toward my

bungalow last week would be my most fearful moment with him. It isn't. The way he's glaring at me and the furious tic his beard-covered jaw is failing to hide has me shaking in my boots more now than when he busted me spying on him in the middle of a lust-hazed romp.

"No." Locks of hair fall into my face when I shake my head. "I write books."

In a flash, the natural beige coloring of Hunter's face returns, closely followed by the normal width of his eyes.

Once the crinkles in his brows smooth, he asks, "What type of books?"

I balk, flabbergasted by the sudden change in his demeanor. He's gone from looking like a man who wants to scoop out my liver and eat it for dinner to the humble boy next door... *if you can look past his tattoos and rough exterior.*

When I remain quiet, he shifts his gaze from my laptop to me. His eyes roam my flushed cheeks, wide eyes, and O-formed mouth before he asks with a cheeky grin, "Do you write mommy porn?"

My dropped jaw gains leverage. "What? No!" *Although some scenes I've written about you are borderline mommy porn.* "I write *romance.*" My tone is as unconvincing as the ruffled expression on my face. It isn't my fault. Adult romance is a new genre I decided to test out last month. It's going well—for the most part.

Hunter's brow cocks. "*Fifty Shades of Grey* was classed as romance."

Now he has me by the throat.

"Did you read it?" I ask as my writer-fighting spirit emerges.

Hunter angles his body to face me. "What? *Fifty Shades?*"

When I nod, his tongue delves out to lick his lips before he turns his attention back to my laptop.

"Well? Did you?" I ask again when he remains as quiet as a baby sleeping. When his bushy beard fails to hide his wry smirk, I tap my boot against his. "Then you can't really call it *mommy porn*, can you? Because I'm reasonably sure you don't have any mommy parts."

My insides do the cha-cha from discovering that he reads. There's nothing sexier than a brute of a man with panty-wetting good looks holding a book in his hand. I'm part of numerous Facebook groups solely dedicated to hunting down sexy man readers. Now I wish I'd packed paperbacks of my books. It could have been a stellar marketing move on my behalf. Although my clean, sweet romance reads may not be up to Hunter's mommy-porn standards.

Another stretch of silence passes between us. Unlike the previous two times, there's a weird sensation impinging the air around us. It's similar to the connection I felt when Hunter peers up at my writing cave window. It's heart-pumping and intense.

Our bizarre kinship dampens when the shrill of a cell phone fills the void of silence. Hunter places parts of my laptop onto the white countertop so he can retrieve a cell out of his pocket. My brows furrow when I notice how outdated his phone is. With a computerized house and obvious wealth, I'm shocked he's carrying a phone similar to the one I had when I was a teeny bopper.

After drifting his eyes to me, Hunter flips open his phone and presses it to his ear. "Boss," he greets. "Hmm, weird... okay, I'll take some equipment to your apartment this afternoon and complete a search." He stands from his chair and walks to the large door at the back of the living room. "What type of devices am I looking for?" he asks before slipping out the glass door.

Surprisingly, all noise stops when he closes the door behind him. I know for a fact that his house isn't soundproof, but his lips are moving, and I can't hear a peep, so I'm going to assume he made his house soundproof from outside noise.

This man just keeps getting more intriguing as the weeks move on.

Once Hunter finishes his call, he returns the phone to his pocket and joins me back by the kitchen. "I have to run a few errands," he informs me, his tone back to its initial gruffness.

"Okay, no worries."

As I slip off the barstool, I glance at my dissembled laptop. Upon noticing my nervy expression, Hunter says, "I'll finish repairing your computer as soon as I get back, and I'll drop it off later tonight."

"That will be great, thanks," I reply, smiling.

I lean in, preparing to kiss him goodbye on the cheek before remembering we're practically strangers. So instead of a friendly kiss goodbye, I wave like a gullible idiot.

I swear I look like a twelve-year-old.

While cringing about my idiocy, I make a beeline for the glass door Hunter just entered. Even with waves crashing to shore and my pulse shrilling in my ears, I still hear his faint laughter as I sprint across the patch of sand separating our patios.

CHAPTER SIX

"Oh my god. I think I'm in love!"

Hunter smirks to hide his grimace from my overly loud voice. "It was nothing major. Just a fuse short-circuiting the tantalum surface mount capacitor, causing…" He stops talking when he notices my baffled expression. It's safe to say computers and I have never been close friends. "It's fixed," he advises in a term I can understand.

I place the switched-on laptop on my entryway table then fire up my Scrivener writing program. I snap my eyes closed and send a prayer to the writing gods for guiding me to Hunter when my manuscripts, both current and old, pop up on my once-again-functioning screen.

"Thank you so much!" I squeal with dramatic flair. "You have no idea how much this means to me."

Caught up by my excitement, I throw my arms around Hunter's torso, then press my lips to his cheek. I smile when his prickles tickle my nostrils. I can't believe how soft his beard is. I was anticipating for it to have a steel-wool feel to it, where it's as soft as a cashmere sweater.

An interesting fact I'll note for future reference.

While doing my best to ignore his noteworthy smell, I pull back from our impromptu embrace and peer into his still mischief-filled eyes. "How much do I owe you?"

Hunter waves off my question as if money isn't an issue for him. "It's fine. No payment is required."

"Come on, I have to pay you something." I drift my eyes to his palatial home while contemplating an appropriate method of payment. When I realize nothing of monetary value would interest him, I mutter, "What about a beer?"

My lips hurt from the vast smile that stretches across my face when Hunter nods. "A beer sounds great."

"Awesome." I clap my hands together like I'm still that annoying twelve-year-old he was introduced to earlier before gesturing my head to the paper-covered two-seater sofa in the middle of the living room. "You take a seat, and I'll grab us a beer."

After gathering bundles of handwritten notes off the couch and coffee table, I sashay into the kitchen to snag two bottles of beer from the sparsely stocked refrigerator. While strolling back into the living room, my heart does a funny flutter. Although Hunter isn't overly large, standing at approximately six feet tall with a moderate build, he swamps the homey living room in my modest rented cabin.

While smiling at the rarity of seeing a woodsy man in the flesh, I hand Hunter a beer before filling the empty seat next to him with my backside.

"Cheers." I clink the neck of my beer against his before downing a generous mouthful.

Malted liquid spurts out of my mouth, drenching Hunter and me when he unexpectedly asks, "How long have you been a voyeur? Just the six weeks you've been here, or is it something you've done before?"

I cough and wheeze while fighting to breathe through the beer now sitting in my lungs instead of my flipping stomach.

"Are you okay?" Hunter asks while gently whacking my back.

Although mortified with embarrassment, my panic doesn't linger for long. Not an ounce of anger reflects from Hunter. He appears more concerned about my near choke than my incriminatory activities the past six weeks.

Once my mini-meltdown simmers, I lock my eyes with the murky blue ones staring at me with worry. "You knew I was watching the whole time?"

A cunning grin etches onto his sinful mouth before he bobs his chin. "For future reference, when you're standing in pitch-black darkness, an iPhone screen can illuminate an entire face."

I gulp loudly.

I have no other defense, so silence reigns supreme.

While eying me over the rim of his beer bottle, Hunter takes a generous sip. I set my beer down on the coffee table, then fold my hands together in my lap, hoping to conceal their shake from Hunter.

When several long seconds pass in silence, I can't help but blurt out. "Why aren't you mad?"

My heart beats double-time as I impatiently wait for him to answer my question. Although he lets me stew for several tortuous seconds, he eventually lets me off the hook. "Your interest gave me a slight curiosity in Martymachlia."

"Marty what?" The tremble of my heart is evident in my voice.

Hunter licks the beer from his lips before explaining, "Martymachlia is sexual arousal from having others watch their *activities*."

My pupils dilate to the size of dinner plates, but in all honesty, even shocked he admitted he gets turned on by people watching him during intimate moments, I'm also incredibly aroused. It isn't the fact he's a little more deviant than expected causing the tingle between my legs. It's because he's so comfortable with his sexual preferences.

It's a refreshing change from what I am used to.

Riley refused to talk about anything relating to sex—in or out of the bedroom.

After swallowing to dislodge the brick in my throat, I ask, "So instead of being angry about me spying on you, you *liked* it?"

He smirks but remains quiet with his eyes locked on me. I inwardly gasp when a warm slickness coats my panties from the hungry look that materializes in his eyes the longer he stares at me. I've watched him in compromising situations for weeks, and my body has never reacted this way.

I begin to wonder if he can read my inner thoughts when he smiles a cocky grin before he takes another swig of his beer. I return his ardent stare, blinking and confused. The *friendship* I created with Hunter's pseudonym, Archer, is a little crazy, but this is ten times weirder. Hunter and I are virtually strangers, but we're sitting in my living room—that now seems two sizes too small from the stifling heat bouncing between us—talking about his sexual preferences as if we're discussing the difference between full cream and skim milk.

Although a little weird, I will admit, I appreciate his frankness. It's rare to find a guy willing to discuss anything these days, let alone sex.

After adjusting my position so my body is facing Hunter, I ask, "How did you discover you had this *marty* condition?" I try to keep my tone neutral and friendly like this is something I discuss regularly.

My efforts are poor. Hunter glares at me over the rim of his beer bottle before muttering against the glass, "Please don't say it like that. It makes it sound like I'm some sort of *freak*."

I arch a brow and stare at him in a sadistic, jeering type of way.

He scoffs. "Who are you to talk?" He returns my leering stare. "You were the one getting *horny* while watching. *I* at least had a partner."

"Partner*s*." I draw out the S with a sneer. "And I wasn't getting *horny.*" My voice sounds like a pre-pubescent teen during my last word. "I was getting inspired."

"Come on, Paige. I'm being honest, and you're spitting out lies like Richard Nixon during the Watergate scandal."

I sneer at him before drifting my eyes to the coffee table to contemplate in peace. I can't look at his handsome face and maintain rational thoughts. I honestly didn't find the interactions between him and his bevy of female companions sexually arousing. I viewed their exchanges as if they were one of the nudes hanging on his walls. I appreciated the smooth lines and fluidity of their connection but didn't get any stimulation from it.

Well, other than mental.

I snap my eyes back to Hunter when he misunderstands my quietness as embarrassment. "There's nothing to be ashamed of, Paige. If watching people is your *thing*, then it's your *thing*."

"I'm not a voyeur."

He slants his head and quirks his lips. "How long have you been staying here? Six weeks now?"

I nod. Nearly seven but close enough.

"Not once have I seen a *visitor* here that entire time." Hunter freezes with his beer resting against his plump lips, his pupils dilating. "Please, for the love of God, don't tell me you've gone six weeks without..." My eyes dance between his, wondering why he suddenly stopped talking.

When I see the mortified look on his face, the rest of his sentence slaps me hard in the face. "No! I'm fine." My roar bounces off the wood-lined walls and shrills into my ears on repeat. "I'm good. I promise."

He glares into my eyes, blatantly calling bullshit.

"I'm *fine*," I assure him again. "I've taken care of *business*." I snap my mouth shut, mortified I said that out loud.

Hunter's pupils dilate even more. "Fuck," he mutters under his breath while adjusting his crotch. "Now *that* is something I'd turn into a voyeur for."

I don't deny his accusation that I'm a voyeur.

I'm too muted by shock to compile a reply to his false statement.

As he scratches his beard, his eyes blaze into mine. "Damn, Paige. You can't tell a guy something like that and not expect some sort of reaction." He licks a droplet of beer from his top lip before muttering, "I could bounce a nickel off my cock just thinking about you touching yourself."

My insides clench, turned on by his admission, and shockingly, the temperature in the room becomes roasting. I'm stunned by my body's reaction to his white-hot gaze, but there's no doubt the tingling in my womb is compliments of his yearning watch.

I can't remember the last time my libido has been this stimulated. I'm fairly certain it's *never* been this intense.

I know people's tastes change. I used to hate eggs when I was younger. Now I'd donate a kidney for eggs Benedict on a lazy Sunday morning. But can your preferences alter so much in a short period? Hunter is *nothing* like Riley, not in the slightest, but I can't deny the prompts of my body. Even though my mind is a jumbled mess of confusion, my body wants Hunter. *Badly*.

Our core-clutching stare-down ends when a cell phone breaks through the silence. Hunter grits his teeth before he fishes his outdated cell phone from his jeans pocket. After locking his eyes back with mine, he flips open the screen and squashes his cell to his ear. "Boss," he greets before waiting a beat. "Alright, I'll head there now. What type of information do you want to unearth?"

I try in vain to keep my interest away from his private conversation, but my efforts are futile. Uncovering the real Archer Boyd is becoming a riveting experience. It is stimulating my mind with more storylines than I can comprehend.

"I'll see you in a few." After disconnecting his call, Hunter places his phone back into his pocket, then stands from the couch. "I have to go."

And just like that, our intense connection is lost.

CHAPTER SEVEN

With a huff, I plop into my writing chair and spin around to face the new Mac I purchased earlier today. Stream upon stream of beautiful words are displayed on the screen in front of me, but nothing can overcome the woeful mood I've been in the last five days. And no, my bad temper has nothing to do with that time of the month and everything to do with the bearded man who lives in the glass house next door.

I haven't seen Hunter in days. Not a single smidge of him. From the number of *activities* he undertook in his private residence the previous six weeks, I can only assume he is avoiding me, or he's taken his lust-crazed romps to another location.

Although I have plenty of inspiration to pen a decent novel, I can't help but be a little peeved.

I don't fully understand what I'm annoyed at, but I am utterly blindsided by my odd behavior of late. I've stated on numerous occasions that Hunter isn't my type, and I'm in no way obsessed with him, but my writing is swaying in the opposite direction. Pages of angst-filled drama and jealousy are the heart of my current masterpiece. Either my subconscious is sounding alarm bells, or I've completely jumped ship from my usual style of writing.

I guess I could rationalize it as a painter working without a muse. I'm sure Leonardo da Vinci didn't paint the *Mona Lisa* without having Lisa Gherardini displayed in front of him, so how am I expected to bring Archer to life on the pages without assessing his finer quirks in full detail? Any artist will tell you it's the minor details that create the biggest impact on any art form.

Oh god. I sound like a grade-A lunatic.

My stern reprimand on the consequences I could face for being charged with stalking is interrupted when a quick tap bellows up the wooden staircase. I save my red editing pen from being gnawed to death by my chattering teeth by using it as a clip to secure a messy bun on my head while trudging down the stairs. My slow pace quickens when I discover who is standing behind the glass door of the wooden deck.

With a broad grin stretched across my face, I unlatch the lock and slide open the door. The smell of the salty ocean and bottled cologne smacks me in the face from my hasty movements.

"Hey, Hunter," I greet, my tone way too high for my liking.

Even with a large scruff of hair on his chin, Hunter can't hide his smile at the eagerness in my voice. He returns my greeting while bouncing his eyes between mine. After a beat, he asks, "Can I come in?"

"Umm... sure." I move out of the doorway to allow him entry, mortified I forgot my manners.

The scent of yummy cologne amplifies the further he enters the cabin.

I close the door to settle the winds whipping inside, then spin around to face Hunter. "Giorgio Armani or Tom Ford?"

His brows furrow as he stares at me in confusion.

"Your aftershave."

I've smelled his scent before, but I can't pinpoint the exact brand of his cologne.

The corners of Hunter's lips curve upwards before he mutters, "Neither."

Not bothering to ease my curiosity, he ambles into my kitchen. It's only when he places a plastic bag full to the brim with Chinese takeout on the tiled counter do I realize he's carrying goodies. My eyes were too invested in the vibrant sparkle in his gaze to notice he was bearing gifts.

"Hungry?" he asks, his voice smoother than melted chocolate.

The instant his murky blue eyes lock with mine, the sweat-producing visual of him in various stages of intimacy smack into me. Unlike the times I watched him have sex in person, the reruns cause a hot trickle of desire to heat my blood and cluster in my womb.

Upon spotting my shocked expression, Hunter asks, "Is eating against the writing code?"

I shake my head, forcefully removing the images of his nakedness from my mind before replying, "No. I'm always up for eating."

I enter the kitchen, happy to use food as a distraction from my out-of-character awkwardness. Hunter eyes me curiously as I move through the compact space, gathering plates, cutlery, and two beers from the refrigerator. The flips of my stomach smooth to a slight twinge when the smell of Chinese food and Hunter lingers through the air, spurring on my rampant hunger... *for food.*

Over the next hour, we devour a wide variety of delicious dishes without speaking a peep. Unlike the last time we undertook a silent stance, it's void of any awkwardness. Hunter has an aura that demolishes my usually impenetrable walls I raise when in the company of the opposite sex.

Normally, I'm more reserved with my food selection. I don't want to appear like a pig at a trough, but I feel comfortable enough around him that I devoured more than my share of the Chinese food he bought without a single qualm crossing my mind.

Stuffed and requiring a nap, I slump low into the two-seater sofa

I'm sprawled on and rest a hand on the curve of my now protruding stomach. "That was... *scrumptious.*"

I make a mental note to ensure I mention the way Hunter's eyes reveal he's smiling without his lips needing to move when a bright shimmer beams from his eyes during my grateful comment.

While gathering our stained plates off the coffee table, he asks, "Full?"

I leap up to help collect our used dishware, mortified that my food-induced coma once again had me forgetting my manners. "I'm more stuffed than my grandmother's overcooked turkey at Thanksgiving." With dishes balancing on my palms, I shadow him into the poky kitchen.

Hunter smirks before he places the dishware into the sink and commences washing them like he's always belonged here. Grinning like a cat staring at a fishbowl, I snag a dish cloth off the kitchen counter and dry the bubble-covered plate he thrusts at me.

"For someone who doesn't know how to *interact* with girls, you're doing a stellar job," I quip, loving that he doesn't see the kitchen as a 'woman-only zone' like Riley quoted numerous times the past three years.

Hunter continues washing dishes like he was born to do it while relishing the peace. On the other hand, I have been cooped up in this cabin for the past five days with no real-life adult interaction, so I'm feeling a little chatty.

We couldn't be more opposite if we tried.

"So where have you been the past couple of days? I haven't seen you around." My pupils widen to the size of the dinner plate I'm grasping. "Not that I've been looking."

As fiery heat creeps across my cheeks, Hunter's breathy chuckle fans a little scattering of hairs curling on his top lip. He must have been busy the past five days because his usually well-kept beard is more bushy than usual. "I've been busy at work."

He hands me the final dish like five little words will ease my curiosity.

It doesn't.

Not in the slightest.

I wait for the gurgling noise of the sink water draining away to vanish before continuing with my interrogation, "Did you go to New Delhi?"

Hunter shakes his head. "No, Paige, I didn't go to New Delhi."

"So where were you?"

After placing the cutlery in the kitchen drawer, I move to the refrigerator for more beer. A whiny groan purrs through my lips when I discover there's only one beer. Not speaking a word, Hunter gathers a glass from an overhead cupboard, snags the beer from my grasp, then pours half of it into the glass before handing it to me.

After a prolonged stare, he mutters, "I've been *working*, Paige." His tone is back to the same edgy one he used during my last interrogation.

"I do not mean to interrogate you. I'm merely being neighborly," I bite back before taking a swig of my beer, desperately needing something to soothe my ravaged throat.

Hunter's nose screws up as he eyeballs me. His ardent stare has my pulse quickening and my pussy throbbing. I freeze when my inner monologue reaches my head.

What the hell is wrong with me? I can't think about Hunter in this manner.

I stop reprimanding myself when he repeats, "You were being *neighborly?*"

The froth in my mouth doubles in size when I rapidly shake my head. "Yeah. It's what neighbors do. We keep an eye on each other to make sure neither of us ends up in any trouble."

A cocky grin etches on his mouth. It's more concerning than the earlier unwanted throbs of my vagina. "Is that why you've been *watching* me for the past seven weeks? Are you making sure I'm not getting into any *mischief?*"

I kick him in the shoe, unappreciative of the humor in his tone. "Not that type of trouble," I say with a roll of my eyes.

Look at me acting all high and mighty when that is *exactly* why I eyeballed him for weeks on end.

"What if I saw a bandit stealing one of your nude paintings? I wouldn't have any way of telling you. I don't even know your full name, let alone your phone number," I gabble out while walking into the living room, saying anything to get the heat off me and my snooping.

I guzzle down the rest of my beer, praying it will stop the word 'vomit' spilling from my lips. I pretty much just asked for his number by dropping hints.

Can anyone say "Loser?"

Hunter runs the back of his hand over his mouth, removing a smidgen of beer from his top lip before he answers, "I have the world's most advanced security system. I'm not the slightest bit concerned about being robbed."

"Good to know." I vainly try to hide the snarl in my tone. I miserably fail.

With a silent huff, I plop onto the rock-hard sofa. My movements are heavy, weighed down by the harsh blow of rejection.

The sting only burns for a second when Hunter mutters, "But for peace of mind, I guess we could always exchange phone numbers?"

A broad grin stretches across my face as my insides break into a jig. "Sure, if you want."

I shrug, hoping it will conceal my happiness.

Just like all my ploys tonight, my attempt at aloofness is woeful.

CHAPTER EIGHT

"*H*ey, Hunter." I pull open the back patio sliding door before gesturing for him to enter.

When he does, my eyes rocket down to the plastic bag in his hand, eager to see what meal he's arrived with today. For the past four days, he's arrived at precisely nine o'clock with a bag full of scrumptious food. The first night was Chinese, the second Italian, and the third was burgers and fries.

At the start, it felt a little odd accepting his generosity. I'd never had a male friend before, so I was a little unsure of the protocol. But as the days move on, our odd kinship is rapidly merging into a close bond. I've only known him in person for a little over a week, but I feel like I've known him for over half of my life. He is the close confidant I once thought Archer was.

"Looks a little plain today," I jest when a loaf of bread is the only distinguishable item in his bag of goodies.

When I lean in to press a kiss to his cheek, Hunter's cheekbone rises under my lips. "I thought we could go back to basics today."

After taking a moment to relish the warmth of his breath on my cheek, I close the door then follow him into the compact kitchen.

As he moves around my kitchen, gathering supplies and unpacking the ingredients from his bag, I leap onto the tiled countertop to watch him in awe.

The Hunter who stated he found it troubling to interact with women while clothed has been nowhere in sight the past four days. He's calm, relaxed, and carefree.

Don't take my admission the wrong way. The sparks of attraction flying between us the night he returned my laptop are still firing, but I'm giving it my best shot to keep them at a dull flame instead of a raging, out-of-control wildfire.

It has been a very hard feat.

Hunter pulls a skillet off the pot rack dangling above the gas cooktop, places it onto the open flame, and dumps a tablespoon of butter into it. After pulling out eight slices of bread, he sets to work on making grilled ham and cheese sandwiches.

When he wordlessly announces the final ingredient, a jar of pickles, I launch off the bench. "No pickles for me, please," I request, my voice high with disgust. "Pickles are gross. Just the thought of their salty ghastliness sliding down my throat makes me gag. Much to my father's dismay, I've never been a fan of pickles."

A smile stretches across my face when memories of my dad sneakily hiding the occasional pickle in my sandwich when I was in junior high creep into my mind. Although he doesn't have the rough and rugged appearance Hunter has perfected, he has no qualms making a mean grilled cheese sandwich. His sandwiches are now just served on a gold-edged plate.

When Hunter flips over the sandwiches, revealing a beautiful golden covering, I remove two beers from the refrigerator. We've quickly slipped into a routine the past four nights. Hunter supplies the food, and I provide the alcohol and conversation. Although Hunter probably wishes I wasn't so fond of the articulate side of my offerings, considering I do most of the talking.

With a stack of grilled sandwiches balancing on a plate, Hunter follows me into the living room. After dumping the beers onto the coffee table, I snag two scatter cushions off the couch and place them on the floor, and hey presto, our makeshift dining area is complete.

Just like the previous four nights, our meal is shared in silence. Too much quiet generally irritates me, but surprisingly, I enjoy small moments of silence when I am with Hunter. So many of his characteristics are exposed through actions more than words. I've added a vault load of mental notes on his finer quirks to my already extensive collection. Like how the small crumbs of bread from his top lip drop onto his beard and become nonexistent, how he wipes the back of his hand over his mouth after every third bite, and how his gulps of beer are so large, he drinks half of the bottle with only one swig.

Once there's nothing but crumbs left on the plate, I crank my elbow onto the couch and rest my cheek on my hand. "So... did anything exciting happen in the telemarketing world today?"

Hunter smirks against the rim of his beer bottle before taking another large gulp. Once his tongue has cleared away a droplet of beer from his top lip, he shakes his head. I inwardly sigh. I've asked him the same question every day for the past four days, and he responds the same every time I ask.

"What about you? Did you smash your word count?"

I smile while nodding. After telling him about my strict deadline the first night we dined together, each day when he leaves, he assigns me a word count I must strive to reach the following day. Since I am super competitive, I give it my all. Yesterday he assigned one of the biggest targets to date—ten thousand words in a day.

Shockingly, I hit my goal by six, meaning I added another two thousand before I showered in preparation for his arrival.

"It may end up being nothing but a whole heap of word vomit, but I smashed it," I inform, my tone high and eager.

Hunter awards me with a playful wink before placing his beer on the coffee table. I eye him curiously when his hand delves into his jeans pocket to remove a small black camera-like device. "I have something that may assist with your writing," he explains to my bemused expression.

After snatching my iPhone off the table, he connects the device to the speaker port of my phone. My brows shoot up to my hairline when he logs into my phone without asking for the lock code. While making a mental note to check the security of my phone, I lean in close when he snaps a picture of one of my many random scraps of paper lying around the living room. "With this device, you can scan your notes and upload them to your phone."

"Kind of like notes to PDF?"

He shrugs. "Not really. This is similar to a scanner, but instead of scanning the documents as an image, it takes your handwritten words and types them into your pages app."

My eyes bug to of my head. "So I can edit the documents?"

When Hunter nods, a massive surge of euphoria pumps into my veins. This will be an ingenious device for me. Normally, I have to type my handwritten notes. This device will save me hours of work.

"Thank you so much," I praise before accepting my phone from him to test how the device works.

The low hang of my jaw increases when I scan one of my hideous sketches, and it converts it to an image below the typed text Hunter just scanned.

Like a kid with a new toy, I continue scanning anything I can get my hands on.

Within minutes, I have pages of notes stored on my phone that would have taken me hours to type.

"This is brilliant. Where did you find it?"

My brows form a small 'v' in the middle of my forehead when a wash of apprehension crosses Hunter's face. After coughing to clear his throat, he quietly mutters, "I designed it."

I stare at him with shock and disbelief tainting my face. "You made this?" I question while jerking my head to the device I'm clutching like it's worth a million dollars.

His eyes flick down to the device before they lift and lock with mine. "Yep," he says with an apprehensive dip of his chin.

I remain quiet, silenced by shock. After he fixed my laptop last week, I knew he had impressive computer skills, but I had no idea his knowledge was this extensive. This isn't an odd-looking home-made contraption. It looks like Apple or Toshiba manufactured it. I'm not ashamed to admit, I am in complete awe that he made this.

After a beat, Hunter mistakes my silence as ungratefulness. "I can take it back if you don't like it."

"No." I shake my head while yanking my hand away from him so he can't make true on his threat. "I love it. Thank you so much."

When I plant a kiss on his cheek, any chances of keeping the flame in my belly to the size of a match head disappear. His delicious smell engulfs my senses. It is unique and intoxicating—a mixture of freshly showered skin, soap, and another smell I can't quite distinguish.

After discreetly inhaling a final whiff of his mouthwatering scent, I pull back from his cheek. When a sparkle in his eyes reveals he caught my sneaky appreciation of his alluring smell, I bounce my dilated eyes around the room, seeking anything but his gaze.

The color of my cheeks nearly matches the vibrancy of my hair when my endeavor not to have my ardent stare witnessed has me stumbling onto another fervent watch. Hunter is watching me from the corner of his eye. His hooded gaze is full of zeal and covetousness.

The mariachi beat of my heart kicks up even more when he leans in intimately close to my side. His unique scent and the grilled cheese and pickle sandwiches he consumed linger in my nose when he props one arm on the sofa while the other one brushes away a bunch of my wavy red hair from my face. Time comes to a standstill when he skims his index finger down my scrunched-up nose.

Before my brain has time to compile an objection, I blurt out, "How come I've never seen you with a redhead?" One of Hunter's heavy brows slants in confusion, but I continue on as if it didn't. "I've seen you with blondes, brunettes, and once you even had a girl with a pink stripe down the side, but not once have I seen you with a redhead." My words come out in a flurry before my brain can stop them. "Do you not like redheads?"

His eyes dance between mine. "I offered, Paige. Remember? It was *you* who turned *me* down."

I shake my head, denying his claim. "I didn't turn you down. I turned down a *threesome*." I squeak on my last word.

Hunter remains quiet, no doubt dazed into silence. My brain is begging me to return his passiveness, but my impulses override it. I scoot across the floor, filling in the minute speck of space between us. I've never been so bold, but I'm fortified and more than ready to begin a new chapter in my life. I want to move on from the stigma of a broken-hearted woman to have an adventure. Hunter seems like the type of guy who could offer me the no-commitment, fast-paced thrill ride I'm seeking. He could invigorate me as I rediscover the Paige I lost years ago.

The muscles in Hunter's thighs flex as his eyes drift between mine. Although he doesn't aid in filling the gap between us, he doesn't pull away either, confirming to my brain that I'm making the right decision with my newly gained boldness.

Just as Hunter's breaths tickle my puckered lips, he mutters, "We can't, Paige. Not now."

I hold back the windless groan his brutal rejection inflicts on my lungs while flopping onto my backside. Even with his cold, hard slap to my ego stinging like a bitch, I'm not desperate enough to request an explanation for his lack of interest.

I threw myself at him.

He denied my advances.

No explanation is needed.

While lifting my half-empty beer to my suddenly parched mouth, I once again seek anything but Hunter's gaze. Although I'm not desperate enough to demand an explanation, it doesn't mean I don't need a few minutes to soothe the sting.

My back molars grind together when Hunter removes the nearly empty bottle from my grasp and dumps it back onto the coffee table. Before any words can spill from his hard-lined lips, I blubber, "I get it. It's cool. You don't have to explai—"

"Shut up, Paige," he interrupts before he pinches my chin between his thumb and index finger and angles my head back to face him.

My mouth gapes, shell-shocked by the bluntness of his reply. Although at times, his moods swing toward grumpy, but he's never been this blunt before.

"If I didn't consider you a friend, my cock would be filling that hole in your mouth."

I snap my mouth closed, equally shocked and turned on by his crude statement.

"But since you're my friend, my cock will stay in my jeans and not in your pretty little mouth where it really wants to be."

I roll my eyes skyward. "Please. We are *not* friends. I hardly know you. You're practically a stranger." My eyes bulge out of my head, stunned that the words I was meant to say inside my head spilled from my mouth.

Hunter coasts even closer to me, absorbing any sense of normality I had left. "We're not friends?"

"Not even close."

My trembling voice gives away my deceit, but Hunter acts ignorant. "So you don't have any concerns about being another notch on my extensively serrated bedpost?"

I cross my arms in front of my chest to hide the quiver of my hands before shaking my head.

His top lip forms into a snarl, but he continues playing it cool. "You wouldn't be at all devastated when I dressed you and walked you to the door the instant I had my fill of your no doubt tight pussy?"

A barrage of emotions smacks into me at once. I'm excited about his dirty words but also devastated by their callousness. I've seen Hunter in his element. I know without a doubt he'd rocket my core to the next galaxy, but I can't comprehend why he believes our kinship requires a no-sexy-time stipulation.

Even with my heart warning me against it, I shake my head, once again denying his claim.

Hunter's hooded eyes blaze into mine, searing my soul from the inside out as he mutters, "And I *never* called you again."

The shake of my head comes to a standstill as does the beat of my heart.

Never?

Upon spotting my shocked response, Hunter mumbles, "Yeah, that's what I thought. I like you, Paige. Surprisingly enough, I don't want to touch you." He waits for our eyes to meet before finalizing his reply, "Because I don't want to hurt you."

My heart recommences beating so it can accommodate the mass surge of blood pumping through it. Although being rejected dents even the world's biggest egos, it's admirable he's being upfront with me. It takes a lot of guts for a man to be honest, let alone to a virtual stranger.

"So... we're going to be just *friends?*" The cheekiness in my voice hides my confusion. I like Hunter more than I probably should, but I also like the idea of being his friend.

Hunter nods. "If you want?"

I lick my lips before replying, "Alright. I think I can handle that."

I hope.

CHAPTER NINE

"*Do* you want to go for a swim?"

Hunter's eyes drift from the suds-filled sink to me. Our routine hasn't altered the past two weeks. He arrives every night at nine bearing scrumptious gifts. We dine together on the floor of my living room, he washes while I dry, and then we snuggle on the couch and watch a movie.

I want to say the fire in my belly has been kept at a dull flame, but that would be a lie. It's expanded to a decent, winter-warming fire, but it's normal for friends to snuggle on the couch every night. *Isn't it?*

I'd also like to say our conversations have exposed sides of Hunter I didn't discover while stalking him, but unfortunately, they haven't. For the most part, he listens while I blubber incessantly, but even with us having an oddly imbalanced friendship, I enjoy spending time with him. I can be myself around him, which is a refreshing change after spending years pretending to be someone I'm not.

Hunter snatches the dish cloth out of my hand to dry his suds-covered one. "You don't have a pool," he replies to my suggestion as his eyes float to the window of my cozy kitchen. "Or a hot tub," he adds when the coolness of a winter breeze sneaks through the cracks of the wood paneling.

I expand my arms to the expansive view of the blackened ocean of Bronte's Peak behind me. "Who needs a pool when you have an entire ocean?"

He eyes me dubiously but remains quiet when I step away from him, walking backward. When I hit the glass sliding door of the back patio, I toe off my shoes and toss them to the side of the cramped living space.

When my hand darts down to the button in my jeans, the glint in Hunter's gaze augments from curious to disbelief. "You're not?" he questions, his usually prominent voice barely a murmur.

His earth-shattering timbre incites my boldness. After flashing him a quick smirk, I hotfoot it across the patio. By the time I make it down the three stairs of the back deck, my jeans have been shimmied off my legs and dumped onto the sandy ground. Sand squishes between my toes as I make a mad dash for the water's edge. I throw off my sweater and long-sleeve shirt on the way.

The coolness of a late fall breeze whizzes through my hair when I increase my speed. My hammering heart nearly blocks out Hunter's wolf whistles and catcalls as I race across the sand like a mad woman on a mission. My smile is as large as the surge of adrenaline pumping through my veins. I hit the edge of the dunes wearing nothing but mismatched cotton panties and a satin bra.

After squealing the loudest squeal I've ever screamed, I charge for the waves crashing on the foreshore. My cheeks burn from the mammoth grin stretched across my face, and my lungs heave as they struggle to fill with air, but I've never felt more free.

When I reach the water's edge, I crank my neck to the left before sliding it to the right. Satisfied no one is watching, I spin around to face Hunter. "Close your eyes, Hunter. Things are about to get scandalous," I warn, my voice dramatic.

With a broad grin on his face, he continues strolling down the sand dunes. When I arch a brow at him, another silent warning on how far I'm willing to stretch my antics tonight, he throws his forearm over his eyes. As my heart hammers my ribs, I unhook my bra and slide my panties down my legs.

If I risk being arrested for public indecency, I plan to give it my all.

Goosebumps prickle the surface of my skin, and a swear word seeps from my lips when I dive into the bitterly cold water. But even with the possibility of getting frost bite increasing by the second, nothing can wipe the grin off my face.

Salty water pummels me when I collide with the waves breaking to shore, but I continue with my mission, fighting against the surge of water trying to sweep me back to reality.

A sense of achievement washes over me when I reach the serene of the flat ocean. "Come on, Hunter!" My high-pitch squeal echoes in the eerie quietness of the almost midnight sky. "It's so beautiful out here!"

The moonlight glistens on my wet cheeks when I spread my arms out wide and float on the surface of the frigid water. I snap my eyes closed then surrender to the calmness of the ocean. My weightlessness adds to the invincibility I'm feeling.

I am unstoppable.

After enjoying the tranquility of being swept away for a few minutes, I slowly flutter my eyes open. The sky is bright with a dusting of stars, and the moon is full. It's truly a beautiful image I'll treasure for years to come.

My stargazing comes to a halt when my name is called out in the distance. While treading water, I crank my neck to the foreshore.

"Paige!" Hunter calls out again, his voice so loud it bellows over the crashing waves in the distance.

As my eyes lock onto a small black speck approaching from my right, I shout, "I'm over here."

The crazy beat of my heart overtakes Hunter's swimming

strokes when the visual of a drenching wet and completely naked Hunter swamps my vision.

Jesus Christ!

Even hidden under the rippling of water, I can see every spectacular inch of his scrumptious chest, bumped abs, and killer arms. It's been weeks since I've seen the glorious visual of a naked Hunter, and boy, I've missed it.

"Holy fuck. It's fucking freezing!" Hunter's chattering teeth don't dampen the deepness of his tone. "I'm pretty sure I won't recognize my dick when we exit the water."

I throw my head back and laugh. Not a slight, dainty giggle, but a full-hearted chuckle that exposes sides of my wittiness I often hide.

Hunter glares at me, his face marred with both shock and concern. I'm sure I look like a grade-A lunatic, but after the day I've had, I needed this. Finding out your fiancé moved his mistress into your shared home ten days after you left him is a shattering blow to any ego.

Memories of the conversation I had with Pepper earlier today make quick work of my laughter. As I battle to hold in the tears I've kept at bay for most of the day, my face scrunches up. Upon sensing a change in my composure, Hunter runs his index finger down the grooves in my nose before drawing me into his chest.

I plaster my body as close to him as I can. I don't allow an ounce of air between us while accepting his comfort.

Sometimes a good hug is the only cure needed for the deepest heartache.

A stretch of silence passes between us as we tread water. It isn't awkward. We're both happy to take a breather from reality to stare at a star-filled sky. It's surreal to think I only met Hunter weeks ago, and I'm already comfortable enough around him to strip naked and dive into a frigidly cold ocean, not to mention snuggle into his bare chest.

And although I try to ignore it, I can't miss certain parts of his body rubbing against mine.

It is unmissable.

After a few more minutes of silent stargazing, Hunter runs his hand down my goosebump-riddled back. "Are you going to use this for a scene in your book?"

I smile, loving that he isn't the slightest bit fazed by my erratic behavior. If I'd pulled this type of stunt with Riley, he would have had a coronary and shipped me off for extensive therapy. Hunter not being concerned shows he gets me and my quirkiness.

"Yeah... it could work," I reply, still smiling. "What do you think? The heroine dives into the water after an argument, and the hero takes off after her. He then shows her what she means to him by making love to her under the stars in the middle of the ocean." I stop talking, and my lips purse. "Although from what you said earlier, I may need to rework the scene. I don't want to factor in shrinkage."

My heart warms when a hearty chuckle rumbles out of Hunter's blue-tinged lips. "It wouldn't matter if they were swimming in Antarctica, Paige, if the woman is who the man desires, shrinkage won't be a problem."

The veins in my neck pulsate when his eyes lower to absorb portions of my naked body plastered to his. Just like my weirdness doesn't daunt him, he has no qualms about openly ogling me without fear of reprimand.

When his eyes lift and lock with mine, after a few seconds of long gawks, the energy between us shifts. It fires the night sky with a cluster of invisible fireworks. "Trust me." His hungry eyes bounce between mine. "He will have *no* problems getting hard."

My heart beats out a rocking tune, beyond smitten by his compliment. "I'll be s-sure to take note of that." The jitteriness of my tone relays my wavering constraint. The energy teeming between us is too great to ignore. It is hammering into me as badly now as it was when he gifted me his latest mastermind invention.

Hunter's eyes shift from a murky blue to a navy blue as they bore into mine. They show so much hunger, I'm shocked by the words he speaks next. I thought they would have been far less tamed. "Now can we get out of here before my cock snaps off?"

Desperate to hide my devastation, I take off for the shore. A winded grunt escapes Hunter's lips when I use his body as a springboard during the commencement of my mad dash. "Loser gets dirty dishes duty for the next week," I yell out between swimming strokes.

"Challenge accepted," I hear Hunter shout over my frantic splashes.

Even with Hunter's rock-hard abs garnering me a decent lead, he overtakes me halfway to shore then emerges from the water before me. When it dawns on me that my defeat is more a victory than a loss, I slow my strokes, giving my eyes plenty of time to drink in every inch of his panty-wetting body when he cups his cock in his hands and races for his jeans and shirt dumped at the water's edge.

His ass—my god. It needs its own entry in the dictionary to explain how scrumptious it is.

The crisp night buds his dark nipples into firm peaks, and goosebumps prickle his torso. His lack of clothing showcases his yummy Apollo belt and spectacular Adonis ass I'll never grow tired of ogling. The visual of him wet and naked is a core-clenching image that makes me completely forget I'm currently submerged in a bitterly cold ocean.

I only continue swimming back to the shore when Hunter's legs slip into his favorite pair of jeans.

Air hisses from his lips when I emerge from the water. Unlike me, he doesn't hide the fact he's eyeballing me. He categorizes and absorbs every inch of my body as I did him without the slightest bit of intimidation. He notices the way my small breasts bounce beneath my forearm as I pad across the sand, the extra swing his hooded gaze instilled on my hips, and that not all the shimmering between my legs is from the water.

"What are you doing to me, Paige," he mutters under his breath before he wraps his plaid shirt around my shoulders. It engulfs me with his delicious scent and makes the throb of my clit even more noticeable.

Since his words come out more as a statement than a question, I don't respond. I merely watch him button up the three buttons on his shirt, gather my panties and bra from the sand and stuff them into his jeans pocket, then guide me to the cabin by curling his hand over mine.

Even the walk up the sandy path between our properties is done in complete silence. Not only has the chattering of my teeth rendered me speechless, so has the tension bristling between us.

When I reach my patio, I press a kiss to the edge of Hunter's mouth. "Thanks for joining me for a swim."

I feel his mouth raise against my lips. "It was my pleasure. But can we do it in summer next time?"

Laughing, I nod while trying not to look too deeply into his suggestion there may be a next time.

After flashing him a quick smirk, I walk up my patio steps. Just as I'm about to yank open the glass door, Hunter calls my name.

I tilt back to face him. "Yeah?"

"Do you have any plans for Christmas Eve?"

While keeping my excitement concealed behind a neutral expression, I shake my head.

A broad grin stretches across his face. "Do you want to come to a party with me?"

My heart rate skyrockets, but I continue playing it cool. "A family thing or just us?"

Hunter throws back his head and laughs. "You just went skinny-dipping on a public beach without a smidgen of concern, but you're freaked about the prospect of meeting some friends of mine?"

I snarl at him, baring teeth. "I'm not *scared*. I was merely making sure this is the type of things *friends* did." I cross my arms in front of my chest, hoisting my little bosoms higher. "It could be because my brain has frozen over, but this kind of sounds like a date to me?"

Hunter smirks while shaking his head. "It's not a date. It is just two *friends* hanging out." His eyes drop to his plaid shirt curled around my body. "It's so casual, you can wear jeans and a plaid shirt if you want."

I tug his shirt in close to my body while stating matter-of-factly, "You're not getting this back."

He smirks a deliciously wicked smile. "Good. 'Cause you're not getting your panties back either."

My jaw drops. I completely forgot my panties are in his jeans pocket.

After propping my hip onto the wall of the cabin, I stare into his jeering face like my heart isn't racing a million miles an hour. "Will you give me back my panties if I go to this party with you?"

"Nope," he replies without a delay, his eyes as scorching as his reply made my body temperature.

Battling to lessen the rush of desire swamping my pantyless crotch from his gleaming gaze, I cross my legs before saying with a snarl, "Then I guess you're going to the party dateless."

I push off the wall and mosey into the cabin, my pace only slowing when Hunter murmurs, "What about a compromise?"

I smile, smitten he isn't giving up without a fight. My nipples tighten when I step back onto the patio. The perkiness of my breasts isn't from the chilly breeze blowing in from the west. It's from the hankering gleam in Hunter's eyes as he dangles my satin bra from his index finger.

"You keep my shirt. I'll keep your panties. You get your bra. I get a date," he negotiates.

My teeth rake my bottom lip while I pretend I wasn't two heartbeats away from spinning around and accepting his date before he suggested the compromise. I won't lie. I love the way sweat beads on the top of his brow from my delay in replying. Even if it's only for a minute, it's nice for the shoe to be on the other foot in our odd *friendship*.

Once I believe he's sweated it out long enough, I say, "You have yourself a deal."

CHAPTER TEN

My leisurely pace up the sand-lined path halts when my eyes lock in on a raw, earth-shattering visual. Hunter is in the shower. Not the shower in his overly priced, pristine glass house. The outside shower nestled in the privacy of his glass and steel patio.

The early morning sun glistens on his wet torso as water from the shower head drenches the long hair framing his face. A breathless moan ripples from my lips when I follow the torrent of water slithering past his smooth pecs and bumps of his six-pack before it gushes over his fisted cock.

His parted lips release quick pants in a rhythm matching his strokes.

No matter how much my conscience tells me to look away, just like the first night I discovered Hunter in a lust-crazed romp, I can't pry my eyes from him. The visual is too primal, raw, and utterly carnal not to devour. His head is lolled to the side, his plump lips are split, and the sexiest groans I've ever heard are rumbling from his throat as he brings himself to the brink of ecstasy.

I lick my parched lips as my eyes drink in every delicious inch of him—his carved, prominent muscles, smooth hairless torso, and a gorgeous face covered by a scruffy beard.

The beat of my heart grows wild when my eyes drop lower. Even his large, manly hand fisting his cock can't take away from the sheer girth and length of his thickened shaft. It's panty-wetting, delicious, uncut, and jutted with the slightest shimmering of pre-cum at the tip. Just watching him pleasure himself brings new understanding to the world of voyeurs. If the visuals I could encounter are this entertaining, I may consider altering my opinion on my voyeurism status.

My throat struggles to swallow when Hunter's pace quickens. He leans deeper into the shower as his hand works his cock from the base to the tip in precise, perfect strokes. I curve my knees inward, battling to ease the crazy pulse surging through my womb when his thumb slides over the crown of his impressive cock to gather a drop of pre-cum beading at the end. Slickness coats my swimwear when I squeeze my thighs together. I am unable to harbor my excitement any longer.

The throb between my legs turns lethal when Hunter hears a moan I fail to stifle. His weighted eyelids pop open before his heavily dilated eyes lock with mine. Another throaty moan topples from my O-formed mouth when the pace of his strokes strengthens from staring into my lust-crazed eyes.

His hips thrust as he guides his magnificent cock in and out of his clenched fist. I stare at him, wide-eyed and open-mouthed, shocked beyond comprehension at the rapid surge of my libido. Just watching him unravel is bringing my climax to the surface at a frantic velocity.

Just as his nostrils flare and the veins in his cock bulge, an annoying buzz blasts my ears.

A rough, tormented groan simpers through my parched lips when I emerge back into the land of the living. Even knowing the glorious visual was nothing but a dream, the wetness between my legs doesn't dampen any. I'm beyond saturated.

I want to say my X-rated dream was the first I've had of Hunter, but that would be a lie. Ever since our skinny-dipping adventure four nights ago, I haven't stopped dreaming about him. And like a sex-deprived nympho, every one of my dreams features Hunter in the middle of a sex act, nude, alone, and handsy.

While endeavoring to ignore the throb of excitement thickening my blood, I throw my legs over the side of the bed and mosey into the bathroom for my fourth cold shower this week.

Pepper's eyes flick between me and a program she's watching on Netflix. "Do a Google image reverse search on him."

I place my bowl of half-eaten cornflakes on my desk then curl my legs under my bottom. "A what?"

"You upload an image onto Google, and it searches for similar images. Maybe it will find him?" she advises after drifting her eyes back to her phone's screen.

We've been FaceTiming the past thirty minutes while watching a recording of our favorite sitcom, *Empire*. We're usually inseparable, spending a minimum of two to three hours together each day, but since I flew to the other side of the country, we've had to resort to FaceTime to keep our unique closeness firmly tethered.

"If he's someone famous, it will find him quick smart," Pepper adds.

I consider her suggestion for as long as it takes me to remember that I don't have a photo of Hunter.

After sharing my dilemma with Pepper, she says, "If you didn't hold out on my request for army porn weeks ago, that wouldn't have been a problem, would it?" Suddenly, her shoulders square and her pupils enlarge. "What's the name of that town near Bronte's Peak? The one you visited to get your laptop repaired?"

"Ravenshoe?" I scrunch up my face, unsure why an unknown town on the other side of the country would be of interest to her.

"Yes!" She jumps from her chair and ruffles through a collection of gossip magazines at her side. Once she finds the article she's looking for, she saunters back to the computer desk and plops into her leather chair. "You know that song blowing up the charts? Umm... what's it called... it's by that group of hotties?"

"Oh... umm... Surrender something?"

""Surrender Me!" That's it," Pepper interrupts, startling me when her loud roar thunders down the line. "I was reading a little article written in a magazine about them this morning. What would you say if I told you the band members of Rise Up live in Ravenshoe?"

My eyes bulge out of their sockets. "Are you serious?"

Pepper waggles her manicured brows while nodding. "Fancy-schmancy house, nice cars, obviously wealthy. Maybe all those women you saw coming and going from Hunter's home those first six weeks were groupies?"

My heart painfully twists during the last part of her statement. Before we became friends, seeing the troop of women come in and out of Hunter's life like a revolving door didn't bother me the slightest. Now... now it stings a little.

"Does the article tell you their names?"

Pepper's eyes scan the document. "Noah Taylor, lead singer. Marcus Everett, bassist. Nicholas Holt, guitarist. And the drummer is Slater Scott."

I slump deeper into my seat. "It's not Hunter then."

"Why?"

My brows inch as high as my voice. "Because he introduced himself as Hunter."

"And? What name did you use when you introduced yourself?"

My heart slithers into my gut. "Paige."

Pepper smirks a winning smile. "Exactly. Maybe you aren't the only one using an alias?"

Keystrokes resonate out of my iPhone speaker as I sit in silence, muted by guilt.

"He isn't the lead singer. Noah is smoking hot but has a dark and moody appearance."

I pull my phone closer to my face. "What are you doing?"

"Googling the Rise Up band members," she reports like it's no big deal she's invading Hunter's privacy. After a small stretch of silence, she turns her eyes to me. "Do you need a visitor? Because I need to see if Marcus is this hot in real life. If he is, I'm giving up my dreams of becoming an actress and taking up the role of Marcus's lead groupie."

I giggle softly. "Better than any cabana boy you've seen?"

"Ah... much better." She returns her eyes to her laptop. "Check your email. I sent you a picture."

I lower the phone and log into my email account. "Wow," I mumble when Marcus pops up on the screen. He has a gorgeous face and seducing green eyes. "I have to write a character with his bedroom eyes."

Pepper laughs. "Hell, yeah. But I think it's safe to say he isn't Hunter. Even with the lack of zoom on your phone, I'm fairly sure Hunter didn't have ravishing African American skin."

I laugh. "No, he's nearly as white as me."

"So that leaves two possibilities. Nick, the guitarist, or Slater, the drummer. Although Nick has similar length hair and coloring, his frame is too small, and his skin is void of any tattoos." Pepper angles her head to the side as she assesses her laptop screen with vivid accuracy. "Does Hunter have dreads?" When she gawks at me through my iPhone screen, I shake my head. "Darn it. I could see a resemblance between Slater and Hunter, but with how tight Slater's dreads are, that's not something he does just for when he's on the road. They're permanent." With a loud sigh, she leans deeper into her chair. "I thought I was onto a winner. I guess you'll have to ask Hunter who the hell he is the next time you see him."

My nose scrunches. "He isn't a fan of sharing personal information."

"What man is?" Pepper shrugs. "I emailed you a photo of each band member. If you see them, be a doll and grab me an autograph. There's a big buzz around them at the moment."

"Alright. I'll keep my eye out," I reply with a cheeky wink.

My attention turns from Pepper's grinning face when a rumbling engine resonates in the silence. I leap out of my chair, eager to see if it's Hunter. I haven't seen hide nor hair of him for the past three days. After spending every night with him for nearly three weeks, I've noticed his absence.

With my phone in my hand, I move toward the arched window of my office.

"Show me," Pepper whispers down the line.

While keeping my eyes planted on the three people emerging from a candy apple red muscle car, I twist my phone around. I'm stunned into silence. In the nine weeks I've been here, this is the first time I've seen a male visitor arrive at Hunter's house, let alone two of them.

"Where the hell are you visiting? Are only hot people allowed to live there?"

I laugh even though I wholeheartedly agree with Pepper's assessment. The brunette standing between the two men is gorgeous. She has light beige skin and luxurious dark hair falling in waves around her shoulders. Even wearing a simple pair of jeans and a long-sleeve shirt, she is stunning. A large brute of a man a good four to five inches taller than Hunter takes the stairs two at a time while the brunette and a handsome blond gentleman lock arms and shadow closely behind him.

A smile tugs on my lips when I spot the brunette's shocked expression from absorbing the enormity of Hunter's house. She looks like a stunned mullet.

"Do you think we should call the police?" Pepper whispers.

I shake my head. "No. Look, the hunky brute is putting in a security code."

Just as I finish speaking, Patricia's computer voice sounds through the quiet.

"That's cool." I can hear Pepper's smile in her voice.

"I told you."

The way the three of them walk through Hunter's residence with wide eyes and open mouths, I can tell this is their first time visiting. Although his house will always be impressive, nothing replicates the first time you've been captivated by something. Their faces display that they're newbies to the grandeur of Hunter's house.

My attention reverts from the beautiful brunette emerging onto the glass deck at the back of Hunter's house to the front of his property when a sports car rolls down the driveway. My heart rate kicks up a gear when a gentleman in a three-piece suit exits the car after parking it next to the shiny muscle car.

"Damn," Pepper draws out in a long, husky drawl. "I'm living in the wrong neighborhood."

She leans in close to her iPhone, ensuring she doesn't miss a thing as the impeccably dressed man makes a beeline for the large glass door. His hair is dark, thick, and luxurious. His body is a similar size to Hunter's, but his choice in clothing accents his god-crafted assets.

Like he can sense us watching, his long strides come to a halt in the marble foyer of Hunter's house, and he cranks his neck to peer at my window. Even knowing he can't see me, I take a step back, unnerved by his powerful gaze.

"Mafia?" Pepper suggests, her voice barely a whisper.

"What? No!" I reply dramatically. "Do you think?"

"He's obviously wealthy, has an edge of darkness to him, and even through your phone, his allure demands my attention. He's either in the mafia or my next sugar daddy."

"Every rich guy is your next sugar daddy," I retort, laughing so hard, I snort.

"Yeah, true. But even if he were as poor as dirt, I'd still let him leave his toothbrush at my place." Pepper's giggling stops when the suit-clad gentleman's intense stare-down of my window is interrupted by a cute blonde wearing a red Chanel suit. "Oh, interesting. It's like watching Lucious and Cookie from *Empire* going to battle," she mumbles when the two engage in a heated argument.

Their discussion is cut short when the dominant one of the duo spots the brunette standing on the glass patio. My insides sigh when the two race to each other. They crash into each other's arms in the middle of the living area. The suit-clad man pulls the brunette into his chest before he takes a seat on one of the white leather sofas in Hunter's living room.

"You need to record that," mutters Pepper, her voice sounding as transfixed as my eyes are. "The sparks firing off those two would make a heart-stopping read."

I nod, even though she can't see me. There's no denying the attraction between the two gorgeous specimens. It's earth-shattering. I've never been much of a crying Nancy, but their closeness is compelling tears to form in my eyes.

"I have to go." I turn my phone screen back to me. "I can't record them and talk to you at the same time."

"Go!" Pepper overemphasizes, excitement heard in her voice.

After air-blowing her a farewell kiss, I disconnect the call and activate the record function on my phone. The blood pumping through my body thickens with excitement, knowing without a doubt I'm in the process of capturing a unique moment between the starring couple of my next alpha male romance.

CHAPTER ELEVEN

"**C**heck the hidden compartment inside your suitcase."

I press my phone nearer to my ear as I saunter to my half-unpacked suitcase in the main suite of my rental cabin. A clink of laughter spills from my lips when I slide open the zipper of the hidden compartment in my bursting-at-the-seams suitcase. "Pepper!" I scoff, my tongue clicking against my teeth. "I think a rodent got into my suitcase on the flight over as most of the material on this *outfit* has been compromised."

"It's supposed to be like that." Just from her tone, I can tell she's rolling her eyes. "It's a crotchless lace teddy."

"Yeah... I worked that out when I noticed the *entire* crotch was missing." I flop onto the bed. "Why in the world did you sneak *that* into my suitcase?"

I turn my eyes to the ceiling when Pepper's contagious laughter barrels down the line. "Because I knew after seven years of dating Riley, that may be the only thing to clear the cobwebs between your legs."

"Thanks for the confidence boost, Pepper."

"Hey, I'm not saying you need any help in being sexy, Paige.

You've got that shit covered. But... you've been living the past three years as if you're my mother. It's time to slip out of the granny panties and add a touch of naughtiness to your ensemble. Wearing sexy clothing isn't about how you look in it. It's how you feel while wearing it."

I remain quiet, contemplating what she's saying.

I can't even remember the last time I wore anything remotely sexy, so she could be onto something.

"Besides, that little number will have Hunter tripping over his feet."

"We're *friends*, Pepper," I quote the same saying I've said to myself numerous times over the past several weeks.

"Friends who eat dinner together nearly every night, go skinny-dipping, and plan dates a month in advance. Yeah... *friends*." Pepper's tone is full of sarcasm. "I've never skinny-dipped with a *friend*." My mouth opens in preparation to dispute her claim, but she cuts me off. "College parties don't count. Your dip in the ocean was only with two people. That's a lot more intimate than a bunch of horny college kids doing a naked swim at Lake George."

Unable to negate her claim, I jump up off the bed and walk to the antique dresser in the middle of the room. My friendship with Hunter has been going great guns. Other than his disappearance for three days earlier this week, we've dined together most nights the past three weeks, have watched a range of movies while snuggling on the couch, and he set up some fandangled thingy on my laptop so my manuscripts will automatically store to my iCloud account, meaning I'll never have to worry about losing any work if my laptop goes kaput again.

It's been a great few weeks that has exposed sides of Hunter I didn't know existed even after weeks of stalking him. He's a great guy—kind, funny, and a little moody. I just wish I could learn to control my libido around him. He wants to be friends, and in all honesty, I want the same, but for some absurd reason, anytime he's around, my sexual appetite rushes to the surface like an out-of-control tidal wave.

I'm beyond flabbergasted by my body's reaction to Hunter. He's *nothing* like the men I usually lust over, but a different side of Paige emerges in his presence. I don't know if my newfound personality is a forced change from leaving a seven-year relationship or a revamp I've been endeavoring to undertake the past three years. Either way, I'm loving it. A change is as good as a holiday.

"Silenced by the truth, hey?" Pepper snickers, reminding me I still have my cell attached to my ear. "If Hunter is only your friend, why can I hear you fluffing your hair? And was that your Sisley Phyto-Lip Gloss being opened? You only wear that brand when you want to get *lucky*."

I screw the stick of my Sisley lip gloss back into its container and throw it into my makeup bag. "God. Am I going crazy, Pepper?" I spit out the only logical reason for my sudden shift in personality. "Maybe I'm attracted to Hunter because he's the only guy within a ten-mile radius?"

"Please," Pepper overemphasizes in a thick drawl. "You like him because he's a hot brute of a man with an Adonis ass. It has nothing to do with loneliness." Even though her tone is friendly, it has an edge of bitchiness attached to it.

"Hunter is *nothing* like Riley."

"Exactly!" she interrupts. "That's what makes him even more attractive." The creak of her leather office chair sounds down the line, closely followed by the padding of her tiny feet. "When you see Hunter, does your heart beat faster?"

I bite my lip and nod.

Even though she can't see me, she continues with her quest, intuiting my reply. "Do your palms get a little clammy and your tummy jittery?"

"Yes," I say in barely a whisper. *Every single time I see him.*

"Those things don't happen because you've been hiding away from society in your writing cave penning your next novel. It's because you dig him. Hunter isn't Riley, not even close, but you're assuming it's Hunter who is the odd man out. Are you sure it wasn't Riley all along?"

My brows furrow, baffled by her statement.

"You started dating Riley when you were seventeen. Did you even know then what your preferences were, or did you alter them to suit the guy shining a light on you?" Pepper questions my silent musing.

I take a minute to consider what she is saying.

"Riley didn't wear a suit until he started working at Leimans," I mumble as the logic of Pepper's statement crashes into me.

Over the seven years I was with Riley, his hair went from a long, wispy style to a short back and sides cut. The stubble on his chin was cleared away, and his clothing selection altered from slacks and printed tees to expensive business suits. But since he was still Riley, I never put much thought into the alteration of his appearance. He was my partner, so I just took it in stride.

"That's right. But for some strange reason, you have it in your head that you're only attracted to business-looking men. If you were to look past Hunter's caveman attire, what would you see?"

I gulp loudly.

"Exactly!" she squeals, scaring the living daylights out of me. "Don't take this the wrong way, as you are in no way ready for a relationship, but that's the brilliance of a friends-with-benefits agreement. You get an award-winning novel, and you may even get your pent-up sexual frustration taken care of."

My nose screws up. "And what does Hunter get out of this?"

Pepper expels a large, frustrated breath. "You, Paige. He gets the pleasure of spending time with a woman as beautiful and as kindhearted as you."

A misting of fluid hampers my vision. I am pleased as punch by her compliment. After my ego copped a severe pounding last week, her littlest compliment has a huge impact on my faltering esteem.

Before I can respond to Pepper's praise, a knock sounds

through my ears. My heart beats triple time when I pop my head into the hallway and discover who is knocking. "I've got to go, Pepper. Hunter is here." Excitement laces my voice.

"Go get him, tiger," she jests.

Her full-hearted chuckle booms down the line when I roar before disconnecting the call. After yanking open the top drawer of the dresser, I ditch the meager scrap of lace material inside before strolling down the hallway. My steps are hurried, surprised by Hunter's impromptu visit. Even though we've hung out numerous times the past three weeks, he's never arrived in the morning before.

"Do you have a dress?" he asks the instant I open the door, not bothering to issue a greeting.

"Hi, Hunter," I retort, my tone jokingly snappy.

He spins on his heels to face me. A grin curls on my lips when he scrubs at his beard. That's a telltale sign that he's nervous. "Sorry. Hello, Paige." His eyes sparkle with candor when he leans in to press a kiss to the edge of my mouth. "Do you have a dress?" he mumbles against my mouth, his beard tickling my lips.

I scrunch up my face and cock my hip. "Not in your size."

Euphoria pumps through my veins when his boisterous chuckle booms into my ears. "Not for me. For you," he retorts between laughter. His cologne I still can't distinguish engulfs me when he stops laughing and takes a step closer to me. "I need your help."

"Okay," I reply without hesitation.

What? It's the neighborly thing to do.

"I need your help in a dress." When I slant my head and stitch my brows, Hunter asks, "If I were to turn up to a high-priced charity function, would I gain unwanted attention?"

I run my eyes over his scruffy jaw, jeans, and plaid shirt-covered body before nodding. Although I've grown accustomed to his unique ruggedly handsome look, the pretentious people who typically attend such events may not appreciate his ruggedness.

"But if I turned up with a beautiful woman on my arm, they'll assume you dragged me there against my wishes, and I'll remain inconspicuous," Hunter continues.

A broad grin stretches across my face, not because his statement is accurate, but because he thinks I'm beautiful.

"That sounds like a great theory, but I don't have a dress," I inform him, cringing.

He stares at me like I just told him I'm not a woman. "You don't have a dress?"

"Nope. I came here to write. You're lucky you see me out of my pajamas." *And with my hair brushed.*

Hunter's sinful mouth curls into a grin.

"But if I have enough time, I could probably rustle something up?" I suggest, eager to do anything to put a smile on his face. My plan works when his grin enlarges to a full, heart-stopping smile. "How fancy?"

Like it could get any bigger, his smile widens even more. "Ten thousand dollars a plate."

My heart fails. "What?" I shake my head, clearing my ears of any congestion to ensure I can hear him properly this time around. "How much?"

"Ten thousand a plate," Hunter repeats.

I swallow the brick in my throat, sending it straight to my swishy tummy. "And how long do I have to prepare for this 10K event?"

"An hour," he states matter-of-factly while curtly nodding.

I double balk. "Are you serious?"

While rubbing his hands together, he nods.

"Well, I guess you better call in a favor from your fancy-schmancy friends to get me a reservation at an overpriced boutique because this doesn't sound like a drop-into-Target-on-the-way type of function."

The smile that etches onto Hunter's face nearly causes me to have a coronary. "Deal." He yanks a smooth black cell phone out of his pocket. His fingers move swiftly over the screen before he squashes it to his ear. "Hey, Cormack, I need a favor," he says into his fancy phone I didn't know he owned.

And just like that, an appointment is made.

Ten minutes later, I've zipped up my half-unpacked suitcase, stored it in the trunk of Hunter's car, and am heading to a dress boutique in the middle of Ravenshoe for an impromptu shopping splurge. This is one of the reasons I love my industry. I can just up and leave on a dime. No excuses needed and no pleading with the boss for time off. Complete control.

My attention shifts from the scenery flying by when the smooth, rich voice of Hunter sounds through my ears.

I crank my neck to peer at him. "Sorry, what did you say? I spaced out a little."

He scrapes his hand along his hairy jaw, making my fingers twitch with envy. "The shopping attendant at On Point Boutique needs to know your cup size." His tone is unwavering, not the slightest bit embarrassed about the sensitivity of his question. "I said a little more than a handful, but for some reason, she doesn't appreciate my candidness."

A feverish heat follows the path his eyes make when they indecently roam my body to gauge not only my cup size but every fine hair on my body as well. When his ardent eyes settle on my face, I cock my brow and return his sweat-impinging showdown. Although our *friendliness* the past few weeks has occasionally stepped over the friendship barrier, he's never taken it this far before.

He must think because we are stuck in traffic and surrounded by cars that he's safe from an attack by a horny writer.

He isn't.

The pegs of his teeth stick out of his bearded face when he asks, "So... what is it? They look like a ten out of ten to me."

I grit my teeth to hide my smile before punching him in the bicep. After mustering a fake snarl, I hold my hand out, requesting his phone. His brash grin enlarges to a shit-eating smile when he secures a device from jeans pocket and hands it to me. My brows furrow when I peer at a small glass bead nestled in my palm. It would be no bigger than half an inch in size.

"Put it in your ear," Hunter instructs to my baffled expression. "It will pick up the vibration of your voice from your inner eardrum."

"So I'll sound like a robot?" I mimic the noises of a robot to enhance my statement.

He chuckles. "No. You'll still sound like you. Trust me."

Grimacing, I place the small bead into my ear. My eyes widen when a nasally female voice shrills down the line, barking orders at someone on the other end.

"Hello," I say, my voice shaky. My heart stops hammering my ribs when my voice sounds eerily similar to how I normally sound, if not more refined. "Umm... Hunter said you needed my cup size?"

The female attendant huffs. "Yes. Due to the *unendurable* short notice we've been given, we will have *no* chance to alter the dress you chose, so we need to ensure we have your correct measurements."

"Okay," I mumble, annoyed at the rudeness in her tone. I cup my hand around my mouth and swivel to face the window. "I'm a B cup," I barely whisper into my hand.

"I'm sorry, I didn't catch that," she replies, her pitch snarky.

I cough to clear my throat. "I'm a B cup," I repeat, slightly louder.

"Nope, still didn't get that."

"B for bonnet," I mutter through clenched teeth.

"You need to talk up."

"I'm a B cup!" I shout, my temper spurred on by the rudeness of her tone.

Because of the loudness of my voice, there's no way in hell Hunter missed my comment.

"Thank you. We will see you in thirty minutes," the boutique assistant snarls before disconnecting the call.

I shake the bead out of my ear. The roughness of my shake

matches the grinding of my teeth. The only way that could have been more embarrassing was if I had Hunter pull over and take my chest measurements himself.

My eyes rocket to Hunter when he says, "I don't know how she didn't hear you the first time. It was crystal clear from my end."

I glare at him, more confused than ever. He grins cockily while tapping on his right earlobe. When I look closely, I see the smallest shimmer of a black bead sitting in his ear. "You were eavesdropping on my *private* conversation," I squeal, shock evident in my voice.

He shakes his head. "No. Eavesdropping means I was spying. I wasn't snooping. I was *observing*." His tone is a mix between facetious and factual.

"How can you hear anything with your ear clogged up by a bead?" I ask in an endeavor to shift the focus of our conversation away from my less-than-stellar chest region.

Hunter purses his lips. "It's no different than a hearing aid. With a microphone on the end, sound waves travel through the amplifier and exit via the speaker. With echo reduction, this device makes everything crystal clear."

"So even if I whispered that you were an asshole under my breath, you'd hear me?" I mumble ever so quietly.

"Yep," he replies with a chuckle.

I roll my eyes and return them to the scenery whizzing by. "Adonis-assed asshole."

"Heard that too."

That was the point, I silently chant to myself.

Twenty minutes later, we pull into a fancy-looking dress shop in the middle of Ravenshoe. Just like the last time I visited this town a few weeks ago, it's a bustling hive of activity. Exhaust fumes linger in the air, and the hum of vigorous activities sounds through my ears. I love the serenity of Bronte's Peak, but if it weren't for Hunter saving me from the solitude, I'd be strapped into a straitjacket by now.

"You're not going to feed the meter?" I ask when he curls out of his car and walks straight past the expired meter.

"Nope," he says with a shake of his head before he pulls open the boutique's heavy glass door for me. "My boss owns this town, so I'm not concerned about getting a ticket."

"Telemarketing my ass," I mumble under my breath while ambling into the opulent surroundings.

Even without his fandangled listening device in his ear, I can be assured Hunter heard my statement because I said it loud enough to ensure he would.

CHAPTER TWELVE

Much to the dismay of Melinda, the dressing hostess from On Point Boutique, I groove out of the dressing room like one of Flo Rida's female entourage, wearing a low-cut dress that shows more of my stomach than my swimwear does.

Just like the movie montage in *Sweet Little Things* with Christina Applegate and Cameron Diaz, I work the immodest dress like it is Julia Roberts's hooker outfit from *Pretty Woman*. While ignoring Melinda's disgruntled snickering, I shake my tushie in front of a wall of mirrors, knowing without a doubt I'd never be caught dead in an outfit as skimpy as this.

Once I've finished checking myself out, I spin around to face Hunter, fully anticipating the thumbs-down signal he's given for the last dozen dresses I've tried on.

Even more shocking than the amount of collagen in Melinda's top lip is discovering his thumb is pointing to the ceiling.

Hold on, make that thumbs.

I cock my hip and glare into Hunter's dilated eyes. "Unless this ten-thousand-dollar-a-plate gala is for the Adult Video Awards in

Vegas, I'm not wearing this dress," I snarl out before pacing back to the curtain to try on another dress.

Hunter leaps off the press-studded chaise and hotfoots it after me. "Come on, Paige, take one for the team. If you wear that dress, no man in the room will pay me any attention."

"The men may not, but I'll be the target of every woman in the room." I spin around, soundlessly requesting he release the hook on the hideous *outfit* I'm wearing. "You may as well stick a bullseye on my back to make sure their daggers have something to aim at."

Hunter chuckles as he slides down the zipper of my dress. The simplest of tasks causes a shift in dynamics between us. It's quick and absolute. We've gone from two friends playing hooky from work to feeling like we're about to star in one of the productions crowned winner at the Adult Video Awards.

I clutch the material of the dress to my less-than-stellar cleavage before spinning around to once again face him. My steps are shaky since I'm balancing on wobbly knees. I stare into his eyes, gauging if he can feel the zapping in the air as well.

His eyes are expressive but not enough for me to garner an answer to my silent interrogation. "Tell me you feel something?" I mutter, my voice barely a whisper, no longer able to harbor my need to know if he can feel the energy in the air or if I'm simply going insane from lack of human contact.

All writers are a little bit quirky. Heck, I'm beyond quirky, but I'm still stumped by the vibrancy that sparks the air when I'm in Hunter's presence. I've never felt anything like this. I've read about it but always assumed it was an overly dramatic way to describe two characters' connection. But this isn't just a feeling in my core. It's real, and it is heart-stopping.

Hunter's top lip twinges as his eyes bounce between mine. Just when I think he's going to say something, his eyes drift past my shoulder to the dark emerald-green satin gown hanging in the middle of the monstrously sized dressing room. It has a gorgeous tight crossover fitted bodice and mermaid tail. Although it's divine, there's no way in hell I'm paying the excessive amount on the price tag for *one* dress. It costs more than all the royalties I've collected from my first novel thus far.

"That one." Hunter's eyes spark with zeal. After pressing his finger to his lips, his fervent gaze turns to Melinda. "We are taking that one."

When he points to the ridiculously overpriced dress, Melinda's eyes flare with excitement. *Obviously, she works off commission.*

Her eagerness doesn't last long when I shake my head. "No. I'm not paying for a dress that costs more than the first car I owned. We will take the azalea guipure-lace illusion dress, but instead of navy blue, I'll take it in cobalt blue and one size smaller." My tone is surprisingly firm, not just spurred on by Melinda's rudeness the past hour but from another brutal rejection by Hunter.

When he attempts an objection, I press my index finger against his lips. "Shut up." I use the same tone he did when he rejected me weeks ago. "I know you didn't like the knee-length skirt, but with the right stiletto heels and a few accessories, it will be a knockout. Trust me."

Not giving him the chance to protest any further, I snap the curtain closed and slip out of the exorbitantly priced stripper dress before sliding back into my stretchy yoga pants and one-shoulder long-sleeve shirt.

Hunter remains quiet as we shadow Melinda out of the dressing room. I vaguely try to pretend I'm not cringing at paying a little over five hundred dollars for a dress. Don't get me wrong, the dress is pretty, but it still isn't worth that price point. The crinkles impeding my forehead deepen when Hunter pulls his wallet out of the back pocket of his jeans when we arrive at the cashier station.

"What are you doing?" I query, my voice snarky.

I need to eat something. I always get a little bitchy when I'm hungry.

His eyes drift between Melinda and me. "Paying for your dress?" His tone is as dubious as his facial expression.

My brows hit my hairline before I ask, "Do I look like a hooker to you?"

My pulse speeds up when his eyes leisurely run the curves of my body. "No. Not a low-end one anyway."

My bitchiness falters from the jaunty gleam in his eyes.

I kick him in the ankle before handing my credit card to a scowling-faced Melinda. "You're *certainly* not Richard Gere, and I'm no Julia Roberts," I mumble under my breath.

From the crass grin that stretches across his face, I can be assured he heard my witty comment.

After gathering my boutique bag from Melinda, I return my credit card to my purse and follow Hunter to his car. The midday sun beaming off the charcoal black coloring gives me a brilliant idea. "I want to drive," I shout, probably a little loud since a little old lady walking by jumps in fright. After issuing an apology to the lady now one step closer to her grave, I lock my eyes with Hunter. "I want to drive your Hellcat. Just the first twenty miles."

"Nope. Not happening," he replies, his tone curt.

I stop my brisk pace to his car and cross my arms in front of my chest. "Then I'm not going to the gala."

"Bullshit," Hunter retorts, not the slightest bit concerned about my threat. "You wouldn't have bought a dress if you weren't planning on coming."

Little does he know acting is another one of my creative arts.

"I can wear that dress to any function," I say, wiping his smug grin right off his face. "Besides, what am I getting out of this deal? I'm helping you out, yet I'm the one being handed the short straw."

I should feel threatened by the glare he's directing at me, but it doesn't hold any heat. The twitching of his lips as he suppresses a smile gives away his true feelings.

"I have to consume food only rabbits should eat and squeeze into a dress two sizes too small so some old geezer can skip his little blue pill for the night. Sounds like a rip-roaring night of fun. *Not.* I'd rather wax my eyebrows and watch re-runs of *Mash*." I spin on my heels, preparing to walk down the cracked concrete sidewalk. "Bye, Hunter."

My brisk pace halts again when the snappiest "Fine" comes out of a pair of stern-lined lips.

I quickly spin on my heels, not wanting to give him the opportunity to recant his statement. His eyes glare into mine as I span the distance between us. "If you get one scratch on my car—"

"You'll spank my bottom?" I interrupt while grinning a victorious smirk before I snatch the keys out of his hands.

"I'll do far worse than spank your ass, Paige," he rebuts, his tone grumbly.

I munch on my bottom lip, feigning that I'm a little sex fiend who has no qualms about a playful spanking. "Oh, well, in that case," I purr, my voice extra throaty.

Not appreciating my attempts at sarcasm, he snatches the keys back out of my grasp. While doing my best to ignore his noteworthy scent, I balance on my tippy toes and brush my lips on the shell of his earlobe. "I promise I won't scratch your car... unless you want me to?"

It takes ten miles for Hunter to release the deathly tight grip on his thighs and another twenty miles before his tight jaw loosens. By the time we're fifty miles out of Ravenshoe, the strain encumbering his gorgeous face slackens, and the standard pre-terrified Hunter re-emerges.

I drift my eyes from the road to Hunter. "What's your interest in the charity gala?" Nothing against him, but he doesn't appear to be a charity function type of guy.

He scrapes his hand along his beard as a smirk stretches across his mouth. "What is it with women judging me this week? First Izzy. Now you."

I smile, loving that he can read my real intentions when I've only spoken six little words. "I'm not judging you." I twist my lips to lessen the size of my smile. "Just *clothed,* you don't seem like the type who'd like this kind of event."

His grin enlarges, either smitten by my compliment or agreeing with it. I haven't worked out the difference between his musing smile and his amused one yet. When I catch the impish gleam in his eyes, I know he's taken my ribbing as playful, not bitchy.

"You, of all people, know you should never judge a book by its cover," he quips.

"Ha," I interrupt with a loud shriek. "That's one of the most inaccurate statements in the writing world. Writers are always judged. Too many commas, not enough commas. Too much sex, not enough sex. Too much description, not enough description, and don't even get me started on the cover. Unfortunately, we live in a world full of critics."

"So you judge a person based solely on the clothes they are wearing?" His tone is a cross between curious and blunt.

"Not all the time, but for the majority, yes." *Wow, that even sounded snobbish to me.*

Hunter briefly nods. "So, what was your first opinion of me?"

"You weren't exactly clothed at the time, so it doesn't count."

The grin on his face turns titanic. "So my nakedness did ignite your stalker obsession?"

I swallow the brick that lodged in my throat from rehashing memories of his nakedness before replying, "Not exactly... it was your Adonis ass."

The stranglehold on my throat lessens when Hunter's chuckle booms around the car's interior. "I like you, Paige," he chokes out between laughter.

"Yep. We've already established that." *That's the whole reason you won't touch me.*

With the fire forming in my belly from his idolatrous glare, I wish I had more of a bitch gene. I like Hunter. He's a great guy. But

I've never had this type of obsession with a man before. It's consuming my every waking moment.

Maybe it's the thrill of the chase? I've never been turned down before, so I don't have anything to compare it to. Since I was with Riley from the age of seventeen, it was normally me turning away tempting invitations, not inciting them.

My attention reverts from planning ways to make myself less appealing to Hunter when he says, "I'm not in the telemarketing industry."

I stray my eyes from the road to him but remain quiet, leaving my interrogation cap where I removed it weeks ago—on the kitchen counter in my rental cabin.

While keeping his gaze planted straight ahead, he elaborates, "My boss has a very important asset attending the gala tonight. I'm to ensure she remains safe." My pulse quickens when his eyes turn to me. They are full of qualm and worry. "I fucked up last month, and the consequences of my actions could have ended up a lot worse than they did. I'm endeavoring to make it up to my boss, but I can't do that without your help."

An inappropriately timed smile etches onto my face. I do not love that he made a mistake, but I'm delighted he needs my help. "So you work in security?" I keep my tone low, feigning disinterest.

Hunter's lips twist as he hesitantly nods.

"Do you carry a gun?" I flick my eyes between the road and him.

He takes his time figuring a response before he mutters, "Yes."

"Cool," I drawl out extravagantly. "Can I see your pistol?"

When he chuckles, the concern hampering his face fades. "Are we still talking about my gun?"

I sock him one right in the arm. "What happened to us being *friends*?" My playful tone hides my excitement.

Hunter smirks while running his hand over his jaw.

After a short moment of silence, he asks, "So what's your deal, Paige? Why books?" completely ignoring my *friends* reference.

I twist my lips. "Name one other profession where you can talk to the voices in your head and not get thrown into a looney bin?"

His brows bow. "True," he says with a nod, not fazed by my reference I am a little loopy. "I also guess you're an only child?"

"What makes you say that?" I ask through furrowed brows. Although his statement is accurate, I'm interested to find out how he reached his conclusion.

My pulse thrums in my neck when his murky blue eyes lock with mine. "We've been driving for nearly an hour, and you haven't stopped fidgeting. You're either an only child or the youngest member of your family. They always have the ants-in-the-pants type of personality."

"Or maybe I'm just horny," I shoot back, my tone teeming with wit. "And all this squirming isn't to settle the ants in my pants. It's to stop the throbbing your sexy car is causing the lower half of my body."

Damn! Where did that naughty devil come from?

The beat of my heart merges into dangerous territory when Hunter's thick fingers grasp my nape. I freeze like an ice sculpture when the softness of his beard tickles the shell of my ear. "Just like my cock, you stiffen when you're horny. You fidget when you are excited," he murmurs into my ear ever so confidently.

My eyes stray from the road to him. "How do you know that?"

What he's saying is true. I'm not a person who fidgets when nervous. I only do it when my insides are bursting with excitement. But the instant I step into the bedroom, my confidence falters, right along with my movements.

Time stands still when he mutters, "Because you're not the only one who's been watching, Paige." My breathing returns in shallow pants when he removes his hand from my neck and slots his Adonis ass back into the passenger seat. "There's a gas station a quarter of a mile out. Pull over, and we will swap places," he instructs, seemingly unaffected by our riveting exchange.

With my mouth refusing to articulate speech, I nod.

Two hours later, we pull into the long driveway of a posh hotel. Although our trip was filled with conversation, we never ventured back over the friends' line Hunter drew in the sand weeks ago.

A grin curls on my lips when a valet opens my door and assists me out. "Welcome to the Wiltshire Hotel, madame," he greets me.

"Thank you," I reply.

After lifting my eyes, I take in the impressive surroundings while shadowing Hunter to the check-in counter. A few dozen people are milling around the expensive-looking checked marble floors and antique furniture. It only takes a matter of seconds for Hunter's attire to gain us the attention of numerous pairs of eyes. Even with the sleeves of his plaid shirt rolled down, the vast collection of tattoos on his hands and the one on the side of his neck are still prominent.

Even being eyeballed like he's a circus act and not a man, Hunter's confidence doesn't falter the slightest. He's so comfortable in his own skin, he doesn't give two hoots about other people's opinions. That's a refreshing change in a world full of judgmental people, and it makes me like him even more.

My eyes bounce between Hunter and the desk clerk when she advises him his room is ready. "Was I supposed to book my own room?" I query, panicked I didn't consider this earlier. I hope the hotel has a vacancy.

"My room is a two-room suite," Hunter advises my baffled expression. "If you don't feel comfortable, I can book you your own suite."

Smiling, I shake my head. "No, it's fine. I'm more than happy to share your suite." My words come out hoarse, strangled with excitement at spending more one-on-one time with him.

"It's a beautiful room," the desk clerk explains while turning her concerned eyes to me. "It has views of the skyline from both rooms, and the doors are *lockable*, so I'm sure you and your *friend* will be very comfortable and *safe*."

When her eyes return to Hunter, they narrow into tiny slits. While returning the hotel clerk's sneer, he snatches the keycard off the polished counter and makes a beeline to the elevator. Unable to come up with a reply to the hotel clerk's bitterness, I give her the stink eye before shadowing Hunter to the elevator banks.

My jaw slackens when we enter the enormous apartment-size suite two minutes later. "Wowsers, this place is huge," I say, my eyes bugging as big as my mouth.

I grin like a kid in a candy store when Hunter flicks a button on the console at the side, and the blinds covering the windows lift. My jaw drops lower the further the blinds rise. The gorgeous city skyline scatters for as far as my eyes can see. Various size buildings of architectural wonder fill my vision. As the lateness of the evening creeps up on us, smog hovers between the buildings. It's both an eerie and beautiful visual.

My attention diverts from the architectural wonder to Hunter when he says, "I've got to run an errand. Are you okay if I leave you here for an hour?"

I nod. "Sure. What time is the gala?"

A clink of laughter topples from my lips when Hunter pulls up the sleeve of his plaid shirt to check the tattooed Rolex on his wrist. After witnessing the grandeur of his house, car, and now this splendid hotel suite, I have no doubt he could afford a real Rolex if he wanted one, but this way, in his eyes, it's always knock-off time.

"It starts in around an hour." He slides his sleeve back down then locks his eyes with mine. "Your room is the one on the right." He points to a set of double doors. "I'll be back in enough time to get ready before we have to leave."

I stiffen when he presses a quick peck to the side of my mouth, but my rigid posture slackens when the hairs on his top lip tickle my nostrils. *Imagine what it would feel like in more sensitive regions of the body?* My stiff stance resumes.

"I'll see you in a few."

Hunter grins before he spins on his heels and strolls out of the room without a backward glance. I kick off my shoes in the entryway then make my way to my bedroom. My toes dig into the plush carpet when I cross the expansive sunken living area. If I hadn't seen the sign in the elevator advising the presidential suite was located on the top floor, I would have assumed this suite was it. It's massive. Body-hugging sofas are scattered through the living area, thick, luxurious furnishings are draped over the floor-to-ceiling windows, and each piece of furniture looks like it was shipped here directly from France. It's gorgeous.

After lowering the gold-embossed door handle, I swing open the white French door of my room. My breath snags halfway to my lungs when the enormity of the space smashes into me. It isn't just the sheer grandeur of the French-designed room that has my breathing faltering. It is the beautiful emerald-green dress from the boutique store in Ravenshoe carefully strewn across the king-size bed.

My heart beats double-time as I pad across the room. I run my sweat-slicked hands down my legging-covered thighs before snagging a small envelope off the high thread count silk. I catch my lower lip with my teeth when my eyes speedread the card.

Wear this tonight.
Hunter.

My eyes roam over the dress, searching for the price tag. If it still has the tag attached, I could return it and get back the exorbitant four-figure price Hunter paid for it.

A sting of pain inflicts my bottom lip when I fail to locate the price tag, but before I can fully register the pain, my cell phone unexpectedly dings, indicating I have received a text message. Because my leggings don't have any pockets, my phone is tucked into the waistband of my pants, which added to my heart attack status from its unexpected ding.

After gathering my heart off the floor, I yank out my phone and peer down at the screen.

HUNTER:

Don't even think about it. They have a no-return policy.

A ridiculous grin stretches across my face. *How does he already know me so well?*

ME:

I don't have the faintest clue what you're talking about.

The monstrous bed dips when I sit on the edge of it.

HUNTER:

The dress.

I smile.

ME:

Dress? What dress?

He only walked me to the foyer, so I make him sweat a little. That's what he gets for paying a ridiculous amount of money for an article of clothing.

HUNTER:

The one in your room.

ME:

???

HUNTER:

The one you're sitting next to.

My eyes snap to the door. When I fail to locate Hunter, I

scramble off the bed and walk back into the living area of the suite. Sweat slicks my skin as excitement overwhelms me.

HUNTER:

Warmer…

I pace deeper into the living room.

HUNTER:

Colder…

Twisting my lips, I change my direction and head for the foyer.

HUNTER:

Warmer…

A broad grin stretches across my face as I quicken my pace.

HUNTER:

Hot…. HOT! Scorching hot!

Laughing, my eyes scope the premises. The smell of freshly cut flowers filters into my nose from the gorgeous bouquet of lilies, roses, and lisianthus on the entryway table. When I stop to admire the beautiful arrangement on the antique rotunda table, my phone vibrates in my hand.

HUNTER:

Bingo.

My heart thwacks against my ribs as my eyes scan the floral arrangement. The beat turns dangerous when I spot the smallest speck of black on one of the lilies' petals. Not long after I screw up my nose, a message arrives on my phone.

HUNTER:

That's not a good look for you.

Holy hell! Is that a camera?
My eyes rocket between the floral bouquet and my bedroom

door. The camera is facing the wrong way, so there's no way he could have seen me sitting on my bed from this angle. I stiffen, and my pupils widen as an improper thought pops into my head.

As I type out a message on my phone, my teeth grit.

ME:

Did you put a camera in my room???

My face reddens as anger envelops me. The living hell is scared out of me for a second time when my cell phone suddenly rings.

After exhaling a calming breath, I hit the call button and press it to my ear.

"Who's the voyeur in this *friendship?*" Hunter's rich chocolatey voice sounds down the line.

I glare at the tiny camera attached to the bouquet while snarling, "Voyeurism and being a peeping Tom are two completely separate entities. Believe me, I've researched them both."

Hunter laughs. "Don't believe everything Google tells you, Paige. Most of the stuff on there is fiction, not fact."

"I don't believe everything I read, Hunter." I draw out his name as he had done to mine. "But even a noob knows you can't photograph someone without their consent."

"Ah... that's where you are *very* wrong. I've not only informed you that you're under surveillance, but the device is also not in a public place or a restroom, so I'm free to invade your privacy as much as I see fit."

"See this." I yank the small black device off the petal and throw it into a bin at my side.

My brazenness freezes when Hunter's growl sounds down the line. "You're even sexier when you're angry."

Frozen from the sexy ruggedness of his voice, my eyes shoot in all directions, searching for more camera devices.

My eyes slant when he says, "You'll never find them all."

Gritting my teeth, I disconnect the call and switch off my phone. You'd think my first reaction would be to grab my bag and request another room, or better yet, the first flight home, but for some reason, unbeknown to me, my feet remain firmly planted on the floor.

It may be imprudent of me, but I already trust Hunter, so I don't believe he'd ever purposely set out to hurt me, let alone spy on me.

I suffer my third coronary failure of the day when the smooth richness of Hunter's voice sounds out of my switched-off phone speaker mere seconds later. "If you don't want me to see you naked, close your bedroom door. The cameras are only in the living areas."

I slide my index finger across my phone's screen, ensuring it's turned off.

It is.

"Then how could you see I was sitting on the bed?" My voice is rickety, confused about how he can talk to me using a switched-off phone.

"Your image was reflecting from the mirror hanging in the entryway."

My eyes rocket to the large gold-embossed mirror hanging in the elegant foyer. The quickening of my pulse settles when I see the emerald-green dress lying on the bed in its reflection.

My bewildered eyes shift back down to my phone when Hunter says, "Paige?"

"Yes," I reply, my voice croaky.

"Stop biting your lip. You're making my teeth jealous."

I release my bottom lip from my menacing teeth as I stare at my phone, incredulous that this is happening. "Who the hell are you?" I barely whisper.

"I'm the man your momma warned you about," he mutters before a click sounds down the line.

"Hello... Hunter?"

When he fails to answer, I dump my phone onto the entryway table and sweep my eyes around the room. My heart is hammering against my ribs, and a fine layer of sweat is misting my skin, but even beyond baffled, I'm also incredibly thrilled. I've never had this absurd amount of excitement thickening my blood before. I feel like an entirely different person around Hunter. I'm not the highly-educated and well-spoken daughter of a much-respected pillar of the community. Nor am I the trophy fiancée on the arm of a cutthroat businessman who only speaks when spoken to and never airs her political objections in public. For the first time, I'm just me. Paige, the quirky novelist.

Squealing, I charge across the monstrous living room and dive onto the enormous bed. The thickness of the fluffy duvet swallows me whole, swamping me with its heavenliness that's nearly as soft as Hunter's beard.

I turn my eyes to the ceiling to silently ponder.

After ten minutes of musing, I reach the same conclusion over and over again.

I may not know who the real Hunter Kane is, but for the moment, I don't care.

CHAPTER THIRTEEN

After telling myself to relax, I release a big breath then flutter my eyes open. The dress is worth every penny just for the way it hugs me in all the right places. The ruched bodice and built-in bra make my less-than-stellar breasts pop, and the fan of the skirt hides my less-desirable assets. Today isn't the first time I've dressed up in a lovely gown, but it's the first time I've wanted to.

Leaning over, I snag a few extra bobby pins from the dresser and pin back a wayward tress of hair that has fallen from my side-swept hairstyle. My lips are a vibrant red, and my eyes have been done with a thick coat of eyeliner and mascara. The darkness gives me the alluring, sex-kitten look I was aiming for while also being classy.

I smile while wondering what Hunter's reaction will be when he sees me. I'm a far cry from the sweatpants-wearing novelist he's used to seeing. My pulse leaps with excitement when a tap sounds on the wooden door of my room. After checking my lipstick in the mirror and ensuring my wavy hair has been wrangled into smooth, glossy locks, I head for the door.

The inane smile stretched across my face dampens when my eyes lock in on Hunter. I cock my hip, wordlessly demanding the focus of his eyes, which are absorbing every inch of my skin. When they finally lock with mine, I observe, "I'm wearing a dress that cost more than my first car, and you're wearing *that*?"

My eyes lower to absorb his long-sleeve button-up shirt and stiff jeans. I appreciate that he at least went to the effort of changing his plaid shirt to a dress shirt, but he isn't even close to being dressed as formally as I am. I look like Cinderella about to attend the ball. He looks like he's a college student heading to a Cold Play concert.

Upon catching my non-amused glare, he scrapes his hand along his jaw then shrugs. "I don't own a suit."

"Then go buy one." I wave my hand around the elegant surroundings. "I'm sure you can afford it."

A spark ignites in his eyes, but he remains as quiet as a grave-yard at midnight.

"If I have to wear this get up, so do you," I respond to his silence. After spinning him on his heels, I nudge him toward the door. "Go down to the lobby and ask the concierge for directions to the nearest suit store. I'll grab my purse and meet you at the taxi stand out front."

"It's eight o'clock on a Saturday, Paige. All the shops are closed," he argues.

As my brisk pace halts, I suck in numerous deep breaths while my muddled brain tries to think of a solution to our situation. It wouldn't matter if I wore more diamonds than Elizabeth Taylor owned in her lifetime. If I turn up to a ten-thousand-dollar-a-plate function with Hunter dressed how he is, he will gain the attention of everyone in the room. Considering his rationalization for bringing me here was to ensure he remained incognito, he needs to wear a suit. There is no other viable option.

"You need to wear a suit," I explain as kindly as possible. I love that Hunter is who he is, but if he wants to fix the mistakes he made with his boss, he needs to do this. "If you want to make things right with your boss, you need to look the part."

"I don't own a suit." He stares into my eyes so I can see the truth in his statement.

"Can you borrow one?" I suggest while returning his sweat-producing stare.

After smiling a traffic-stopping grin, he nods.

Ten minutes later, we enter the presidential suite. My breath hitches when he enters the suite without bothering to knock. I'm at a complete loss for words when my eyes take in the grandeur of the room. I thought the views were spectacular from Hunter's suite, but these are ten times better.

My dress swishes on the pristine marble tiles as I shadow him deeper into the suite. Three large plush leather sofas line the space of the sunken living room. A baby grand piano sits in one corner, and a crystal bar is in the opposite one. The suite screams of wealth and superiority.

The heels on my stilettos snag in the thick carpet when we step into the sunken living area. When we round the corner, my leisured pace comes to a complete halt. Standing in the corner of the room, talking on a cell phone is the dark and mysterious stranger I spied on in Hunter's glass house three days ago.

When he notices Hunter and me approaching, the alluring stranger finalizes his call and places his cell into the breast pocket of his suit jacket. In contrast to Hunter, he looks dressed to impress in a full black tuxedo, white dress shirt, and bowtie.

My eyes rocket to Hunter when he asks, "Hey, boss, can I borrow a suit?"

So this is Hunter's boss?

Hunter's boss arches his brow and peers at Hunter in shock. My heartbeat quickens when an ostentatious smirk etches on his mouth before he nods. After gesturing his hand to a set of double doors on the other side of the suite, he says, "Help yourself to anything you like."

Hunter's brows bow. "Don't even think about it." His tone is laced with cheekiness. "After tonight, you won't catch me in a suit *ever* again." While ignoring the jeering look stretching across his boss's face, he shifts on his feet to face me. "I'll be back in a minute."

I smile and nod, relieved he's finally accepted there's no other viable attire for him tonight than a suit. When he struts into the room, his boss moves to stand in front of me. The smell of expensive cologne smacks into me. Unlike Hunter, I can recognize his scent. Clive Christian 1872.

He offers me his hand to shake. "Isaac Holt."

"Paige," I introduce before accepting his handshake.

Isaac is gorgeous in a dark and mysterious way. His eyes are dark gray in color, and his hair is thick and luxurious. I smile when I notice he has a cleft chin hiding behind a few days of stubble.

I've always wanted to pen a book with a male lead who has a dimple in his chin.

"How do you know Hunter?"

Isaac strides to a crystal bar set up in the room's corner. After pouring himself a generous helping of whiskey, he dips the tumbler toward me.

I wave my hand in front of my body, denying his offer of a whiskey before answering, "I'm his neighbor."

A smirk etches on Isaac's mouth before he downs the generous helping of whiskey in one hit. After running the back of his hand across his lips, he questions, "You're the tenant staying in my cabin?"

My eyes balk with surprise. "You own the cabin?"

He smirks while pouring himself another whiskey. "Yes. I own most of the houses in that gated community."

From the way he carries himself and the aura of wealth permeating from him, I'm not astonished by his admission. "Do you own Hunter's residence as well?" I ask curiously.

"No." He places the decanter of whiskey onto the bar and

ambles closer to me. "Don't let Hunter's appearance deceive you, Paige. Under his ruggedness is a man with a brilliant mind and even sharper ethics."

"Then why do you have him working your security? Why not put his brilliant mind to good use?" I blurt out before my brain can cite an objection.

Just from Isaac's demeanor alone, I know he isn't a man I should spar against, but I'm curious as to why he'd say Hunter is a brilliant man but then only use him as a protective detail. Let alone the fact Isaac doesn't seem like the type of man who requires the aid of a bodyguard. He looks more than capable of taking care of himself.

"Hunter told you he works for me?" Isaac's brow is arched, and his words are clipped.

After swallowing to relieve my parched throat, I nod.

Isaac huffs, seemingly stunned Hunter shared that information with me, but before he can configure a response, Hunter strides back into the room. Every limb in my body becomes immobile as he spans the distance between the master suite and the sunken lounge. When his murky blue eyes lift from securing the button on the cuff of his midnight black suit, an asinine grin tugs on his lips, no doubt loving my muted reaction.

I'm speechless and utterly flabbergasted, unable to relay the core-crunching visual in front of me. My body slicks with sweat as a frenetic rush of desire swamps the lower regions of my body. The suit he chose to wear fits him like it was tailored specifically for his body shape. The darkness of the crisp blue dress shirt makes his eyes more effervescent, and the cut lines of the luxurious fabric showcase his body as if he were standing before me naked as the day he was born.

It's a riveting visual, and it has my heart racing.

Hunter winks cockily as he glides past me to join Isaac by the bar. I stand frozen at the side of the living room, muted by rampant horniness. Isaac's eyes flick to me, glaring at me and my awkwardness for several uncomfortable seconds before he turns his gaze back to Hunter. I'd normally respond to an inquisitive stare, but I'm too stunned at the desire coursing through my veins to form words.

Blood floods my heart when Hunter says, "She's okay. You can speak in front of Paige. I trust her."

I smile, beyond pleased I'm not the only one who's issued the trust card so early in our newly formed friendship.

Isaac curtly nods. "Although my empire has contributed a significant amount of money to this foundation, my focus is not on business tonight."

"You're going in for Izzy," Hunter intuits.

"Yes," Isaac answers. "Hugo has advised she's en route. Even though she will be in my sight at all times, I still want eyes surrounding her. Until we know who is following her, everyone around her is to be treated as a threat."

"I understand," Hunter replies with a nod. "Unfortunately, the hotel the gala is being held at has top-notch security. I can only access the data center from the server in their security office. Once I infiltrate their system, I'll have complete access to their security feeds and monitoring stations. Anyone arriving or leaving will be caught."

Relief fills Isaac's expressive eyes. "Good."

My expression changes from curious to excited. When Hunter said he worked in security, my first thoughts drifted to Kevin Costner in *The Bodyguard*. But the mention of servers and other computer gobbledygook I've never understood makes his job sound a lot more integral than merely protecting an asset from overzealous fans. It has my interests immensely piqued on exactly what he does for a living.

My eyes stray from the ground to Hunter when he says, "I also have an extra set of eyes that have agreed to help me tonight."

My heart beats triple time when he swings his eyes to me and smiles. Giddiness clusters my brain as I return his smile.

"Okay. Good." Isaac's tone is slightly reserved as his eyes bounce between Hunter and me. "Then let's head out. I want to arrive before Isabelle."

With a nod, Hunter encloses his hand around mine then guides us back into the elegant hallway. My excited fidgeting becomes distracting when we enter the elevator behind Isaac. I've never had so much energy coursing through me.

"Stop fidgeting," Hunter mutters while ushering me to the back of the elevator.

Leaning in close to his side, I mumble, "I can't help it. I'm too excited."

I bounce on my heels as my eyes drift between the elegantly dressed men and women in the car with us. Even with the dense aroma of wealth hampering my senses, eagerness beams out of me.

The tic impinging Hunter's jaw gains intensity when he catches the curious glare Isaac is directing at me. His brows are furrowed. He appears utterly baffled. I can understand why. I'm sure I look like an absolute twit.

Hunter and Isaac's moods are somber and brooding, whereas I have a gigantic smile stretched across my face, and my eyes are full and bright. The intrigue, mystery, and vibrancy are too much for me to handle. I have more storylines swirling in my mind than I've ever had. If I didn't have the curious eyes of Hunter and Isaac eyeballing my every move, I would have whipped out my phone and jotted down some notes, but not wanting to encourage more curious rubberneckers, I keep my cell in my clutch and my eyes straight ahead.

After lessening the size of my smile, I inwardly battle to get my childish antics under control. My fidgeting only halts when a warm hand heats the skin high on the back of my thigh. All cogent thoughts disappear when it glides up the silkiness of my dress, stopping once it hits the curve of my backside. A breathless moan ripples through my O-formed mouth when my ass cheek is squeezed by a rough hand. It kneads away my giddiness and replaces it with rampant horniness.

While keeping my head facing the front of the packed car, I shift my eyes to Hunter. He's also facing forward, seemingly unaware of the sweat-forming friskiness happening right next to him, but the gleam in his eyes and the twitching of his top lip leaves me no doubt that it is his hand feeling up my backside.

"I thought you wanted us to be friends?" The tremble of my voice shamefully exposes my excitement to his tease.

"We *are* friends, Paige," Hunter replies with his eyes planted straight ahead.

"So groping my ass is your idea of friendship?" I strangle out quietly, shocked I can articulate speech. Usually, it isn't just my body that freezes during sexual contact. My words fail as well.

I grimace when the lady standing next to me takes a step forward. *Obviously, my quiet declaration wasn't that quiet.* Then I freeze like a statue when Hunter's fingers dip lower, inching closer to the one region of my body that's paying careful attention to every movement he makes.

The heat in the car turns rife, and it feels like the walls are closing in on me when he continues his endeavor of ceasing my childish fidgeting. Through heavy pants, my eyes drink in Hunter's handsome face. I have no idea how he's maintaining his calm, cool demeanor. The slickness that coated my panties when he walked out of the suite wearing a tailored suit has doubled, and my throat is hoarse from the blazing heat warming my body. I'm an utter wreck.

"All this to stop me fidgeting?" I choke out, my voice strangled by arousal.

The corners of Hunter's lips tug higher. "That, and the fact I couldn't resist seeing if your ass felt as good as it looks in that dress." The exultant smirk curving my mouth turns into a full grin when he mutters under his breath, "It does."

My attention sidetracks from his teasing hands when the elevator dings, announcing we've arrived at the lobby. As a congregation of people exit and enter the elevator, I stand still, frozen in place with desire. If Hunter didn't relinquish my bottom from his magic hand, I would have spent the remainder of my night riding the elevator. That ride was more enthralling than any rollercoaster I've ever been on.

The trip to the gala is made in complete silence, my mind too baffled to configure speech. The confusion about my friendship with Hunter has reached a level of weirdness even someone as quirky as me can't comprehend. Hunter is giving me different signals, left, right, and center. He pulls out the friend card but then lavishes me with more attention than Riley ever gave me. He denies my advances but then gets friendly with my backside in an elevator full of strangers.

He's confusing the heck out of me.

By the time we arrive at the hotel thirty minutes later, my excited fidgeting returns, although not as paramount as it was earlier. It is still weighed down by the lust thickening my blood from Hunter's earlier tease. After a quiet word with Isaac, Hunter crooks out his elbow in offering.

See? Mixed signals.

Smiling to mask my confusion, I accept his offer. Excitement sparks my veins, but I ignore the wooziness his touch caused to my brain as I glide into the hotel foyer. The aroma of overpriced champagne lingers in the air as he guides us into the heavily populated space housing hundreds of well-dressed patrons.

Just as Hunter predicted, numerous gala attendees turn their eyes to him when he graces them with his presence. Once their judgmental eyes finish assessing him in great detail, they study me with just as much depth.

Although most of the eyes he gained are from snobbish, prudish people, a handful of the women's gazes don't loiter on him because of his tattooed hands and rugged appearance. They appreciate the core-tightening view.

I can't blame them. There's nothing as sexually stimulating as a stealthy brute of a man in a refined suit. Hunter's aura no doubt implies he's a man of great stamina, but his eyes expose his true self. Underneath his rugged appearance is a soul worth exploring. *A soul I plan on unearthing.*

"I told you..." Hunter leans in close to my side, "... they're either assuming you're a little rich girl who is out to make Daddy mad, or I'm some rich schmuck with a trophy wife on his arm."

"So which one am I? Rich bitch with Daddy issues, or money-hungry trophy wife?" I jest, trying to lighten the somber mood encroaching our intimate gathering.

His eyes swoop down to mine. "Yeah... I'm not falling for that one." He guides us to the corner of the room. "No matter which way I answer, I'd be digging my own grave."

I elbow him in the ribs but don't bother refuting his statement since it was acutely accurate. When we reach a small alcove in the corner of the space, Hunter relinquishes me from his side. While holding back the whine his loss of contact compelled, I eye him curiously. He digs his hand into the breast pocket of his suit jacket and produces a diamante-encrusted black satin mask.

"It's a masked gala," he explains before spinning his finger, wordlessly requesting me to turn around.

Excitement thickens my blood when I twirl around as requested. After tucking a stray tress of hair behind my ear, Hunter slips the mask in front of my eyes and fastens the straps at the back of my head. I smile when I feel the heat of his body on the smooth coolness of the satin material.

Once the mask is secured, I spin back around to face him. I wobble in my stilettos halfway around. He also put on a mask similar to mine, minus the diamantes. The blackness of the mask on his already concealed face makes his blue eyes even more sharp-witted and bright.

My grin tugs higher when I remove a frayed strand of silk off his cheek, and his muscles twitch in response to my touch.

Maybe he's a sexual fidgeter?

The twitch impinging his cheek grows when he slips his hand

into the pocket of his trousers and produces a silver necklace. The chain is so thin, it's nearly invisible, but the gorgeous murky emerald-green stone clasped in the middle of a twisted silver design is mesmerizing.

Warmth glows on my cheeks when he places the pendant on the curve of my pushed-up breasts before fastening the clasps at the nape of my neck. His citrus-smelling mouth fans my lips when he says, "There you go," under his breath.

I'm honestly at a loss for words. Not just at his generosity, but the way he instills it—no fanfare, no groveling, not even a jewelry box. He just presents it as if he placed a vending machine prize around my neck and not a precious gem.

"Thank you." I adjust the pendant so it sits in the middle of my chest. "It's breathtaking."

My words come out weak, strangled by emotions. I'm not used to being awarded gifts without a penance attached to them. If I were smart, I would have realized sooner why Riley always arrived home from weekend meetings with a gift in tow.

"You're welcome." Hunter cups my jaw to lift my downcast head. "It's a necklace, Paige, not an engagement ring."

"Yeah, but with the dress, you don't think it's all a little too much?"

"No." He shakes his head. "But if it makes you feel better, you can class it as a partial payment for your *services* tonight." His voice is jam-packed with sexual innuendo.

When I kick him in the ankle, he chuckles a full-hearted laugh.

There's no sexier sound in the world than Hunter's chocolatey-smooth chuckle.

CHAPTER FOURTEEN

"*I*f they would just leave their post for twenty seconds, I'd be set," Hunter grumbles.

We've spent the last thirty minutes in the opulent foyer of the hotel, waiting for two security officers to move away from the only door housing the server room for the hotel security. I've downed four Long Island iced teas during the sweat-mustache-producing surveillance. I needed something in my hands to stop my fidgeting. Now, I'm more jittery from the alcohol pumping in my veins than euphoric.

"We have to do something." I slide off the barstool. "Because they look settled in for the night, and I've reached my quota on iced tea." My voice slightly slurs, exposing the truth of my statement.

I yank Hunter off the barstool by the lapels of his suit. His delicious aftershave swamps my senses, adding to the giddiness clustering my brain and twisting my stomach. Once I have the lapels of his suit jacket smoothed back where they're supposed to be, I lock my eyes with his amused gaze. A smug smirk is etched on his face.

Even hidden under a beastly beard, his smile makes my knees weak and my panties moist.

As his eyes bounce between mine, the grin on his face turns mocking, no doubt perceiving what has instigated my recent bout of stiltedness. Hunter isn't reserved or shy, which isn't surprising. A man with his stamina requires a sense of assertiveness and dominance. If he lacked either of those, the skills I witnessed many times in my first six weeks at Bronte's Peak wouldn't have been as fire-sparking as they were.

The twisting of my stomach winds up to the base of my throat. Before Hunter and I became friends, his *liaisons* never bothered me. Now they sting a little. Not at all similar to the heartbroken angst Riley pummeled me with, but the sting of a paper cut—small but still painful enough to feel.

"Paige," Hunter mutters, his tone flat like he can sense where my thoughts drifted to without a word spilling from my lips.

He's so much like Pepper.

He doesn't know about Riley, but I may have been a little snarky to him last week about his *numerous* female companions. I didn't mean to get snippy at him, but with it being that time of the month, the occasional bitchy comment slipped from my lips before I had a chance to rationalize my jealousy. Thankfully, Hunter took my snide remarks in stride by completely ignoring them or changing the course of our conversation, but only now am I wondering if my bitterness is why I haven't seen any visitors at his place the past few weeks?

Ignoring the outlandish beat of my heart, I return Hunter's flirty smile before saying, "I'll give you thirty seconds, but any longer than that, you're on your own."

Feeling brazen from the buzz of alcohol warming my blood, I press a kiss to the side of his mouth before sauntering away from him.

I don't need to turn around to know his eyes are on me. I can feel it in my bones.

With a vivacious smirk, I greet the security officers guarding the door as I saunter by with an extra swing to my hips. I roll back my shoulders, hoisting my bosoms out further. Their small size is at least two cups bigger, thanks to the aid of a strapless silicone-padded bra.

I inwardly cheer when my prance gains me the two extra sets of eyes I was endeavoring to secure. Just as I reach the middle of the foyer, I inhale a nerve-cleansing breath before throwing my arm up to my forehead and collapsing to the ground.

Half of the grimace crossing my face is thanks to the acting classes Pepper dragged me to during our college years, but the other half is from the rigid hardness of the marble floor.

I think I'll be sporting a bruise for that effort in the morning.

Stomping feet boom into my ears as the security officers and Hunter rush toward me. I lock my eyes with Hunter and squint before inconspicuously nudging my head to the security office the guards just left unattended. When a smirk peeks out from beneath his newly trimmed beard, I switch my small whimpers to a pained howl.

Upon hearing my devastating sobs, the security officers increase their already brisk pace, whereas Hunter slips into the office undetected.

"Oh dear, they must have over-polished the floor," I sob, my voice as pathetic as my excuse for falling on the world's most level surface.

The security guards fuss over me and request I remain on the floor as they call in assistance from the medical team on the radios strapped to their shoulders. I continue with my over-the-top performance for nearly thirty seconds, giving it my all. I even manage to pick up a southern accent I've never had merely to increase the authenticity of my Oscar-worthy performance.

Just as I've finished giving the security officers a rundown of my clumsiness the past twelve months, Hunter emerges from the security office. The smile on his face when he taps two fingers on the breast pocket of his jacket is the largest I've ever seen. After jerking his head to the ballroom entrance at my nine o'clock, he returns to his original station at the bar.

"Stay on the ground, honey. We have confirmation the medic is close by," one of the security officers with gorgeous dark skin says when I scurry onto my hands and knees.

"Oh, I'm fine. It was just a little tumble." I scamper to my feet, which is no easy feat in a dress that weighs nearly as much as I do. "See." I step forward three paces before spinning around and sauntering back. "I'm perfectly fine. It must have been all the wonderful help you fine gentleman issued. How could I possibly thank you?"

The cheeks of the second officer with pasty white skin and rich hazel eyes turn a shade of pink, but I don't give him the chance to issue whatever reward he's formulated in his wicked mind when I say, "I'll be sure to fill in a guest comment card at the reception desk for the pleasing service I have received before leaving this evening." My southern accent is still in full effect.

While sweating like a pig on a stick, I make a beeline for the double doors of the ballroom the fundraiser is being held in. A blast of fresh air from the over-door air conditioning gives my sweat-slicked skin a small moment of reprieve as I glide into the room. My eyes shoot in all directions, eager to absorb the grandeur of the space. Mirrored balls, crystal vases, and black long-stemmed roses give the room a sleek, masculine appearance.

The squeal rippling from my lips is only just heard over Rhianna's song "Love on the Brain" being played over the speakers when my elbow is suddenly grasped. After muttering an apology for scaring me to death, Hunter guides me toward a set of concealed doors on my left.

On our journey, I catch the quickest glimpse of Isaac dancing in the middle of the dance floor with the beautiful brunette I saw at Hunter's house earlier this week.

Once we enter the room, Hunter pulls down two white catering chairs from a wooden tabletop, removes his suit jacket, and dumps a hemp bag I didn't realize he was carrying until now onto the table.

"Where were you hiding that?" I ask while watching him set up a mini surveillance site.

He takes a seat behind a clunky-looking laptop. "I had a contact in reception hold it for me." He removes his mask before his luminous eyes lift from the monitor to me. "How many chips will that riveting performance cost me?"

I nudge him with my hip. "Ask me after the bruise on my ass heals."

He chuckles before turning his eyes back to the computer, where his fingers move across the flat silicon keyboard at lightning speed. I watch him carefully, categorizing every expression that crosses his face as he merges into a world I've never seen him in before.

Now I understand what Isaac meant about not letting Hunter's outward appearance deceive me. He's in his element, and it's a spellbinding visual. In minutes, he has a state-of-the-art security monitoring station set up on the catering table. All the attendees mingling at the gala or within the hotel have their faces captured, even the couple getting a little handsy in elevator number six.

"They are a cute couple." I wave my hand to an image in the corner of one of the screens capturing Isaac and his female date. "Is she the asset you were referring to earlier?"

Hunter nods. "Yes, that's Izzy. Isaac's Aphrodite."

"So who is Isaac? Hephaestus, Aries, or Adonis?"

He smirks. "You studied Greek mythology?"

I screw up my nose. "Not really. I attended a handful of lectures while waiting for the creative writing class to have an open seat my first semester in college. It wasn't my thing."

Hunter laughs again, but his focus remains arrested on the computer monitors. I'm shocked he can maintain a conversation while working. I've never been able to work and communicate at the same time. More often than not I found myself typing the conversation around me instead of the scene my characters were acting out.

"Isaac would like to say he's Poseidon, the ultimate protector, but I'd say he's Aries, her one true love," Hunter says after a short stint of musing.

My mouth gapes, surprised by his extensive knowledge. "Greek mythology major?"

"Nope." He shakes his head at my arched brow. "I just have a bad habit of reading something once and never forgetting it."

I giggle while nudging his broad shoulder with my elbow, assuming he's pulling the wool over my eyes. It's only when he locks his truth-bearing eyes with mine do I realize he's being serious.

"You remember everything you read?" Disbelief taints my voice.

Hunter's lips tug higher in one corner as he nods.

"How many floors are there at the hotel we are staying at?"

"Sixty-eight," he answers without delay. "The pool, gym, and sauna are located on the twelfth floor, and there was a pamphlet for a Thai restaurant at 1917 Markwell Street sitting on the entryway table of the presidential suite when we entered."

My mouth gapes. "What was the hotel check-in clerk's name?"

"Mischa."

My lips twist. I wasn't paying much attention when we checked in, so I have no way of gauging his accuracy.

"Did you want to dance?"

His eyes rocket between mine, and astonishment from the sudden change in conversation is evident all over his face. Since I've secured his devotion, I snatch the piece of paper sitting next to his silicon keyboard and hold it close to my chest.

"What's the first sentence of this document?" I ensure my hands are covering the document from both sides just in case the paper is see-through.

Hunter's lips quirk as he stares into my musing eyes. "I can't answer that."

The rough grittiness of his voice sets my pulse racing, but it won't stop me from saying, "Ha! Proof you were telling porkies!" My loud voice booms around the room.

My earlier dizziness comes rushing back to the surface when his cloudy blue eyes stare steadfastly into mine. Even having a mask covering most of my face, I feel exposed, almost naked from his greedy gaze. "I can't answer... as there are no words on that paper. It's all code."

I furrow my brows together before I sneakily pull the paper away from my chest.

The groove in the middle of my forehead deepens when Hunter recites, "55321667A2245B."

It is the exact code on the first line of the document.

I place the paper onto his makeshift desk. "That's cool and a little bit freaky."

"Kind of like you penning a novel about a bearded billionaire living in a crystal house?"

I cringe, but my panic is kept at bay when I realize he doesn't seem the slightest bit angry. "You know about Archer?" My voice is scratchy, hampered by the barrel of emotions pummeling into me at once.

He smiles before nodding.

"And you're not angry?"

"No, Paige. I'm not angry. Although the billionaire title is a *slight* exaggeration," he replies with a chuckle.

My mouth gapes further. "What the hell is wrong with you? I'd be beyond pissed if I discovered someone was invading my privacy."

"I live my life as an open book." Hunter's tone isn't hindered by the slightest bit of anger.

I cross my arms in front of my chest, faking annoyance. "Then why did you give me the telemarketing line the first day we met?"

"I live my life as an open book. He doesn't." He nudges his head to Isaac and Izzy floating across the computer monitor as they move toward a set of double doors similar to the ones we're hiding behind.

Too shocked by his latest revelation to remain standing, I take the spare seat next to him and watch him work in silence. Although I am surprised by his admission, I'm not totally stunned by it. Hunter has been nothing but forthright the past few weeks. He has the type of personality that people are either drawn to or repelled by. Grouchy Hunter scares me, but frank Hunter sucks me right into the Hunter vortex. He should come with a warning because once you've been swept into the Hunter vortex, there's no possibility of breaking free.

"Where are they going?" I ask when Isaac and Izzy slip behind a set of doors.

Hunter doesn't need to reply. The crass grin stretching across his face is all the answer I need.

My pulse quickens, surprised by their audacity to get *friendly* in a public place.

"Is Izzy really in danger or is Isaac being overcautious?" My voice is weak, strained by excitement.

Hunter's lips twist. "I wish he was."

"Is it your job to protect her?"

"For now, yes, it's my main priority."

"Sounds like an exciting job?" I'm an outsider to this uniquely dynamic group, but my heart is still hammering my ribs.

"It is, for the most part," he answers, his tone reserved.

I eyeball him, silently demanding further explanation.

"I like the parts where I'm not forced to wear a suit," he explains, unamused. "Isaac has been trying to get me into a monkey suit for years."

"Well, I think you look very handsome," I add an extra dose of sugar to my voice. "You look an intriguing mix of mountaineer and—"

"I look like Wolverine stuffed in a suit."

"Exactly! What woman doesn't want a rough and rugged Hugh Jackman in a suit? Roar!"

His laughter bellows over the music streaming through the double doors.

A small stretch of silence crosses between us. It isn't awkward or stuffy. I just don't feel the need to fill the void with noise.

After a few more minutes of quiet, I nudge him with my elbow. "You never answered my initial question."

"Which one?"

From the gleam in his eyes, I know he's acutely aware of which question I'm referring to, but feeling playful, I play along with his little ruse. "Did you want to dan—"

"No," Hunter interjects before the whole sentence spills from my lips.

"Why not?" I shoot back.

His brows bow. "Because I don't dance. Period." He sounds disgusted that I even suggested it.

"We can dance in here where no one will see us," I suggest with a shrug.

"No."

"Hunter—"

"No, Paige."

"Dancing is just like sex, you just keep your clothes on," I continue to argue.

"No, Paige."

"I've seen you move your hips. You could totally work it on the dance floor."

"Paige," Hunter drawls out in a long angry snarl, his frantic pace on the keyboard halting. "I don't dance."

I huff and cross my arms in front of my chest, hoisting my small bosoms higher. He's discreet, but I don't miss his quick glance at my chest region. My insides sigh from his adroit glimpse.

When his eyes return to my face, his thumb twangs my lower lip. "Suck your lip back in. Pouting isn't sexy when you're..." He stops talking, and his face screws up. After a brief shake of his head, he turns his attention back to the computer monitor.

I watch him in silence, confused as to why he stopped midsentence.

Then it dawns on me.

He doesn't know how old I am.

Smiling at the memories of the time I asked him his age, I mumble. "I'm twenty-five."

Hunter peers up at me. "What?"

"I'm twenty-five, a Virgo, love long walks on the beach, and have no siblings." I lock my eyes with his amused gaze. "I think that about covers it. Unless you have any other questions you want me to answer?"

"Only one," he replies, which shocks the contemptuous look right off my face. "What's your opinion on going undercover?"

My eyes widen until they're nearly as large as my mouth.

"So all I have to do is walk around the room?"

"Yes." Hunter adjusts my hair so the bead in my ear is concealed. "I'll keep in contact with you by the listening device. If you think someone is acting suspicious or you feel uncomfortable, scratch your right collarbone, and I'll move in."

"Should I be concerned for my safety?" I question after swallowing a lump in my throat.

He shakes his head. "No. But you'll garner some attention."

My heart rate increases. Not just from the way his eyes rake over my body but from the increase of adrenaline pumping through my veins.

This is more exciting than watching the Super Bowl.

After he finishes his avid assessment of my body, Hunter locks his eyes with mine. "In that dress, you'll gain the devotion of a lot of old geezers who want to skip their little blue pill for the night."

Grinning, I kick his borrowed polished black shoes with the toe of my stilettos. Hunter smiles and returns my kick with a gentle nudge to my pumps. "I appreciate you doing this, Paige." He adjusts the pendant on my necklace. "I have twelve cameras uploaded from the hotel's main server in the ballroom, but with the blind spots and poor lighting, I can't get everyone's faces. You doing this will ensure I capture every attendee in the room."

"And you call *me* a voyeur," I jest, my tone drenched in wit. When the entirety of his statement hits me, I freeze. "Hold on, how will you capture everyone's faces just from having me wandering aimlessly around the room?"

Hunter's lips quirk as he returns his focus to the computer equipment. After a few quick strokes on the keyboard, the side of his well-formed torso fills the main screen of his security monitor.

A groan I've never heard before rumbles from my throat when I realize where the new image is projecting from. "You put a camera in my necklace?" I squeal, sending my voice ricocheting off the whitewashed walls. "What if I wore it in the shower?"

The shit-eating grin on his face enlarges. "I could only hope."

This time when I kick him, I aim for his shin, and I add more force. "*Friends* don't see their *friends* naked."

The scowl on my face fades when Hunter says, "I was just evening the score between us."

Although his voice is full of playfulness, I remain quiet, muted by guilt.

Not even the world's best lawyer could win this case.

After a beat, he mumbles, "Don't feel guilty, Paige. If I didn't want you to see me naked, you wouldn't have." He locks his eyes with mine so I can see the honesty behind them. "You saw what I wanted you to see."

"You wanted me to see that you're a manwhore?" I query with my nose scrunched up tight.

He laughs. It isn't his usual boisterous chuckle, being more reserved and apprehensive. "No. I wanted you to see me at my worst."

My brows furrow. "Why?"

Hunter sets a contraption down on the desk and shifts on his feet to face me. He fiddles with my necklace while muttering, "Because I didn't want you to like me."

He's so quiet, if I didn't have his listening contraption in my ear, I wouldn't have heard him.

"You didn't have to be a manwhore for that. I don't like you." Even I can hear the deceit in my voice.

He chuckles again. This time it's his proper laugh. "That's good to know," he mumbles under his breath as he places his palm on the curve of my back and guides me to the set of double doors. "Remember, scratch your collarbone if you're worried," he instructs, his tone more serious than earlier.

I exhale a deep breath and nod. "Let's do this." I lean in to press a kiss on his hairy cheek. He spins me on my heels and shoves me toward the mass gathering of gala attendees when I guess, "Creed Aventus?" When I twirl back around to face him, the fan of my skirt flares out. "One day I'll learn what your scent is," I quip, walking backward. "Then all your greatest secrets will be exposed." I make my voice super dramatic like I'm the voiceover for the newest sci-fi movie about to hit the cinemas.

He winks before closing the door between us.

After running my sweaty hands down the front of my dress, I mosey around the room filled to the brim with sparkling gown-wearing ladies and gentlemen dressed to the nines. The room has the distinct aroma of wealth and superiority, which isn't surprising considering the required donation per attendee.

I've attended numerous functions similar to this in my lifetime, but not one the past two years. Nothing against the organizers, but it doesn't seem like I've been missing out on anything. These types of events aren't about having fun. They are either to network or drain your bank balance for a worthy cause.

My heart leaps out of my chest when Hunter's chocolatey-rich voice unexpectedly sounds through my ear. "That's a good pace, Paige, just be sure to circle the entire room."

"Okay," I barely whisper, ensuring I don't look like a loon talking to herself.

By the time I've made it halfway around the room, I've dipped my chin in greeting to many inconspicuous gawkers and altered the course of my direction when a few inquisitive stares lasted longer than I was comfortable with.

As I make my way toward a bar set up in the corner of the ballroom, I freeze, and my hand clamps over my chest.

"Everything alright?" Hunter asks not even two seconds later.

My lips quiver when I begin to speak. "Yes. Everything is fine."

I can hear Hunter running his hand over his beard. "Are you sure everything is okay? Your pendant isn't responding."

"Everything is fine." My voice jitters as I track two females crossing the space between the bar and the dance floor.

"Paige," Hunter drawls out in his smooth, rich voice. "What's going on?"

From his tone alone, I can tell he isn't buying the explanation I offered.

I huff. "Two Victoria's Secret models are walking by."

"So you covered your pendant to stop me from seeing them?" he asks with amusement in his tone.

"Yep," I snarl, the 'P' having an extra pop to it.

"I have at least another ten cameras in your region alone. Covering your pendant was utterly pointless."

Upon hearing the laughter in his voice, I lower my hand from my chest. Alessandro Ambrosio graces me with her perfect smile as she saunters by. Just from the way her god-gifted assets jiggle, I have no doubt she didn't need the help of silicone to achieve her alluring curves. She's downright gorgeous.

"Although I don't quite have the angle you do," Hunter growls, his voice low and clearly aroused. When my hand snaps back up to cover the pendant, his chuckle jingles through my ear and clusters in my core. "I'm joking, Paige."

Even with hearing the truth in his tone, his little taunt bruised my ego.

Any concerns about my faltering esteem diminish when he says, "There's only one girl my eyes are tracking in that room."

"Izzy," I respond after recalling why I'm aimlessly wandering around like a loser without a date.

"No, Paige. *You*," Hunter replies. The beat of my heart shrills in my ears, and I have no chance of hiding the smile spreading across my face when he says, "Now hurry up so we can get out of here. This bowtie is cutting off my circulation."

Grinning like an idiot, I continue with my original endeavor.

CHAPTER FIFTEEN

*H*unter's eyes track me when I enter the room and glide across the floor. Although his gaze spurs a rush of goosebumps to prickle my skin, the usually frozen stance a coveted glance like his would incite is surprisingly void.

I tug on the untied bowtie dangling around his broad shoulders. "Get too restrictive?"

His smile makes me giddy. Something has changed between us this weekend. I don't know if it stems from his generous gifts or the honesty he's bestowed upon me, but whatever it is, I like it.

"What will you do with these images?" My voice is high with excitement as image after image flicks across the multiple monitors in front of him.

"I'll run them through facial recognition. If anything triggers a flag, I'll run an additional search on a more advanced program," he replies with his gaze locked in on a dark-haired gentleman sitting on a barstool.

"Have you done that to me?" I endeavor to keep suspicion out of my voice. I fail.

His eyes drift to mine. "No." He shakes his head. "You're the first girl I've propositioned *before* running a background search." A cheeky glimmer shimmers in his eyes. "And look where that got me."

I rib him with my elbow. "I'm not the one who pulled out the *friend* card."

My nipples harden when he quietly mutters, "Biggest fucking mistake I ever made."

Not willing to let his little comment slide, I ask, "Not running the background check? Or the friend card?" I tap on the listening device in my ear, ensuring he's aware I heard his sneaky comment. "And by the way, I'm keeping this. It's nearly as good as having eyes in the back of my head."

He chuckles. "It's only a prototype at the moment, but once I have them manufactured, I'll be sure to give you a friend's discount."

"There you go with the *friend* card again," I say with a roll of my eyes. Heat pulses through the middle of my legs when Hunter laughs. When his focus returns to the bank of computers, either refusing or choosing not to answer my earlier question, I ask, "Is skirting questions a hobby of yours or more of a career?" My tone is full of wit.

"There's only one skirt I like getting into, sweetheart, and it isn't an interrogation." When I screw up my nose and snarl at him, he runs his index finger down the grooves indenting my nose. "I like that you're a mystery, Paige. That's why I didn't run a background search on you. It kind of sucks knowing everything about someone. You're an unknown. A little onion I'm unraveling one layer at a time."

Warmth blooms across my chest. "Oh, that's so sweet, except for the smelly onion reference. You couldn't have said I was a beautiful rose you're removing one petal at a time?"

The covetousness in his murky blue eyes spears me into place. "Are you asking me to deflower you, Paige?" he asks, his voice rough and gravelly.

I stare at him, blinking and confused. From the impish glimmer in his eyes, I have no doubt there's a whole heap of hidden innuendo in his statement, but I'm wholly stumped at what it is. Even after watching him in meticulous detail for months, I still haven't learned how to read his prompts yet. Unless he lays his cards out on the table for me to see, I have no clue what he's thinking.

It's only when the corners of his lips flitter and his rascal eyes lock with mine does the sentiment of his question slam into me, closely followed by a fiery heat.

I swallow, feeling the warmth pumping through my veins extending to my cheeks.

"And Paige finally clicks on," he mutters, tapping the heel of my stiletto with his boot. Before any response can dribble from my mouth, Hunter's attention turns back to the computer monitor. "Isaac is on the move. It's time for us to go."

He stands from the chair and rapidly gathers his equipment. I'd offer to help him, but I don't want to impede his technical-looking dissembling, so I just stand to the side and watch him in awe.

In record time, he has everything stored back into his hemp bag left slouched on the floor during his surveillance.

After ensuring everything in the room is back to its original configuration, appearing as if we've never been here, he holds his hand out in offering.

It's the simplest of gestures, but it causes the biggest dose of excitement to heat my blood.

My head lifts from the extensive room service menu when Hunter walks into the living room of our shared suite twenty minutes after we've returned. A grin curls on my lips when I notice he's back in his usual attire—jeans and a blue and black plaid shirt. His hair is wet and flopped to the side, and he smells freshly showered.

"Going to work?" I ask while trying to ignore the drumming of my heart from his invitingly wet appearance.

He shakes his head. "Not yet. Knowing my boss, he'll be a while."

I freeze. "Twice in one night? Lucky girl," I mumble under my breath.

"You hungry?" Hunter jerks his head to the menu in my hand.

I nod. "You?"

He smiles while housing a black firearm in the drawer of the entryway table. "Yep. But not for anything they're selling." He snatches the menu out of my hand and throws it onto the coffee table. "No pickles, right?"

I smile and nod.

"Alright. Let's get you fed." His fingers fumble over his phone's screen. Not even ten seconds later, he returns his phone to his jeans pocket. "Done."

My brows meet my hairline. "Did you order us dinner or get directions to the closest deli?"

He runs his hand along the edge of his jaw, infusing the air with his scent I still haven't distinguished. "I not only ordered dinner, but I also arranged to have a case of Richart chocolates delivered for dessert and sold half a million in stocks."

My eyes bulge, but I maintain a silent front, incapable of articulating a response.

"I'm joking," he jests, hurdling over the couch and slipping into the spare seat next to me. "I didn't order the chocolates."

I stare at him, more confused than ever. I really need to work on unlocking his many facial expressions because I can't tell if he's joking or not.

The groove in the middle of my forehead smooths when Hunter playfully yanks on a wayward curl of my wet hair. I've also showered and changed, wearing my standard attire consisting of a pair of stretchy black pants and a loose t-shirt.

"Have you ever shopped online?" he questions after lifting his gaze from my beaming lips to my eyes.

I stare at him in a sadistic jeering type of way.

He grins. "How many websites do you normally visit before you finalize your purchases?"

My lips quirk. "Depends. Sometimes one, but if it's an expensive purchase, I normally shop around to make sure I'm getting a good deal."

"Well, if you download my app, you'll never have to search for the best deal again," Hunter states matter-of-factly.

"You develop apps as well?"

He grins as he digs his cell back out of his pocket and opens an app. "Name one thing you really want right now, and I'll have it delivered within twenty minutes and at the lowest price guaranteed."

My eyes rocket to his. "No way. Are you serious?" Lucidity smacks into me. "Is that how you got my dress here so quick?"

Hunter waggles his brows as a chortling grin etches behind his shaggy beard. "Although don't tell Melinda. She won't be impressed with the loss of commission."

"Serves her right," I mumble under my breath.

While he chuckles at my snide comment, I tap my index finger on my lip, trying to think of something I could order that will stump Hunter and the egotistical glint brightening his handsome face. "A signed copy of *The Weekend Romance* by Rachel Maloney." My voice is weak from struggling to conceal the rush of emotions pummeling into me.

Hunter's grin enlarges as his fingers fly across his phone's screen, completely unaware I just assigned him an impossible task.

Not wanting to be the cause of his disappointment when he fails to procure my eccentric demand, I say, "Hold on, scrap that. Umm..."

My eyes scan the room while thinking of something unusual for an online order.

My pulse quickens when I think of the perfect item.

"Schweddy Balls," I squeak out, my voice high. "Vanilla ice cream—"

"Loaded with fudge-covered rum and malt balls," Hunter interrupts, his tone as playful as the cheeky grin on his sinful-looking lips.

The smile on my face turns cataclysmic. "It went to Ben & Jerry's ice-cream graveyard back in 2011, so I don't like your chances of getting it here in twenty minutes."

"Done," he states, his tone condescending.

"Bullshit," I retort, shocking myself with my foul language.

Hunter winks before swiveling his phone screen around to face me. My pupils enlarge when I see he has purchased a one-pint limited edition batch of Schweddy Balls for two hundred and thirty-eight dollars.

"Two hundred and thirty-eight dollars is *not* the best deal," I mock.

"It's for an ice cream flavor that's been defunct since 2011," he disputes.

I giggle. "It's probably out of date."

My small giggle turns into a full-hearted laugh when Hunter says, "I don't care if it's covered in mold. For two hundred dollars, you're going to eat every spoonful."

In sync, our necks crank to the door when a doorbell rings through the suite.

Hunter's eyes drop to the phone in his hand. "Wow, that's a new record."

After snagging his wallet off the coffee table, he heads for the door. My brow cocks when he walks back into the living room with a plastic bag in one hand and a bottle of Dr. Pepper sarsaparilla in the other. The grumbling of my stomach intensifies when the smell of creamy pasta and freshly baked bread ignites my senses.

Remaining quiet, Hunter moves his computer equipment, which is still scanning faces, off the coffee table to place it on the six-seater table in the dining area. Once the coffee table has been cleared, he nudges his head, requesting me to join him on the floor for supper.

This is nothing out of the ordinary for us. All the meals we've shared the past few weeks have been on the living room floor of my rented cabin.

Smiling, I slide off the leather couch and plop my backside onto the floor next to him. With a cheeky expression on his face, Hunter pulls out two Styrofoam containers from the plastic bag. "Just remember, you can't judge a book by its cover. It looks disgusting, but it tastes so fucking good." He slides a container with a Gray's Papaya logo on the top to me.

He watches me curiously as I lift the lid. "What is it?" I slightly gag. It looks like someone's stomach overloaded on mac and cheese and *dispelled* the excess pasta onto a hotdog.

"Trust me. It's the bomb."

I giggle over his eccentric pronunciation of the word 'bomb.'

"A carbohydrate bomb."

Hunter doesn't grace me with a reply. He merely lifts the sticky mess from the container and inches it toward my lips. My mouth hesitantly opens. I'm not eager to taste something that looks like it belongs in the bottom of a spew bucket.

"Come on, Paige. I know your mouth opens bigger than that," he jests.

My mouth dangles open larger, more from the cheekiness of Hunter's statement than his request. After pinching the bridge of my nose, I take a large bite of the unappealing feast. My mom always taught me that plugging your nose dulls your taste buds. I used to think she was fibbing just to force me to eat my vegetables at dinner, but after testing her theory on a Brussel sprout, I realized it had some legitimacy. Although I could still taste their horrid flavor, they weren't as potent as normal.

Hunter shakes his head at my eccentric behavior but remains quiet, waiting for me to express an opinion on his meal of choice.

When the messy concoction hits my taste buds, my first response is hesitance, closely followed by shock.

Hunter cocks his brow when a deep moan rumbles from my stuffed mouth. "Good?" he asks.

I don't issue a reply. I'm too eager to devour another bite than spark a conversation.

Removing the bun from his grip, I take another mouth-filling bite of the unique-flavored meal. I moan even louder. My taste buds love it just as much the second time around.

"Told you." Hunter flops onto his backside. "That shit is the *bomb*!"

For the next twenty minutes, we sit on the floor eating ourselves into a carbohydrate coma while sharing the Dr. Pepper sarsaparilla he ordered—minus any glasses. I smile every time Hunter takes a swig before handing the bottle to me, not the slightest bit concerned our lips are sealing over the same rim.

Upon noticing only a mouthful of soda left in the bottom of the bottle, he kindly offers the bottle to me. I screw up my nose and shake my head. "Google says the last five percent of a bottle is pretty much just backwash, so I'm good."

He laughs. "So you're saying your spit is in this bottle?"

"Not just mine, yours as well," I reply, holding back a gag.

"Our spit combined? Sweet."

Heat slides through my veins, warming my pussy when he downs the remainder of the soda with a deep moan. His Adam's apple bobs up and down in an erotic way, quickening my pulse. When a bead of pop shimmers on his top lip, an overwhelming desire to crawl into his lap and lick it off his plump lips smashes into me.

For every second that passes, my restraint falters more and more. I can imagine how delicious his mouth will taste. Creamy goodness from the pasta, sickly sweet from the soda, and a taste that belongs solely to him because he's unique in every possible way —his smell, his looks, and his personality.

A groan rumbles from my lips when Hunter runs his hand over his mouth, gathering the small droplet of soda my tongue was begging to lap up.

With my fantasy crashing to oblivion, his curious eyes bounce between mine. "You alright?" The smoothness of his voice adds to the dampness of my panties.

I swallow to relieve the dryness in my throat before replying, "Uh-huh."

While he gathers our rubbish, I battle to calm the crazy pulse surging through my body. Earlier today, I rationalized to Pepper that my attraction to Hunter may be based on being isolated at Bronte's Peak. Tonight, I realized it isn't. Not the slightest. My eyes absorbed hundreds of well-dressed, handsome men at the gala this evening, but my interests never wavered from the smooth chocolate voice in my ear. He's different from every other guy I've met. Not just his appearance, but his personality as well, and I really like that about him.

Just as Hunter dumps our trash into a bin in the entryway, a ringing cell phone shrills from his jeans pocket. My breathing levels when I realize it's the ringtone on his ancient 'work' phone. Delving his hand into his pocket, he pulls out his cell. His eyes lift and lock with mine as he flips the screen and presses it to his ear. "Hey, Hugo," he greets, his tone jovial.

I release the breath I'm holding in, grateful he seems carefree. I've noticed the past few weeks that Hunter's moods swing toward the negative after he takes a call on that phone.

My relieved breath is quickly redrawn when a fretful mask slips over his face, and he scrapes his hand along the edge of his jaw. "Alright, I'll go and check on him," he mutters, his tone concerned.

He disconnects the call without issuing a farewell to his caller. I remain quiet, watching his throat work hard to swallow.

After a short period of contemplation, he asks, "Are you alright if I leave you here for a few?"

I nod. "Yeah, sure. Is everything okay?" I ask, my tone reserved.

I don't want to force him to open up to me, but I'm worried about the unease clouding his eyes.

"I'm not sure," he replies. "Hugo asked me to go check on Isaac. Something is going on between him and Izzy."

My eyes dance between his. "Did you want me to come with you?"

The darkness of the cloud in his eyes lightens from my offer. "Thanks for the offer, but Isaac's a pretty guarded man, so he wouldn't appreciate an audience. I'm also not too sure what I'll be walking in on."

When he gathers his pistol from the entryway drawer and houses it in the back of his jeans, I step closer to him while nodding. Most men I've met are guarded.

Hunter takes a step closer to me, standing so close, the garlic from the creamy sauce on our hotdogs filters through my nose. "Are you sure you're alright staying here by yourself?"

"Yep. I'm going to write," I reply with excitement in my voice.

All day I've had a truckload of storylines bouncing around in my head, dying to be let free. But not wanting to be rude, I left my laptop stored in my suitcase instead of on my lap where it really wanted to be.

He smirks at my excitement. "Alright, I'll see you in a few."

My pulse quickens when the lips I'd been fantasizing about earlier incline closer to me. Unable to harbor the desire to find out if his lips have their own unique taste, I adjust the tilt of my chin, forcing his lips to land smack bang on mine. Air hisses out of his mouth, fluttering my lips with the flavor of the meal we just shared and a tangy citrus scent.

Elation swamps me. Even though he doesn't increase the intensity of our kiss, he doesn't pull away either. We stand still, completely motionless in the middle of the foyer with our lips joined and our hands fisted by our sides. I don't know how much time passes. I'm too busy fighting the urge to run my tongue along the seam of his mouth to keep time. Although our kiss is as basic as an innocent schoolyard peck, it's still heart-stopping. It is also our very first kiss.

Only after enough time passes that our lips have nearly become one does Hunter pull back. His massively dilated eyes bounce between mine, reflecting a range of emotions. Shock and apprehension are there, but the one making me giddy is the yearning. I just hope it isn't there because of his lack of female contact the past few weeks.

I know from experience he's a sexually motivated creature, but ever since our friendship formed, his female *visitors* have become extinct. I'm not sure if all contact has ceased to exist, but he certainly doesn't bring them back to his glass house anymore.

"I'll be back as soon as I can." Hunter's voice is deeper than usual. When I nod, he places another kiss on the edge of my mouth. My laughter vibrates on his lips when he mutters, "Not going to pull another fast one on me?"

I draw back and peer into his eyes. "It's no big deal. *Friends* kiss *friends* on the lips all the time. It is only once tongue gets involved does it cause issues."

I'm so full of shit. If the hot trickle of desire dampening between my legs isn't enough of a clue to my deceit, the galloping of my heart is a surefire indication.

A bolt of lightning shoots through my pussy, aiding my eagerness when Hunter responds, "So I could have been tasting your lips the entire time I've been friends with you?"

The smug grin on his face enlarges when I nod. "If you wanted to?"

My heart beats wildly when he says, "Fuck Isaac. I think a night in is on the cards."

I laugh even with my insides twisting in excitement. "Go and do what you need to do." I nudge him toward the door. "I'll be here when you get back."

I'm not going to lie. I love that he seems hesitant to leave.

Once he slips behind the door, I bolt back into the living room, eager to FaceTime with Pepper.

I've only just finished replaying every event that has happened for the past twelve hours to Pepper when a doorbell buzzes into the room.

Pepper inhales a quick breath as her mouth forms an 'O.' "Do you think it's Hunter?"

"Why would he ring the doorbell?" I ask through scrunched brows.

She shrugs. "Only one way to find out."

"Do I look okay?" I check my hair and face in the small video of me in the top corner of my phone.

"You look gorgeous! Go get him," Pepper replies.

After air kissing her farewell, I place my phone on the coffee table, leap off the thick woolen rug, and head for the door. The pulse between my legs thrums more the closer I get to the foyer. My excitement is short-lived when I swing open the door to find a bike messenger in a super tight pair of bike pants and a reflective vest standing in the hallway. His outfit is so tight I can see every detail of his body.

Every.

Single.

Detail.

"Hi," I greet him with unease in my voice.

After the bike messenger finishes absorbing my flushed expression, wide eyes, and panting chest, his gaze shifts down to a clipboard in his hand. "Paige?" he asks.

"That's me," I reply, smiling.

He stores his clipboard under his arm, then digs his hand into the backpack resting at his side. "I'm sorry it took us longer than quoted, but your order was a hard one to fill."

A small giggle spills from my lips when he hands me a one-pint serving of Schweddy Balls ice cream with a silver catering spoon dangling on the top. I giggle loudly when I read the gift tag attached to the spoon.

Eat this.
Hunter.

"A man of many words," I mumble to myself. I return my eyes to the bike messenger. "Thank you."

My interest piques when the bike messenger holds his index finger in the air, requesting a minute before he goes digging through his bag again. My nose gets a twinge when he pulls out an item covered in brown paper and twine. I can tell from the shape alone that it's some type of book.

Moisture forms in my eyes as my heart rate climbs astronomically. While juggling the ice cream and spoon in one hand, I attempt to open the package with my other.

"Thank you," I mumble to the bike courier when he removes the ice cream from my unstable grip.

Through shaking hands, I untangle the twine and tear a large section of brown paper away from the middle of the parcel. Tears prick my eyes when a familiar ocean side cover of a first edition copy of *The Weekend Romance* comes into my vision.

After running the back of my hand over my cheeks to remove my tears, I crack open the pristine cover. A whizz of air parts my lips when I see Rachel's signature scribbled across the front page. Although Hunter found a signed first edition of the book I wanted, it isn't the exact one I've been searching for over the past three years.

CHAPTER SIXTEEN

"*H*e opens the petal of her flower, searching for the sweet nectar of her rosebud. What the fuck is that?"

My heart leaps out of my ribcage. "Oh my god, Hunter, you scared the shit out of me!" I shriek while clutching my chest with my hand. "You can't do that to someone. Jesus Christ." I sink deeper into the reclining chair I'm sitting on and suck in deep breaths to calm the mad beat of my heart. "For future reference, never sneak up on a writer when they're in the zone. It could end up very poorly for you and your package."

Hunter moves around the reclining chair to sit on the coffee table opposite me. When his eyes lift to me from the devoured ice cream container I licked clean, I rub my stomach. "It was *sooo* good," I drawl out. "I was planning on saving you some, but I got a little bit eager."

He chuckles, but it isn't his full-hearted laugh. It's reserved and with a bit of hesitation. I return his passiveness while I study him in great depth. Although his eyes are still sparked with their normal vivacity, it isn't as potent as normal. His brows are hanging a little lower, and his aura points to his mood swinging more toward the moodier, grumpy Hunter than the chipper one who left here earlier.

When my eyes drift to the clock hanging in the middle of the living room, I balk. He has been gone for a little over three hours, and I've been writing nonstop for two.

After returning my eyes to Hunter, I ask, "Is everything okay with Isaac and Izzy?"

"Only time will tell," he answers while rubbing a kink out of the back of his neck.

From his short response, I know he doesn't want to continue our conversation, so I flash him a quick smirk, silently relaying I'm here if he needs to talk before returning my focus to my laptop. I don't type. I just pretend to work on my novel as I keep an eagle eye on him over my Mac screen.

His eyes remain planted on his black boots for several minutes before they lift and lock with mine. "If you're writing a story about a bee falling in love with a human, it's already been done."

I slant my head and cock my brow. "What?" I query with a screwed-up nose.

"*The Bee Movie*, starring Jerry Seinfeld," he elaborates.

I snarl at him. "I know what movie you're referring to, but what does it have to do with my WIP?"

"Whip?"

"WIP. W. I. P. It means work in progress," I advise after remembering that most people don't understand author talk.

Hunter's hand drops from his neck, and he scoots a little closer to me. "If this is a romance book, what's the whole petal-rosebud referring to?"

Heat creeps across my cheeks. "It's the beginning of a *bedroom* scene I'm working on."

I endeavor to keep my voice confident.

I miserably fail.

"Scrap it and start again." Hunter's tone is blunt and straight to the point.

I balk. "No way! I've been working on that scene for over two hours," I blubber out. "You only got one small snippet of it. You can't judge an entire scene from one line."

He props his elbows onto his knees and tilts his torso closer to me. "Read it to me then."

"Ah... no," I reply with a brisk shake of my head.

"Paige."

"No, Hunter. I'm not reading it to you." I snap my laptop screen shut and hold it in close to my chest.

Hunter cocks his brow and bores his eyes into mine. "Read it to me... or I'll hack into your cloud backup and send your manuscript to every email recipient in the country."

My mouth gapes. Shock is all over my face. I don't need time to deliberate if his threat is idle. The frivolous look on his face is all I need to know he intends on doing as pledged if I don't read it to him.

Snarling, I huff, "Fine!" After opening my Scrivener program, I commence reading the steamy scene I just created. "He lays her on the bed, her hair a rich molten waterfall crescent on the pillow. He eyes her delicately, absorbing the softness of her skin, smooth and velvety like a plucked rose petal. His lips press on her neck, collarbone, and right rib before they lower even further. Her breath stiffens when he reaches her lady parts, brushing his fingers on the undergarments hiding the petals of her flower."

I stop reading and glare at Hunter when his body shakes as he fights to hold his laughter.

Upon spotting my furious glare, he coughs, clearing his throat. "Sorry. Please continue."

After snarling at him, I stray my eyes back to my laptop. "Her insides sigh in happiness, like a child making a snow angel in an abandoned field when he slides her modest underwear down her legs. She moans his name in a soft whisper when he opens the petals of her flower, searching for the sweet nectar of her rosebud.

He wants to taste the sweetness of her pollen, devour the nectar of her delicate flower."

My teeth grit, and I slam my laptop shut when Hunter's loud chuckle bellows through my ears. Even copping the wrath of my knee-clattering stink eye doesn't lessen his uproarious laughter.

"You're an asshole," I mutter before dumping my laptop on the coffee table and storming into my room, slamming the door behind me.

When he doesn't attempt to follow me, I make my way into the bathroom, deciding a nice hot shower may be the only thing to lessen the anger boiling my blood.

I take my time in the ginormous double shower attached to my room, letting the steaming hot water drain away the negativity of Hunter's response. I'm sure with a bit of tweaking and some word alterations, the scene will be beautiful and poetic, a real justice to the connection my characters have.

I stop lathering my breasts with body wash as a whiny moan spills from my lips.

There's no saving that.

It's rubbish.

Total rubbish.

This is the reason I penned young adult romance—to avoid the stupid sex scenes.

After dumping the shower puff onto the tiled marble floor, I step under the spray. Water gurgles in the back of my throat when I let out a long, deep scream, expelling the negativity choking my writing inspiration. I wouldn't have any issues writing a half-decent sex scene if I had some real experience. I'm not saying Riley was a dud in the bedroom...

... actually, yes, I am.

Riley was as plain as they came. Missionary every Tuesday night, lasting for approximately four minutes, give or take a minute or two. I'm fairly sure Riley didn't understand the meaning of the word *foreplay*. His routine never altered the entire three years we lived together, so I wasn't at all surprised when I walked in on him and Beth Millner in the obligatory missionary position in the bed I only emerged from an hour earlier.

If my neighbor, Mrs. Peters, hadn't stopped me that morning for a friendly chit-chat on my way to have brunch with Pepper, I have no doubt I'd still be unaware of Riley's indiscretions to this day. Our impromptu chat meant I caught sight of Beth's car pulling into the driveway of the home I shared with Riley.

Although Beth and I were friends in high school, we rarely saw each other since senior prom, so I knew in that instant she wasn't there to visit me.

"The same time, every Sunday morning," Mrs. Peters muttered while tapping my forearm gently.

Even seeing Riley's affair firsthand, it still took four weeks of deliberations before I built up the courage to leave him. It wasn't a lack of self-esteem that had me delaying the inevitable. It was because it was seven years of my life I was walking away from. That may not seem like much time over an eighty-year lifespan, but when you're only twenty-five, seven years seems like a lifetime, and when every detail of your life is played out in public, a failed relationship is the last thing you want to add to your list of achievements.

After crashing at Pepper's house for three weeks, plotting my next move, she suggested I rent the cabin and get away from it all to solely concentrate on my writing. And that's exactly what I've been doing the past few months.

Although this weekend away was never figured into my plans, I would have never said no to Hunter's request. That, in itself, is truly astounding considering how long it usually takes me to make a decision, but I owe Hunter a lot. Without him and his bevy of female companions, I'd still be penning my own rendition of *Basic Instinct*, ice picks and all. So even though Hunter thinks my sex scenes are laughable, I appreciate his honesty.

I'd rather have one person laughing at me than an entire reading community.

I step out of the shower, wrap a towel around my body, and finger comb my hair before wandering into my room. My brisk pace halts when I walk into the main area of my room and find Hunter leaning on the doorjamb. His shoulder is propped on the wall, and my Mac is balancing precariously on his palm.

Sensing my presence, his head lifts from the screen of my laptop. "This is really good, Paige." My chest swells, honored by the praise in his voice, but my happiness is short-lived when he continues, "It's just the sex scenes."

"What's wrong with them?" I ask, my tone hesitant.

Hunter's brows furrow together. "They are good, just too... *flowery*. You have these two amazing characters who have fire-sparking passion that dulls the instant they step into the bedroom."

"That's life," I argue as my eyes bounce between his. "Sometimes that's just the way it is."

He shakes his head. "No, it isn't." His tone is blunt and without hesitation.

I cross my arms in front of my chest. "Maybe not for you, but for *real life* relationships, they can be just like that. Not every guy is an Adonis in the bedroom. Some are just... *duds*."

Hunter places my Mac on the dresser to his left before his eyes lock with mine. "You need to write from experience, Paige. Write what's in your heart."

"I'm trying," I snarl through gritted teeth while battling to keep my tears at bay. "But when you've got nothing to go off, it makes it a little hard."

Hunter eyeballs me. Not just a general stare—he *stares* at me for numerous heart-clutching seconds. When his eyes drop, reality slams into me. I'm standing in front of him in nothing but a fluffy hotel towel with a wet, shaggy mane. *Like my night could get any worse.*

My throat struggles to swallow when he pushes off the wall and prowls toward me. Even with the air conditioning set to a reasonable level, it becomes muggier with every step he takes. I attempt to speak, but the fervor in his eyes renders me speechless. My mouth moves but refuses to relinquish any words.

"The sexual connection between a couple should increase the closer they get to each other." His voice is smoother than melted chocolate. "The sparks, the desire... they should grow with every minute they spend together until neither can resist the urge any longer."

He cups my jaw, redirecting the mad pulse surging through my body to my aching-with-desire pussy. "They fight their attraction for as long as possible, but when the pull becomes too great, they stop fighting and give in to their desires."

A speckling of goosebumps follows the trail his beard makes across the corner of my mouth, past my inflamed cheek until he stops at the shell of my earlobe. "If you want to write about the connection a couple feels during sex, you have to experience it. *Taste* it. *Devour* it. *Feel* what they are feeling."

Excitement darts down my spine when he repositions himself to stand behind me. He's standing so close I feel the heat of his thickened cock against the curve of my backside. Air puffs from my lips when his hand slithers up the planes of my stomach to unknot the twist in my towel, sending it toppling to the floor.

You'd think my first reaction would be to dive for the towel or the bathrobe sprawled on the monstrous bed I'm standing next to, but it isn't. I stand still, frozen in place with both desire and shock, and for once, allowing my body to overrule my head.

My pulse shrills in my ears when he curls his hands over mine and guides them over the silky smoothness of my skin that's still damp from the shower. My heart thrashes against my ribs, matching the pulse of my clit when he uses my hands to cup my breasts. He kneads and caresses them until my nipples bud painfully.

"A woman's body was created to be worshiped, Paige. Your body was created for pleasure. To both give and take."

My mouth waters, turned on by his words and the softness of

my hands fondling my breasts. Although I told him weeks ago that I'd "taken care of business," it was a lie. I've never brought myself to climax. But with his rich, velvety voice whispering in my ear, the roughness of his beard scratching my neckline, and the way my breasts feel larger and sexier in my smaller hands, I'm already tiptoeing to orgasm station.

My thighs shake when Hunter glides my right hand away from my breast, directing it toward the wetness dampening the insides of my thighs. A breathless, throaty moan simpers from my lips when he places his boot between my bare feet to spread them with a gentle kick. My pupils dilate when he cups my drenched pussy with my hand. When he guides my index finger through the folds of my pussy, coating both of our fingers with the evidence of my excitement, the quiver of my thighs intensifies.

"This is not a flower. It's a gift. Every drop of liquid is an unspoken promise of impending pleasure." His voice sends a surge of red-hot desire to my already slicked pussy.

I rest my head on his shoulder when the weight of my legs becomes too much for me to handle. My muscles are exhausted from fighting to stay upright as all the energy in my body focuses on more needy regions.

"Touch your pussy, Paige. Feel the way it clings to and massages your finger. What makes it wetter. Learn what it likes, then work harder to unravel its greatest desire. What it loves. No man can tell you what *you* want, crave, or desire. Only you can."

When my knees falter at his words, he releases my hands from his grasp and secures them around my waist, keeping me upright. Unashamed and on the brink of ecstasy, I use him as an anchor while I continue fondling my breasts and playing with my pussy.

Normally, I'd never be so bold, but with his head buried in the crook of my neck and us surrounded by nothing but cream-colored walls, I feel no embarrassment or shame. Oddly, I feel desired and sexy.

The heat in the room becomes stifling when I thrust my finger in and out of my clenching pussy in rhythm to Hunter's heavy breaths hitting my neckline when he bombards me with a flurry of dirty compliments. He says my body deserves nothing but perfection, how good it feels against his, and how I should never let another person's opinion alter my own on what is or is not right for my body.

The heaviness of my breasts increases as the first signs of an orgasm rises. My thighs shake, and my breaths become more labored.

"Do you feel it? The spark? The loss of control?" he mutters in my ear, intuiting that I'm close to the brink.

"Uh-huh," I pant between breaths.

"That's what you write about, Paige. What you're feeling right now. How good you feel. How desirable your body is."

The warmth of his breath on my ear sets me off. I moan as an orgasm rushes over me. It buckles my knees and sends a noise I've never heard before into the silence of the night. Hunter groans as he tightens his grip on my hips. His probing fingers add even more strength to the climax shimmering new life into my emotionally drained body. My body shatters, sexually satiated and emotionally appeased at the same time.

The blissful haze of an orgasm keeps me floating on cloud nine when Hunter gathers me in his arms and strides toward the large bed. While keeping his heavily dilated eyes arrested on my idyllic face, he yanks back the thick duvet cover and places me beneath it. The fog of my climax slowly dissipates when he lifts the covers, presses a kiss on the edge of my temple, then he ambles to the door.

I lurch from the bed, exposing my naked breasts to his view. "Where are you going?" My voice is hoarse, scorched from the erotic screams that shredded from my throat during climax.

He doesn't spin around.

He doesn't grace me with a reply.

He just stalks out of the room without a backward glance.

CHAPTER SEVENTEEN

*A*wkward.

That's the only word I can use to describe the thick stench plaguing the air between Hunter and me as we make the two-hundred-and-fifty-mile journey home. He's barely spoken a word to me since last night. And since I don't know exactly how to apologize for bringing myself to climax in front of him, I've also maintained a quiet front.

He is mere inches from me, but it feels like we're worlds apart.

For every mile we travel, my annoyance firms. I didn't ask Hunter to touch me last night. *I didn't stop him either.* But we're grown adults, so the fact he's acting so childish is irritating the shit out of me.

Huffing, I turn my attention away from the scenery of Ravenshoe whizzing by and focus it on Hunter. "Who is watching Charlie?" I ask, endeavoring to spark some type of conversation between us before I die of asphyxiation from the tension depriving the air of enough oxygen to maintain life.

His eyes drift from the road to me. "Who?"

Even though his reply is short, I'm grateful I've pried a response from him.

"Charlie. Your dog."

His shoulders stiffen. "Oh... umm... he isn't my dog."

"Huh?"

Hunter scrapes his hand along the edge of his jaw. "I kind of borrowed him."

My brows furrow. "You borrowed a dog? Why?"

His eyes drift between the road and me. "Because I saw you sitting in the sand dunes."

"And you wanted to talk to me, so you used Charlie as a way in?" I interrupt, wanting him to hurry up and get to the heart of his story. I'm not a sitting-on-the-edge-of-your-seat suspense type of girl. I like to get straight to the nitty-gritty, often jumping ahead in any books I'm reading just to find out what happens before going back and reading the entire chapter.

"No, Paige." When Hunter shakes his head, confusion swamps me. "I wanted to *fuck* you. So I used Charlie as my way in," he clarifies, his voice stern. "I wanted to fuck you from the very first day I spotted you."

I'm shocked, not just from the crudeness of his reply but his admission as well.

To be honest, I don't know whether to be pissed or happy.

"So everything... Charlie, fixing my laptop, the app, the gifts were all because you wanted to get into my panties?" I ask, my tone a cross between curious and astounded.

If his sole purpose was to get me between the sheets, why didn't he take advantage of the opportunity last night?

He swallows before turning his eyes back to me. "Charlie was a ploy. The rest was me. I like you, Paige. The stuff I've given you is because I wanted to, not because I want to fuck you."

His statement should bristle my spikes, but they don't. Because he didn't say he *wanted* to fuck me. He said he *wants* to fuck me.

My happiness doesn't last long when he mutters, "But what happened last night won't happen again. I was supposed to show you the connection your characters should feel. To explain the dynamic, not do it. I took it too far."

"No, you didn't." My squeal bellows through the thick stench of awkwardness plaguing the air. "You didn't even touch me."

Technically, I was the only one doing the touching.

Hunter's face lines with anger. "Oh, but I fucking wanted to," he mutters under his breath. After firming his grip on the steering wheel, he turns his hardhearted eyes to me. "Do you have any idea how hard it was for me to walk away last night? Seeing how your eyes spark and your lips part when you're about to come? It fucking killed me walking away."

"Then why did you?" I reply, both angry and confused. Angry for the way I felt when he walked out without a word escaping his lips and confused as to why he keeps fighting this unique draw we have toward each other.

"Because a girl like you doesn't belong with a man like me!" His angry roar rumbles through my heaving chest.

I laugh in disbelief, a crazy cackle that exposes my nuttiness. "Are you seriously giving me that line after spending weeks telling me how I should never let another person's opinion alter my own?"

"It's not a line, Paige. It's the truth. I have nothing to offer you."

"Bullshit, Hunter. You blew my mind last night. Made me achieve something I've never done before."

"As you said earlier, that was all you, Paige. I didn't touch you." His voice is a vicious snarl and full of maliciousness that maims my heart.

My back molars smash together. "Oh. Okay. I guess my opinion on you has changed," I retaliate before swinging open the passenger door of his car with brutal strength, forcing him to slam on his brakes halfway down his gravel driveway. "Because here I was thinking you were a *smart* man. Obviously, you're more *stupid* than I initially perceived."

I grit my teeth, suffocating a squeal when he snarls, "And quick-witted Paige *finally* clicks on."

"Fuck you, Hunter," I snarl before curling out of his car.

After slamming his door shut, I storm toward the back deck of my rented cabin. Hot, salty tears are threatening to spill down my face at any moment, and the only thing keeping them at bay is the potent anger boiling my blood.

My frenzied pace falters when gravel crunching under feet sounds through my ears as Hunter chases to catch up with me. "You saw how many women I've fucked, Paige! You witnessed it first-hand, yet it still isn't enough to scare you away from me." His fury is easily heard over the crashing waves in the distance. "Then what the fuck will it take?"

"You don't need to ask for help, asswipe! You're doing a stellar job right now!" I retort as I continue with my brisk pace, not bothering to turn around and face him. "You want to scare me away? Guess what, you have!"

While willing myself not to cry, I rush into the cabin. I grab everything and anything I can get hold of before shoving it into my half-packed suitcase. My movements are chaotic and filled with devastation.

Once I have my clothing packed, I drag my suitcase into the small living area. I don't need to lift my eyes to know Hunter is present. I can both sense and smell him.

"Where are you going?" he asks, his voice gruff.

I place my suitcase next to the entryway table before locking my tear-glistening eyes with his. His face is stern and lined with anger, but his eyes give away his true self.

They are full of worry.

"I can't do this anymore, Hunter. You keep drawing me in, then pushing me away in the same breath. You need to either let me in or let me go," I plead as my heart cracks along with my voice.

His stern mask momentarily slips, revealing a flicker of panic he rarely exposes. I hold his gaze, ensuring he's aware my words aren't an idle threat. I can't keep doing this pulling and pushing routine of the past four weeks. It's exhausting, and I'm burned out.

"Do you feel anything for me?" My heart hammers against my ribs. "Anything at all?"

His jaw muscle ticks when he begins to speak. "Of course I do, you're my friend—"

"Stop giving me the stupid fucking friends' line," I interrupt, my voice rising in anger. "You know as well as I do that you're using it as a barrier between us because you're too scared to admit your true feelings."

My firm stance eases when anger floods Hunter's eyes. He glares at me, issuing me the same threatening stare he gave me during my last round of interrogations, but even with my heart hammering against my ribs, I maintain a strong front, pretending his ardent glare isn't affecting me.

In reality, it's causing a sick feeling to spread through my stomach.

When the dense stretch of silence passing between us becomes too suffocating to ignore, I spin on my heels and gather my suitcase. My steps are frantic as I battle to hold in the tears threatening to spill down my face. Hunter has openly expressed on numerous occasions that he hates talking about himself, but now is different. This weekend shifted our relationship out of the friendship zone, and I'm no longer willing to hide my feelings.

I did it for years with Riley.

I refuse to do it with Hunter.

Hunter's indistinguishable smell hits my senses the closer I get to him. My steps are hurried since I'm desperate to escape the room that's shrinking by the minute. My chin quivers when I dip it in farewell while racing to the door. I need privacy before I'll allow my tears to fall.

Just as I hit the edge of the patio door, Hunter catches my wrists. A whimper scuttles from my lips when he pins me to the wall with his imposing body. I go from steaming in anger to frozen with desire in seconds from being trapped by six feet of pure man.

His eyes are wide, his nostrils flaring, and his whole composure screams of nothing but fury, but instead of being unnerved by his intimidating stance, I'm excited and incredibly turned on. My breasts are heavy, my clit is throbbing, matching the mad beat of my heart, and my body is acutely aware of every inch of him pressed up against me.

I'm not the only one aroused by our closeness. Hunter's cock is thick and hard against my stomach. "Do you have any idea what you're fucking doing to me?" The hotness of his breath adds to the intense heat radiating from my cheeks. "You've sent me into such a tailspin, I can't think straight anymore. I fucked up at my job as I was too fixated on you, yet you feel the need to ask if I have feelings for you. I can't breathe, sleep, or eat without thinking about you. You're driving me fucking crazy."

"Good. It's about time you joined the crazy club because I've been here for weeks." My words come out fast, spurred on by the desire to unravel him, to force him to finally admit the undeniable connection between us.

"I've been there from the fucking start, Paige. From the moment I saw you." He steps closer, pinning me more firmly to the wall. I feel the surge of his pulse streaming through his body via his hands clamped around my wrists. "The instant I saw you, I wanted you. The way the moonlight caught your hair, your smooth, soft skin, your beautiful face. I wanted it all."

My breaths come out in ragged pants, my chest not able to fully expand with how close he's standing. "Then why did you throw down the friend card? Why have you kept me at arm's length?"

"Because I knew you'd ruin me," he mutters, his words hurried.

My pupils widen as shock spreads across my face.

"For over ten years I've kept everyone at arm's length. I tried to do that to you as well. For weeks, I kept my distance, but the pull became too great. It became too much."

I nod in full agreement. Even shocked beyond hell at how quickly my feelings have developed for him, I can't deny the draw between us. We're magnetized to one another.

He stares at me, his gaze smoldering with lust and anger. "I don't just want to *feel* you, *taste* you and have you beneath me, Paige. I want to have *all* of you."

"Then have me," I mumble, unable to understand why he's holding back.

He angrily shakes his head. "That's not me, Paige. I don't want a relationship. I've never wanted that."

"That's because you hadn't met me." My voice is low, overcome by the barrage of emotions barreling into me. "I want you to *touch* me, *feel* me, *taste* every single inch of me, Hunter. I want you to have *all* of me."

Incapable of moving my arms since he has my wrists pinned at my side, I flex out my chest, urging him even closer, giving him that final push. A brutal grunt escapes his lips when my budded nipples crash into his firm pecs, and his tightness around my wrists firms.

I moan, incredibly turned on by the roughness of his hold. Upon hearing my shameful response, the anger lining his face lessens, and a new glint brightens his eyes. As though he could find any more space between us, he leans in even closer. "Don't destroy me, Paige."

"Never." My voice is shaky, shocked he'd ever think I'd hurt him while also wondering who already has.

His eyes search my face, seeking any untruth. When he fails to locate any deceit, he slowly and possessively seals his lips over mine. I gasp out the word, "Finally," when his tongue delves into my mouth, stepping us over the friendship line he drew in the sand weeks ago.

The roughness of his beard is unlike anything I've ever experienced, but it heightens my excitement, adding more giddiness to his heart-twisting kiss. The inside of his mouth has the same citrus freshness as his lips, a scrumptious mix of flavor and heat.

He relinquishes my wrists from his rigid grip to band his arms around my waist, drawing me nearer. Every nerve in my body goes haywire, incapable of grasping what to do first. I want to run my fingers through his thick mane and nibble on his lips. I also want to grind against his thick cock rubbing the seam of my panties while he holds me against the wall, devouring every inch of my mouth in perfect, lengthened strokes.

There are too many choices, and my mind is fritzed on which item to select first.

Why can't I do them all?

So I do exactly that. I run my fingers through his hair, securing his mouth to mine so I can nibble on his delicious tangy lips while I grind my throbbing pussy on the impressive thickness in his jeans.

When he tries to pull away, I hold on, refusing to relinquish his mouth from mine. It's taken him this long to revoke the friendship card he issued, and I haven't had nearly enough time to ensure he never wants to use it again.

"I want you in bed so I can take my time with you," Hunter mutters against my lips. "Screaming my name in a place where no one else will hear it."

My nipples bud even harder as a needy moan topples from my lips. "My bed, not yours." I suck his bottom lip into my mouth. *He can't dress me and walk me to the door if it isn't his house.*

He's walking through the living room of my cabin before I even realize he's moving, too engrossed with sampling every inch of his mouth to maintain rational thoughts. Just like he made himself at home in my kitchen and living area the past few weeks, he enters the cabin's main bedroom, not needing to ask for directions.

The thick duvet cover on my bed feels cold against my feverish skin when he places me down on the edge. A cringe crosses my face when I catch my reflection in the full-length mirror in the corner of the room. My hair is mussed from his large hand tugging it during our kiss, my lips are swollen and red, my eyes are wide, and my pupils are heavily dilated. But even looking the most frazzled I've ever been, I also feel incredibly desirable. That probably has something to do with the way his dark, possessive eyes are scanning my face, adding to the thickness his jeans are failing to conceal.

"You shouldn't let me touch you," he mutters, his voice deep and raspy. "I shouldn't be allowed to fucking touch you."

My breathing sharpens, panicked he hates what he's seeing.

When my hands dart up to my hair, vainly trying to smooth the frazzled pieces into manageable locks, Hunter mutters, "You're fucking beautiful, Paige. Don't ever doubt it."

"Then why did you say that? Why would you say that?"

"Because if I get one taste of you, I'll never let you go." His voice is low and full of worry. "You don't need a man like me, Paige. You deserve someone better than me."

"What are you saying? I need a man in a suit, clean-shaven, and with no tattoos?"

My teeth grit when he nods.

"Been there. Done that," I snap, my tone brittle like cracked glass. "Didn't make him any better of a man."

His murky blue eyes flash, and his nostrils flare as jealousy swamps him. The raging beat of my heart speeds up when he removes his gun from the back of his trousers and places it on the table at his right. His eyes scorch into mine as his fingers make quick work of the buttons on his red and black plaid shirt. The wetness between my legs multiplies when the smooth ridges of his torso become exposed, closely followed by the bumps of his stomach.

I moan, a needy, raspy groan when his shirt falls off his shoulders, puddling around his boot-covered feet. When he steps toward me, my eyes devour how his muscles flex with every long stride he takes.

When he reaches the end of the bed, I glide my eyes from the band of his jeans to his vehement gaze. "I warned you," he mutters while staring straight into my eyes.

I nod. "And I didn't listen. Lucky you seem to like my defiance."

A ghost of a smile sneaks out from behind his beard. "I like you any way I can get you," he barely mutters before clasping my hand in his and hoisting me off the bed.

"Lucky me, 'cause I don't like you at all." The laughter spilling from Hunter's mouth simmers when I grip his erect crotch and squeeze it in my hand. "This, on the contrary, I think I could *really* like this."

His lips quirk. "Nah. That won't happen anytime soon."

I stare at him with alarm on my face. I thought with the removal of his shirt I was making headway in my endeavor to have him stepping over the friendship line. Now, I'm not so sure my ploy is working.

Any concerns about my lack of seduction vanish when Hunter says, "You won't like it. You'll *love* my cock by the time I'm finished with you."

CHAPTER EIGHTEEN

*J*ust like the carefree Paige who only emerges in Hunter's presence, a new, unstiffened Paige surfaces in the bedroom as well. It might have something to do with the way his eyes devour every inch of me as he removes my shirt. Or how he loosens the elastic holding my hair so my wavy locks can spring free. Or the fact the thickness in his jeans gets larger with every second that passes as he wrangles my skin-tight jeans down my quivering thighs.

Whatever it is, I'm loving the newly found, relaxed Paige.

For the first time, I feel desired.

I'd even go as far as saying I feel sexy.

The warmth of Hunter's breath adds to the misting of sweat on my skin when he stands from his crouched position. His trek is slow since he stops at several intimate spots on the way to press a kiss or a nip to my heated and aching skin.

Just like last night, he moves to stand behind me before pressing his body firmly to mine, engulfing me in his hot, manly form. Shivers rack my body when the bristles of his beard tickle my neck a mere second before his teeth sink into my shoulder blade. Excitement surges through my blood when his tongue lavishes the spot, both soothing my skin and adding to my lightheadedness. One of his hands grips my neck, securing my body to his, while the other curls around my chest to cup my breast. He teases and caresses my nipple until it puckers in desperation.

Desire pummels through me when Hunter mutters on a breathy groan, "I love your fucking tits, Paige. I knew they'd be ten out of ten. I can't wait to see my cum smeared all over them."

His clever fingers work me into a frenzy while his crass words add to the dampness of my panties. As his lips pay dedicated attention to my neck, his hand moves away from my breast to follow the path he guided mine down in our hotel room last night. Goosebumps follow the trail his hands make over the small swell of my breasts, down the smooth plains of my stomach before stopping at my aching-with-desire pussy.

A hiss of air parts his lips when his fingers run over the dampness of my panties. My core tightens with every soft stroke he makes. When he slips his hand inside my panties, breaking through the small cotton barrier between us, my nails bend while securing a rigid hold of his thighs.

"You're so fucking wet." He rolls his hips so his thick cock grinds into my backside. "Are you dying to *feel* this, *taste* it, *fuck* it?"

Unashamedly, I nod. "Yes... so what's taking you so long?"

His beard scratches my neck when he smiles at my eagerness. "In time, Paige." He pushes his finger inside me in a slow and unbridled thrust. "First, I'm going to make you come like you did last night, but I'll use my hands this time. Then, I'll make you come again... *on my face.*"

I moan and buck against him, turned on by his promise. My entire body is pulled taut, aroused, and close to the brink. The combination of his words and the way he is finger fucking me has me racing to climax. I am ready and eager to topple into oblivion.

The buildup of tension in my core strengthens when he squashes the pad of his palm firmly onto my throbbing clit. Then, when he adds another finger into the mix, my race for release becomes frantic, almost uncontrollable.

"Open your eyes, Paige. See how beautiful you are when you come," Hunter mutters into my ear.

When my eyes flutter open, heady desire scorches through my veins. My knees buckle, and my orgasm comes to fruition as I catch sight of our reflection in the full-length mirror in the corner of the room. Hunter's manly body overpowers mine as he arches over me. He sends me to the brink with nothing but a talented pair of hands and a dirty, wicked mouth.

I climax with a hoarse cry, shameless and free of doubt. Hours of tension is swept away in an instant when my body is engulfed by a mind-shattering orgasm, stronger than any before it.

I've barely had time to emerge from the clouds when my feverish body is swamped by the softness of a cloud. My panties are snapped off, and an eager mouth dives onto the cleft of my trembling pussy. I secure a firm grip on Hunter's hair before trying to pull him away. I'm too sensitive, too overcome, too spent for my pussy to handle this type of attention so soon after a mind-hazing climax.

He pins me to the mattress by my hips before his tongue delves inside me. He laps up the residue of my orgasm while also adding to my wetness.

"I warned you, Paige," Hunter mutters against my drenched lips, forcing a tremble to roll down my spine. "I told you what I was going to do."

I come for the second time when his lips circle my pulsating clit, and he sucks down hard. As my body shakes, I scream his name. Every muscle contracts while battling through an orgasm even more intense than the one before it.

Hunter's deep growl ripples through my pussy when he places a final set of teasing licks to my swollen clit before he stands from his crouched position. His beard is wet and glistening, shamefully exposing the power he has on my body. His torso is slicked with sweat, and the front of his jeans is extended and taut.

When my eyes lock with his, a shudder runs through my exhausted body, invigorating it with renewed excitement from the hankering look in his eyes.

One of his hands runs over his beard, clearing away the evidence of my arousal while the other gathers it from my pussy. "How long has it been?" he asks while lowering the zipper of his jeans so he can transfer some of the slickness on his hand to his cock.

The deepness of his voice makes my insides clench, not to mention the imminent removal of his impressive cock from his trunks, but not enough for me not to seek clarification to his question. "Since?" My voice is scarce from the loud screams torn from my throat during my climax.

"Since you've been fucked?" he replies, not the slightest bit ashamed.

I swallow the brick suddenly lodged in my throat. "Umm... I don't... ah..."

"So a while?" he fills in.

While biting on the inside of my cheek, I briefly nod. Deep down inside, I knew something wasn't quite right with Riley, so our Tuesday night schedule came to a grinding halt a good six months before I discovered him in bed with Beth. Although I'm certain Riley blames my 'lack of interest in sex' as the downfall of our relationship, rumors are Beth wasn't the first affair he undertook during our seven-year relationship.

My mind snaps back to the present when Hunter asks, "Doggie? Or do you want to ride on top, cowgirl style?"

My eyes bounce between his, shell-shocked he's seeking permission as to what position we're going to do. Even with our sex life replicating a married couple in their eighties, Riley never once asked for my input.

While ignoring the nerves hampering my boosted self-esteem from two mind-blowing orgasms, I suggest, "Missionary?"

Locks of Hunter's sandy blond hair fall into his face when he shakes his head. "No. It's not a good position for getting reacquainted with sex. Doggie is a good angle to loosen your pelvis a little, or if you're on top, you can control how much you can handle."

You'd expect me to be annoyed at his comment, considering he's pretty much throwing it in my face that he's more sexually experienced than me, but I'm not. He only stopped touching me mere seconds ago, and my body is already missing his touch.

"You pick," I blurt out, too embarrassed to admit I don't know which position would be most enjoyable.

A smile creeps across Hunter's face before he mutters, "Cowgirl, it is." His tone is as thick and rugged as his cock. "Then I get to see your beautiful face while I'm fucking you."

When his jeans clatter to the floor, my eyes widen and drop, eager to see him in his full naked glory. I frantically assess and categorize every delicious inch of his body. Although I've seen him naked on numerous occasions, it's never been this personal. Tonight, I not only get to see his body, but I also get to feel it as well.

Above me.

Beneath me.

Inside me.

A crass grin etches on Hunter's face when he notices my ogling eyes. He stares straight at me, all rugged, primal, and one hundred percent masculine as he releases his cock from his cotton briefs. I squeeze my thighs together, vainly trying to lessen the dampness puddling there when I'm confronted with the full and gloriously satisfying visual of his naked package. His cock is just as impressive, if not more so than I remember—thick, lengthened, uncut, and rugged—just like its owner.

A condom wrapper being torn open diverts my attention from his thickened shaft. After awarding me with a cocky wink, Hunter rolls the condom down his girthy cock before he prowls toward me.

My lungs burn as they strive to secure a full breath when he places his knee between my legs before gliding his body along mine. His hair is wet at the ends, and he smells musky and intoxicating.

Every inch of my skin he touches sets on fire. His touch moistens my skin with more perspiration as it battles to calm the raging heat shooting through it.

I wrap my legs around his waist and guide his head down to mine, more eager to taste his delicious lips again. The smell of my arousal mixed with his unique scent intensifies when his lips inch closer to mine. A throaty moan roars from my throat when he seals his lips over mine and spears his tongue in my mouth. I buck against him, loving the heat of his cock nestled between the wet folds of my pussy.

Every brush the crown of his cock makes to my aching clit has me tugging his hair harder.

He doesn't seem to mind. The more I tug, the more his crotch pins me to the mattress.

After quickening the thrusts of my hips, I run my hands over the ridges of his back. I love feeling his heated skin under mine. His back is as bumpy as his muscular midsection, and it sets my pulse racing.

When Hunter flips us over, swapping our position so I am on top of him, a squeal abruptly leaves my lips. With a grin, he bands his arms around my back, then scoots up the bed until his torso is resting on the headboard, and my thighs are straddling his wide hips.

I angle my chin down low so my thick red hair acts as a shield for my aroused face. Normally, my face was buried in the crook of Riley's neck during sexual encounters, so this feels very open and unguarded.

We are face to face, mere inches from each other.

Hunter grips my chin and jerks it higher. "No hiding, Paige. I want to see your beautiful face while you fuck me."

When he rocks his hips, stroking his cock along the folds of my wetness, my head flings back, and a husky moan spills from my mouth.

"That's it, baby," Hunter coaxes, his throat a sexy purr. "Sex is just like dancing, remember? Now we're dancing. Dance with me, Paige."

I unclench my fists and roll my shoulders back to ease my stiffened posture. "Sex is just like dancing," I mutter to myself before moving my hips in a similar rhythm to Hunter.

One grind of my pussy against his stiffened shaft has my next chase to climax ramping up a gear. He is so thick and heavy beneath me, I'm suddenly a little wary of taking a man so adequately hung.

Before my worries can get the better of me, Hunter takes my pert nipple into his warm and inviting mouth. He nibbles on the stiffened peak, making it even harder before he circles it with his tongue. The talents of his mouth are mind-blowing. He only lathers my breasts with core-shattering devotion for seconds, yet I'm already on the cusp of climax again.

Moaning, I rock my hips faster, needing something to lessen the insane throb between my legs. My breathless whimpers turn into feral groans when the crown of his cock connects with my clit. With his mouth and hands on my breasts and his fat cock stimulating my clit, I'm on the verge of free-falling into ecstasy again at any moment.

After leaning back, I balance my hands on his thighs before increasing my pace even more. I'm not the slightest bit ashamed I'm about to get off like a teen at prom. I rub myself along his hard-as-stone shaft in a rhythm so fast, my topple into climax occurs quicker than I'm expecting.

When an orgasm crashes into me, I moan a long and shuddering groan. None of my usual stiffness is present—not a single ounce as I shudder and shake above Hunter. I scream his name over and over again as white-hot passion overtakes my body.

Once the tremors racing through my body simmer, I flutter open my eyes and stare into Hunter's heavily dilated gaze. Any concerns tempting to surface vanish when he says, "Holy fuck, that was the sexiest thing I've ever seen. Now you need to do it again with my cock inside you."

I lift myself off the bed on a pair of shaky knees, gaining the height needed so the crown of his cock can nestle between my legs. Desire shoots through me when I slowly lower down to take in the first inch of his thick shaft.

"Slower," Hunter demands, his voice strangled with lust.

My breath hitches as I continue lowering myself down. Even with experiencing countless orgasms and being drenching wet front to back, his girthy cock still causes pain to rocket through my core as much as ecstasy.

"You need to relax, Paige. Breathe and relax."

While licking my parched lips, I nod before inhaling a deep breath of air.

Just granting my body permission to breathe loosens the walls of my clamped vagina, and I glide down another two inches.

"That's it, baby, nice and slow."

When my pussy hits the base of Hunter's cock, I gasp in a deep breath. I didn't think I had it in me.

A smile stretches across my face, pleased as punch that I've taken him all the way to the root. Although painful, it's also incredibly arousing.

I've never felt so full.

When my eyes lock with Hunter, I see that he is also smiling. I understand why when he twitches his cock to ensure I know exactly how deeply seated he is.

He throws his head back and groans when I swivel my hips to return his tease.

"Fuck, Paige. Unless you want me to come this instant, you better not do that again."

As my smile enlarges, I swivel my hips again, wordlessly denying his request. When his eyes snap open and bore into mine, my pulse hastens. His gaze is greedy and wanting and solely devoted to me.

With a wicked smirk on his ruggedly handsome face, he props his hands at the side of his splayed hips before he swings his legs over the side of the bed.

I cry out when he thrusts into me again. He's even deeper this time around.

My pussy ripples around him, squeezing him tight when he drags his hips back before launching them forward again. "You're so fucking tight," he mutters, his voice rough and one hundred percent sexy.

My head lolls to the side, and my lips part when he increases the tempo of his pumps. Even though I'm riding on top and am technically supposed to have control, my playful tease has switched things up. The reins have been handed to Hunter.

After a handful more mind-hazing pumps, one of Hunter's hands guides my shoulders back, opening me to him even more while the other lowers to the region where our bodies are connected in the most intimate way. Any pain I'm experiencing is voided when he rolls his thumb over my throbbing clit. He stimulates it at the same teasing pace his cock consumes my pussy.

As my body temperature rises, a musky smell invades my senses. My skin is covered with a fine misting of sweat, and my heart is beating wildly. It almost matches the insane throb of my pussy.

My eyes snap shut when Hunter's tongue delves out to lick a bead of sweat rolling between my breasts. I thrust my chest out, loving the sensation of his beard scratching the stiff peaks of my nipples.

"Oh god," I pant when he scrapes his beard across my chest, firmly tightening my coil. "Again. Please. Do it again." When he does as requested, blistering lights shatter in front of my eyes. "Oh. Oh. Oh."

"Ah. Fuck. Christ," he mutters when his cock gets strangled by my pussy from another climax shimmering through my body.

His fingers dig into my nape as his pumps grow wilder. He pushes me over the edge, his wordless demand for me to scream his name as brutal as my hazy head. I become lost in an orgasm as his lunging thrusts have the crown of his fat cock hitting the tender spot inside me. My core spasms, launching a pleasurable pulse to every region of my body, spurring all the fine hairs on my skin to bristle.

While fucking me senseless, Hunter holds my gaze. He watches me unravel, absorbing and categorizing every shudder he instigated.

His ardent stare lengthens my orgasm before catapulting it to a never-before-reached level. It is a beautifully long climax that zaps every bit of my energy.

Just when I think the shudders will never end, my body goes lax, and I slowly come down from the blessedness. I lean into Hunter, unable to hold up my head, let alone continue fucking at the ruthless pace he's undertaking.

I take a few minutes to breathe before the wondrous circumstances of our exchange pulls me out of the trenches. After regaining control of my wild heart, I push off Hunter's torso then meet his pumps thrust for thrust. I bounce on and off his cock at the same speed he pounds into me. I feel him get thicker as his chase to release deepens.

I sling my arms around his damp shoulders then lock my eyes with his, desperate to see him lose control as I had. To watch him come undone.

His gorgeous face constricts as his hips jerk faster. He slams into me with brutal force, causing another tidal wave of excitement to scorch through my exhausted body.

While moaning a feral groan, he does one final thrust, impaling me to the very base of his fat cock before the tremors of my body extend to his. "Fuck, Paige," he roars. "Fuck, fuck, fuck!"

My pussy ripples around him, squeezing and massaging every drop of cum firing from his throbbing cock. Once every bead has been expelled, he draws me in closer then nuzzles his damp head into the nook of my neck. I smile when his breath hits my neckline in hard, ragged pants. It is similar to his twitching cock as it endeavors to deflate.

He's still hard enough to drill a mine, and although round two shouldn't be on my mind right now, it appears as if my once misplaced libido has other ideas.

"Jesus Christ, Paige," Hunter mutters against my neck when I slowly commence rocking against him. "You're going to fucking destroy me."

CHAPTER NINETEEN

My taps on the keyboard stop when I sense another presence in my writing cave. When I lift my eyes from the stream of words in front of me, I discover an even more awe-inspiring visual than an almost completed novel.

Hunter's shoulder is propped on the doorjamb. He's wearing nothing but a pair of unbuttoned jeans and a cocky grin. The low hang of his jeans means his scrumptious Apollo belt is on full display, his drool-worthy tattooed pecs, and the breathtaking bumps of his impressive six-pack.

After giving my eyes plenty of time to absorb the panty-wetting visual, I lock my eyes with his face. Guilt smashes into me when I notice how tired he looks. His eyes are plagued with dark rings, and his beard is more unkempt than normal.

I grimace when I realize it's a little after four in the morning. "Did my typing wake you?"

With a shake of his head, he pushes off the doorframe and enters my writing space. "No. Just a cold bed."

"I figured you'd be used to that with how quickly you kicked your conquests out." I snap my vindictive mouth shut before lifting my apologetic eyes to his. "I'm sorry," I mumble, my voice sincere. "I get a little bitchy when I'm hungry."

His plump lips not hidden by his scraggly beard tug into a smirk, silently accepting my apology. He plucks me out of my hideous writing chair, takes a seat, then pulls me down to sit on his lap. Any concerns about him being upset by my snarky comment vanish when the bristles of his beard scratch my neck. He nuzzles into my side then presses a succession of feather-like kisses to my jaw.

The softness of his prickles reminds me of a tabby cat curling up against its owner. The only difference is I'm the one purring instead of Hunter.

The past two weeks have been crazy. Yeah, I know what you're thinking—*Paige, my dear, you were already crazy*—but it's been a different type of crazy. After the gala, Hunter's work schedule turned hectic, meaning I only see him when he crawls into my bed in the wee hours of the morning, and more often than not, he leaves before I'm awake.

Our regular dinner dates have become nonexistent, meaning I've resorted back to peanut butter and jelly sandwiches to get me by. But even with our conflicting schedules, I wouldn't change a thing.

The past two weeks haven't just been crazy. They've been staggering as well. Our budding relationship is unlike anything I've ever experienced. It's filled with moments of discovery and Hallmark-movie cheesiness. I don't know if Hunter classes us as a friends-with-benefits arrangement or something more, but whatever it is, it is wonderful.

"What are you working on?" Hunter's voice isn't as smooth as normal due to the early hour.

When I close my notes on my Scrivener writing app to bring up the draft of my current manuscript, Hunter wheels in close to my desk. He props his elbows onto the edge of my writing chair then speed-reads my rough first draft.

I don't breathe or make a sound while scrutinizing every expression crossing his face. He's reading a newly created bedroom scene I just penned, and I'm nervous as hell he is going to tear it apart like he did the last naughty scene I wrote.

I can tell the exact moment he reaches the raunchy part of the story just from how his lips twitch, but he remains quiet, reading the three-thousand-plus word scene in absolute silence.

Even with his response hard for me to gauge, this is ten times better than sending my draft to a group of beta readers. This way I get to see how a reader may react while reading my work. It's an exceptional experience, one I'm sure authors would pay bucketloads of cash to experience.

Once he finishes reading the scene, Hunter slumps back into my chair, taking me with him. I wait impatiently for him to give his feedback. Although his expression doesn't allude to the humor he experienced the last time he read my raunchy scene, I'm still braced for impact. It isn't that I haven't put my heart and soul into this piece as he suggested—I have—but my writing skills are lacking in the steamy romance department, so I'm expecting some type of negative rebuttal.

Which I don't get.

"It's really good, Paige." Hunter locks his glistening-with-pride eyes with my shocked ones. "Really, *really* good."

I search his eyes for any untruths. When I fail to discover any, I suck in a large breath that puffs my chest out. "You're not just telling me that because you want to get into my panties, right?"

He throws his head back and laughs. "No, Paige. But if I'd known I only had to compliment your writing to get into your panties, I would have done it months ago."

I rib him in the elbow, pretending not to love his playfulness. Once his chuckles die down, he pulls me deeper into his chest. His raging heart confirms my story has the impact I'm looking for. "They have it all... spark, intrigue, fire-heating passion. It's a good scene. You should be proud," he says a short time later while running his hand down my back.

I pop my head off his chest. "I can't take all the credit." I waggle my brows while peering into his lust-filled eyes. "I kind of stole a lot of the scenes from what we've created the past two weeks."

My heart beats double-time when an impish gleam brightens his murky eyes. "Do you want to add another scene to your book?"

He bucks his hips so I can't mistake that he's primed and ready to go. While biting my bottom lip, I nod. A girlie squeal topples from my mouth when he abruptly stands, taking me with him. My ear-piercing shriek turns into laughter when he snags the open jar of Nutella off my writing desk. I don't eat it while writing. That would just create a mess. It's merely there so I can sniff it. It's a weird approach, but it keeps my hunger at bay long enough I can get down a chapter or two between breaks.

Tiny, breathless pants ripple through my lips when Hunter gallops down the stairs with me still in his arms. The frigidness of the tiled counter cools my backside when he places me down before moving to the refrigerator. Just like the past six weeks, he moves around my kitchen with ease.

The puffiness of my chest, compliments to his accolade about my writing, increases when I watch him prepare eggs Benedict. It only took me ordering it at the hotel the morning after our first *interaction* for him to know it's my favorite breakfast food.

Hunter stops stirring the hollandaise sauce when I dig my finger into the jar of Nutella and scoop out a large chunk. My Nutella-loaded finger freezes halfway between the jar and my lips when I catch his cajoling gaze. He isn't a man of many words, but his eyes alone are sweet-talking enough. He doesn't even need to speak, and I'm willing to do anything he requests.

After removing the saucepan from the heat, he places it onto the wooden cutting board then prowls my way. My pulse quickens to match the throb awakening in my clit. "I was planning on serving you breakfast before eating mine." His voice is smoother than the hazelnut spread dripping off my finger and onto my thigh. "But you've convinced me to revise my tactics."

When my eyes snap to the counter next to the open-flamed cooktop, my heartbeat intensifies. Only one plate is sitting next to the discarded saucepan. When I return my eyes to Hunter, the meaning behind his comment crashes into me.

Food isn't on his breakfast menu.

I am.

After stopping to stand in front of me, he pushes my legs apart so he can slot between them. My knees hit the hard curves of his waist when he pops my Nutella-covered finger into his mouth and sucks down hard. As he licks off the nutty goodness on my finger, he makes quick work of the satin tie cinching my knee-length dressing gown to my waist. Air hisses from his lips when he discovers I'm completely bare under the smooth material.

"You can never be too prepared for late-night visitors," I murmur, wanting to ensure he's aware I'm only dressed like this for him.

Although his late-night visits are every night, he rarely wakes me, believing I'd be too tired for extracurricular activities. What he doesn't realize is that I'd refrain from sleeping for a year just for the energy his contact invigorates me with. Even the simplest of gestures, like how he runs his index finger down my scrunched nose, sparks my body with renewed hope. He gets me like no one else ever has. He understands me, and the depth of his knowledge is both shocking and exciting, especially when another reality smashes into me.

I'm falling in love with him.

I tried not to fall for him, but with every day that went by, I fell harder and harder. I often joke with Hunter that I don't like him. But I do. I like him a lot—a *real* lot.

I also love him.

Mistaking my stiffened stance as nervousness, Hunter mutters against my heated skin. "Dance with me, Paige."

Although I am nervous, this time, it isn't from sexual contact. It's being scared to death that I'm placing my heart on the line again only to risk it being shattered.

After recalling the words he spoke to me only two short weeks ago, I whisper, "Don't destroy me, Hunter."

"Never."

His warm breath fans my earlobe before he tugs it with his teeth. I melt into his embrace, purring even louder than I did when he drew me into his chest in my writing cave. The way my body reacts to him is genuinely terrifying. My nipples bud painfully, my pussy aches for him, and my entire body pulls taut, dying to be consumed by him. I always knew he'd rocket my core to the next galaxy. I just had no clue it would be this profound. He hasn't just rocketed my core, he's demolished and destroyed it for any man who may come after him.

As his fingers travel up the grooves of my ribcage, Hunter's lips suck, nibble, and bite on my neck. A moan spills from my lips when his exploring hands stop at the swell of my breasts. While sucking on my neck firm enough to mark, he fondles and tweaks my nipples until their hardened peaks.

I thrust out my chest, loving how his big manly hands swamp my less-than-stellar anatomy. Even though his previous companions were big-breasted ladies, he's never once shown a lack of appreciation for my smaller assets.

For that alone, I *like* him even more.

With devotion focused on marking my neck with his touch, he curls his arms around my waist and lifts me from the counter. A broad grin stretches across my face when he murmurs, "Grab the Nutella," into my ear a second before he whisks me out of the kitchen.

As his big hands knead and caress my ass, he moves through the cabin. His steps are as slow and lazy as the teasing kiss he gives after sealing his lips over mine. My stomach grumbles when his citrus-flavored mouth combined with the Nutella he sucked off my finger hits my taste buds.

It's the perfect combination, ensuring I'll never eat Terry's Milk Chocolate Orange Balls again without getting horny.

A grin tugs at my lips when Hunter deposits me onto the bed right in front of the mirror. He even angles my backside so not even the wide span of his shoulders can hide the glistening wetness between my legs.

After giving both our eyes enough time to enjoy the scandalous image in front of us, Hunter mutters, "I still shouldn't be allowed to touch you, but fucked if I can stay away. You've put me under a spell, Paige. Every minute of every day is spent thinking about what I've done to you, what I want to do to you, and for exactly how fucking long I'm planning to do it."

"Yet, you're still making me wait."

The flare darting through his eyes heats me up everywhere. "I'm just making sure you know what you're getting."

"I know what I'm getting..." I drop my eyes to his impressive crotch. "And then some."

His growl activates every one of my hot buttons. With his eyes fixed on mine and the rock behind his zipper growing larger for every second we stare at each other, Hunter lowers the fastener in his jeans, then frees his dick from its tight constraints. "Are you sure you're ready for this, Paige? Ready to *taste* it, feel it—"

"And be thoroughly *fucked* by it." My crudeness should shock me. I should be scampering across the mattress and hiding under the bedding, but for some reason, I'm not. Hunter's attention has done wonders for my self-esteem over the past two weeks. I feel confident and beautiful and one hundred percent sexy. "So, once again, what are you waiting for?"

When Hunter wedges his knees between my legs, air whistles between my teeth, stopping their press mid-squeeze. "I was just waiting for your fantastic tits to be fully exposed. I think it's about time I see them covered in my cum."

I don't care that his knee is wedged between my legs. They're squeezing together no matter the firmness of the obstacle between them. His voice was too knee-quaking for a nonchalant response, and it was even hotter than usual since it occurred at the same time a droplet of pre-cum beaded on the end of his fat cock. "What do you say, Paige, a tit fuck for breakfast?"

I almost reply, *I doubt there's enough there to satisfy your hunger*, but I hold back. The image of Hunter stroking his cock is already mesmerizing, but it is even more perverse when I notice the direction of his hooded gaze. He's staring at my chest, and nothing but admiration is beaming from his lusty eyes. "A tit fuck then reverse cowgirl on the edge of the bed. That way, we both get to enjoy watching each other's face in ecstasy without bringing boring missionary into the equation."

Hunter's voice is rough when he mutters, "Missionary isn't boring when you're doing it with the right person." His change in tone isn't because he's worried he is once again reminding me about his previous promiscuity. It is from me scooting closer so the droplet of pre-cum that's about to drip from his cock can fall onto my breasts.

Desire surges through me when Hunter gathers the drop of pre-cum with his thumb before he transfers it to my nipple. The sticky goodness aids in his endeavor to have my nipples standing at attention and ready to be devoured.

Once the second nipple is coated with the same gooey substance, he nudges my shoulder. His shove doesn't have my back bracing the bedding, but I'm far enough away from him, my shoulder blades touch and my breasts push forward.

"Such perfect tits, Paige. They're going to look so good with my cum smeared over them."

There's enough pre-cum leaking from his cock to lube up the small gulley between my breasts, but Hunter acts as if there isn't. With a smirk as panty-wetting as it is playful, he dips two fingers in the jar of Nutella, scoops out a generous serve, then raises it to my chin.

It feels like lava scorches my veins when he drags his Nutella-covered hand down the pulse in my throat and between my thrusting chest before he pops his fingers into his mouth to lick up the leftovers.

"Hmm…" he groans in a throaty moan. "Paige and Nutella, my new favorite combination."

Either forgetting his pledge of a tit-fuck or blindsided by the same rampant horniness making a mess between my legs, he drags his tongue up the path his fingers just took, only stopping when he reaches my mouth. "Want a taste?"

I barely breathe out, "Yes," when he spears his tongue between my lips and drags it against the roof of my mouth.

Good lord, he tastes good. Sweet and chocolatey—just like his scrumptious voice.

By the time he pulls back from his arousing kiss, his beard is as dark as the mess between my breasts and as matted as he makes my heart feel.

There's no denying my earlier assumption. I am in love with a man I barely know even with me knowing almost all his infamous quirks.

It's incredible what you can unearth when you stalk someone for weeks.

"That's it, baby, dance with me," Hunter groans as his lips drop from my mouth to my neck before they eventually lower to my chest.

He sucks my nipple into his mouth, not the slightest bit confronted that he smeared his pre-cum on it only seconds ago while he rocks his cock in and out of his clenched hand. The visual of him jacking off is so enticing, tingles race to the lower half of my stomach as my hips begin to naturally rock. We move as one for several long minutes, my pace only slowing when Hunter's rocks between my breasts bring the crest of his cock to within an inch of my mouth.

He grunts an undecipherable word when my tongue delves out to lick up the sticky goodness pooling at the end, then he doubles the shimmers sparking every inch of my body by instructing me to roll my shoulders forward.

"Yes... just like that," he murmurs when the slightest movement causes my breasts to cup his thrusting shaft. "Now squeeze them together for me. Milk my cock with your tits like your pussy does every time I fuck you."

I almost fall back onto the bedding when I do as instructed, but before my shoulder blades get close to the duvet, Hunter bands his arm around my back and holds me in place.

"I got you," he mutters between the long plunges of his cock, both the roughness of his voice and his pace picking up. "I got you real fucking good."

When I drop my eyes to the scene causing his murky blue eyes to become the color of the ocean in the dead of night, rampant horniness clusters low in my stomach. My breasts are less than impressive, they barely fill a B cup, but the image of Hunter's cock sliding in and out of them is panty-wetting delicious. Not even the odd coloring of our lubricant of choice detracts from the awe-inspiring visual. It has me on the cusp of ecstasy in an embarrassing amount of time and desperate to witness the contrast of Hunter's milky white cum against the darkness of the Nutella.

"Fuck, Paige," Hunter grunts between grinds when each rock of his hips has my tongue connecting with his enlarged knob. "If you keep doing that, I'm going to come in your mouth instead of over your tits." His threat excites me more than it scares me, and he knows it. "If that's what you want, I'll have to even the score. I'm all about fairness."

With my breasts no longer on his radar, he scoots forward until more than the tip of his cock encroaches my lips. Several inches break past the barrier I'd never keep fully shut from him.

My moan vibrates down his silky shaft when the combined taste of Hunter and Nutella activates my taste buds. It is a manly, virile palette that has me forgetting I have a gag reflex.

"Sorry."

He isn't sorry. He's as desperate for me to swallow him down as I am for him to make true on his promise to return the favor. The rock of his hips as he stuffs inches of his cock down my throat assures me of this, not to mention his firm hold of my hair. Even if I wanted to pull back, his hold would never allow it.

Hunter gives fantastic head, and a part of his skills is directly attributed to his hairy chin. Even if I hadn't added back the detail of Archer's furry face, I would have eventually written about a character with a full beard because there's nothing more appealing than a rough and rugged man with his head between a woman's legs other than evidence of their exchange still lingering on his face hours later.

Hunter's beard often smells like me, and I like that almost as much as I love the salty liquid pumping onto my tongue.

"This is your final warning, Paige," Hunter warns between big breaths. "If you don't want to eat me for breakfast, I suggest you lay back and thrust those fantastic tits into the air." When I grip his Adonis ass and yank him forward until my eyes are on the verge of popping out of my head, he curses into the cool morning air before he surrenders to the sensation keeping his balls close to his tattooed thighs.

It takes his torso rising and falling several times in a row before his chin eventually balances on his chest, and he smiles a deliciously wicked smirk. "Now it's my turn for breakfast," he mutters before he hooks my ankle out from beneath me and yanks me down the bed.

When my hands shoot to his hair, the sensation of his mouth on the cleft of my pussy almost too much to bear, he snatches up my wrists and pins them to my sides. As he holds me hostage to the bed with both his strength and the desire making my limbs double their weight, he stabs his tongue between the folds of my pussy before he drags it up to my clit.

"Do you feel it, Paige?" he murmurs against my aching-with-need skin before he hits my clit with back-to-back flicks of his tongue. "The desire. The connection. The uncontrollable urge to fuck like nothing else in the world matters."

"Yes," I reply with a faint bob of my head. "I feel it."

I feel it so much, I rock against his mouth without a care in the world and dance on his face void of a single qualm. Then, not even a minute later, I shimmer through an orgasm so strong, the scream that rips from my throat could be heard in Ravenshoe.

"One more," Hunter growls against my dripping center a mere second after I've descended from blessedness.

I shake my head, certain I don't have another orgasm in me today. That one was the strength of three, so I could possibly be out of cum for another hour or two.

"One more," Hunter growls against my throbbing pussy again before he locks his eyes with mine over the goopy mess between my breasts. "Then I'll show you that the magic has nothing to do with your chosen position and everything to do with how a woman's body was created to be worshiped. Doggy, cowgirl, or missionary. It doesn't matter when the fireworks start long before a couple enters the bedroom." He licks my cleft, pokes his tongue inside me, then gently grazes my clit with his teeth before muttering, "I should know. I felt them the moment I saw you. The nerves. The butter-flies. The desire to make you mine. I felt them all with one fleeting glance."

His confession sets me off. With an arched back and a moan unlike any I've heard leave my mouth, I come with a hoarse cry. Hunter groans when my wetness soaks his lips. After holding down my bucking hips to make sure he doesn't miss a drop, he drags his beard along the cleft of my pussy, coating it with my scent.

His bristles push my orgasm into a record-breaking shimmer. I shake for several long seconds, equally exhausted and ecstatic that nothing inside me is broken. It was merely the wrong man holding the key to my greatest desires.

Pepper was right.

Hunter isn't the odd man out.

I just didn't know what I was looking for until his naked backside was thrust into my peripheral vision. But now that I do, I won't let it go for anything.

Not even a *New York Times* No. 1 best seller.

CHAPTER TWENTY

I'm lying in the crook of Hunter's arm, sexually satiated and gorged. After we feasted on each other's bodies for breakfast, he made an extra-large helping of eggs Benedict for us to share in my bed. Even feeling like a sticky mess from the smears of Nutella still covering my body, I am content and happy.

Who wouldn't be after numerous mind-altering orgasms?

After lifting my head off Hunter's chest, I peer into his eyes. He's drinking in the popcorn ceiling of the cabin, seemingly deep in thought. Even with his warm hand running down my back, a chill runs through my body, bristling every fine hair. Upon feeling the quiver racking my body, his eyes drop to mine. They're more clouded than usual, and his demeanor is swaying toward Grumpy Hunter instead of the Dominating Hunter I was handling only an hour ago.

"Rough week?"

I keep my question wide open so he can answer any way he chooses, which he does two seconds later. "More like one shit storm after another."

I prop my elbow next to his naked torso and balance my cheek on my palm. With a playful smirk, I say, "I've heard the telemarketing industry is pretty cutthroat."

My tease has the effect I'm aiming for when a hearty chuckle rumbles out of his stern lips. His laughter is so boisterous, it vibrates through my body, warming both my heart and my pussy.

When his laughter eventually dies down, he says, "That it is... that it is."

"Then why do it?" My tone has not an ounce of probing associated with it. I want to ensure he knows I'm not interrogating him into revealing guarded secrets. I am genuinely interested to learn why he stays in an industry that exhausts him so much. "With your skills in app development and all your other computer knowledge, your career possibilities are endless."

Just from his assets alone, I'm reasonably sure he doesn't work for Isaac for a monetary value, so it must be something greater keeping him there.

"I've considered leaving," Hunter replies, his tone still somewhat apprehensive. "Mainly after I screwed up last month."

I nod but remain quiet.

"But after talking to my mom, I realized I don't work for Isaac for the money. I work for him because I like him."

I run my thumb over the groove in the middle of his forehead. "Enough that it's worth all this heartache?"

His eyes drift between mine before he curtly nods. I smile, appreciating his honesty and understanding what he's saying. My job is not nearly as important as his, but I sacrifice a lot to do it. I often canceled engagements when my characters were talking or wake up in the middle of the night to jot down notes, so I can relate.

Hunter scoots down the bed so we come face to face. Air whizzes through his lips when his shuffle causes the sheet to fall to my waist, and he spots the smallest portion of my side boob.

"My eyes are up here, *buddy*," I jest while pulling the sheet up to cover my chest.

Although I'd love nothing more than to spend a few more hours with Hunter between the sheets, I don't want anything to interrupt the conversation we're undertaking. Even knowing him for months, there's still so much about him I haven't unearthed. I don't know what month he was born, let alone why he hates tea and coffee.

I run my finger past his slanted brow, over the scruffiness of his dark beard before stopping at the tattoo on the side of his neck. "What does this say?" I trace the word *traicion* integrated into his tattoo. "It's not English, is it?"

Hunter's throat works hard to swallow as he shakes his head. "It's Spanish." His tone is back to a sternness I haven't experienced in weeks. "It translates to 'betrayal.'"

My nose scrunches up, and dread swishes in my stomach. "Why would you have that tattooed on you?" I blurt out before I can stop myself.

When the heat in the room turns stifling, I lift my eyes to Hunter's face. He's glaring at me like he's silently daring me to continue with my interrogation. His gaze is so furious, my pulse quickens and my pussy throbs.

After wearily smiling, I scoot down the bed and burrow my head into his chest, not game enough this early in our... *friendship*... to confront Grumpy Hunter. I'm not a confrontational person as it is, but sparring against a man like Hunter when he's tired and withdrawn seems like a stupid move to make.

"I'm not saying I don't like your tattoo. I'm simply trying to understand why you'd mark your skin with such a hurtful word," I mumble into his chest a short time later. "Betrayal is a terrible thing. No one should ever have to experience it." *I most certainly wish I never did.*

Hunter exhales a deep breath of air that rustles my already tousled hair. After a few moments of silence, he slips out of bed. My heart thrashes against my chest when he throws his legs into the jeans he discarded on the floor earlier. Tears prick my eyes as my panic skyrockets, but in my distressed state, I've lost the ability to articulate speech.

If I'd known he'd have such an adverse reaction to my wish to know him a little better, I wouldn't have done it. I don't want to know all his secrets—I just want to know him better than anyone else.

"Hunter, I'm sorr—"

"Shut up, Paige."

My mouth gapes, not solely shell-shocked by bluntness but also surprised when he lifts me out of bed and dresses me in the satin dressing gown I was wearing earlier. His movements are fast and efficient, the tie knotted around my waist within a matter of seconds.

I will not cry. I will not cry, I silently chant to myself.

"This is my house, so you can't kick me out," I mutter as my voice quickly converts from devastated to anger.

My chin quivers when Hunter cups my jaw and lifts my downcast head. "Don't." His tone is a cross between stern and apologetic, and it sends my head into a tailspin.

After enclosing his hand around mine, he exits the cabin's main bedroom. Since he's clutching my hand to near death, I follow him.

My panic simmers when we walk toward the stairs that lead to my writing cave instead of the back patio door. My heart pounds my ribcage with every step we climb as does my curiosity.

When we enter the space that now seems two sizes too small from the awkwardness plaguing the air, Hunter sits on my writing chair then pulls me onto his lap. After wrapping his hands around mine like he did weeks ago at the hotel, he fires up the Internet Explorer program on my laptop. His pulse is surging through his body so rapidly, it pulverizes my hands.

The heavy pants of his breath blast my neck when he types a long string of code into the search bar using my index fingers. I know from experience he can type faster than this, but by going slow, I can memorize every keystroke he makes.

Once the search engine bar is filled with code, he releases my hands, grips my waist, then swivels me to face him. "I don't like talking about my past." He coughs to clear his throat. "I don't like talking about my life in general."

"Okay," I faintly murmur.

"But that doesn't mean I don't want you to know me, Paige. I want you to know me."

A small grin curls on my lips, glad he realized I wasn't trying to interrogate him. I merely want to know him.

Hunter's eyes flick to the monitor of my laptop before he returns them to me. "If you hit enter, every detail of my life will be displayed on your laptop's screen." His grip on my hips tightens, sending a ping of pain through my body. "*Every* detail, Paige. The good and the bad."

He tries to hide away the flare of emotion tainting his face, but he isn't quick enough for me to miss it. Just from the concern clouding his eyes, I know he's worried I'll discover something about him I don't like.

I hold his gaze for several minutes, waiting for his panic to pass before asking, "Is this similar to the search you typically conducted on your... *dates?*" When he curtly nods, I ask, "Will you run this search on me the instant I hit the enter button?"

His head bob switches to a shake. "No. Because unlike me, you don't have any issues communicating."

Even in the tenseness of our conversation, a small giggle rumbles up my chest.

The strain hampering Hunter's face eases when I hold down the delete button on my laptop until every digit and letter of the code is removed. After shifting my eyes from the now blank screen to him, I say, "I don't want to find out about you from anyone but you."

"That could end up being a very long time, Paige." His tone exposes the truth of his statement, much less his candid eyes.

I shrug. "Then I guess that just means you'll have to keep me around a little longer than originally intended."

A trace of a smile peeks out from behind his beard when he mutters, "And Paige finally clicks on."

CHAPTER TWENTY-ONE

$\mathcal{A}$ chilly winter wind sifts through my hair as Hunter and I walk down a bustling sidewalk in Hopeton. For Christmas Eve, the streets aren't as jam-packed as they usually are, but there are still a notable number of people mingling in the space.

I lean in close to Hunter's side, craving his body heat while also happy to have him standing beside me. I thought the first two weeks of our relationship was a crazy rollercoaster ride, but they had nothing on the past week. Hunter's work meant I didn't see hide nor hair of him the five days following our exchange in my writing cave, but he didn't need to explain the extenuating circumstances of his absence.

The media handled every aspect of it.

Isaac's partner, Isabelle, the asset Hunter was assigned to protect, was kidnapped. If that wasn't already daunting, it was by a well-known and much-feared mob boss.

I remained glued to the broadcast the entire day of Izzy's kidnapping. I searched every station for a play-by-play rundown of the events that transpired that afternoon. For the most part, I was seeking any signs if Hunter was a part of the operation that killed

Col Petretti and the arrest of two of his assailants, but a part of me was watching purely for storylines.

Even tragedy can appear beautiful to the right eyes.

The news of Isabelle's kidnapping wasn't solely contained to the local news channels, though. It spread across the country, even reaching Pepper.

"I told you he was mafia!" she screamed down the phone when Isaac's face was blasted across multiple channels while carrying an unconscious Izzy out of an abandoned warehouse in Harbortown.

My heart was maimed when I saw Isaac's devastated face as he placed Izzy onto a medical responder's stretcher. I've only ever seen that look once before. It was when my father said his final goodbye to my mother before she slipped into her unconsciousness a little over three years ago after a brief two-year battle with ALS.

My mother was a beautiful woman. A true gift from God. I miss her every single day, but for the past three months, I've been following the pledge I made to her in her final days—I'm living my life how I want to live it instead of what is expected of me.

My brisk strides down the cracked concrete path slow when we pass a small bookshop. It won't matter how many copies of *The Weekend Romance* I purchase, I won't stop looking until I find the exact one I'm searching for.

Upon sensing my slowed pace, Hunter stops then peers down at me. His eyes drift between the bookstore and me for barely a second before he jerks his head to the glass entry door, wordlessly encouraging me to enter.

"Are you sure we have enough time?" I don't want to be late to the Christmas party we've been planning to attend for the past six weeks.

Hunter places his hand on the curve of my back and guides me to the single door of the bookshop. "We have plenty of time."

When he opens the door for me to enter, the smell of vanilla and almonds smacks into me. My eyes shoot in all directions, absorbing the lines of bookshelves that fill the small space before they lock with a lady with black ringlet hair greeting us with a broad smile. "We're twenty minutes from closing. Are you looking for anything in particular?" she questions, stepping closer to us.

Hunter shakes his head at the exact moment I say, "*The Weekend Romance* by Rachel Maloney."

As his eyes snap to me, confusion mars his ruggedly handsome face. Oblivious to his odd expression, the owner directs me to a large section of romance books near the front window of the book-store. Tears well in my eyes when I see over two dozen books with the familiar coastal cover in a prime position in the romance section. Even decades after it was released, it continues to be a favorite amongst readers.

My hand shakes when I remove the first book off the shelf and crack open the pristine condition hardcover. When I fail to locate an inscription inside, I pop it back on the shelf before pulling down the one next to it.

After my third removal and replacement, Hunter mutters, "You're looking for a particular signed copy?"

I bite the inside of my cheek in warning for my tears to stay at bay before nodding. "My mom wrote a message inside a first edition copy. I didn't realize its importance until it was too late. During a move from college to my family home, it became lost in transit."

Hunter moves to the other end of the bookshelf housing first edition copies of *The Weekend Romance* before pulling down a copy. "What does the inscription say?"

Heat creeps across my cheeks, closely followed by a large grin. "Be yourself. No matter what. Some will adore you, and some will hate everything about you, but who cares? It's your life. Make the most of it. I love you, Pookie Bear."

Hunter places the book back onto the shelf then moves to stand next to me. His eyes shift between my tear-welling ones as he promises, "You'll find it one day, Paige." He drags his eyes over the impressive collection before adding, "It may even be here."

Twenty minutes later, we've checked every copy of *The Weekend Romance* on the shelves. Unfortunately, none had the inscription I was searching for. Feeling slightly deflated, I nuzzle into Hunter's side before continuing our original journey.

Music blasts into my eardrums when we enter the head office of Destiny Records in Hopeton half an hour later than planned due to an impromptu stop at the bookstore. Compared to the gala we attended weeks ago, this event has a relaxed, cheerful vibe. The women are still dressed elegantly, but their hemlines are a little riskier, and instead of wearing tuxedos, the men are wearing suits—some with jackets, some without.

After slinging off my coat, I offer it to the attendant standing by the door as my eyes scan the room. Hunter's brows furrow when he witnesses an exchange between the tall brute of a man I saw at his home weeks ago and a gorgeous African American man near the bar.

"I'll be back in a minute."

He presses a quick kiss on the edge of my cheek before he strides closer to the two men. He doesn't interrupt them. He just stands to the side, scrutinizing their confrontation.

After a minor bout, the African American man puts on his suit jacket and strides to the door, tipping his chin in greeting to me on the way by.

"Everything okay?" I query when Hunter returns by my side.

His brows slant. "Maybe ask me in a year or two... because with all the shit that's been happening the past two months, I honestly don't know how to answer."

I fight to hide my delight that he believes I'll be around in a year or two to ask.

My brow bows when Hunter runs his shaky hand along his beard. This is the first time I've seen him genuinely nervous.

A grin curls on my lips when the reason for his nervousness is revealed. "Do you want to dance?"

There's no chance of hiding the grin attempting to stretch across my face, so I set it free before nodding.

My smile sags when Hunter directs us away from the dance floor. I shoot my eyes between his amused gaze and an office door marked *Boardroom* when he swings open the door before gesturing for me to enter before him.

"There's no chance in hell I'm going to make a fool out of myself, so we either dance in here, or we don't dance."

I drag him into the boardroom before he can change his mind. "Here is great."

As I wrap my arms around his broad shoulders, I inhale a large breath of air through my nose, drinking in his delicious scent.

"Million by Paco Rabanne."

Hunter smirks before shaking his head.

Darn it! One day I'll guess his scent.

"Ready?" Hunter asks while curling his arms around my waist.

I smile and nod, hopeful some playfulness will ease the tension fettering his face.

We're dancing, not swimming with sharks.

I smile to hide the cringe attempting to cross my face when Hunter stomps on my foot for the third time in the past ten minutes. I'll be honest. I now understand his hesitation to dance. He has two left feet and absolutely no dancing abilities whatsoever. He's stiff, robotic, and the look on his face is anything but pleasant. But since I appreciate that he went to the effort of attempting to dance with me, I'm going to keep my big mouth shut.

Well, I would have if the tempo of the song didn't change.

When the techno crap booming out of the speakers in the

ceiling changes to a faster beat, I unwrap my arms from Hunter's girthy shoulders then take a giant step backward.

"Moving out of the danger zone?" he questions.

Since half his words were chopped up by laughter, I gabble out, "Something like that."

After recalling Hunter gently guiding me through my awkwardness weeks ago, I interlock our hands and sway them into a wavy pattern.

"If you start doing the sprinkler, I'm fucking out," he warns, chuckling.

I hit him with a frisky wink before spinning around and plastering my backside to his crotch. I sway my hips in beat to the music but in a slower, more sensual pace to ensure Hunter can keep up.

"Dancing is just like sex, remember. I've experienced your moves. I know you have no problems swinging your hips."

Hunter's citrus-scented breath hits my neckline when he laughs, but as the song progresses, the stiffness of his hips relaxes. He bends his knees, aligning our bodies better before adding a grind to my sensual sways. Although his feet remain planted on the floor like concrete, his hips, torso, and hands loosen up.

One hand lingers on my hip, keeping me firmly attached to him while the other conducts an in-depth frisk of my body. Even with our bodies flushed with heat, my nipples tighten like a chilly wind is blowing into the enclosed room when he briefly brushes past them.

As the music overtakes me, I lean deeper into Hunter. I mold my body as close to his as possible, loving his sweat-slicked skin wrapped around mine. We dance so near, not even air exists between us. The sweat dampening me from head to toe causes my dress to cling to my skin, but nothing can dull the excitement thickening my blood.

My dance moves become more sensual, almost sultry when Hunter mutters, "God, Paige. Will I ever get enough of you? I just had you before we left, and I already want you again. I want to *feel* you, *taste* you, *devour* you." He grinds up against me, ensuring I can feel his thick, hot rod behind his zipper.

"Here?" The breathy deliverance of my question divulges my excitement about his inability to reel in his eagerness in my presence. I love that he craves me as much as I do him. It is a nice change.

"Would you let me?" His beard scrapes my cheek when he drags his lips from my ear to the base of my throat. "Would you let me fuck you here?" His warm breath on my neck and the roughness of his beard as he nibbles my skin dampens my already slicked panties.

When I attempt to spin around to face him, he firms his grip on my hips, both keeping me facing the front and denying me access to his truth-revealing eyes. "Answer me, Paige. Would you let me fuck you here, where you could get caught with my cock between your legs, pounding your sweet, tight little pussy? Would you let me scandalize you that much?"

My eyes snap to the frosted glass wall sheltering us from the other partygoers. Although no one has disturbed us in here, I've heard numerous muffled voices walking by the past thirty minutes, and considering the glass door doesn't have a lock, the possibility of getting caught is credible.

When Hunter leans in closer to me, the vicious shudder that racks through my body gives me the answer I'm seeking.

"Yes," I murmur, allowing my body to overrule my astute brain.

When he releases my hips from his grip, I spin around to face him. My movements are slow and unbalanced, compliments to a wobbly pair of legs.

The quiver of my thighs intensifies when my eyes lock with Hunter's. His gaze is sparked with unbridled hankering that is brightening his eyes beyond their normal murkiness.

I peer into them while declaring, "I'll take you any way I can get you."

The music dulls to barely a hum when I'm overwhelmed by hands, teeth, salivating lips, and the roughness of a full beard. Just like every other kiss we've shared, this one is dominating and skilled. Its wildness makes me forget that we're in a glass box surrounded by partygoers, and it proves I made the right decision.

A disappointed groan spills from my lips when Hunter pulls his talented mouth away from mine. I'm panting, dying to secure a full breath, and every nerve in my body is sparked.

His eyes flick between mine, his face a cross between confused and aroused. "Not here." His voice is as strained as the zipper in his jeans. "I don't want anyone to see you."

I stare at him in utter shock. He never voiced a single qualm about having spectators during the sexual rendezvous he hosted at his house, so what's changed now?

"They weren't you, Paige," Hunter replies to my quiet ramblings. "I didn't care who saw them, but I don't want anyone seeing you."

Even though my bitchy spikes should be hackled from his comment, they aren't. The fact he isn't treating me as if I am one of the numerous notches on his bedpost keeps my anger at bay.

After leaning up on my tippy toes, I press my lips to the shell of his ear. "Then take me home."

Smiling, he encloses his hand over mine and guides me back out of the boardroom. Even though we only arrived at the party forty minutes ago, and I haven't been introduced to any of his friends or work associates, I'm too horny to care.

There will be plenty of time to mingle with his friends at a later date.

The suspicious eyes of the lady who housed my coat earlier bounce between Hunter and me when I hand her my ticket. Clearly, we haven't done a good job concealing the lusty gleam in our eyes.

With the feverish need still warming my body, I don't bother putting on my coat when she hands it back to me.

I'm still trying to reel in a sense of normality when Hunter pulls his Hellcat away from the curb and commences our thirty-minute trip home. Hoping some music will distract my lust-riddled mind long enough to rein in my unbridled horniness, I switch on the radio.

Nothing works.

I can smell Hunter's delicious scent, taste his tangy flavor on my lips, and feel the slickness between my legs.

When Hunter slows his speed for some pedestrians crossing the road, he shifts his eyes to me. They expose he's fighting the same struggle, walking down the same beaten path.

His grip on the steering wheel tightens when I unlatch my seat belt and reposition myself so I'm kneeling on the seat instead of sitting, then he holds it even firmer when I say, "I can't wait any longer." As my hand slithers down to the crotch of his trousers, I nibble on his hairy jaw. Desire twists in my stomach when I discover he's already hard, heavy, and thick. "I want you now."

The excitement heating my skin intensifies when he pulls down a deserted side alley, yanks his seat back, then pulls me into his lap. My dress bunches around my waist when my knees wrap around his bulky hips, then he steals the moan escaping my mouth when he seals his lips over mine. I groan when his delicious taste and smell engulf my senses. Then I moan some more when he rubs his cock against my aching pussy in a rhythm to match the pace of his tongue in my mouth.

An exciting mix of speed and skill builds the tension in my womb rapidly. As one of his hands fists my hair, holding it to his mouth, the other gropes my breast. He pinches my nipple into a tight, hardened bud before doing the same to my left side.

While keeping my mouth arrested with his, I fumble with the buttons on his shirt. I'm dying to feel his firm, tattooed skin under my hands again.

Just as the last button on his shirt is undone, Hunter yanks down the front of my dress, fully exposing my breasts. He groans a rough grunt when he realizes I'm not wearing a bra. After tearing his mouth away from mine, his eyes lower to my chest. I feel the twitches of his cock when he drinks in my small yet still adequate breasts.

The dampness of my silk panties increases when he mutters, "Fuck, you're beautiful. I don't know what I ever did to be able to touch you, but I am sure damn fucking grateful I did it."

"You're not too bad yourself," I say as we engage in another long, lingering stare.

He flashes me a flirty grin when I drag my damp panties down the length of his thickened shaft. I go extra slow to ensure he feels the effect he has on me.

"If we weren't trapped in the confines of my car, I'd be laying you out and devouring that sweet pussy of yours until you begged me to stop."

I thrust against him harder. "You make me want to whip out my notepad and take notes. My readers will love this scene."

He laughs, not at all shocked by my comment. Lucky because I wasn't joking. Many of the bedroom scenes I've written in the past few weeks are based on my interactions with Hunter.

"Then we better make sure it's a good one." After slipping my panties to the side, he strokes the folds of my drenched pussy. "As I know how much those romance readers love a good mommy-porn book."

Once the dampness he gathered from between my legs has been gobbled up by his mouth, Hunter adjusts the rearview mirror so it is elongated and faces us, then he weaves his hand through my hair and tugs my head back.

The unsteady rhythm of my heart breaks into a new beat when the reason behind the adjustment of the rearview mirror comes to light. Even with my head thrust back, I can see Hunter's face as clearly as he can see mine.

"I know how much you love throwing your head back and howling while riding my cock. This way, I still get to see your beautiful face."

My nostrils flare in an attempt to cool my skyrocketing body temperature when he removes a condom from his jeans pocket before he guides the rigid material over his glorious backside.

"Can I?" He stares up at me with the condom wrapper between his teeth and a curious stare. "I've just never done it before. It would be good for research."

"Research?" he double-checks, his voice as raw as my throat feels.

I lift my chin. "For the book I'm writing." I snatch the condom out from between his teeth, grinning when it rips open before adding, "Although they may be a little lax on protection from time to time, Archer would never be so foolish."

An unknown glint darts through Hunter's eyes, but I don't have the time to ask what it is. His eyes drop to the panties doing a poor job of hiding my throbbing pussy from his hooded gaze a mere second before I pinch the tip of the condom and roll it down his veiny shaft.

"Make sure it goes all the way down," he murmurs when I stop rolling the latex half an inch from his balls tucked up underneath him.

I can barely breathe through the brutal grunt that rumbles in my chest when he raises his ass out of his seat, exposing another two inches of his cock. I've ogled him naked more times the past couple of weeks than I did when he was unaware I was watching, and it still isn't enough. I'll never grow tired of watching the veins in his cock throb harder the longer I stare or how the tip becomes wetter with only the slightest brush of my thumb. I could stare at him for twenty-four hours a day and not grow tired.

"What did I tell you, Paige?" Hunter mutters as the smell of my arousal filters in the air. "I said you'd love my cock once I was done with you, and you do."

"I do," I concur. "Very much so." Before I can utter another declaration far too early to express, I lock my eyes with Hunter's, then murmur, "But once again, you're leaving me hanging."

He mutters something under his breath, but I don't quite hear what he says. My ears are too battered by the throaty groan whimpering from my lips when he snaps my panties off after only the quickest glance of our surroundings.

He wasn't lying when he said he didn't want anyone to see me. He wants our escapades solely between us, and I can't fault him for that. I've only just stopped clamming up, so I'll never do anything to have my adventurous side backtracking for even a second. Heck, Pepper will burn me on a stake if I slow down the climax train now. She said it would be a long, satisfying track since it was decommissioned for so long.

I'm beginning to believe her.

When he mistakes my shock about my unexpected happiness as worry, Hunter assures, "You don't need to worry about anyone seeing you. In two clicks, I had surveillance shut down three blocks over before I pulled down the alleyway."

"Three blocks over?" I spit out, shocked. When Hunter jerks up his chin, I giggle. "Your cock is impressive, but three blocks is a little overkill, don't you think?" I peer around the car's cab, certain the confident, carefree voice I just used doesn't belong to me. I've never sounded so liberated from responsibilities.

Hunter's beard can't hide his smile when he mutters, "If I had done it just to conceal my dick, perhaps... but not for your screams." After opening me up for him by spreading his thighs as far as they can go, he braces the head of his fat cock against the entrance of my pussy before disclosing, "They could be heard three towns over, but since I'm planning to suffocate them with my tongue, I figured it was best not to break every one of Isaac's protocols."

He displays precisely what he means when he jerks his hips upward, impaling me with one breathless thrust. My moan only rolls halfway up my throat before Hunter's tongue licks it up. He scoops it into his mouth with a long, greedy lick before he swallows down the rest as effectively as my pussy chokes his cock.

His kisses are always overwhelming, growing better and better the more we do, but this is different. It is almost too much. He's assaulting my pussy and mouth with the same level of savagery, and it has me on the brink of climax in a short time.

When the sensation becomes too much, I pull back so I can secure a full breath.

It is a tragic waste of time when Hunter drops his devotion to my breasts. The instant his beard scratches over my puckered nipple, I moan like I'm possessed.

"Keep them down," Hunter pleads a mere second before the flicks of his hips have me on the verge of screaming.

While biting my lip hard enough to mark, I shake my head, silently advising him that his request isn't possible. I can't have the best sex of my life and be quiet. That is absurd even to consider.

With a smirk that has me wondering if I said my thoughts out loud, Hunter curses under his breath. I join him when he stills the thrusts of his hips. The tingles low in my womb are still paramount, and my body is coated with a misting of sweat, but I need more than the scratchiness of his beard as he leans across my body to fiddle with the console in the dashboard to freefall into ecstasy.

I need every inch of him.

Mercifully, whatever Hunter is doing only takes him a minute. After a handful of keystrokes and the silencing of his cell phone, the rocks of his hips return more potent than ever—as does the gleam in his eyes.

"What did you do?" I query, sure there's more to the glint in his eyes than an impending orgasm. Mischievous Hunter has arrived a day early, and I'd be a liar if I said I was upset by the prospect.

"Nothing." He is a terrible liar. His chest shudders as he strives to hold in his chuckles exposes this, much less the drop of my jaw when an ear-piercing siren almost bursts my eardrums.

"You activated the tornado warning system?" When he nods, unaware I wasn't asking a question, I shout, "It's December! No one is going to believe there is a tornado in December. They're going to come out to investigate, and when they do..." I gulp. My breasts aren't extraordinary, but I still don't want them eyed by random strangers.

I'm lost for words, but Hunter picks up the slack for once. "They'll see a car parked down an alleyway but not hear a single peep of what's going on inside." His lips tug at one side when I arch a brow in confusion. It is settled when he mutters, "Patricia, activate central command security for my vehicle."

"Yes, Mr. Kane," she answers half a second before the windows of Hunter's ride blackout completely. The tint is so dark, the only visible objects are my white breasts and cheeks.

"None one can see us."

"No, they can't," Hunter agrees as he takes my budded nipple back into his mouth. "And thanks to the siren, no one can hear us either."

I won't lie. The thrill racing through my veins gives credit to Hunter's claims that my watch gave him a slight fascination with Martymachlia. The risk that we could be caught is already thrilling, much less knowing we're possibly surrounded by people none the wiser about the scandalous activity occurring next to them.

Hunter moans against my aching breasts when I squeeze the walls of my pussy around his still hard shaft instead of yanking away from him. "I should have known not all the heat on your cheeks when you were watching me was because of voyeurism. You like the idea of being watched as much as I loved knowing you were watching me."

Jealousy is the only thing heard in my tone when I reply, "I didn't like watching you with th—"

Hunter squashes his index finger against my kiss-swollen lips. "I wasn't talking about them. I was referencing the times I was alone, doing the most mundane things."

"Eating peanut butter toast every morning isn't mundane," I mutter against his finger. "Sometimes it is the littlest detail that makes the biggest impact."

"Mm-hmm," he murmurs again before he drops his finger from

my lip to my less-than-ample breasts. "Because these exposed your desires long before your mouth."

He brushes the back of his hand down each of my nipples before doing the last thing I expect him to do. He covers my chest with my dress, lifts me off his cock, then deposits me onto my seat like the stretchy rubber at the end of the condom isn't digging into his throbbing cock.

"Hu—"

Before I can get half his name out, he interrupts, "Your body was designed to be worshiped, Paige. I can't do that in a car parked down a dirty alley."

After tucking away his cock, he pushes a handful of buttons on his electronic console before demanding Patricia to deactivate the security program she had only just implemented. I try to lessen the redness on my cheeks when the tint on the windows clears away enough to spot a handful of residents milling outside of the apartment buildings Hunter's Hellcat is wedged between.

I shouldn't have bothered to act cordial because more than my cheeks heat up when Hunter finalizes his sentence, "But on the beach responsible for re-sparking some of the life in your eyes, I reckon I could worship you there." As he guides his car between the residents, grateful the siren was a false alarm but still peeved about the inconvenience, Hunter strays his eyes to mine. "What do you say, Paige? Shall we test out if shrinkage will be an issue before placing it in your next novel?"

Too horny to care about how many sand-loving crevices my body has, I nod.

CHAPTER TWENTY-TWO

*A*fter lifting my arms out of the duvet covering my bed, I have a long, leisurely stretch. My muscles are delightfully sore from hours of lovemaking on the beach that went well into the wee hours of this morning. Christmas morning will never be viewed in the same light again after my magical night with Hunter.

When I lower my arms, crinkling paper catches my attention. A grin curves onto my mouth when I discover a handwritten note sitting on the spare pillow next to me.

My grin enlarges to a full-toothed smile when I read what it says.

Call me.
Hunter

Hunter is understandably spending the day with his mother and sister two towns over. Most of my adult life I've returned home for Christmas, but it doesn't feel right this year with a failed relationship under my belt. I also agreed to go to the Christmas Eve party with Hunter last month, and I planned on keeping my word. My dad and I will have a belated Christmas celebration when I return home in mid-January. Although he was disappointed I decided not to come home, he said he understood.

After placing the note on the bedside table, I scoot up the bed until my back rests on the headboard. The happiness twisting my stomach increases when I dial Hunter's number and squash my phone to my ear.

I smile when his rich, chocolatey voice sounds down the line. "Good morning, Sleeping Beauty."

"Good morning, Hunter. Merry Christmas." My voice is husky, still raw from the erotic screams torn from my throat last night.

"Merry Christmas, Paige."

Hunter scrubbing his beard is the only noise that sounds through my cell for the next several minutes.

"Umm..." My heart rate climbs astronomically when I'm unable to miss the nervousness in his voice even with him only speaking one little word. "My mom wants me to invite you to her place for dinner tonight. I told her you might have plans, but she made me promise I'd ask, so I'm asking. There... I asked."

A giggle spills from my lips when a young female voice says, "She won't come if you ask her like that." When she makes a *tsking* noise, I imagine his sister from the photo on his mantelpiece crossing her arms in front of her chest and tapping her foot. "Ask her again and do it properly this time."

My cheeks burn from the size of the smile etching onto my face when Hunter asks, "Will you please come to my mother's house for dinner tonight, Paige?" His voice is the smoothest I've ever heard it. "My mom and little brat of a sister would love to meet you." I laugh when a rough groan sounds down the line, closely followed by, "I'll get you back for that, squirt." Hunter's stomping feet sound down the line before quiet encroaches. "She kicks harder than you." His voice has a hint of laughter behind it. After coughing to clear his throat, he mutters, "I understand if you don't want to come, Paige, I know it's ear—"

"I'd love to come," I interrupt, my smile radiating through my voice.

"Okay." His voice is deeper than normal but just as pulse-quickening. "I'll pick you up in a couple of hours?"

I smile larger. "Alright. I'll see you then."

"Bye, Paige."

"Bye, Hunter."

Just as I pull my phone away from my ear, I hear Hunter call my name.

"Yes." I squash my cell back to my ear so fast, I bet I get a bruise.

My eyes bulge when Hunter mutters, "Stop biting your lip. My teeth are getting jealous."

Stealing me the opportunity to reply, he disconnects our call. I stare at my phone, blinking and confused before remembering a time when something similar happened. My eyes rocket around my room as my suspicions pique.

When I fail to locate any type of electronic device hidden in the wooden walls, I scoot across the bed, adamant a more avid inspection is required. The sun beaming in the open curtains warms my chilled skin as I pad around the room, seeking anything that could house a small camera.

During my third trip past the large window stretching across the entire wall of the bedroom I catch the quickest glimmer reflecting from the corner of Hunter's property. After sheltering my face from the blinding sun's rays, I adjust my eyes. My heart beats triple time when I realize there is a black security dome mounted on the corner wall of Hunter's home, but before half my shock can register, my cell phone unexpectedly vibrates in my hand, scaring the living daylights out of me.

When I peer down at the screen, the insane beat of my heart climbs even more.

HUNTER:

Bingo.

I screw up my nose then turn to face the camera. Instead of the lens facing Hunter's property, it's pointing directly at my bedroom window. My mouth gapes when the camera swivels a few seconds later like it's being controlled remotely.

After sticking out my tongue, I yank the thick curtains shut.

My phone dings not even two seconds later.

HUNTER:

Killjoy.

I smile while my fingers fumble over the screen.

ME:

Peeping Tom.

Hunter must text as fast as he types code because his next message comes through remarkably fast.

HUNTER:

Only for you, Paige. I'll see you soon.

Smiling, I reply.

ME:

Yes, you will. In person.

A happy sigh fills my chest when his reply pops up on the screen.

HUNTER:

Can't wait.

I spent the first hour of my morning preparing for my dinner date with Hunter. Then the next two hours are spent in front of my Mac, adding a decent number of words to the already impressive word count of my manuscripts.

Usually, I only pen one novel at a time, but with the range of storylines hammering me since I arrived at Bronte's Peak, I'm currently juggling two manuscripts. One is a contemporary romance piece on Archer Boyd, and the other is a romantic suspense novel about a millionaire businessman and his Aphrodite.

When the sound of the cabin's back sliding door opening bellows up the stairwell, I hit save on my manuscripts. "Hey, Hunter, I'm in my writing cave," I shout while impatiently waiting for my program to save everything before shutting it down. With a threat of a storm looming, I don't like leaving my imperative electronic devices plugged in.

A smile sweeps across my face when big stomps echo through my ears.

Someone's a little eager.

After powering down my laptop, I yank the cord out of the wall and spin around to face Hunter. My breath snags halfway to my lungs when I run smack bang into a solid, suit-covered chest. I linger my eyes on the well-formed chest for several heart-thrashing seconds so my heart has a chance to settle down before I hesitantly lift them to a face I can recall in photographic memory.

"Merry Christmas, Candace." Riley swoops down and plants a kiss on my O-formed mouth.

If he'd slapped me in the face, he couldn't have shocked me more.

When I yank away from him, I stumble over my feet and fall into my leather writing chair.

"Woah, careful there, darling. You'll hurt yourself." He thinks he sounds endearing, but all I hear is the condescending tone of a horrid man.

"What are you doing here, Riley?" I stammer out through the mad beat of my heart.

When he takes a step closer to me, I hold out my hand, demanding for him to stop.

He doesn't.

"It's Christmas, Candace. I've spent every Christmas with you the past seven years. I didn't want to miss one." He shoves his hands into his pockets. "Unfortunately, I've arrived late because it took me this long to track you down." He rocks on his heels, his entire composure screaming of superiority and arrogance.

Oh my god, is that how Hunter saw me the first time? As a rich, condescending snob?

When he interprets my silence as an open invitation, Riley takes another step closer to me. "God, I've missed you, darling."

My spikes bristle. "Oh, I'm sure you did while you had Beth sleeping in my bed."

His pupils widen, and he gasps in a quick breath, seemingly shocked I knew about his affair with Beth, let alone him moving her into our shared home.

"Yeah, I knew all about Beth. Why do you think I left?"

His smug smirk weakens as he swallows bleakly. "It was a mistake, Candace. I love you. I realize that now. It won't happen again," he replies, his pitch as arrogant as the pompous look on his face.

He actually believes I'll forgive him just from hearing that one pathetic apology. If you can even call it that. It was more a statement than an attempt of pleading for forgiveness. He didn't even say he was sorry.

My teeth grit when he hoists me from my writing chair with a firm grip on my wrist. Air hisses from my mouth when my chest crashes into his. Unlike the times I've collided with Hunter, this is a hiss of anger, not excitement.

Riley's cagey eyes bounce between mine. Even though he only turned thirty last year, he looks at least five years older. *Deceit does age you.* "I promise you, Candace, there's no other woman in the world for me but you."

When he tightens his grip around my waist, I attempt to yank away from him, but the more I fight, the harder he holds me. "You have to believe me, Candace."

The air is vehemently removed from my lungs when Hunter's rich, chocolatey voice sounds through my ears. "Who is Candace?"

When I swing my eyes to the entrance of my writing cave, I spot Hunter standing at the stoop of the stairs. One of his arms is hanging at the side of his body, his fist clenched tightly, while the other is slipped behind his back, no doubt bracing the gun he houses in the back of his jeans.

His ticking jaw intensifies as his eyes dart between Riley and me. After pushing off Riley's chest, I take a giant step backward, wanting to ensure Hunter doesn't misconstrue our position as intimate.

I breathe a sigh of relief when Hunter's eyes lock with mine before he silently asks if I'm okay. When I nod, his hand slides deeper into the back of his jeans before his eyes shift to Riley. His jaw is tense, and his gaze is dangerous. "Who are you?" he asks, his voice rough and brimmed with anger.

"Riley," Riley responds cockily, his arrogance not as tarnished as it should be for a scorned man. "Candace's fiancé." He cranks his neck to me. "Candace, who is this guy?" His voice is as uneased as the mask slipping over Hunter's face.

"Who the fuck is Candace?" Hunter snarls, his loud voice booming through my ears, startling me.

I stand still, frozen in shock. I demand my mouth to work but seeing Hunter and Riley side by side has muted me into silence. I knew it would be like comparing day to night, and it is, but every point is being awarded to Hunter even with him wearing a plaid shirt and a pair of ripped designer jeans. His feet are covered with the black motorcycle boots he regularly wears, and although his beard was recently trimmed, it covers a vast majority of his gorgeous face. His hair is longer than when I first spotted him, hanging an inch below his ears. Whereas Riley is decked out in a navy-blue pinstriped suit with a ghastly Christmas-themed tie. His shoes are so polished, I can see my reflection in them. His model-inspired face is void of any type of facial hair, and his hair is cut in a short back and sides style.

They couldn't be any more different if they tried, but Riley's smooth, sophisticated look isn't winning him any brownie points this time around.

I step between Riley and Hunter when Riley steps up to Hunter like he regularly did our gardener when he trimmed our lawn shorter than he liked. "I'm Riley," he advises again like Hunter is hard of hearing. After gesturing his hand to me, he says, "Candace's fiancé."

Hunter balks, physically impacted by his lie. His pupils widen, swamping the corneas of his murky blue eyes. I shake my head, soundlessly denying Riley's statement, but before Hunter spots my silent response, Riley asks, "And you are?"

My heart shatters into a million pieces when Hunter answers, "I'm Hunter. Candace's *friend*." He glares at me over Riley's shoulder with nothing but resentment reflecting from his shattered eyes. "Just thought I'd come check on my *friend* since it's Christmas, and she was alone. You know, it's the *friendly* thing to do." He locks his shattered eyes back to Riley. "But you look like you've got this covered."

"That I do."

I'm desperate to slap the haughty expression off Riley's face, but a far more dire situation demands my utmost attention. "Hunter," I squeak out when he spins on his heels and gallops down the stairs. "Wait! Hunter, please."

I yank my arm out of Riley's firm grip when he tries to stop me, then barge him out of the way. My heart races a million miles an hour as I chase after Hunter. I beg my legs to continue moving as a barrage of emotions slams into me at once—fear, resentment, confusion. It all smashes into me.

"Hunter, wait," I call out again when I catch him in the driveway of his home, my words trembling through the fear clutching my throat. "Give me a chance to explain."

A small moment of relief washes over me when his furious pace slows. After inhaling a big breath to replenish my lungs with air, I span the distance between us. The pain in Hunter's eyes matches mine to a T. His fists are balled just as tight, and his facial expression is anything but pleasant.

"That wasn't what it looked like—"

"Is your name Paige or Candace?" His raspy tone is full of warning that his anger is rapidly surging.

"It isn't that simple."

"Yes, it is," he sneers, once again cutting me off. "Is your name Paige or Candace?"

"If you'll give me a chance to explain—"

Hunter's eyes scorch into mine as he shouts, "Answer the fucking question! What is your name? Your *real* name."

As I fight back tears, I faintly murmur, "It's Candace."

The anger projecting out of Hunter strangles the oxygen out of the air. It makes it hard for me to breathe. Even with his jaw covered by the thick beard I've grown to love, I can't miss the furious tic inflicting it. He glares at me for numerous heart-pounding seconds before he turns on his heels and continues his original journey without speaking another word.

I try to go after him. I want to, but my legs refuse to move. They're weighed down by the pain stabbing the middle of my chest.

"I'm sorry, Hunter," I strangle out a second before he curls into his car and slams the door shut.

His car fishtails out of control, barely missing the large steel gate at the entrance of his property when he flattens his foot onto the accelerator.

Burning rubber lingers in the air for several minutes after his dramatic exit. I remain motionless in the driveway while desperately striving to find a way through what just transpired. I am truly at a loss, both dazed and confused.

I snap back to reality when an arm unexpectedly curls around my shoulders. When I recognize the bottled cologne I've grown to hate infiltrating my nostrils, I brutally yank out of Riley's embrace.

"Oh, come on, Candace, if I can get over you sleeping with a lumberjack, you can get over my affair with Beth," Riley snaps, his voice back to the normal condescending tone I was accustomed to hearing the past seven years.

I spin on my heels. My movements so quick and manic, my hair slaps my face. After pointing to a dark gray rental car sitting at the front of the cabin, I sneer out, "You need to leave."

"Candace—"

"Stop calling me that! No one calls me Candace anymore."

He glares at me. "It's your name, isn't it?"

My sadness about Hunter's abrupt departure is overtaken by anger at Riley's sudden arrival. "You don't call me Candace because it's my christened name. You use it for the social status associated with it." Anger burns through me when he doesn't attempt to negate my claims. "That's why you came back, isn't it? It's just dawned on you the extent of your unfortunate timing." When a mask of panic slips over his face, a cunning grin curls on my lips. "Well, now that we have that settled, let's hash out a few more points. This..." I gesture my hand between us, "... will never happen again. As far as any media is concerned, we never happened to begin with. And for every second you delay leaving, you're lowering your political chances more and more." My tone should alert him to the fact I'm not joking. The Candace he remembers is long gone, and I plan to show him that.

Riley's eyes slit like he can cut down my determination with a stare. "The bitterness of a scorned woman will have no influence on my future candidacy bid."

"I may not, but what about my father?" I cross my arms in front of my chest. "I'm fairly confident when he hears about the extracurricular activities you've undertaken the past three years of our relationship, he'll be more than happy to have a friendly chat with your campaign supporters." The panic in his no-longer slit eyes increases with every syllable that seeps from my lips. "And what's that saying you've always quoted?" I tap my lips, pretending I've forgotten the quote he cited numerous times over the past three years. "Without power, you'll never have money, but without money, you'll never have power." I straighten my spine and stare him straight in the eyes. "You'll have neither money nor power if you don't leave this instant!"

He glares at me with nothing but unbridled disdain on his face, but I don't back down. I am a stronger, more determined, kick-ass Paige than he knows, and I'm not putting up with his shit anymore.

Air wafts me in the face when Riley finally gets the hint that he isn't wanted. He storms by me and marches to the rental car sitting in the driveway.

I try to hold in my smile, to show a small snippet of the class my mother ingrained in me, but no matter how hard I fight, I can't stop a victorious grin from etching onto my face. Victory is too good to contain.

"I hope your fall into the gutter doesn't hurt too much," Riley snarls before curling into the car.

Incapable of letting him have the last word, I shout, "It couldn't any more than it did with you."

CHAPTER TWENTY-THREE

Vying to stop the winter chill blowing in from the west, I tug my knitted cardigan in tighter. I've been sitting in the sand dunes in front of my rented cabin, watching the waves tumble to shore over the past two hours. Bronte's Peak is the quietest it's been since I arrived here months ago.

Usually, too much silence makes me crazy, but I needed fresh air. I was hoping it would lessen the swirls hampering my stomach the past six hours. Although the cramps encumbering my tummy have eased, the crisp winter air has done nothing to reduce the pain inside my heart.

I shouldn't be surprised. Even a pep talk from Pepper didn't settle the pain.

I've been calling Hunter's cell nonstop for the past six hours, and every one of my calls have gone directly to his voicemail. When I text, I get an automated response saying my text has bounced and to try later. The only godsend I have is knowing I'm his neighbor. Sooner or later, he will have to return home, and when he does, I plan to beg for the chance to explain why I lied.

My little fib isn't as heinous as Hunter thinks it is. When he gives me the opportunity to defend myself, I am sure he'll see the funny side to it.

The Weekend Romance by Rachel Maloney is a loosely based fictional story of how the governor of New York City's daughter—my mom—fell madly in love with the gardener's son—my dad. The story includes numerous real-life facts about their relationship, like the first day they met when my dad fell off a ladder pruning the bushes at my grandfather's estate when he spotted my mom sauntering by the large, elegant windows to the precious words they spoke to each other when they discovered they were going to become parents.

My mom penned *The Weekend Romance* as a gift to my father for their tenth wedding anniversary. My dad was so impressed with her work, he encouraged her to have the book published. He never expected it to be a *New York Times* number one best-selling book for eight weeks in a row, be translated into thirteen foreign languages, and made into a blockbuster motion picture.

If he had known, he might have pleaded harder with my mom to reconsider her decision to leave the characters' names as the original names she used in the manuscript.

Actually, scrap that.

I don't think he'd change a thing.

I was only a child at the time my mom penned *The Weekend Romance*, and even I knew she was creating brilliance, so I'm sure my dad was even more aware.

For the six months following the novel's release, my father playfully called me by my middle name—Paige. As the months went by, the name stuck.

Those nearest and dearest to me call me Paige. The only person in my inner circle who hasn't the past fifteen years is Riley, and that was purely for political gain. He used me as I am sure Hunter thinks I used him.

The twisting of my heart amplifies when an engine rumbles through the quietness surrounding me. I leap up from the sand dunes and crank my neck to Hunter's house. When I spot Hunter's Hellcat gliding down the driveway of his home, I sigh in relief.

I knew you'd eventually come home.

After gathering the picnic blanket from the ground, I wrap it around my arm before urgently striding up the sand-lined path between our properties. My pace quickens when the rich smoothness of Hunter's voice slides through my ears. It's like melted chocolate on a hot summer day.

I've just cleared the opening of the sand dunes when a light in his house flicks on, illuminating his property with an artificial glow. My heart skips a beat when I catch the quickest glimpse of him moving toward the bi-fold doors at the back of his living space, then it completely stops beating when my stalking gaze captures another person in his presence.

Jealousy twists my stomach before winding up to my throat when a beautiful woman with waves of red hair enters the living area. Her eyes are zipping around the surroundings with eagerness, absorbing the enormity and grandeur of Hunter's house.

I stand frozen, hidden in the shadows of his patio when the cute redhead removes her shoes and jacket. She looks set for an extended stay.

When my pulse races, sending my heart rate to a dangerous level, I attempt to suck in some deep breaths. It is a woeful waste of time. Nothing can settle the morbid fear crippling me from the inside out.

I beg for my eyes to look away when a set of privacy curtains I didn't know Hunter owned roll down the large panels of glass his house is designed with. Even though the blinds slide fluidly into place, they aren't quick enough to conceal the image of the redhead slinging her arms around Hunter's shoulders and nuzzling into the crook of his neck.

When the pain becomes too much for me to handle, I throw the blanket to the ground and scream bloody murder. I thought walking in on my fiancé in the midst of an affair hurt, but this is ten times more. I trusted Hunter. I showed him the real Paige, a side hardly anyone gets to see, and he still betrayed me.

That hurts more than anything.

After angrily flinging a rogue tear off my cheek, I rush into the cabin and crank the stereo as loud as it will go. I refuse to hear another moan of ecstasy screamed from my neighbor's house.

The pain knotted in my throat intensifies when I enter my writing cave to hide from the image I know will rip my heart straight out of my chest. When I slide down to sit on the wooden floor, my eyes catch sight of my storyboards of Archer Boyd—the bearded billionaire who lives in a crystal house. Even though most of the board is made up of handwritten notes, I've studied Hunter in so much depth during the past three months, I can physically see each expression I jotted down.

Like a movie playing before my eyes, each scribbled note is displayed in graphic detail.

The storyboard causes even more anger and despair. I leap up from the floor and yank down every shred of paper from it. I rip them into tiny specks that float into the air like snowflakes falling from a darkened sky. Even though I am destroying hours of hard work, the triumphant feeling is worth the loss in research.

Once the storyboard has been destroyed, I focus my attention on removing every bit of information about Hunter from my laptop. I delete the scanned handwritten notes and sketches I placed on there with the app he created for me, then I trash any notes and references in my writing applications.

My manic behavior only ends when I open the nearly finished manuscript about Archer Boyd. I've been working on it nonstop for the past three weeks and only have the final chapter and epilogue to go.

When my eyes scan the beautiful words in front of me, a new idea formulates in my head. After twisting a red editor's pen into my hair to hold it off my face, I pull my writing chair in close to my desk and set to work. Everything I'm feeling is put down on paper, and every word I type loosens the restrictive hold Hunter has placed on my heart.

I type and type until I have nothing left to type, and six hours have ticked by on the clock, then I sink into my writer's chair and stare at the incessant blink of a black cursor on a white screen.

Since my manuscript is finished, my writing application requests that I fill in the title page. My heart beats wildly as the events from the day I arrived at the cabin until now roll through my head. When the scene stops on the day I spotted Hunter on the back patio of his glass house, the perfect title smacks into me.

While exhaling a big breath, I type the name of my newly penned novel:

Spy Thy Neighbor

The smell of warm paper and fresh ink filters through my nose when the inkjet printer at my side sets to work on printing the one hundred and fifty A4-sized pages of my manuscript. I save the one and only original copy onto a spare USB before deleting it from my writing application.

I only have one plan for this book.

It isn't publishing it.

Leaving the printer to do its job, I trudge down the stairs and head to the main bathroom. I shed my clothes on the way, not wanting to waste any time. The thought of a heavenly, hot shower is the only thing keeping me motivated.

As I lather my body with soap, I try to keep my focus off Hunter, but it's a fraudulent mission. I've showered with him numerous times in this very shower.

It's crazy to think how much things have changed in twenty-four hours. This time yesterday, I was waking up sexually satiated, and now it feels like I haven't been touched by him in months instead of hours.

God, I am pathetic.

I thought the weeks it took to leave Riley were pitiful, but this beats that tenfold. Hunter only betrayed me mere hours ago, and I'm already missing him.

I am better than this.

I am stronger than this.

And it isn't just Riley about to learn this.

After remembering the promise I made to my mother three years ago, I switch off the water and step out of the shower. Once I have a towel wrapped around my body, I walk into my bedroom. My steps are more determined than they were before I entered the shower. After dressing in a wool skirt, lace-topped stockings, and a cashmere two-piece cardigan, I call for a taxi before I commence packing my belongings.

It's time for me to go home.

Unlike the time I packed in a frenzied haze only weeks ago, this time, I ensure I collect every item I arrived with. My clothing and laptop will travel with me on the plane, but my writing chair, printing equipment, and storyboards will be collected by a transport company later in the week.

A grin curls on my lips when I open the top drawer of the dresser and discover the crotchless teddy Pepper snuck into my suitcase three months ago. "I don't think I'll need you anytime soon," I mumble to myself while placing the lingerie onto the unmade bed in the middle of the room.

I inhale deeply, gathering the quickest scent of my last sexual encounter with Hunter still lingering in the air before making my way to the taxi parked at the front of the cabin.

"Thank you," I say with a smile when the cab driver with kind eyes removes my suitcase from my hand to place it into the trunk.

I race back into the cabin to gather the freshly-inked

manuscript from the printer and the USB from my writing cave before making my way back outside. "Could you please start the meter? I'll only be a few minutes," I request to the driver.

His eyes connect with mine before he curtly nods. I leave my laptop and handbag in the taxi's backseat before sauntering toward Hunter's house. He isn't home. One of the garage doors of his four-car garage has been left open, and his Hellcat is nowhere in sight.

A swear word seeps from my lips when I bob down to place the manuscript on the doormat and Patricia's computerized voice sounds through my ears. "Welcome, Paige."

My eyes dart to the security panel at the side when it flashes up a message stating that the front door has been unlocked.

"Thank you." I catch my eye roll halfway that I'm communicating with a computer program before pushing open Hunter's heavily weighted front door. I shouldn't be entering his residence unattended without permission, but curiosity killed the cat.

My heart bleeds more with every step I take. Cheap floral perfume is trapped in the space since the privacy blinds are still lowered, and no windows have been opened.

I feel physically ill when I enter the living area and see that the couches are askew. The thick Persian rug is indented from where the sofas used to lie. The coffee table is upturned, and some of the paintings adorning the walls are crooked.

It looks more like a fraternity house after a raging party than a private residence.

After pushing aside a champagne glass that has a coating of red lipstick on the rim, I place the manuscript and USB for *Spy Thy Neighbor* onto the counter Hunter eats his three slices of peanut butter toast at. While ignoring the pain splitting my heart in two, I snag a pen from a computer desk in the corner of the room and write an inscription on the title page of the one-of-a-kind book.

In true Hunter style, I keep my message brief:

Enjoy.

Paige Turner
New York Times Best-selling Author

The hairs on the nape prickle when I sense a presence standing behind me shortly before cruel words are spoken by a voice I'll never forget. "What are you doing in my house, *Candace?*"

$\mathcal{A}$ shiver moves through me from the anger projected in Hunter's low, sharp tone. I don't need to turn around to know he's angry. The terse crackling in the air makes me acutely aware of the anger flowing out of him in tiny, invisible waves.

He isn't the only one angry, though. My blood hasn't stopped simmering since last night, adding to the pain festering in my heart. He betrayed me and played me for a fool. He doesn't deserve an explanation for my intrusion. He deserves nothing.

After squaring my shoulders, I pivot on my heels and make a beeline for the front door. I keep my head low, using my hair as a shelter to ensure he doesn't see the pain not even the world's most scalding shower couldn't remove from my face.

The smell of hot, sweaty skin and alcohol increases the further I move as does the knot in my stomach.

I jerk to a halt when my wrist is suddenly seized, and I'm pinned to the wall by Hunter's imposing frame. Furious heat sweeps through my body when I realize he's shirtless and barefoot, wearing nothing but his favorite pair of jeans. His hair is wet and flopped to the side, his face is sleepless, and the other half of the almost empty bottle of liquor he's grasping is seeping from his pores, suffocating his normally alluring smell.

Even knowing I'll never budge a man of his size, I push on his torso with my hands while barging my hip into his waist. His stance remains firm, not the slightest bit intimidated by my fight. His eyes are wild, and his nostrils flare with every breath he takes.

His boozy breath flutters on my overheated cheeks as his furious eyes scorch into mine. "What are you doing here, *Candace?*" he asks again, his voice just as vicious as it was the first time he interrogated me.

"I came to say goodbye." My lips thin with annoyance, hating that my voice came out in a quiver.

Hunter's furious mask slips for the quickest second before it returns stronger than ever. When he sucks in a deep breath, he pushes me into the wall more firmly. His fierce gaze sears into mine, pausing the frantic beat of my heart. "You had your fun, and now it's time to leave?"

My stomach recoils from the bitterness of his words. "Yeah, I had my fun," I sneer as my anger steamrolls back in from catching the quickest whiff of the floral perfume still lingering on his skin. "Because being *betrayed* is a rollercoaster ride every woman lines up for."

He takes a step back, balking at my allegation. I use his unsteadiness to my advantage. After pushing on his chest with all my might, I slip under his arm and race to the door.

Just as I grasp the steel bar door handle, Hunter commands, "Patricia, commence security lockdown."

"Yes, Mr. Kane," replies the computerized voice of Hunter's home security system.

The clicking of locks overtakes the shrilling of the pulse in my ears. I furiously yank on the door, endeavoring to open it. It remains shut, locked tighter than Hunter's mouth during interrogation.

While grinding my back molars together, I twist around to face

Hunter. "Let me out." The quiver of my words is more from anger than devastation. My body is shaking and slicked with sweat, and my eyes are welling with tears as every emotion I've ever felt hammers into me.

"Patricia, play the surveillance of my arrival home last night," Hunter instructs, completely ignoring my request to be released.

"Yes, Mr. Kane," Patricia replies.

I blink, reeling back the tears looming in my eyes when I am confronted with the image of Hunter arriving home with the pretty redhead last night. The gut-wrenching video is projected onto a white screen that has lowered from the ceiling in his living room. It's so large, it covers the entire span of the window in Hunter's living area. Unlike last night, this visual gives a bird's eye view of the incident captured by the surveillance cameras installed in Hunter's house.

Blood roars in my ears when the pretty redhead removes her coat and tosses it onto one of the leather couches in Hunter's sunken living area. I try to tear my eyes away. I beg them to look at anything but the screen, but no matter how hard I plead, my eyes refuse to budge.

My throat tightens painfully when the redhead slips off her shoes and pads closer to Hunter. Eagerness beams out of her when she curls her arms around his neck. My breathing halts, preparing for the brutal blow I am about to be dealt.

The commands of my lungs are fruitless. The event unfolds differently than I imagined hundreds of times last night. Hunter doesn't return the redhead's embrace. He pulls away from her before stalking toward a bar in the corner of the room.

After his fingers punch something into his phone, he places it on the counter and snags a liquor bottle from the small selection in front of him. Undetermined, the redhead pouts before she prances after him. My brows furrow, utterly mortified that she can't take a hint.

Even with her ego copping a hard blow, she continues with her endeavor of seducing Hunter. After molding the generous curves of her body with Hunter's side, she runs her fingers through his beard. I clench my jaw before snapping my eyes to Hunter. That may not seem like an intimate act to most people, but to me, it hurts like a million bee stings.

Hunter watches me with dark, troubled eyes while guzzling down mouthfuls of the amber liquor from the bottle he's clasping but remains quiet.

Against the suggestion of my smart head, I turn my eyes back to the video. The Hunter in the surveillance video replicates the one standing at my side. He's gulping down large swigs of brown liquid, but he's using a glass instead of a bottle.

The swirling in my stomach intensifies when the redhead loosens the buttons of his shirt. When inches of his smooth, tattooed torso are exposed, and her efforts shift to the belt holding up his jeans, it lurches into my throat.

Confident I've seen enough, I snap my eyes closed. The brisk movements of my eyelids send a couple of tears rolling down my cheeks, but I brush them away without fear, certain no woman could watch such a horrifying image and not be upset.

My eyes pop back open when glass smashing filters through my ears. Brown liquid seeps down one of the nude paintings lining the walls, pooling around the shards of glass sprawled across the floor.

When I lift my tear-swamped eyes from the bottle of alcohol Hunter broke on the wall to him, my heart cracks. He looks so broken, both angry and hurt.

"Watch it," he demands, his tone flat and brimming with anger.

I shake my head, which sends more tears dropping onto my cheeks.

Either blind to my rejection or fuming mad about it, Hunter quickly spans the distance between us. His furious pace helps him reach me in under a heartbeat. After curling his body around mine, enveloping me with his feverish heat, he grips my chin and forces my head back to face the projector screen. "Watch it," he commands again, his hot breath fanning my earlobe.

His furious pulse adds to the quiver of my chin when my eyes return to the projector screen. I flinch in the same manner as the redhead in the video when Hunter upends one of the couches in his living room and sends it sailing across the room. It hits the wall with such force, one of his nude paintings topples to the floor.

Hunter snaps his eyes closed and inhales numerous big breaths as the redhead stands to the side of him with her mouth gaped open in surprise. Once he's reined in some sort of composure, he flutters open his eyes and locks them with the redhead. I can't hear any of the words he speaks, but I can tell he's apologizing. His mortified expression displays his remorse for scaring her, not to mention the shame in his eyes.

After doing up the buttons on his shirt, he gathers the redhead's coat from the untouched couch, places his hand on the curve of her lower back, then walks her to the door.

"Patricia, play the surveillance video from the Dungeon nightclub at sixteen times the speed from four o'clock this morning," Hunter requests, his words slurred but still crammed with anger.

"Yes, Mr. Kane," Patricia complies.

Even though my gaze remains fixated on the screen, Hunter keeps his hand wrapped around my throat and his index finger and thumb pinching my chin. Although his hold could be construed as aggressive, my body isn't registering it like that. It's excited by his domineering nature.

My heart was shredded last night, but as the footage of Hunter downing drink after drink, alone, at a bustling nightclub filters before my eyes, the uncontrollable thud in my chest transfers to another region of my body. This one is much lower.

"You didn't sleep with her?" I mumble more to myself than Hunter.

"I fucking wanted to, but I couldn't," he responds to my silent interrogation. "She wasn't who I wanted."

The sweat rolling down his torso is absorbed by my cardigan when he molds his body to mine. I try to suppress it, but the faintest moan topples from my gaped lips. Even being angry that he purposely set out to hurt me last night, my body melts when his beard scratches my neck. When he sinks his teeth into my shoulder blade while his erect cock grinds my backside, my panties dampen.

"Can I have you, Paige? Can I scandalize you some more?"

When I nod, the hand wrapped around my neck lowers to my breast while the other one slides beneath the hem of my skirt. When his thick fingers brush over my panties clinging to the folds of my pussy, my knees shake. I grind down on his hand, my earlier pain a forgotten memory.

I throw my head back and pant when his finger slips inside my panties before he slowly enters my clenching core. As his thumb and index finger roll my budded nipple, his finger fucks me at a rapid yet also leisurely pace. He curls his fingers at the tip, making sure he gets the tender spot inside me while his mouth lavishes my neck with bites and kisses.

The tension bristling between us is incredible, and within a short time, I'm on the verge of a climax.

Just as I'm about to announce that I'm close to detonation, Hunter mutters, "One last fuck before you run back to your country club friends to tell them how you spent Christmas slumming with the less fortunate."

My orgasm comes to a screeching halt—as does my heart. I lurch away from him, both disgusted and shocked by the callousness of his words.

When I spin around to face him, I nearly lose my footing. I'm dizzy from the closeness of a climax and the anger roaring through my veins. Heat rises from my gut to my cheeks when I catch sight of his mocking smirk. His eyes are blazing, and his entire composure screams of arrogance.

He is the ugliest I've ever seen him.

"Candace Paige Maloney, daughter of Gerald Maloney, Senator

from California." His tone is dangerously even. "Prestigious grand-daughter of Richard Breene, ex-governor and oil tycoon with an estimated worth of over three billion dollars." He drawls out my grandfather's worth like he's announcing the jackpot in the lottery. "Her major at college was political science before she changed it to creative writing after her mother was diagnosed with ALS."

Tears prick my eyes at the mention of my mother's name. The only thing keeping them at bay is the remorse that flashes through Hunter's eyes for the tiniest second before he continues his malicious drunken tirade. "Candace's best friend since kindergarten is Quinn Peters, crowned Miss Daisy Beauty Queen in 2017. She currently works at a local coffee bean chain while attending audition after audition after audition, as she, along with the other eighty-eight percent of Los Angeles residents, is an aspiring actress. Surprise. Surprise."

I cross my arms in front of my chest. My anger is so paramount, my face is red, and steam is nearly billowing out of my ears. "Are you done?"

"Just one last thing." He lifts his index finger into the air—the same finger still glistening with evidence of my near arousal. "Patricia, bring up the last-searched item on my home server," he requests, his words slurring.

My pulse is pounding in my ears so efficiently, I don't hear Patricia agreeing to his command. I am beyond ropable that he invaded my privacy like this. He had no right to do this. I don't care how angry he is.

The fevered heat slicking my skin with sweat intensifies when image after image of my engagement to Riley fills the projector screen. Most are magazine articles, but the occasional random picture from attendees who came to our small and highly unrated engagement party pops up. Even the obligatory newspaper announcement Riley's mom placed in the local paper of her home-town has been included.

"I find it interesting I could locate hundreds of articles on your engagement to Riley Smith, but I failed to find one mention of it ending." Hunter's slur doesn't affect the maliciousness of his words. They're as stinging as ever. "So what was I, Paige? The cold feet before the wedding fuck? Or the shmuck you used to get back at your daddy for spending too many hours in the office playing sergeant to his little minions?"

"Neither," I say with a shake of my head.

The quickest spark of relief brightens Hunter's eyes.

It's short-lived.

"You were the stupid fuck I used to fill my scrapbook with storylines." My tone matches his earlier maliciousness. "You were the one who said I had to write from experience. And boy did I experience it. I *felt* it, *tasted* it, *devoured* it. I took every inch you were willing to give *all* just to fill the blank pages of a book."

When Hunter balks as if my words physically slapped him, I smirk a grin I've only ever been on the receiving end of before strutting to his front door. I keep my eyes straight ahead, ensuring he won't see the hot, salty tears threatening to spill down my cheeks. I've never been a confrontational type of person, but after what I've endured the past twenty-four hours, my claws are bared, and my inner bitch has been unleashed.

After inhaling a big breath to rid my voice of nerves, I say, "Let me out so I can go share my newly-discovered mommy-porn stories with my rich country club friends."

The cracks in my heart enlarge when Hunter snarls without pause for thought, "Patricia, disarm all security locks."

The heat of the midday sun does nothing to lessen the dampness of my cheeks as I race down the stairs of Hunter's residence and hotfoot it to the taxi still idling at the front of the cabin. As I slot into the back seat, I tell the driver to take me anywhere but here.

He does precisely that without seeing hide nor hair of Hunter.

CHAPTER TWENTY-FIVE

"*W*ow. Swanky view." Pepper peers out of the supersized double windows of my hotel suite at Oceana Beach Club Resort in Santa Monica. The dull hum of tourists chatting filters into the room when she opens the bi-folding doors and steps onto the patio. The sun setting in the distance bounces off her dark chocolate hair, haloing her in a luminous glow. "Have you spent any time out here?" She cranks her neck back to peer at me, her eyes rolling when I shake my head. "Miles of beautiful beaches and even more pristine men, and you've cooped yourself up in a hotel room. If you wanted to spend your days looking at ugly, bland walls, you could have just stayed at my apartment."

I shrug and turn my eyes to the makeshift writing cave I created in the living area of my suite. I've rarely ventured from my laptop the past five days, only leaving it to shower and have the occasional bite to eat.

"I came here to write, not look at the scenery," I blubber, blurting out the same excuse I gave her when I shut myself off from any form of communication.

I've spent the last five days doing what I was supposed to do while at the cabin. I finished penning a steamy romance novel. I switched off all electronic devices, completely hiding away from social media, and kept my focus solely on my manuscript.

I'm not saying my mind didn't stray to Hunter numerous times the past five days, but I vied to keep it as irregularly as possible, deciding nothing but my work would be my primary focus.

When Pepper saunters back into my room, leaving the patio door open, I push off my chair and close it. Usually, too much quiet is my archenemy, but for the past few days, I've discovered the enjoyment you can achieve from little bouts of solitude.

Sometimes the most powerful thing you can say is nothing at all.

Pepper snags a stone-cold French fry off the room service tray before padding to my makeshift writing cave. "Did you get your manuscript in on time?"

I nod. "Yep. I emailed it to my editor this morning. The hero is no Archer Boyd, but I think the storyline will keep my readers enthralled."

"I told you you've never missed a deadline," Pepper replies, her brow arching high.

I narrow my eyes at her. "I only made it by the skin of my teeth. I've hardly slept a wink the past five days."

She tugs on a strand of my hair that hasn't been washed in nearly a week. "Even without your deadline looming, you wouldn't have been getting any sleep. You know it, and so do I."

I plop into the hard office chair the hotel chain supplies, hating the way my backside doesn't mold into the deep crevices of the padded chair as did my old writing chair.

At my request, the transport company shipped my favorite chair back to my father's residence. Until I can decide on my next move, I'm technically homeless.

"Now I just have to think of a title," I mumble after returning my focus to the only thing that will ensure I don't end up homeless and jobless.

I spin around to face the blank white page I've been staring at for the past two hours as Pepper's bare feet move soundlessly across the plush carpet. With a huff, she props her hip onto the side of my desk and purses her lips. "Do you have any idea what you want to call it, or are you just sending me into this bad boy blindfolded?"

I smile, loving that she can drag my mind away from any negativity attempting to surface in it. "I've been tossing around a few ideas, but nothing has stuck. I want the title to be mysterious and intriguing."

"Mystery Man!" Pepper pipes up, scaring the living daylights out of me.

I shake my head. "Already done by Kristen Ashley."

"Oh yeah, I love that book," she replies, smiling.

I waggle my brows. "Me too."

Pepper taps her index finger on her red-painted lips. "Mad... *man?*" I cock my brow and glare at her. "No?" she asks with a shake of her head and a cheeky grin.

When she snags my iPhone off the table and switches it on, I ask, "What are you doing?"

This is the first time my phone has been switched on the past five days. I cut off all communication after receiving a three-word text message from Hunter the night I left the cabin.

It simply said, *I'm sorry, Paige.*

I try to pretend my lack of electronic communication is to spite Hunter, but in reality, I know he's capable of reaching me, switched-off phone or not. I merely turned it off to stop myself from messaging him.

I've undertaken numerous personal battles the past few days about whether I should contact him to negate the false statement I gave him the last time we talked. The only thing that has stopped me is my pride... and perhaps a little bit of bitchiness.

When my phone fails to ding, indicating it has a new voicemail or text message, I slump deeper into my chair as rejection maims my already disfigured heart. Half of me tries to pretend I don't give two hoots about Hunter, where the other half—mainly the writing half —is dying to know if he read the manuscript for *Spy Thy Neighbor*.

I poured my soul into that book. The promise I made to my mom to live the life I want to live, not the one I felt compelled to live because of my family name, Riley's betrayal, and the most important of all—how I fell in love with a bearded man who lived in the glass house next door.

If I did my job as a writer, Hunter would no longer have any doubts about my intentions. He'd realize his assumptions were wrong and that I was with him because I wanted to be with him.

He also should have manned up and apologized in person.

Obviously, my writing isn't quite the caliber I thought it was.

"Oh, here we go," Pepper says, drawing my thoughts back into the present. "Dr. Google has supplied us with a broad range of words matching mystery. We have puzzle, conundrum, riddle, enigma, problem—"

For the first time in days, my heart beats faster. "Enigma," I say, testing the word out for size. "I like that. It's mysterious, dark, and alluring... just like my main character."

A broad grin etches onto Pepper's mouth. "It has a sexy feel to it too. Like you're expecting to meet Mr. Dark and Handsome between the pages."

I smile. "That is the *exact* response I want from my readers, so I guess that's it. *Enigma*."

"And who says Google is hopeless?" Pepper places my phone back onto my desk just as a knock taps on my suite's door. Her face brightens as excitement sparks in her eyes.

"Don't get too excited. Cabana boys don't do house calls. It's probably just room service coming to collect their cart."

With a pout, she pushes off the desk and moseys to the entryway. I gather some small bills from my purse in the desk drawer before following her.

My steps falter, closely followed by my breathing when my eyes lock in on a pair of murky blue eyes I'll never forget. *Hunter.*

His eyes are plagued with dark circles and crammed with remorse, and his beard is scruffy and unkempt. Even heartbroken and still harboring anger at him, I hate seeing him hurt.

Pepper's eyes bounce between Hunter and me like she's watching a tennis match between Roger Federer and Novak Djokovic. When she catches Hunter's curious glare, she mumbles. "I'll be... *downstairs.*"

She snags her purse off the entryway table, glides past Hunter, and slips out the door. My lips struggle to hold back a smile when she silently mouths, "He's so hot," behind Hunter's shoulder while hooking her thumb at him.

After doing an impromptu grind-up behind a completely oblivious Hunter, she disappears down the hall. I shake my head. Only Pepper would find time for banter during a heart-strangling confrontation.

Once she's no longer in sight, I return my focus to Hunter. When I spot a glint of amusement in his eyes, I realize he's aware of Pepper's spontaneous dance-off.

As his intoxicating smell quickly swamps the suite, I roll my shoulders while remembering the pledge I made to myself five days ago. Quirky. Eccentric. A little nutty. I'll happily accept any of those names, but doormat is one I'll no longer tolerate. Not from Riley and most definitely not from Hunter—the man who taught me I'm more than enough.

A bout of silence stretches between us, neither willing to show their hand first. It's thick and heavy, which weighs down my already crippled heart. Hunter isn't a communicator, but this should be different. Why come all the way here to continue with the same tactic that divided us to start with? If he'd just given me the chance to explain that afternoon, things wouldn't have gone as far as they did.

No longer able to stand the quiet, I mutter, "What do you want, Hunter?"

He digs his hand into the front pocket of his beloved jeans before taking a step closer to me. "I wanted to give this back to its rightful owner."

My heart whacks my ribs when he pulls out the USB I left on his kitchen counter. It holds the only digital version of *Spy Thy Neighbor*.

"Did you read it?"

He nods. "Every word, Paige." He licks his dry lips before adding, "It's *really* good. Although your readers may kill you if you blindside them with that cliffhanger." His tone is aiming for cheeky, but it still sounds pained.

Air escapes my nostrils, my body's only visible response to the hurt stabbing in my chest. "Well, I didn't know how it would end," I answer truthfully. "I hadn't planned on an ex-fiancé crashing back into the picture."

He tries to tuck it away, but I don't miss the quick flash of anger crossing his face.

"Riley isn't my fian—"

"I know. I read that," Hunter interjects as his remorseful eyes bounce between mine. "I'm so sorry, Paige. For not giving you time to explain. For the hurtful things I said."

When he cups my jaw, I beg for my body to pull away, to reject his touch, but I can't. My body doesn't care how angry he makes me, it will never deny his touch.

As his sorrow-filled eyes silently plead for forgiveness, he murmurs, "I fucked up, Paige."

"Yeah, you did." I wipe away a tear dribbling down my face from my quick head bob. "You hurt me, Hunter. Even if you didn't betray me like Riley, you still purposely set out to hurt me... that's something

I don't know if I can forget." My words come out rough, hampered by the sob sitting in the back of my throat, dying to break free. "Then you invaded my privacy. You didn't need to do that. I would have answered any questions you had, all you had to do was ask."

"I know. I made a mistake, but I'm here trying to make it right."

"Don't," I plead when he presses a kiss on the side of my mouth. "Don't," I beg again when I lean into his second kiss instead of repelling from it. "You hurt me." The pained sob of my words exposes the truth of my statement. "You're still hurting me."

An unexpected whimper seeps from my lips when his beard inches away from my cheek. Although it is what I wanted, the disappointment roaring through my body would have you believing the opposite.

With his hand still curled around my jaw, he pleads, "Tell me how to fix this. I want to fix the mistakes I made."

More tears spill from my eyes when I shake my head. "I can't tell you how to do that, Hunter. Only you can work out how to fix the wrongs you made."

After faintly cursing under his breath, he removes his cold hand from my face, scrubs it across his beard, then speaks a bunch of truths I never thought he'd share. "I thought you made me my father. That you forced me into a twisted love triangle I would have never chosen to be a part of." I try to deny his claims, but he keeps speaking before I have the chance. "For the first four weeks of my sister's life, I thought she was my daughter." His devastated laugh sucker-punches the wind out of my lungs. "Turns out the girl I had been dating since junior high was more interested in the refined Mr. Kane than me."

Instinctively, one of my hands fists his shirt while the other flattens against the area just above his heart. "They had been having an affair for a year prior to my sister's birth. The confusion about April's paternity was only discovered when she required a blood transfusion shortly after birth. Her blood type was A negative... just like my dad. That was the beginning of a bitter paternity battle."

He stops talking, and his throat works hard to swallow. "When the results came back exposing my father as April's biological parent, my mom sought the aid of a divorce attorney. I supported her all the way, more concerned about the pain she was experiencing than my own." His words are hurried like they're spilling from his mouth before he has the chance to stop them. "When my mom's lawyer filed the official divorce papers, she discovered my dad had taken everything my parents had accumulated in their twenty-year marriage and signed it all into his mistress's name months earlier. He was not only planning on leaving my mom heartbroken but broke as well."

The thick beard covering most of his face is unable to hide the tic of his jaw. "It was the night I arrived home to my mom crying over an eviction notice that my true hacking abilities became unearthed. I'd dabbled in hacking in my early teens, but nothing more than issuing free cinema tickets for my friends and me or changing the grades of some college friends' papers." A smile tugs on his lips when he continues to talk, "Within three hours, the house my parents purchased a year after marrying was returned to my mother's name, and my dad's bank accounts were wiped clean. I took every penny he had." His wild smile enlarges. "The look on his face when I told him I was the one who cleaned him out was priceless. The sweetest revenge."

He exhales a big breath before relocking his eyes with mine. "But the downfall of youth is being too cocky. I was sloppy, leaving a paper trail a mile long. I paid for the consequences of my actions. Two years in county jail."

I try to speak, to say something, but for once in my life, I'm truly at a loss for words.

After a small stint of silence, the smile Hunter was wearing earlier returns. "But even with me leaving a massive paper trail behind, they still couldn't find where I hid his money. That's when my dad got desperate. He gave me two options. Either tell him where the money was, or he would have me prosecuted."

"You chose option B," I whisper when my mouth finally cooperates with my brain.

Hunter nods. "I hated him so much, to me, there was only one option." His chest expands when he inhales a large gulp of air. "I got served a four-year sentence. I was out in two for good behavior."

"Did they ever find the money?" I query when my curiosity gets the better of me.

"No," he replies with a shake of his head. "It's been hiding in plain sight for over ten years, but since my dad is so blinded with rage, he can't see the signs flashing before his eyes."

I stare at him, shocked and confused.

"It's in a trust fund in my sister's name," he elaborates. "The interest from her sizable bank balance gets deposited into my mom's account every month. If my dad had any concerns for the welfare of his youngest child, he might have realized an unemployed divorcee left penniless after her husband fleeced her for every dime couldn't raise a small child without assistance. But since his gaze has been rapt on the wrong child the entire time, he's none the wiser to the substantial trust fund his daughter now has."

"Does he not see her?" I ask, my voice pained for April growing up without a father.

Hunter shakes his head. "No. Last I heard, my dad is in Cuba living off the money he swindled from a group of investment bankers."

"What about April's mom?"

He once again shakes his head. "She hasn't seen her since the day she left her on my mom's doorstep with a note pinned to the blanket wrapped around her."

"So your mom raised April as if she's her daughter?"

The smile that etches onto Hunter's mouth makes my knees weak. "Yep," he breathes out. "Even though April doesn't have my mom's blood running through her veins, she has part of mine, and that's enough for my mom."

"Sounds like an incredible lady," I murmur as fond memories of my mom pummel into me.

"She is."

Another stretch of thick silence greets us. Although heartbreak is still heating my blood, it isn't as potent as it was when Hunter first entered the room. It has simmered from his honesty.

After a short stint of contemplation, Hunter locks his remorseful eyes with mine. "When I read your manuscript, I realized how fucking stupid I had been. But I was hurting, Paige. I thought I'd finally allowed someone in, only to have the door slammed in my face." His eyes float between mine. "I was wrong, and I'm sorry for that."

I nod, soundlessly accepting his apology. I had forgiven him the instant the first "sorry" spilled from his lips. The final quote my mom gifted me before she passed has been running on repeat in my mind for the past five days. "You've got to take the good with the bad, smile with the sad, love what you've got, and remember what you had. Always forgive, but never forget. Learn from mistakes, but never regret."

Although I am angry at how Hunter handled the situation, I can't say I don't understand his reaction. He was hurting, believing I had betrayed him. But if he had talked to me instead of relying solely on the false documents in front of him, he would have realized I never betrayed him.

I guess I can't talk. I knew the cruel words fired off my tongue during our argument had no factual basis, but I still spat them out, forgetting that two wrongs don't make a right. If anything, I'm not the only one who deserves an apology. Hunter does as well.

"Hunter, I'm so—"

"Don't," he interrupts, his tone both stern and remorseful. "I unleashed my anger about what had happened ten years ago on the wrong person. Don't apologize for reacting the way you did, Paige. I deserved it. Hurting or not, I was in the wrong."

This time when he cups my jaw, I don't pull away. I relish it.

Another stretch of silence passes between us. It isn't riddled with anger and pain like earlier. It's filled with forgiveness and another feeling I can't quite recognize.

My eyes bounce between Hunter's as I try to comprehend what the unidentifiable glimmer in his eyes is.

When it smacks into me, I inhale a sharp breath while stepping backward. It isn't his remorseful eyes that have my heart stuttering. It's the glint he's trying to conceal with a repentant look causing my greatest concern. "You're expecting me to run."

"No, I'm not expecting you to run," he denies with a shake of his head. "But I want you to."

"Why?" My words strangle in my throat as my eyes shimmer with new tears. "And don't you dare give me the same pathetic excuse you did last time about me deserving a better man." When grimness thins his lips, I know that's the exact line he's planning to issue. "Stop, Hunter! Haven't we been through enough? Did you not read a word I wrote?"

"You wrote that before you knew I spent time in jail, before you knew of the viciousness I unleash when angry." His hard-set eyes are incapable of concealing the hurt he's feeling. "Your dad's biennial election is also looming, so it would be an injudicious time for you to expose your connection to a criminal."

"What happened to not judging a book by its cover? You don't know my dad, but you're judging him by his outward appearance. He didn't become a senator for the title or the fanfare. He did it because he loves his state and country. You might see him as a sergeant playing with his minions, but underneath the suit is a man who has many similarities to you."

Unlike Riley, my dad never used my grandfather's influence to secure his position. It was years of hard work and the love and devotion of a dedicated partner that made him the man he is today. I can see so many likenesses between my dad and Hunter. That's one of the reasons I was myself around Hunter so quickly.

And why I fell in love with him even faster than that.

I cup Hunter's jaw similarly to how he held mine. A grin tugs at my lips when his cheeks twitch from my briefest touch. "You use your appearance as a shield, but you can't fool me. Just like you saw the real Paige, I see you, Hunter. The *real* you." The cracks in my heart are filled by the massive surge of blood pumping through it. "You might have an Adonis ass and a body crafted to make my knees shake..." a smirk etches on his mouth from my playful comment, "... but it is your insides I fell in love with. Not the cover of your story. The heart of it, cheeky Hunter, playful Hunter, mysterious Hunter, and even grumpy Hunter... I love them all the same."

He draws in a long, shaky breath, showcasing that hearing my feelings in person has more impact than reading them off a sheet of paper.

The repairs to my heart increase when I notice the painful glimmer in his eyes dampens with every second we stand across from each other. I've only known him for a few short months, but I can't deny the prompts my heart is relaying.

I love him.

Unequivocally and without a doubt.

I've never had these types of feelings before. Not even for a second of the seven years I was with Riley. I knew from the moment I saw Hunter he would be my greatest risk. I just never knew it would also be so substantial.

The stranglehold that's been crippling my heart for the past five days eases when Hunter murmurs, "Don't destroy me, Paige."

"Never," I reply before sealing my lips over his.

CHAPTER TWENTY-SIX

Two hours later, I am beyond exhausted and content. After requesting VIP cabana status for Pepper and booking her own room, Hunter spent the next ninety minutes issuing his apologies with his body.

It was the most riveting apology I've ever been given, and it's seen me spend the last ten minutes working out a way to make him need to apologize again and again.

The lazy beat of my heart quickens when Hunter enters the suite's main room. He's shirtless and barefoot, and his cell phone is attached to his ear. Just like five days ago, his body is glimmering with wetness, but it isn't from a shower. It's from the exhaustive activities we've just undertaken.

A chill runs down my spine when I realize he's talking into his untraceable cell.

After scampering off the sweat-dampened sheets, I pad across the floor. The muscles in Hunter's back tense when I mold the curves of my body with his.

He tugs my arms around his waist firmer before he mutters, "Can't. He's in Vegas helping Parker secure Isaac's asset."

Once I've wrangled my hands free from his painless clutch, I slither them down the damp ridges of his abdomen before slipping past the waistband of his unbuttoned jeans. He inhales a quick, sharp breath when I stroke his cock through his jeans, priming him for round two.

The vibration of Hunter's chuckle rumbles through my chest when he says, "I'm a little *indisposed* right now."

Oh, yes, you are.

I curl around to the front of his body and stare into his murky blue eyes while lowering his zipper. He smiles a heart-stopping grin but continues with his conversation like nothing scandalous is about to occur.

I have news for him.

"That means you're fifteen hundred miles closer to Izzy than me. I've tried everyone, but being New Year's Eve, I'm running out of options. Besides, you're the only man Isaac trusts with Izzy."

His thighs prickle with goosebumps when I lower his jeans down his legs, then my eyes bulge when I realize he isn't wearing any briefs.

After lifting my hunger-filled eyes to Hunter, I whisper, "Hurry up. I want to suck your cock."

Pre-cum pools on the tip of his fat cock before he says with urgency, "I've got to go. Can you do this or not, Hugo?"

I lower myself onto my knees before wrapping my hand around the base of his throbbing shaft. His musky, manly scent deepens when I hover my lips over his glistening knob.

"I'll add it to the long list of favors," Hunter pushes out, his words so fast they sound like cracks of a whip.

Stealing his caller's chance to reply, he disconnects his call, throws his phone onto the crumpled bed, then secures my hair into a loose ponytail by using his fist as a band. A feral groan leaves his mouth when I suck down hard. I'm more than eager to see the expression that only crosses his face when he's coming.

A pleasurable shudder darts through me when his delicious cock swamps my taste buds. He tastes tangy and salty, and he smells intoxicating. It's a unique scent of cologne, soap, sweat and... *me*.

I work him hard and fast, loving the thick veins throbbing under the smoothness of his skin that's taut, jutted, and hot. When my sucks become more forceful, he rubs his thumbs over the hollows in my cheeks, softening them for the exhaustive activity they're undertaking.

I take him deeper and harder, moaning through every drop of pre-cum expelled onto my tongue.

I can't get enough. I love that I can make him so open and raw. That I can unravel him.

Tasty drops of salty goodness spurt onto my tongue as I pump him faster. My jaw is aching from sucking him so furiously, but my pace doesn't slow in the slightest. I take him to the very back of my throat before swiveling my tongue around his veiny shaft.

A rough groan tearing from his throat has Hunter's grip on my hair tightening. He's getting close to the end, and the knowledge has my nipples budding with excitement and my pussy slicking with moisture.

"Fuck, Paige." His hips jerk forward, ramming even more of his cock into my mouth. "You suck dick so good." After another three rocks of his hips, he murmurs, "In or out, baby? I can't hold back much longer." My eyes bulge when I grip his Adonis ass and thrust his hips forward. His cock is jammed down my throat, but the pain is worth the smile that etches onto his ruggedly handsome face when he says, "In it is."

The muscles in his stomach contract and his head drops back as the first spurts of cum explode onto my tongue. I struggle to swallow the thick stream pumping from his engorged knob, but I continue working my throat until every drop has been consumed.

When I slowly glide his still hard cock out of my mouth, I lift my eyes to Hunter's face. He grins a deliriously delicious smile before banding his arms around my waist and hoisting me off the ground. "My turn for dessert," he mutters into my ear while making a beeline for the bed.

I squeal into delight when he tosses me onto the springy mattress. It switches to a moan when his beard is scratching the cleft of my pussy before I've even done one whole bounce.

"Mmm," he growls against my aching slit when he discovers how aroused I am from sucking his dick. I'm dripping back to front, and despite a tinge of modesty demanding I close my legs to a ladylike width, I sweep them open so they can accommodate the wide span of Hunter's shoulders. "Do you feel it, Paige?" he asks before spearing his tongue between the wet folds of my pussy and dragging it up to my clit. "The excitement? The rush? The desire?"

Incapable of speaking, I nod before weaving my fingers through his hair that's damp at the tips.

Even with his eyes on my breasts instead of my face, Hunter must intuit my reply. "That's why your story was so good. It has the connection a couple should feel. The bond that can't be made up on a whim." He peers at me over the blobs of flesh he admires as if they're far more luscious than they are before muttering, "The love."

Before I can identify the glimmer in his eyes or demand him to spell it out for me, he bombards my clit with back-to-back rapid-fire hits. I scream his name as my body shakes through a long, revitalizing orgasm.

I've barely returned from the blessedness when Hunter crawls up my body. His beard is glistening with evidence of my arousal, and the cutest gleam is brightening his dark eyes.

"Nuh-uh," he murmurs when my spent body naturally rolls to locate a more enjoyable position. "Stay right where you are." He snags a condom from the box on the bedside table, rips it open with his teeth, then rolls it down his fat cock all the while returning my stare.

We've never done missionary.

Not once.

"Don't look so surprised, Paige. I said missionary isn't boring if you're doing with the right person."

After curling my legs around his sweat-slicked waist, he lines his cock up with the entrance of my pussy, then lifts his eyes to mine. When I jerk up my chin, silently granting him permission to enter me, he slowly notches inside me.

I dig the pads of my feet into his perfect ass when his hips sink low enough, his Apollo belt rubs my overstimulated clit. "That shouldn't feel so good."

Good lord, he brought out his shy smirk.

As he sinks my body into the mattress with perfectly constructed pumps, Hunter lowers his forehead to rest on mine. "Now I can't miss a single expression that crosses your beautiful face."

I can smell my arousal on his beard and breath, but since it's mingled with the musky scent of his overheated skin, it's almost enticing.

We breathe as one for the next several minutes while he makes love to me like actions will always speak louder than words. Since I believe that, I bestow the same amount of devotion on him that he's awarding me. I run my hands down his back before gripping his ass cheeks and giving them a gentle squeeze. He soundlessly laughs like he can't understand my obsession with his butt, but his cock also throbs, which gives away his true response.

He loves that I am as smitten by his cock and ass as he is my breasts and pussy.

He may even love something more than them.

"Slower," Hunter barks out when my excitement gets the better of me. "Nice and slow, baby. We're not fucking. *We are making love.*"

I don't know if he speaks his last four words or if my lusty head made them up, but they are the final push I need for the wave in my womb to spill over.

That, along with the words he speaks next, "You ruined me, Paige. You fucking ruined me for eternity. But despite that, I promise to love you even longer than that."

CHAPTER TWENTY-SEVEN

*I*ncapable of leashing my curiosity for a second longer, I pop my head off Hunter's chest, bend an elbow, and peer into his sexually satiated eyes. "When did you read my manuscript?"

"The day you left," he answers while scraping a hand over his unshaven jaw.

"Five days ago?" I try to keep bitchiness out of my tone. It's a waste of time. My words are smeared with annoyance.

When Hunter nods, I climb out of bed and pace the room. "Then why are you only arriving now? Why did it take you five days to realize you were wrong?" He tries to interrupt me, but I keep rambling. "You knew I did nothing wrong, yet you left me wallowing in self-pity and stupidly feeling guilty for lashing out when *you* were the one being an unreasonable asshole." My hair swishes against my naked back when I twist around to face him. "I've barely slept or eaten the last five days because of *you*. And don't think it was just my writing stopping me from ordering the biggest burger on the room service menu. It was the twisted, sick feeling in my stomach. I was lost. Hungry. Pissed off! How could you leave me hanging like that? That's the mother lode of all cliffhangers. The ultimate betrayal."

I get ready for a second tirade when Hunter slips off the bed, enters the living room of the suite, and gathers up his hemp bag he dumped near the entryway table. If he thinks he's walking out on me, he has another thing coming. I don't care what obstacles come at me, after the words he spoke last night, I will fight for us. It won't be fair, and it won't be clean, but my god, I will fight.

My clenched fists unfold when Hunter strides back into the room, his cock swinging with every step, to place a heavy rectangular object into my palm. "This is why it took me five days to get here." He nudges his head to the wrapped product. "It took a lot longer to find than I was anticipating."

Tears well in my eyes as they roam the brown paper and twine-covered parcel. From its size and weight alone, I can easily derive that it's a book.

I bite the inside of my cheek before carefully tearing open the top corner of the parcel. Time comes to a standstill when the spine of *The Weekend Romance* peeks out from behind the paper.

A tear rolls down my cheek as I lift my eyes to Hunter. He's watching me with a reserved yet poignant stare. He looks more fearful now than he did when he first arrived at my door.

After wiping away the tears from my ashen cheeks, I continue removing the paper covering my mom's book. My chest heaves up and down when I crack open the spine to discover her handwritten inscription inside, the one she wrote for me.

As a sob tears from my throat, I hug the book in close to my chest before slinging my spare arm around Hunter's broad shoulders. "You found it," I barely whisper, my lips quivering against his neck.

My body shudders in the shock that he found something I've been searching for years to find. Not trusting my legs to keep me upright, Hunter gathers me into his arms, then sits on the bed. He doesn't speak. He simply runs his hand down the curve of my back, silently supporting me.

While endeavoring to get my sobs under control, I listen to the frantic beat of his heart.

It takes several tedious minutes, but once again, it doesn't feel awkward.

It just feels right.

By the time I've settled my emotions, Hunter's torso is wet with my tears, and his eyes are more pained than earlier. "I wanted to give it to you earlier, Paige, but I didn't want you to think I was using it as leverage to force you to forgive me."

"I know," I interrupt, not requiring further explanation.

Hunter is the first person I've met who gives gifts without any stipulations attached.

That's another reason I fell in love with him so quickly and the sole reason I'll love him for eternity as well.

Six months later...

*H*unter's fingers fly over the keyboard. His brows are knitted, and his concentration is solely focused on the laptop in front of him. He is in his element.

I don't mind that he's distracted. I'm too busy drinking in the way his crisp black suit showcases his Adonis ass in panty-wetting detail to worry about his focus being on anyone but me.

His beard is neatly trimmed, and both his hair and his tattoo collection have grown the past six months. He looks so scrumptiously delicious, if we weren't in a church about to attend the wedding of his work colleague and friend, Hugo, I'd have a hard time keeping my hands off him.

The past six months have been staggering.

Day after day is filled with nothing but joy and adventure.

The morning following Hunter's reappearance, we traveled back to the cabin.

What? I had two weeks remaining on my lease so it would have been heinous of me not to take advantage of the spectacular views of Bronte's Peak.

Once my contract expired, and against Hunter's wish, I begrudgingly returned to my hometown. I lasted all of three days before I stood on the stoop of my neighbor's glass house with a suitcase in one hand and delivery slip for my writing chair in another.

I'll never forget the smile that etched onto Hunter's face when Patricia announced my arrival. It's a memory that will remain ingrained in my mind until the end of time.

Only one other memory comes in a close second. It was the day Hunter and my dad met. To say I was surprised when my dad introduced himself to Hunter like he already knew him would have been an understatement. I was flabbergasted.

When Dad noticed my shocked expression, he simply said, "Did you really think I'd let you fly to the other side of the country without first checking who you may be associating with?"

I wasn't the only one stunned by his admission. Hunter looked mortified, and while I am being forthright, he looked a little scared. Not a single spark of hesitation crossed my dad's face when he accepted Hunter's handshake, proving what I already knew. My dad would never judge a book by its cover.

My focus returns from reminiscing when Hunter says, "Done." He lifts his eyes from the laptop screen covered in code to me. "Are you sure this is what you want to do, Paige?"

I nod without hesitation. "Yep. He deserves it." I kick his black polished dress shoe with my pricy pumps. "Don't tell me you're backing down. Riley is a cheater and a retiree bank swindler. He's the very epitome of your dad."

When Hunter and I left my hotel in Santa Monica, we were inundated with reporters. Malicious questions regarding my so-called 'affair' with Hunter fired off their vindictive tongues as Hunter guided me from the hotel's foyer to an awaiting town car.

Just from the range of questions, I could tell Riley leaked news of my connection with Hunter, but instead of acknowledging that our engagement ended four months prior, he made out as if I was the adulteress in our relationship.

While I sat in the back seat of the town car, stunned like a fish out of water, Hunter hacked every newspaper in the country, endeavoring to remove the false reports made about me.

My shock at the reporters' inaccurate statements turned into awe as I watched him work his magic on a small handheld device he created. Within forty minutes, he shut down every article regarding my alleged affair for the eastern side of the country and was rapidly making his way through the west. It was only once I scooted across the leather seat and curled my hand over his did his mission stop.

"Let them run the story," I said while peering into his eyes.

Hunter's lips thinned. "No, Paige. He's making you out to be the one who betrayed him."

"So?" I shrugged. "We know that isn't true, and that's all that matters." My eyes danced between his. "Besides, I've always believed in Karma." I grinned a sly smirk. "Once the dust settles, Karma can step in." I dropped my eyes to Hunter's large black boots tapping the floor of the town car. "With a boot that big, I'm pretty sure Karma's kick will hurt."

That day was a little over six months ago. Today, Karma will finally see sunlight. Not just for me but for the hundreds of retirees Riley fleeced of their retirement funds before he relocated his financial services business to Spain.

Hunter's eyes lock with mine. "I'm not backing down. I'm just making sure you're aware once I push the enter button, everything he has will be gone. I can't bring it bac—"

His words stop when I lean over his shoulder and hit the enter button, wiping Riley clean of every penny he has. "Oops," I breathe out like my insides aren't dancing with happiness that half of Riley's money is being returned to its rightful owners while the remaining half is being distributed to numerous orphanages around the world.

Within ten seconds, Riley's *supposed* hidden bank accounts go from high seven figures to one. Three *measly* dollars.

"I had to leave enough so he could pay for a balance slip." Hunter's smooth as chocolate tone is incapable of hiding the hilarity in his voice.

After closing his laptop screen, he places it into his hemp bag before standing from the pew he's sitting on. I purr like a cat when he wraps his arms around my torso and burrows his head into my neck.

I purr louder when his beard scratches my earlobe. "You're a bad girl, Paige. I think I like this new naughty side."

Cranking back, I peer into his eyes. "Really?" I query as my hands move for the buttons of his suit.

He smiles as lust fires in his eyes. "What are you doing?"

"Research for my next novel." I walk backward, silently praying the confession chamber is unlocked and empty.

Hunter bows his brows, but it can't hide the girth growing behind the zipper of his fancy-schmancy trousers. "In a church?"

My teeth munch on my bottom lip before I nod. "I'll take you any way I can get you."

And I did. Not once but twice in the little white church in the middle of Rochdale, New York.

The next story in the Enigma series is a brand-new character, Brax.
You can find his book here:
The Opposite Effect

Facebook: facebook.com/authorshandi

Instagram: instagram.com/authorshandi

Email: authorshandi@gmail.com

Reader's Group: bit.ly/ShandiBookBabes

Website: authorshandi.com

Newsletter: https://www.subscribepage.com/AuthorShandi

The Way We Were

Sugar and Spice *

Lady In Waiting

Man in Queue

Couple on Hold

Enigma: The Wedding

Silent Vigilante

Hushed Guardian

Quiet Protector

Enigma: An Isaac Retelling

Twisted Lies *

Bound Series

Chains

Links

Bound

Restrain

The Misfits *

Nanny Dispute *

Russian Mob Chronicles

Nikolai: A Mafia Prince Romance

Nikolai: Taking Back What's Mine

Nikolai: What's Left of Me

Nikolai: Mine to Protect

Asher: My Russian Revenge *

Nikolai: Through the Devil's Eyes

<u>Trey</u> *

<u>The Italian Cartel</u>

Dimitri

Roxanne

Reign

Mafia Ties (Novella)

Maddox

Demi

Ox

Rocco *

Clover *

Smith *

<u>RomCom Standalones</u>

Just Playin' *

<u>Ain't Happenin'</u> *

<u>The Drop Zone</u> *

Very Unlikely *

False Start *

<u>Short Stories - Newsletter Downloads</u>

Christmas Trio *

Falling For A Stranger *

<u>One Night Only Series</u>

Hotshot Boss *

Hotshot Neighbor *

<u>The Bobrov Bratva Series</u>

Wicked Intentions *

Sinful Intentions *

Devious Intentions *

Deadly Intentions *

ΛΕΣΒΟΣ
Φυγή στην Ερεσό

ΑΡΤΕΜΗΣ ΑΡΤΕΜΙΑΔΗΣ

ΠΕΡΙΕΧΟΜΕΝΑ

ΠΡΟΛΟΓΟΣ

Η φυγή από την πραγματικότητα είναι το τελευταίο, αλλά και το πιο ελπιδοφόρο καταφύγιο του ανθρώπου. Σε αυτήν καταφεύγουν οι καταπιεστές και οι καταπιεσμένοι, οι ευχαριστημένοι από τη ζωή τους, αλλά και όσοι δεν γνώρισαν την ευτυχία, οι κυνηγημένοι από τις ενοχές τους, αλλά και οι εφησυχασμένοι από τη μακαριότητά τους.

Οι ήρωες του μυθιστορήματος ξεκίνησαν, ο καθένας από διαφορετική αφετηρία, να ξεφύγουν από τα προσωπικά τους προβλήματα. Πίστεψαν ότι η φυγή θα ήτανε η σωτηρία τους.

Η Σόνια προσπάθησε να απαλλαγεί από τις τύψεις της για τη συμμετοχή της σε ένα αναίτιο έγκλημα.

Ο Μάικ θέλησε να την ακολουθήσει ψάχνοντας κοντά της την ερωτική χίμαιρα. Ο Αλέξανδρος ξεκίνησε ένα μακρινό ταξίδι κυνηγημένος από το θάνατο που καραδοκούσε.

Η Λάουρα βρέθηκε σε μόνιμη φυγή, αρχικά από την άθλια ζωή της, στη συνέχεια από τη χωρίς προοπτικές ήρεμη ζωή στο απόμακρο ταβερνάκι του νησιού και, τέλος, από τη σκληρή ζωή της μεγαλούπολης, από τον ίδιο της τον εαυτό.

Η μοίρα τούς ένωσε για να βρουν καταφύγιο στην πατρίδα της Σαπφούς, την Ερεσό. Επηρεασμένοι από τη ζωή της ποιήτριας και τις θεωρίες της, αλλά και παρακολουθώντας σεμινάρια στο εκεί κέντρο διαλογισμού των Ινδών γκουρού, βρήκαν λύση στα αδιέξοδά τους επηρεασμένοι από την ποίηση της Σαπφώς, καθώς και από τις διδασκαλίες της ινδικής φιλοσοφίας.

Η απέραντη ομορφιά, αλλά και η αγριάδα του τοπίου, η ερωτική ατμόσφαιρα του νησιού, η γαλήνια και ατάραχη ζωή κοντά στους απλούς και αγαθούς ανθρώπους του χωριού και, κυρίως, η ανθρώπινη επαφή που απέκτησαν μεταξύ τους, τούς πρόσφεραν αυτό που έψαχναν στη ζωή τους.

Η φυγή έπαψε πια να έχει κάποιο νόημα για αυτούς.

ΜΕΡΟΣ ΠΡΩΤΟ

ΣΟΝΙΑ ΚΑΙ ΜΑΪΚ, ΜΙΑ ΠΡΟΒΛΗΜΑΤΙΚΗ ΣΧΕΣΗ

1

Η ΣΟΝΙΑ ΤΗΣ ΖΩΗΣ ΜΟΥ

Εκείνη τη χρονιά, ο βαρύς σκανδιναβικός χειμώνας είχε πλακώσει από νωρίς και δεν έλεγε να τελειώσει. Δυνατοί άνεμοι σταλμένοι από τον Βόρειο Πόλο λυσσομανούσανε ασταμάτητα. Η βροχή που έπεφτε μέρες τώρα άλλαζε σε χιόνι μόλις πλησίαζε στη γη και το χιόνι γινότανε αμέσως πάγος. Οι δρόμοι ήτανε ερημικοί, οι ψυχές των ανθρώπων παγωμένες. Δεν άκουγες πουθενά γέλια, αλλά μόνο κάποιους ψιθύρους να σπάνε τη νεκρική σιωπή. Παντού επικρατούσε σκότος λες και η παγωνιά δεν άφηνε να προβάλλει ο ήλιος.

Η Σόνια έγινε πανύψηλη και πανέμορφη τώρα που έφθασε στην εφηβεία. Το μπόι των κοριτσιών του βορρά, το οποίο στους Λατίνους άντρες προκαλεί ερωτικές ανατριχίλες και τούς κάνει να ποθούν τα θηλυκά σαν αφιονισμένοι, αυτές οι λυγερές όμορφες, σαν αγγελικές υπάρξεις, που με το μπόι τους γεμίζουν κρεβάτι, εδώ στην παγωμένη πατρίδα τους περνάγανε απαρατήρητες ή μάλλον πολλοί θεωρούσαν το ύψος τους μειονέκτημα για μια γυναίκα.

Οι συμπατριώτες της Σόνιας εστίαζαν τις φαντασιώσεις τους στις ολοστρόγγυλες κοντούλες, γεμάτες χυμούς υπάρξεις του Νότου, τις κατακόκκινες και πικάντικες, χαρούμενες νεαρούλες ίδιες ντοματούλες γεμιστές της γιαγιάς, που γελαστές και ζωηρούλες, καθώς ήτανε, άναβαν μέσα τους φωτιές.

Όσο ψήλωνε η Σόνια τόσο γινότανε και πιο κομπλεξική για το ύψος της. Τί κι αν η φύση τήν είχε προικίσει με μία σπάνια ομορφιά, με ένα αγγελικό πρόσωπο στεφανωμένο με το χρυσάφι των μαλλιών της, πρόσωπο στολισμένο με τα τεράστια γαλαζοπράσινα μάτια της; Τί κι αν το σώμα της είχε τις τέλειες αναλογίες; Η αδιαφορία των συμπατριωτών της, αδιαφορία, το δικό της κόμπλεξ, κόμπλεξ.

2

Ο ΜΑΪΚ ΑΝΑΠΟΛΕΙ ΤΗ ΣΟΝΙΑ

– Διατηρούσα την ανάμνησή σου άσβεστη μέσα μου, αγαπημένη μου Σόνια. Είχανε περάσει πέντε χρόνια από τότε που χάθηκες από κοντά μου– ή μήπως ήτανε και έξη, δεν είμαι σίγουρος,– όμως η μορφή σου δεν έλεγε να σβήσει με το χρόνο. Σε ένοιωθα να είσαι δίπλα μου σε κάθε στιγμή ακόμα και στα όνειρά μου. Δεν μπορώ βέβαια να πω ότι με ενοχλούσε η συνεχής παρουσία σου στο μυαλό μου, παρ όλο που ήτανε στιγμές που ευχαρίστως θα απόδιωχνα την ανάμνησή σου για να λυτρωθώ από τις εμμονές μου.

– «Καημένε Μάικ. Απόψε την ένιωθες πάλι κοντά σου. Τα χρόνια που περάσανε δεν έχουνε σβήσει καμία λεπτομέρεια από τις αναμνήσεις σου. Σου λείπει πάντα ο εύθυμος χαρακτήρας της, η αγάπη της για τη φύση και τα αδέσποτα ζωάκια που θαρρείς και έκανε συλλογή από δαύτα, οι απότομες μεταπτώσεις της διάθεσής της, ο τρόπος που απολάμβανε την κάθε ερωτική πράξη είτε γινόταν στην ακρογιαλιά είτε στο κακόφημο εκείνο ξενοδοχείο για ζευγαράκια που πηγαίνατε, είτε στον καναπέ του σπιτιού σου. Ο νους σου είναι στραμμένος σε εκείνη ακόμα και όταν πετυχαίνεις να εξασφαλίζεις μια ευκαιριακή ερωτική σύντροφο ακόμα και όταν απολαμβάνεις προσωρινά μια άλλη γυναίκα απάνω σου, κάτω σου, η και πλαγιασμένη δίπλα σου. Ώρες ώρες έχεις την πεποίθηση ότι μόνο εκείνη αντιπροσωπεύει το γυναικείο φύλο. Όλες οι άλλες είναι φαντασιώσεις που σβήνουν μόλις κορεστεί η σεξουαλική σου επιθυμία. Δεν της κράτησες κακία ακόμα και όταν σε παρέσυρε σε εκείνη την τραγική, την απίθανη περιπέτεια που συνέβαλε στη φυγή και των δυο σας. Φυγή που για εκείνη ήτανε μία λύτρωση από το αθέλητο έγκλημα, αλλά και από την πατρίδα και τους ανθρώπους της. Φυγή που για σένα ήτανε κάτι το αναπάντεχο, μια πράξη πανικού να γλυτώσεις την τιμωρία, να απομακρυνθείς από τις τύψεις σου, να χωρίσεις από εκείνη που με την προσωπικότητά της σε είχε καταντήσει πειθήνιο όργανό της. Το «έγκλημα» έμοιαζε να έχει γίνει ο συνδετικός κρίκος που θα ένωνε για πάντα τις ζωές σας. «Ή μήπως δεν ήτανε έγκλημα, μήπως κατά βάθος δεν είχε την πρόθεση να σε παρασύρει σε μια τέτοια αποτρόπαιη πράξη!

– Άβυσσος η ψυχή σου, Σόνια. Κανείς ποτέ δεν θα κατορθώσει να σε ψυχολογήσει... Θα σε κυνηγάνε για πάντα τα γεγονότα εκείνης της βραδιάς που, όσο ακριβά και να τα πληρώνεις ακόμα, ποτέ δεν θα καταφέρεις να απαλλαγείς από την τραγική τους ανάμνηση. Αγαπημένη μου, εσύ που έφερνες τον ήλιο στα σκοτάδια της ψυχής μου, εσύ που με έκανες να καταλάβω τί θα πει Ανατολίτης και τί αντιπροσωπεύει στη ζωή μας η Ανατολή, μια Ανατολή που λατρέψαμε και οι δύο μας ύστερα από μια σύντομη επίσκεψή μας εκεί. Θυμάμαι τον ενθουσιασμό σου όταν καθισμένοι στο κατάστρωμα του ποταμόπλοιου ανακαλύπταμε μαζί τη γοητεία του ηλιοβασιλέματος στο Νείλο, όταν μαγευόμασταν από τις επισκέψεις μας στους μεγαλοπρεπείς ναούς της αρχαίας Αιγύπτου, όταν εκστασιαστήκαμε στο αντίκρισμα των Πυραμίδων και στο μυστήριο της Σφίγγας. Θα μου μείνει αξέχαστη εκείνη η επίσκεψή μας στη μακρινή Ανατολή και, στη συνέχεια, στα νησιά του Αιγαίου με την ασυνήθιστη ομορφιά τους, τις ιδιομορφίες τους, τη διαφορετικότητα των άγονων τοπίων, τον πληθωρικό ερωτισμό των κατοίκων τους που ήτανε διάχυτος στα πεινασμένα για σεξ βλέμματά τους, στην ατμόσφαιρα, τους αρχαίους ελληνικούς μύθους και θρύλους, που μου διηγιόσουνα με πάθος, τους γεμάτους από περιγραφές για την υπερσεξουαλικότητα των θεών. Περιγραφές που ακόμα και σήμερα επηρεάζουν τη γεμάτη πάθος ερωτική ζωή των θνητών και συνδυάζει την ερωτική πράξη με το συναίσθημα ξεχωρίζοντας τον άνθρωπο από το ζώο μια και εκείνο λειτουργεί μόνο με το ένστικτο. Σε θυμάμαι να μού παρουσιάζεις τα συμπεράσματά σου για τη σεξουαλική πράξη που τής αποδίδουν τόση σπουδαιότητα εκεί στην Ανατολή, ώστε να την περιβάλλουν με μυστήριο, με ίντριγκες, με υποκρισία, αλλά και συναισθήματα αγάπης, να τη θεωρούν σαν την ύψιστη ηδονή τυλίγοντάς την συγχρόνως με το μανδύα του μυστηρίου, του παράνομου και της αμαρτίας. θυμάμαι εσένα που με έκανες να κατανοήσω το γυναικείο οργασμό και από πού πηγάζουν οι γεμάτες πάθος, πρωτόγονες – συχνά υστερικές – γυναικείες κραυγές που διαλαλούν αδιάντροπα την κορύφωσή του, εσένα που με έκανες να συγκινούμαι με την ποίηση και τις καλές τέχνες που απογειώνουν από τις ανθρώπινες καθημερινότητες. Ίσως για αυτό το λόγο μιλάνε μόνο σε ορισμένες ψυχές κατορθώνοντας να τις κάνουν να δακρύζουν από αισθητική συγκίνηση.

Μια μορφή ποίησης γεμάτη μυστήριο, μου ανέφερε συχνά η Σόνια μου, είναι και αυτή που σου μεταδίνει και η μονότονη, λατρευτική και αργόσυρτη φωνή του μουεζίνη – απαραίτητο χαρακτηριστικό στις χώρες της Ανατολής – που αρκεί να τήν ακούσεις μια φορά για να σφραγίσει το είναι σου και να την κουβαλάς πάντα μαζί σου. Χαράματα, πριν ακόμα αρχίσουν το κελάηδισμά τους τα πουλιά, κυριαρχεί στην πλάση το άκουσμά της που σε παρασύρει σε μιαν απόκοσμη νιρβάνα. Μια φωνή που έφθανε στ' αυτιά μας από το πουθενά, που ξεχυνόταν μέσα στην ατμόσφαιρα και ανακατευόταν με τις γεμάτες μυστήριο πρωινές ομίχλες και με τα αρώματα της φύσης που ξυπνούσε. Η θαυμαστή προσευχή χάραζε το δρόμο της μέσα από τις αποκοιμισμένες ακόμα αισθήσεις μου, σκέτο φίδι που τρυπούσε τα αυτιά μου για να εξελιχθεί στη συνέχεια σε νότες πιο χαμηλές μέχρις ότου φθάσει σε κορεσμό και σβήσει μέσα στους ήχους της φύσης, όταν εκείνη σιγά σιγά συνερχόταν από το νυχτερινό της λήθαργο σηματοδοτώντας μία θεία χάρη ξαφνική και απρόσμενη. Εξυμνούσε ο μουεζίνης μέχρι να δύσει ο ήλιος το θεό της Ανατολής, το λατρεμένο, τον αιώνιο, τον ένα και μοναδικό. Αυτόν που δεν έχει όμοιό του ούτε και ισάξιο. Και εμείς οι άπιστοι και άθεοι, νοιώθαμε, όχι χωρίς κάποια απορία, τη συγκίνηση να μας πνίγει μπροστά στο μυστηριακό μεγαλείο.

Κάτι τέτοια ποιητικά και απόμακρα σε απασχολούσαν, αγαπημένη μου Σόνια, και με παρέσυρες και εμένα στους κόσμους σου μακριά από τις μικροαστικές καθημερινές έννοιες της μικρής μας κοινωνίας. Ζήσαμε οι δυο μας έναν μεγάλο έρωτα μόνο που αλίμονο κράτησε για ένα τόσο μικρό διάστημα. Κρίμα! Και όμως αυτό το ελάχιστο διάστημα έμελλε να σημαδέψει για πάντα την ζωή μου. Και να που τώρα αισθάνομαι απελπιστικά μόνος. Κατέφυγα σε όλες τις λύσεις για να πετύχω το αντίθετο. Έφυγα μακριά σου, διάβασα, άκουσα μουσική, θαύμασα τα αριστουργήματα της τέχνης ψάχνοντας να βρω ένα καταφύγιο. Παρ' όλα αυτά το νοιώθω ότι ματαιοπονώ, μακριά σου με πνίγει ο ίλιγγος της μοναξιάς μου.

***

3

ΠΡΟΒΛΗΜΑΤΑ ΤΗΣ ΕΦΗΒΕΙΑΣ

– Γκρίνιαζε εκείνο το δειλινό η μητέρα σου στη βόλτα που έκανε παρέα με την κολλητή φίλη της την Κίρστεν Δίπλα στη λίμνη ήσουν, λέει, απόμακρη, ασυνεννόητη, ζούσες στο δικό σου κόσμο διαβάζοντας μόνο ποιήματα και έχοντας για μοναδική σου απασχόληση τα ταξίδια, τα ζώα και την ποίηση.

– Εμένα, είτε με αγνοούσε είτε προφασιζόταν ότι με αγνοεί, παραπονιόταν η μητέρα.

– Μην ανησυχείς – την παρηγορούσε η κολλητή της φιλενάδα. Όλα αυτά οφείλονται στη σύγκρουση της πρόωρης εφηβείας της με τη δική σου καθυστερημένη κλιμακτήριο. Όλα θα τα διορθώσει ο χρόνος. Μην νομίζεις, έχω και εγώ παρόμοια προβλήματα με τον γιο μου τον Γουστάβο. Είναι και αυτός μοναχικός, μελαγχολικός, αποφεύγει να συζητά μαζί μας, μένει ώρες κλεισμένος στο δωμάτιό του παρέα με το κομπιουτεράκι του και το κινητό του τηλέφωνο. Αυτή είναι η μόνη του επικοινωνία με τον έξω κόσμο. Κυρίως με απασχολεί η παντελής αδιαφορία του για το σεξ, σε σημείο που ο άντρας μου άρχισε να φοβάται ότι είναι σεξουαλικά ανώμαλος.

– Μητέρα, μού παραπονιέται συχνά. Δεν καταλαβαίνω τί μου συμβαίνει. Μου προξενούν απέχθεια τα κορίτσια που συνέχεια μου κολλάνε. Θέλουν να βγούμε σε ραντεβουδάκια, προσπαθούν να με αγκαλιάζουν, να με φιλάνε στο στόμα και εγώ νοιώθω μιαν απέραντη σιχασιά. Ανατριχιάζω στην παραμικρή επαφή μαζί τους, μου προκαλεί αηδία η μυρωδιά του ιδρώτα τους, προσπαθώ συνέχεια να αποφεύγω τις παρέες τους. Αντίθετα, βρίσκω μεγάλη ευχαρίστηση να κάνω παρέα με αγόρια, συχνά αφαιρούμαι θαυμάζοντας τα δυνατά τους σώματα, ενώ τα «ποντίκια» στα χέρια και στα πόδια τους μου προξενούν μιαν ανεξήγητη αναστάτωση. Μου αρέσει να παλεύω μαζί τους, να τα αφήνω να με νικάνε, να με ρίχνουν κάτω ακόμα και να με δέρνουν. Δεν τολμάω να ομολογήσω στον εαυτό μου ότι κάτι αφύσικο μού συμβαίνει. Νοιώθω απέραντη μοναξιά. Τα αγόρια συχνά με κοροϊδεύουν και με αποφεύγουν, τα κορίτσια τα αποφεύγω εγώ. Βοήθησέ με μητέρα, δεν είναι ζωή αυτή, μόνο σε εσένα μπορώ να στηρίζομαι.

– Έχω και τον πατέρα του που έχει αρχίσει να καταλαβαίνει τί συμβαίνει στο παιδί. Αντιδρά με βιαιότητα, άλλοτε προσποιείται τον αδιάφορο και άλλοτε τρώγεται με τα ρούχα του. Μοιάζει να αδιαφορεί για το πρόβλημα του παιδιού. Πιο πολύ τον απασχολεί το πώς θα αντιμετωπίσει την κοινωνία, τους φίλους του, τα αδέλφια του. Δεν θέλει να με ακούσει όταν ζητάω τη βοήθειά του. Εθελοτυφλεί και προσπαθεί να παρηγορήσει τον εαυτό του.

– Θα συνέλθει, όταν βρεθεί καμία «ξεπέτα» να τον συνεφέρει» μού λέει και σταματά εδώ τη συζήτηση. Εγώ τον προτρέπω να μην τον πιέζει, να μην τον αντιμετωπίζει με το γνωστό ειρωνικό του ύφος. Πανικοβάλλομαι με τις εφηβικές αυτοκτονίες που μαθαίνω ότι συμβαίνουν κάθε μέρα γύρω μας...

– Βλέπεις, λοιπόν, φιλενάδα, ότι κάθε μία έχουμε τα προβλήματά μας με την εφηβεία των παιδιών.

– Εγώ σκέφτομαι να πάω τη Σόνια στον Βέρτη, τον ψυχολόγο, να με βεβαιώσει ότι δεν πάσχει από κατάθλιψη, να ησυχάσω τουλάχιστον από αυτή την άποψη. Γιατί δεν κάνεις και εσύ μια τέτοια προσπάθεια;

– Καλή ιδέα, κάτι τέτοιο θα προσπαθήσω να κάνω και εγώ!

***

4

Η ΣΟΝΙΑ ΑΝΤΙΜΕΤΩΠΗ ΜΕ ΤΟΝ ΨΥΧΙΑΤΡΟ

– Με κουβάλησε με το ζόρι η μητέρα μου να επισκεφθώ τον Βέρτη. Υποχώρησα μόνο και μόνο για να απαλλαγώ – έστω και προσωρινά – από τη συνεχή γκρίνια της. Περιμέναμε αρκετή ώρα στο σαλόνι του, η μητέρα μου ξεφυλλίζοντας αφηρημένη ένα περιοδικό και εγώ παρατηρώντας τους συμπάσχοντες μανιοκαταθλιπτικούς, άλλον να κοιτάζει επί ώρα το ταβάνι, άλλον να τραντάζεται συχνά από διάφορα «τικ», άλλον να είναι συνέχεια δακρυσμένος και τέλος τον διπλανό μου μια να γελάει και μια να αναστενάζει δακρύβρεχτα. Επιτέλους ήρθε η σειρά μου και με βάλανε στο χώρο που εξέταζε. Σηκώθηκε και η μητέρα μου να με συνοδεύσει, αλλά η νοσοκόμα με μια ευγενική χειρονομία την απέτρεψε. Ευτυχώς! Ο Βέρτης με κάρφωνε με το βλέμμα του σιωπηλός και απόμακρος. Περνούσαν τα λεπτά γεμάτα αμηχανία, ενώ εγώ μάταια προσπαθούσα να ανταποδίδω τη ματιά του μήπως και το εκλάβει σαν αδυναμία μου.

– Λοιπόν, είπε στο τέλος, ενώ έδειχνε να τον απασχολεί περισσότερο το άναμμα της πίπας του παρά η δική μου αντίδραση. Πες μου, λοιπόν, πιο είναι το πρόβλημά σου;

– Ένοιωσα ένα κύμα θυμού να με πνίγει. Σηκώθηκα να φύγω λέγοντας ένα ειρωνικό ευχαριστώ. Με κοίταξε χαμογελαστός και επιτέλους μίλησε.

– Άκουσε καλή μου, ήρθες εδώ για να συνεργαστούμε, να βρεις λύση στα προβλήματά σου. Μίλησέ μου, λοιπόν, αν θέλεις να σε βοηθήσω. Έλα σε ακούω.

– Ξαφνικά τον συμπάθησα. Κάτι έκανε «κλικ» μέσα μου, λειτούργησε ένα είδος χημείας ανάμεσά μας, πίστεψα στην ειλικρίνειά του να με βοηθήσει, αποφάσισα να του μιλήσω.

– Γιατρέ, τελικά όσο πνίγομαι μέσα στο πέλαγος της εφηβείας, τόσο συνειδητοποιώ ότι δεν ανήκω σε αυτόν τον τόπο. Πρέπει την προηγούμενη ζωή μου να την έζησα εκεί στη Μεσόγειο, κοντά στον ήλιο, παρέα με τους ζεστούς ανθρώπους, τους ζωντανούς, τους πλημμυρισμένους από αισθησιασμό, τους φωνακλάδες, τους ανεπρόκοπους, τους ανθρώπους που εύκολα γελάνε και ακόμα πιο εύκολα κλαίνε.

Η Σόνια σταμάτησε το μονόλογό της εντυπωσιασμένη και η ίδια από τα λόγια της, κάτι κουνήθηκε στο βάθος του δωματίου και την τρόμαξε.

– Είναι ο Χανς ο γάτος, της εξήγησε ο ψυχίατρος. Μην τρομάζεις, συνέχισε για να την καθησυχάσει.

– Το βλέπω ότι δεν ανήκω στον εδώ κόσμο, συνέχισε. Είμαι η μετεμψύχωση μίας κόρης του ήλιου και της θάλασσας, ακούω Λάτιν μουσική και ανατριχιάζω σύγκορμη, Νοιώθω το αίμα μου να βράζει, το κορμί να σείεται και να κουνιέται, ολοκλήρωσε.

Τώρα κανείς δεν διέκοψε τη σιωπή που έπεσε. Ακουγότανε μόνο το τραγούδι της φωτιάς στο τζάκι. Το χιόνι φάνταζε να πέφτει πυκνό και βελούδινο πίσω από την τζαμαρία. Το ρολόι του τοίχου σήμανε τελετουργικά το τέλος της ώρας.

– Συμφωνώ ότι οι περισσότεροι από εμάς εδώ θα θέλαμε να είμαστε

Λατίνοι – αν φυσικά, δεν ήμασταν αυτοί που είμαστε. Η τάση της φυγής κυριαρχεί σε πολλούς από εμάς. Όμως ο χρόνος μας τελείωσε, ραντεβού σε μία εβδομάδα, είπε.

Ο ψυχίατρος σηκώθηκε και της έσφιξε το χέρι, σηκώθηκε και εκείνη να φύγει, η επαφή των χεριών τους της ζέστανε λίγο το μέσα της.

– Θα φύγω, δεν τον μπορώ τον βορρά. Θα πάω να ζήσω εκεί από όπου νοιώθω ότι κατάγομαι, είπε, καθώς η παγωνιά την χτύπησε καταπρόσωπο μόλις βγήκε από το ιατρείο.

– Δεν ανήκω εδώ, επανέλαβε μέσα της.

– Εδώ οι άνθρωποι είναι ψυχροί και ουδέτεροι, αδιαφορούν για το διπλανό τους και αυτό το ονομάζουν πολιτισμό, πρόσθεσε. Οι έρωτές τους είναι πιο ψυχροί και από αυτό το χιόνι. Οι οικογένειες δημιουργούνται για να διαλυθούν μόλις τα παιδιά ενηλικιωθούν. Οι γονείς και τα παιδιά αποξενώνονται, ίσως να τηλεφωνιούνται για τις εορτές. Οι διασκεδάσεις γίνονται και αυτές μέσα στην ψύχρα, στηρίζονται αποκλειστικά στα ναρκωτικά και το οινόπνευμα. Δεν υπάρχει αίσθημα, δεν υπάρχει ρομαντισμός. Το σεξ είναι και αυτό μέρος της ρουτίνας, κάτι χωρίς σημασία, σαν μία χειραψία, σαν ένα φιλί στο μάγουλο.

Βάδιζε με γρήγορα βήματα. Τα μακριά, ατελείωτα, πόδια της ήτανε μαθημένα από χιόνια. Δεν γλίστραγε, απλώς κρύωνε. Όμως η απόφασή της την είχε ενθουσιάσει, έδινε φτερά στα πόδια της να τρέξει, να μην χάσει λεπτό, να φύγει μακριά. Οι σκέψεις καλπάζανε μέσα της.

– Τέλος τα συνεχή σκοτάδια, τόνισε. Θέλω ήλιο και ζέστη. Τέλος οι ψυχροί άνθρωποι. Θέλω αίσθημα και φλογερά πάθη. Τέλος τα ανόητα σπορ να σέρνεσαι ατελείωτες ώρες μέσα στο χιόνι και τους πάγους. Θέλω μπάνια στη θάλασσα και ψήσιμο στον ήλιο. Με αφήνει αδιάφορη το σεξ που εξαρτάται από το πόσο έχει μεθύσει ο τυχαίος ερωτικός σύντροφος της βραδιάς. Θέλω έρωτα παθιασμένο, θέλω σεξ να ξεχειλίζει από συναισθήματα, να το απολαμβάνω κάτω από τα άστρα, στις αμμουδιές, στο πάτωμα τού σπιτιού, στην κουζίνα, παντού. Τον θέλω απρογραμμάτιστο, άγριο και γεμάτο πάθος. Νvα φτάνω στα άκρα της αντοχής.

Επιστρέψανε αμίλητες, μάνα και κόρη βαδίζοντας ζωηρά μέχρι που φτάσανε στο σπίτι. Η μητέρα, μόλις μπήκανε στο φιλόξενο σαλόνι τους, άναψε το τζάκι και κάθισε βιαστικά στο πιάνο της. Είχε την ελπίδα ότι μόνον έτσι θα απέφευγε τις ατέρμονες συζητήσεις με τη Σόνια και τα προβλήματά της. Όμως ματαιοπονούσε. Η Σόνια είχε πάρει τις αποφάσεις της και ανυπομονούσε να τις ανακοινώσει στη μητέρα της.

– Μητέρα, πρέπει να σου μιλήσω, έχω αποφασίσει να πάρω την ζωή μου στα χέρια μου, έσπευσε να μιλήσει..

– Έλα τώρα, μωρέ Σόνια. Άσε με να γαληνέψω λίγο στο πιάνο. Μη μου αρχίσεις πάλι τα ίδια και τα ίδια. Συνέχισε με τον κύριο Βέρτη και θα δεις ότι σύντομα θα συνέλθεις.

– Μητέρα, θα φύγω. Δεν την μπορώ τη σκοτεινιά σας εδώ και τους μονόχνοτους ανθρώπους. Θα πάω στην Ανατολή, να ζεσταθεί η ψυχή μου, να ζήσω ανάμεσα σε κόσμο γεμάτο αυθορμητισμό, κόσμο χαρούμενο και ανέμελο, σε ανθρώπους που γελάνε και κλαίνε με το παραμικρό, που αγαπάνε και μισούνται συχνά χωρίς σοβαρό λόγο, ανθρώπους που ζούνε μια έντονη ζωή.

– Φύγε αν θες. Δεν σε κρατάει κανείς. Μόνο πρόσεχε μην το μετανιώσεις.

Η μητέρα της απάντησε αδιάφορα προσπαθώντας να μπλοφάρει. Πόσο λίγο την ήξερε, πόσο ξένη τής ήτανε αυτή η μητέρα!

*****

5

ΕΝΑ ΕΓΚΛΗΜΑ ΧΩΡΙΣ ΔΟΛΟΦΟΝΟ

Ο Μάικ συνέχιζε τις αναμνήσεις του.

– Είχα φτάσει απρόσμενα να τη βρω στο ξενοδοχείο, εκεί όπου την είχανε παρασύρει οι γονείς της για την «κυνηγητική» τους εκδρομή.

– Έλα μια τελευταία φορά μαζί μας πριν πάρεις την οριστική σου απόφαση και μας εγκαταλείψεις, τής έταξε η μάνα της.

Η Σόνια μου είχε γίνει έμμονη ιδέα. Έπαιζε μαζί μου σαν τη γάτα με το ποντίκι. Άλλοτε τρυφερή και αγαπησιάρα και άλλοτε χωρίς λόγο απόμακρη και ψυχρή. Δεν άντεχα να είμαι μακριά της για πολύ. Εκείνες οι τάσεις της για φυγή με είχανε αναστατώσει. Φοβόμουνα! Με έπιανε πανικός με την ιδέα ότι θα μπορούσε ξάφνου να εξαφανιστεί από τη ζωή μου. Πήγα να τη συναντήσω στην οικογενειακή εκδρομή όπου είχε καταφύγει. Δεν μπορώ να πω ότι η υποδοχή που μού έκανε ήτανε ιδιαίτερα θερμή. Είχε εκείνο το γνωστό ύφος το απόμακρο και προβληματισμένο, το σχεδόν ονειροπόλο. Προσπάθησα να τήν κάνω να μου ανοίξει την καρδιά της μήπως και ξαλαφρώσει από τους εφιάλτες της., και για μεγάλη μου έκπληξη εκείνη ανταποκρίθηκε. Σιγοπερπατούσαμε στην όχθη της λίμνης και μαζί με το θρόισμα του ανέμου άκουγα την ψιθυριστή φωνή της. Μου μιλούσε με ένα ύφος εμπιστευτικό, σαν να μού αποκάλυπτε ένα μεγάλο μυστικό. Άρχισε με την περιγραφή της επίσκεψης στο γιατρό τον Βέρτη και την εξομολόγηση που τού έκανε. Ύστερα συνέχισε με τον αποχαιρετισμό με τη μητέρα της, η οποία το μόνο που τής ζήτησε ήτανε να τη συνοδεύσει στην περίφημη εκδρομή που είχε προγραμματίσει με την παρέα της πριν πάρει την τελική της απόφαση, και κατέληξε με τη φρίκη της περιγραφής των σκηνών που παρακολούθησε αντάμα με το μικρό της ξάδελφο τον Γουστάβο. Τέλος, διστακτικά προχώρησε στην περιγραφή της σεξουαλικής της εμπειρίας με το μικρό. Μιλούσε σα να περιέγραφε μια φυσιολογική εξέλιξη των γεγονότων χωρίς να δείχνει να ενδιαφέρεται για τις δικές μου αντιδράσεις. Τότε ήτανε που κατάλαβα ότι η Σόνια δεν θα γινότανε ποτέ δική μου, διότι ο εγωισμός της δεν θα τής επέτρεπε ποτέ να ανήκει πουθενά. Την συνόδευσα προβληματισμένος στο ξενοδοχείο και καθόμαστε σιωπηλοί σε δύο πολυθρόνες αποφεύγοντας να διασταυρώσουμε τα βλέμματά μας. Ξάφνου, εμφανίστηκε ο μικρός κραδαίνοντας ένα όπλο.

– Είναι το όπλο του παππού. Το βρήκα κρυμμένο στο συρτάρι του, είπε με ύφος θριαμβευτικό. Πάμε να τους σκοτώσουμε όλους και να τους εξαφανίσουμε μέσα στη λίμνη, συνέχισε με τα χέρια τρεμάμενα από μίσος.

Στα μάτια της Σόνιας φάνηκε μια περίεργη αστραπή σα να της κατέβηκε μια ξαφνική ιδέα.

– Εντάξει Γουστάβο, τού είπε. Όμως, ας κάνουμε πρώτα μια προπόνηση. Θα βάλουμε στο «μύλο» του πιστολιού μία σφαίρα και τις υπόλοιπες θέσεις θα τις αφήσουμε κενές. Ύστερα, θα πυροβολούμε ο ένας τον άλλο με τη σειρά για να δούμε ποιοί είναι οι τυχεροί και ποιος ο άτυχος. Άμα είσαι άντρας και αρκετά γενναίος έλα να βάλουμε στοίχημα...

Ο μικρός χωρίς να έχει πολυκαταλάβει έδειξε να συμφωνεί και τότε η Σόνια έβαλε τη μοναδική σφαίρα στο όπλο. Μού έγνεψε να γυρίσω το «μύλο» ώστε η σφαίρα να βρεθεί στην τελευταία θήκη και υπολογίζοντας ποιο θα είναι το θύμα μού έδωσε το όπλο να πυροβοληθώ πρώτος. Ακούστηκε ένας ξερός ήχος του πιστολιού που δεν είχε σφαίρα. Ακολούθησε ο μικρός με τρεμάμενα χέρια, τίποτα και αυτός. Ούτε βέβαια η Σόνια πέτυχε το εαυτό της. Συνεχίσαμε με ένα δεύτερο γύρο γνωρίζοντας ότι πλησίαζε η μεγάλη στιγμή. Ο Γουστάβος είχε τώρα αναθαρρήσει, η παιδική του επιπολαιότητα τον έκανε να νομίσει, δεν ξέρω και εγώ τί... Η πιστολιά που ακολούθησε, τράνταξε το μικρό χώρο. Στον τοίχο απέναντι από τον Γουστάβο σχηματίστηκε ένας μικρός λεκές από αίμα... Τότε, εγώ παρασυρμένος από το ένστικτο αυτοσυντήρησης, έβγαλα το μαντήλι μου και σκούπισα καλά το όπλο. Ύστερα το στερέωσα με τρόπο στο νεκρό χέρι του παιδιού. Αυθόρμητα σηκώσαμε το πτώμα του νεκρού παιδιού και με χίλιες δύο προφυλάξεις το μεταφέραμε στην όχθη της λίμνης απ᾽ όπου και το πετάξαμε στο νερό. Κατόπιν χωρίσαμε πανικόβλητοι. Η Σόνια γύρισε στο δωμάτιό της και εγώ πήρα το δρόμο για το αεροδρόμιο να φύγω με την πρώτη πτήση. Πέρασε κάμποση ώρα. Κάποια πουλιά πετάξανε πάνω από τα παγωμένα νερά της λίμνης κράζοντας αλαφιασμένα, τα κυνηγόσκυλα αρχίσανε να γαβγίζουν προσπαθώντας να ελευθερωθούν από τις αλυσίδες τους. Όμως και αυτά δεν επέμειναν για πολύ. Ακολούθησε μια νεκρική ησυχία. Τα αγριοπερίστερα του βορρά παραξενεύτηκαν με το θέαμα. Παρατηρούσαν κάτι που επέπλεε πάνω στη λίμνη, κάτι μεγάλο και ακίνητο. Όρμησαν καταπάνω του με φόρα. Δεν υπολόγιζαν κανένα κίνδυνο μπροστά στην πείνα τους. Τα νερά είχανε αρχίσει να παγώνουν, σε λίγο οι πάγοι θα σκέπαζαν τα πάντα και θα χάνανε την ευκαιρία να χορτάσουν την πείνα τους. Πέσανε σαν βολίδες πάνω στα ανοιχτά του μάτια και τα εξαφάνισαν στο λεπτό. Έπειτα προχώρησαν με κραυγές θριάμβου και με μανία άρχισαν να ξεσκίζουν τις παγωμένες σάρκες του. Σε λίγο το πτώμα του δεκαπεντάχρονου Γουστάβου είχε μετατραπεί σε άμορφη σάρκα, τα ρούχα το σε χιλιοτρυπημένα κουρέλια. Από το τσιμπούσι δεν απουσίασαν και τα ψάρια της λίμνης. Αυτά θα συνέχιζαν το μακάβριο έργο τους μέσα στη θανάσιμη σιωπή που επικρατούσε κάτω από τους πάγους.

– Καλλίτερα έτσι παρά να τον φάνε τα σκουλήκια, μονολόγησε με κυνισμό η Σόνια, που παρατηρούσε με αφύσικη αδιαφορία το θέαμα από το μισάνοιχτο παντζούρι του παραθύρου στο δωμάτιό της όπου είχε επιστρέψει.

Κατέβηκε περπατώντας στα νύχια των ποδιών της στον κάτω όροφο μην και την πάρει κανένας είδηση. Όμως τα τρία ζευγάρια, οι γονείς και οι θείοι της Σόνιας παρέα με τους γονείς του Γουστάβου, δεν υπήρχε περίπτωση να την αντιληφθούν. Συνέχιζαν το ομαδικό τους όργιο – άλλωστε γι' αυτό είχανε κάνει αυτή την εκδρομή, όχι για το κυνήγι που είχανε προφασισθεί – τρυγώντας ο ένας το κορμί του άλλου και στενάζοντας ελαφρά από το πάθος, ένα πάθος συγκρατημένο και πολιτισμένο κατά πως συνηθίζεται σε εκείνα τα βόρεια μέρη. Η Σόνια είχε συγκλονιστεί, όταν ένα προηγούμενο βράδυ, αγριεμένη από τους απόκοσμους αναστεναγμούς που αντηχούσαν στο μικρό ξενοδοχείο, είχε πάρει το νεαρό Γουστάβο από το χέρι και μαζί αντίκρισαν από μια χαραμάδα της πόρτας το «παιχνίδι» των μεγάλων. Τα δύο παιδιά παρακολούθησαν αποσβολωμένα σε κάθε του λεπτομέρεια εκείνο το «παιχνίδι» μέχρις ότου η Σόνια τράβηξε λαχανιασμένη το μικρό από το χέρι. Τον πήγε σπρώχνοντας στο δωμάτιό της και τον έριξε στο κρεβάτι. Ο μικρός τα είχε χαμένα, κάποια στιγμή προσπάθησε να αποφύγει τη δοκιμασία, αλλά γρήγορα οι εφηβικές ορμόνες τον πρόσταξαν διαφορετικά. Βιαστικά το ζευγαράκι άρχισε να επαναλαμβάνει το παράδειγμα των μεγάλων.

– Σαν τα ζώα παρακινούμενοι μόνο από το ένστικτο, χωρίς κανένα αίσθημα χωρίς να νοιώθουμε το παραμικρό ο ένας για τον άλλον, αναλογιζόταν αργότερα η Σόνια.

Όμως σύντομα κατάλαβε ότι ο ευκαιριακός ερωτικός της σύντροφος δεν ανταποκρινότανε στα χάδια της και στην προσπάθειά της να τον ερεθίσει. Τον φιλούσε σε όλο του το κορμί, τον παρακινούσε με λόγια τολμηρά, όμως εκείνος.. τίποτα. Στο τέλος απηυδισμένη έφυγε από πάνω του και ξάπλωσε δίπλα του. Χωρίς καν να το συνειδητοποιήσει άρχισε να του λέει λόγια προσβλητικά. Μέχρι και … «αδελφή» τον είπε! Εκείνος σηκώθηκε και κλαίγοντας βγήκε από το δωμάτιο. Ο Μάικ έφερνε συχνά στο νου του εκείνες τις εφιαλτικές στιγμές του μακάβριου παιχνιδιού που ακολούθησαν...

Ακόμα δεν μπορώ να εξηγήσω τον παραλογισμό της πράξης που κάναμε οι δύο μας. Η Σόνια με παρέσυρε, εγώ μετατράπηκα σε άβουλο όργανό της, δεν την εμπόδισα, αλλά σαν ναρκωμένος υπέκυψα στις προσταγές της. Κουβαλήσαμε το πτώμα του Γουστάβου στην όχθη της λίμνης και το πετάξαμε μέσα στο νερό. Με κοίταξε άγρια αμέσως μετά σαν να έγιναν όλα από δική μου πρωτοβουλία. Ο κόσμος σκοτείνιασε μέσα μου, έφυγα πανικόβλητος Η Σόνια δεν μπορούσε να ξεχάσει τις στιγμές που έμεινε μόνη να ατενίζει το θέαμα έξω από το παράθυρο. Τα πουλιά που πετούσανε κράζοντας απαίσια, το χιόνι που έπεφτε ακατάπαυστα, τα σύννεφα που παίζανε κυνηγητό με τον άνεμο. Μέσα της ένοιωθε την απουσία κάθε συναισθήματος. Ούτε λύπη, ούτε τύψεις, ούτε κανένα ίχνος συγκίνησης. Δεν άργησε την πιάσει πανικός, να νοιώσει την ανάγκη της φυγής. Το ίδιο συναίσθημα – ίσως πιο δυνατό τώρα – που την ταλάνιζε εδώ και καιρό. Άφησε δύο λέξεις πάνω στο κομοδίνο της.

– Μάνα φεύγω, όπως σού είχα πει.

Τίποτε άλλο. Μάζεψε τα πράγματά της και κατευθύνθηκε όσο πιο αθόρυβα μπορούσε στην έξοδο. Κάπως έτσι χώρισαν οι δρόμοι τους. Η Σόνια είχε ξεγράψει για πάντα τους δικούς της, δεν είχε καμία διάθεση να τους ξαναδεί πια.

* * *

6

ΓΙΑΤΡΕ ΒΟΗΘΕΙΑ!

Ο γιατρός Βέρτης δεν έδειξε καμία έκπληξη όταν άκουσε εκείνη την ακατάλληλη ώρα το δυνατό χτύπο στην πόρτα του. Δεν ήτανε η πρώτη φορά που κάποιος απελπισμένος από τους ασθενείς του, κάποιος κυνηγημένος από τον ίδιο τον εαυτό του, θα ζητούσε τη βοήθειά του. Η έκπληξή του ήτανε όταν αντίκρισε τη Σόνια, η οποία αναμαλλιασμένη και ξεπαγιασμένη όρμησε μέσα στο ιατρείο.

– Γιατρέ βοήθεια, ψιθύρισε με σβησμένη φωνή πριν σωριαστεί στον καναπέ.

Άρχισε να τού διηγείται την εμπειρία της εκδρομής και το συγκλονισμό που ένιωσε παρακολουθώντας τους γονείς και τους φίλους τους στις ερωτικές στιγμές τους. Δεν τόλμησε ακόμα να προχωρήσει στην περιγραφή του τέλους του Γουστάβου.

– Δεν είναι αηδιαστικές, γιατρέ, οι σκηνές που σού διηγήθηκα; Εσύ πώς θα τις αντιμετώπιζες;

– Ας μην είμαστε απόλυτοι στις κρίσεις μας, γλυκιά μου. Η κάθε φάση της ζωής έχει και τα άγχη και τις ιδιομορφίες της. Προσπάθησε να κατανοήσεις αυτούς τους ανθρώπους. Βλέπουν με την κάθε μέρα που περνάει τη ζωή τους να πλησιάζει προς το τέλος της. Δεν υπάρχει μέλλον για αυτούς, προσπαθούν να επωφεληθούν από το παρόν για όσο αυτό διαρκεί. Εδώ που ζουν υποφέρουν από την έλλειψη δυνατών συγκινήσεων. Έρωτες και πάθη, χτυποκάρδια και αγωνίες, φιλοδοξίες, σχέδια και όνειρα τρελά, ακόμα και αν τα έζησαν ανήκουν πια στο παρελθόν. Είναι γλυκές αναμνήσεις για όσους τα δοκίμασαν, αλλά και απωθημένα όνειρα για τους άλλους τους περισσότερους που απλώς τα έζησαν με τη φαντασία τους. Το συζυγικό σεξ, για όσους επιμένουν σε αυτό, είναι ένα αναμασημένο φαγητό, αναμασημένο και άνοστο. Όσοι διατηρούν ψευδαισθήσεις για κάποια τελευταία εμπειρία, καινούργια και συγκλονιστική φτάνουν στα άκρα μήπως και την πραγματοποιήσουν. Ας μην τους κατακρίνουμε. Μαζί με τα χρόνια που περνάνε ελαχιστοποιούνται και οι δυνατότητες για καινούργια σχέδια, για όνειρα για δυνατές συγκινήσεις. Και οι άνθρωποι μέσα στην απελπισία τους καταφεύγουν σε διάφορες λύσεις, την αυταπάτη, την άρνηση κάθε κανόνα ηθικής συμπεριφοράς, τον ασκητισμό και τελικά τη φυγή. Οι δικοί σου και οι φίλοι τους επέλεξαν τη φυγή για να ανακουφίσουν τις ανησυχίες της ηλικίας τους. Κατέφυγαν στη λεγομένη εμπειρία του τίποτα, ενός κενού που υποσκάπτει ύπουλα τα θεμέλια της ύπαρξής τους. Πελαγοδρομούν στην αναζήτηση νοήματος για τη ζωή. Εσείς οι νέοι δεν φαντάζεστε πόσο σκληρό είναι να αισθάνεται κανείς ότι πλησιάζει το τέλος του, χωρίς να έχει προλάβει να χορτάσει τη ζωή, όπως την είχε φανταστεί, με τις άπειρες συγκινήσεις που θα μπορούσε να τού προσφέρει, γιατί σας είναι δύσκολο να τους κατανοήσετε.

Η Σόνια τον άκουγε βυθισμένη σε περισυλλογή. Άρχισε να βλέπει ότι κάθε πρόβλημα έχει δύο όψεις. Αναθάρρησε διαπιστώνοντας ότι ο Αλέξανδρος είχε την ικανότητα να την κάνει να δει τη ζωή από την σκοπιά του ώριμου ανθρώπου. Παίρνοντας θάρρος, προχώρησε ακάθεκτη τη διήγησή της με την περιγραφή της στιγμιαίας επαφής της με τον Γουστάβο για να καταλήξει στην εξομολόγησή της.

– Με είχε καταλάβει η διάθεση να κάνω κάτι ακραίο, ίσως ένα φόνο, να σκοτώσω κάποιον χωρίς να μου φταίει σε τίποτα, είπε. Με πιάνει αυτή η επιθυμία, κυρίως όταν ξυπνάω το πρωί από έναν ύπνο έτσι κι αλλιώς ταραγμένο από εφιάλτες. Θέλω να σκοτώσω, θέλω να ξεράσω ελπίζοντας ότι μαζί με το διαταραγμένο στομάχι μου θα ξαλαφρώσει και το διαταραγμένο μου μυαλό. Θέλω να ξεφύγω από την τωρινή μου πραγματικότητα, θέλω να φύγω, να κρυφτώ...

Συνέχισε περιγράφοντας το θανάσιμο «παιχνίδι» των τριών τους και την τραγική του κατάληξη.

– Τώρα, εκτός από τις τύψεις που με κυνηγάνε, νοιώθω και μία απέχθεια για την σεξουαλική πράξη. Στο μυαλό μου έρχεται η λαχανιασμένη ανάσα του μικρού, οι γεμάτες αμηχανία κινήσεις του. Παγώνω αμέσως κάθε φορά που νοιώθω κάποιον ερεθισμό, στο μυαλό μου συνεχίζουν να έρχονται εκείνες οι σκηνές και αηδιάζω. Γιατρέ, φοβάμαι ότι έχω γίνει ψυχρή και αυτό με γεμίζει πανικό.

– Παρασύρθηκες από ένα στιγμιαίο πάθος, θέλησες να εκτονώσεις το μίσος σου για τους μεγάλους αφαιρώντας τη ζωή του Γουστάβου, έσπευσε να πει ο γιατρός. Δεν το τόλμησες μόνη σου, παρέσυρες και τον Μάικ που θύμα του έρωτά του σε ακολούθησε σ' αυτόν τον κατήφορο. Τώρα νομίζεις ότι θα γλυτώσεις με τη φυγή. Μια φυγή που την δικαιολογείς με χίλιους δύο τρόπους.

Ο γιατρός δίστασε πριν συνεχίσει, όμως τελικά το αποφάσισε.

– Έλα να φύγουμε μαζί, αν θέλεις., της πρότεινε. Είναι για μένα μια απόφαση που την έχω πάρει και εγώ από καιρό χωρίς να την πραγματοποιώ κυριευμένος από την αβουλία της ηλικίας. Να που εσύ μού δίνεις την ευκαιρία. Θα ταξιδέψουμε μαζί και συγχρόνως με την αλλαγή περιβάλλοντος θα προσπαθήσω από μέρους μου σιγά σιγά να ξαναφέρω τη γαλήνη μέσα σου. Σού υπόσχομαι ότι θα κάνω ό, τι περνάει από το χέρι μου...

Έτσι που αντίκρισε τη γλύκα του προσώπου της, με αποτυπωμένη την αγωνία στα όρια πανικού, ένοιωσε την ανάγκη να την αγκαλιάσει και να την χαϊδέψει τρυφερά. Όμως αμέσως κρατήθηκε. Η δεοντολογία του επαγγέλματός του δεν επέτρεπε τρυφερότητες και ιδιαίτερες σχέσεις με τους «ασθενείς». Πολλοί, όταν τούς έδινες κάποια ένδειξη ιδιαίτερης συμπάθειας, έπαιρναν αμέσως θάρρος. Πολλοί αποκτούσαν πλήρη εξάρτηση από το γιατρό τους, φαντασιώνονταν διάφορες καταστάσεις και κατέληγαν πολλές φορές να παρασύρουν και το γιατρό σε ένα δεσμό χωρίς νόημα και συχνά με πολύ κακή κατάληξη. Ωστόσο, το διαισθανότανε ότι με τη Σόνια τα πράγματα θα μπορούσανε να είναι διαφορετικά. Συχνά την έφερνε στο νου του μετά την πρώτη τους συνάντηση και ένοιωθε να υπάρχει ανάμεσά τους μια ταύτιση. Η ανάγκη της φυγής, όπως τού την είχε περιγράψει και εκείνη, είχε φέρει στην επιφάνεια τα παλιά δικά του όνειρα.

– Να ένας άνθρωπος που θα μπορούσε να με συντροφέψει στη φυγή που ονειρεύομαι. Ίσως να είναι ο ιδεώδης σύντροφος για την τελευταία περιπέτεια της ζωής μου, μονολογούσε.

Ο Βέρτης ήτανε άνθρωπος των γρήγορων αποφάσεων. Αα αποτολμούσε το πρώτο βήμα. Την έπιασε από τα δύο χέρια και όταν ένοιωσε κάποια σημάδια ανταπόκρισης την πήρε στην αγκαλιά του.

– Λέγε με Αλέξανδρο, είπε στοργικά!

***

7

ΤΟ ΠΡΟΒΛΗΜΑ ΤΟΥ ΓΙΑΤΡΟΥ

Είχε και ο Αλέξανδρος τα προβλήματά του, για τα οποία έψαχνε συνέχεια να βρει κάποια διέξοδο. Οι στιγμές που τον έπνιγε η τρομερή μοναξιά γινόντουσαν όλο και πιο συχνές. Η αίσθηση του κενού, η βεβαιότητα ότι η ύπαρξή του βάδιζε καλπάζοντας προς την ανυπαρξία, τον βύθιζαν όλο και πιο συχνά σε μια άβουλη απελπισία.

Οι παρατεινόμενες ώρες της ανίας τον οδηγούσαν – το ένοιωθε – στο επόμενο βήμα, την κατάθλιψη. Πλησίαζε ο Δεκέμβριος, ο μήνας που η θλίψη γιγαντώνεται μέσα στην ψυχή αυτών που δεν έχουν λόγο να περιμένουν τις γιορτές. Ο καιρός, που όλο και χειροτέρευε, έπαιζε και αυτός το ρόλο του στην ψυχική του διάθεση. Άρχισε να ενδιαφέρεται καθημερινά – όπως πολλοί συνομήλικοί του – με την πρόβλεψη του καιρού ή να παρακολουθεί τις ειδήσεις που δεν τον αφορούσαν μια και ενδιαφερόταν για άλλα, πιο ουσιαστικά, γεγονότα. Οι κλιματικές αλλαγές έμοιαζαν να έχουν πάρει μια σημαίνουσα θέση στη ζωή του. Το σώμα του τού έστελνε τα πρώτα θλιβερά σημάδια για τα χρόνια που περνούσαν καλπάζοντας. Τελευταία ένοιωθε μια συνεχή κούραση. Τον τυραννούσε ένας επίμονος βήχας, το στήθος του πονούσε συχνά.

Πήγε σε ένα γνωστό του γιατρό και έκανε εξετάσεις. Η καθημερινή του ρουτίνα άλλαξε δραστικά τη μέρα που ο γιατρός του τον κάλεσε να του ανακοινώσει τα αποτελέσματα. Με την ωμή ειλικρίνεια που διακρίνει τους γιατρούς στη χώρα του τον άκουσε να τού ανακοινώνει το συνταρακτικό νέο.

– Δεν μου αρέσουν οι εξετάσεις σου, φίλε, τον άκουσε να λέει. Πολύ φοβάμαι ότι δεν σου απομένει πολλή ζωή. Τα πλεμόνια σου είναι γεμάτα σκιές, η αξονική δείχνει ότι είσαι γεμάτος καρκίνο. Λυπούμαι...

Ξεροκατάπιε, ένοιωσε τη γη να φεύγει κάτω από τα πόδια του. Σχεδόν αυτόματα έκανε τη γνωστή ερώτηση.

– Γιατρέ πόσος χρόνος μού απομένει;

– Έχεις τουλάχιστον ένα χρόνο μπροστά σου να ζήσεις μια κανονική ζωή, ύστερα πια δεν σού εγγυώμαι τίποτα... Πρέπει να αρχίσεις αμέσως θεραπεία μήπως και μπορέσουμε να προλάβουμε κάτι, ίσως και να παρατείνουμε για λίγο την ζωή σου.

Ο νους του έτρεξε στα νοσοκομεία, τις επίπονες θεραπείες, το μάταιο αγώνα.

– Δεν αξίζει τον κόπο γιατρέ, τού απάντησε σχεδόν αυθόρμητα. Δεν βλέπω το λόγο γιατί να τυραννιστώ, να περάσω όσο χρόνο μού απομένει στα νοσοκομεία και να τυραννιέμαι με μάταιες θεραπείες. Καταλαβαίνω ότι το τέλος μου είναι σχεδόν σίγουρο, αλλά και αν ακόμα γίνει το θαύμα να παραταθεί η ζωή μου, θα ζήσω κάποια χρόνια αγωνίας και ταλαιπωρίας στα νοσοκομεία με μια ζωή αναμονής του τέλους χωρίς καμία χαρά. Όχι, προτιμώ να τον αξιοποιήσω καλλίτερα αυτόν τον χρόνο που μου απομένει, να πάρω σιγά σιγά τον δρόμο της επιστροφής για την πατρίδα, όπου ονειρεύομαι να με θάψουν. Δεν θα βιαστώ να φτάσω, θα κάνω κάποιο γύρω προηγουμένως να γνωρίσω τον κόσμο που δεν γνώρισα, θα προσπαθήσω να μαζέψω όσες εμπειρίες θα προλάβω, ώστε να φύγω τουλάχιστον ευχαριστημένος.

– Δική σου η απόφαση φίλε μου, δεν σου δίνω άδικο, κάνε ότι νομίζεις καλλίτερο.

Ο γιατρός σηκώθηκε από την καρέκλα του με ανακούφιση, είχε ξεπεράσει τις δύσκολες στιγμές και ένοιωθε ξαλαφρωμένος.

– Όποτε με χρειαστείς, εδώ θα είμαι, τον αποχαιρέτησε δίνοντάς του κάποια ισχυρά παυσίπονα.

– Πάρε αυτά, τού είπε, φοβάμαι ότι θα σού είναι απαραίτητα.

Ο Αλέξανδρος παρέμενε διστακτικός.

– Κάτι τελευταίο, φίλε μου. Αποτείνομαι στον φίλο, όχι στον γιατρό. Μη με αφήσεις να τυραννιστώ, όταν πλησιάσει η κακιά ώρα. Δώσε μου την ευκαιρία να διαλέξω εγώ πότε θα φύγω από τη ζωή. Ξέρω ότι υπάρχουν κάποια χαπάκια...

Ο γιατρός τον έκοψε.

– Φίλε, εγώ σπούδασα γιατρός, μην μού ζητάς να κάνω το δήμιο.

– Μα δεν σού ζητώ να κάνεις τίποτα παραπάνω απ ό,τι θα έκανες – ο μη γένοιτο– σε κάποιον πολύ δικό σου, στη μάνα σου, στην αδελφή σου.

– Δεν θα έκανα ποτέ κάτι τέτοιο, σε βεβαιώ. Με έχει προβληματίσει πολλές φορές το θέμα και έχω καταλήξει στις αποφάσεις μου. Χρησιμοποιώ τις επιστημονικές μου γνώσεις για να προσφέρω ανακούφιση στους ασθενείς μου, όχι για να τελειώνω μια ώρα αρχύτερα μαζί τους. Το μόνο που μπορώ να κάνω– και αυτό μόνο για σένα– είναι να σού δώσω τη διεύθυνση ενός «ειδικού» στην Ολλανδία που έμαθα ότι ασχολείται με αυτές τις περιπτώσεις. Δεν συμφωνώ αλλά θα το κάνω στο όνομα της παλιάς μας φιλίας.

Αυτό ήτανε! Ο Αλέξανδρος σημείωσε το όνομα και την πολύτιμη

γι' αυτόν διεύθυνση, και αποχαιρετιστήκανε και φιληθήκανε σταυρωτά, στο κάτω – κάτω παλιοί φίλοι ήτανε. Και τώρα ήρθε η στιγμή που το αποφάσισε. Ο παλιός Οδυσσέας ξύπνησε μέσα του. Θα έκανε – έστω και πολύ αργά – την προσωπική του επανάσταση. Θα άλλαζε ζωή. Θα έφευγε όσο πιο μακριά θα άντεχαν οι δυνάμεις του, θα επέστρεφε επιτέλους στην πατρίδα του την Ελλάδα... Μακριά από τον παγωμένο βορρά με την ψευδαίσθηση ότι έτσι απομακρύνεται και από τη σκληρή του μοίρα. Ούτε και αυτός καταλάβαινε πως καλυτέρευσε η διάθεσή του μόλις πήρε τις αποφάσεις του. Άλλαξε το αυτοκίνητό του αγοράζοντας ένα τζιπ της μόδας, προμηθεύτηκε χάρτες και ταξιδιωτικούς οδηγούς, ξαγρυπνούσε κάνοντας προγράμματα και σχέδια για το τελευταίο του ταξίδι, θαρρείς και το τελεσίγραφο του γιατρού τον είχε ξυπνήσει από ένα χρόνιο λήθαργο και του άνοιγε καινούργιες, ενδιαφέρουσες προοπτικές για όση ζωή του είχε απομείνει. Από μια άποψη σκεφτότανε ότι μάλλον την καλοδέχτηκε την ετυμηγορία του γιατρού. Έως τώρα δεν πίστευε σε κανένα θεό, πίστευε στην επιστήμη και στις ανθρώπινες δυνατότητες. Τώρα που αντιμετώπιζε τη σκληρή αλήθεια ένοιωσε μια αλλαγή να γίνεται μέσα του.

– Δεν είναι δυνατόν, σκεφτότανε, η μεγάλη πλειοψηφία της ανθρωπότητας να ζει με την ψευδαίσθηση κάποιας θρησκείας, να αντλεί από αυτήν ελπίδες για τη συνέχιση με άλλες μορφές της ύπαρξης μετά τον σωματικό θάνατο. Ας μην είμαστε τόσο εγωιστές εμείς οι φιλοσοφούντες άθεοι, δεν είναι καθόλου σίγουρο ότι το δίκιο είναι με το μέρος μας. Ας αρχίσω να δίνω κάποια πίστη σε αυτό που διδάσκουν οι περισσότερες θρησκείες του κόσμου. Μπορεί να έχουν κάποιο δίκιο. Τελικά, την ίδια αδυναμία που έχουν οι πιστοί να αποδείξουν την ύπαρξη κάποιου θεού, ακριβώς την ίδια έχουμε και εμείς να αποδείξουμε τη μη ύπαρξή του. Ίσως σε λίγο καιρό που θα απαλλαγώ από το σαρκίο μου, ίσως τότε μάθω την αλήθεια.

Όπως όλοι οι θνητοί, άρχισε μπροστά στο θάνατο και ο Αλέξανδρος να ελπίζει αυτό που εκείνη τη στιγμή τον συνέφερε περισσότερο.

Ανθρώπινο ήταν.

– Το είχα αποφασίσει να ξεφύγω από την πραγματικότητά μου, αλλά άλλο είναι να το αποφασίζεις και άλλο να το πραγματοποιείς. Ακούγοντας την αλλοπρόσαλλη ιστορία της Σόνιας, μια τρελή ιδέα κυριάρχησε μέσα μου. Η Σόνια λαχταρούσε να φύγει όσο και εγώ. Μέχρι τώρα διατηρούσα ένα δισταγμό να ξεκινήσω μόνος. Λαχταρούσα μια συντροφιά, αρκεί να ταιριάζανε τα χνώτα μας. Ξάφνου συνειδητοποίησα ότι η Σόνια έμοιαζε να είναι η σύντροφος που μού έλειπε. Δεν δίστασα να τής το προτείνω. Χάρηκα όταν εκείνη δέχτηκε χωρίς δισταγμό.

– Φύγαμε Αλέξανδρε, με έναν μόνο όρο. Θα είμαι ελεύθερη να κάνω ό,τι θέλω, να γνωρίσω ανθρώπους και καταστάσεις, να πλουτίσω σε εμπειρίες. Έχω μάθει να είμαι ανεξάρτητη, δεν θέλω δεσμεύσεις.

– Τής το υποσχέθηκα. Άλλωστε τήν είχα ήδη ψυχολογήσει. Ήξερα ότι η Σόνια ήθελε να ανήκει μόνο στον εαυτό της.

Ξεκινήσανε αμέσως σαν κυνηγημένοι, αφού για άλλη μία φορά αγκαλιαστήκανε και φιληθήκανε σαν παλιοί γνώριμοι –«σαν εραστές που ξανασμίγουνε»; – πέρασε από το μυαλό του η σκέψη σαν αστραπή. Συμφωνήσανε να μην σταματήσουνε καθόλου στην Κοπεγχάγη. Άλλωστε δεν είχε τίποτα το διαφορετικό να τούς προσφέρει. Καταχνιά και κρύο, άνθρωποι κουμπωμένοι και βιαστικοί στους δρόμους, κατήφεια παντού.

Η Σόνια ένοιωθε την έντονη επιθυμία να ξεκινήσουν αμέσως προς τα Νότια. Ο νους της ήτανε προσανατολισμένος προς τα εκεί σαν τη βελόνα της πυξίδας, που όσο και να τη γυρίζεις, εκείνη στρέφεται να δείξει το σημείο της γης που την τραβάει σα μαγνήτης. Εκείνος πάλι δεν έβλεπε την ώρα να φθάσει στην Ολλανδία, να βρει στο Άμστερνταμ τον ειδικό που θα τόν λύτρωνε από το άγχος ενός θανάτου βασανιστικού και επώδυνου «όταν θα έφθανε η ώρα.»

Μόνον έτσι, σκεφτόταν – έχοντας το λυτρωτικό χαπάκι στην τσέπη του – μόνον τότε θα μπορούσε να «απολαύσει» τη ζωή που τού υπολειπότανε να ζήσει. Φυσικά και δεν ανέφερε τίποτα από αυτά στη σύνοδό του. Ήταν πολύ νωρίς για τέτοιου είδους εξομολογήσεις. Άλλωστε, δεν μπορούσε να μαντέψει πώς θα αντιδρούσε εκείνη. Ίσως έπρεπε να κρατήσει το μυστικό του ως το τέλος. Την παρατηρούσε τώρα να καταβροχθίζει με όρεξη το πρωινό της, να φλυαρεί περί ανέμων και υδάτων, να σταματά μόνο για να του χαμογελάσει, να ξεσπάει σε γέλια μόλις εκείνος διακόπτοντας τις θλιβερές σκέψεις του τής πέταγε κάποιο αστείο.

— Σε ζηλεύω, τής έλεγε από μέσα του. Εσύ πάς να βρεις τη ζωή, εγώ πάω να την αποχαιρετήσω...

Το ύφος του τον πρόδωσε, η Σόνια το παρατήρησε.

— Πολύ σκεφτικό σε βλέπω σήμερα, σαν κάτι να σε τυραννάει, τού είπε αγγίζοντας τρυφερά το χέρι του.

— Δεν είναι τίποτα, έσπευσε να δικαιολογηθεί. Απλώς, ανυπομονώ και εγώ να βρεθώ σε πιο χαρούμενα μέρη.

Εκείνη δεν επέμεινε, δεν πείστηκε βέβαια, μόνο το άφησε να περάσει έτσι. Ανακουφίστηκε ο Οδυσσέας με τη διακριτικότητά της, Είχε ανάγκη μια τέτοια διακριτικότητα. Το τζιπ καταβρόχθιζε τώρα με άνεση τα ατελείωτα χιλιόμετρα, ενώ οι επιβάτες του, βυθισμένοι ο καθένας στις σκέψεις του, απολάμβαναν την απαλή μουσική που ακουγότανε από το ραδιόφωνο. Η Σόνια είχε σπεύσει να αλλάξει τη συμφωνία του Μάλερ, η οποία ακουγότανε με μία ζωηρή Λάτιν μουσική.

***

8

ΣΤΟΥΣ ΕΥΡΩΠΑΪΚΟΥΣ ΠΑΡΑΔΕΙΣΟΥΣ

Αμστερνταμ. Η πόλη έσφυζε από ζωή. Το χιόνι που έπεφτε κατά διαλείμματα είχε στολίσει τα κανάλια με ένα πέπλο φαντασμαγορικό. Από τα διάφορα γεφυράκια, που ένωναν τις όχθες, έβλεπε κανείς να κρέμονται σταλακτίτες και να τούς δίνουν μία παραμυθένια όψη. Οι δύο κυνηγοί της χίμαιρας είχαν γίνει ένα με το χαρούμενο πλήθος που σουλατσάριζε στις όχθες των καναλιών χαζεύοντας τις βιτρίνες με το ζωντανό εμπόρευμα και σχολιάζοντας τα εκθέματα.

– Μου προξενεί αηδία η ελευθεριότητα αυτού του λαού, σχολίαζε η Σόνια. Βρίσκω ότι η δημοκρατία τους έχει ξεπεράσει τα όρια της πολιτισμένης ζωής. Η εκμετάλλευση του ανθρώπου από τον άνθρωπο, με το πρόσχημα της απόλυτης ελευθερίας, βρίσκω ότι τούς έχει οδηγήσει σε ακραίες καταστάσεις. Δεν νομίζω ότι το σεξ είναι εμπόρευμα να αγοράζεται και να πουλιέται. Δεν μπορεί να ονομάζεται αυτό το πράγμα πολιτισμός. τού μιλούσε ακατάπαυστα δείχνοντάς του τη βιτρίνα με την ολόγυμνη κοπέλα να προσποιείται ότι αυνανίζεται με μία μπανάνα, ενώ τη χάζευε το φιλοθεάμον κοινό.

Ένας τερατόμορφος μελαψός τούς έφραξε ξάφνου το δρόμο. Πρότεινε με απειλητικό τρόπο τα ναρκωτικά που πουλούσε στον Αλέξανδρο, ενώ συγχρόνως έσπρωχνε το ζευγάρι προς το κανάλι. Τρομάξανε και με χίλια ζόρια απαλλαγήκανε από αυτόν και από τις απειλές του. Η Σόνια σχεδόν σε κατάσταση πανικού πρόσεξε με φρίκη ότι κανένας από τους περιπατητές δεν έδωσε σημασία. Ούτε βέβαια εκδήλωσε την παραμικρή διάθεση να παρέμβει βοηθώντας το ζευγάρι.

– Τι καλά που θα βρεθούμε στη Μεσόγειο. Όχι ότι και εκεί δεν γίνονται του κόσμου τα εγκλήματα και οι εκβιασμοί. Όμως ο κόσμος είναι διαφορετικός.Δεν προσπερνά όσους κινδυνεύουν σφυρίζοντας αδιάφορα. Συντρέχει το διπλανό του, προσπαθεί να τον βοηθήσει στη δύσκολη ώρα, είπε.

 Ο Αλέξανδρος τής χαμογέλασε πατρικά. λέγοντας:

– Συγκράτησε τις ψευδαισθήσεις σου, μικρή μου. Ο κόσμος είναι ζούγκλα, είτε στο Βορρά βρεθείς είτε στο Νότο.

Μπήκανε βιαστικά σε ένα κινέζικο εστιατόριο. Ήταν ένα από αυτά τα εστιατόρια πολυτελείας του Άμστερνταμ που έχουνε βαφτίσει Κινέζικα τα διάφορα φαγητά ανατολίτικης έμπνευσης που σερβίρουν και που εξάπτουν τη φαντασία και τη γεύση των καλοζωισμένων πελατών τους.

– Αν έτρωγαν έτσι οι Κινέζοι θα ήτανε πολύ διαφορετικός ο κόσμος, παρατήρησε ο Αλέξανδρος γευόμενος την πεντανόστιμη πάπια με μέλι που άχνιζε τώρα στο πιάτο του.

– Ας μην είμαστε σε όλα αρνητικοί, καλέ μου, τού αντέτεινε η Σόνια. Ας ζήσουμε λίγο το όνειρο που μας σερβίρουν έστω και αν αυτό δεν είναι παρά ένα ψέμα, μία χίμαιρα.

Ο Αλέξανδρος ένοιωσε ένα ξεχείλισμα στοργής για το νέο κορίτσι που έβλεπε τόσο χαρούμενο απέναντί του. Τής έπιασε το χέρι και το φίλησε τρυφερά

– Καλή σου όρεξη, κούκλα μου, να είσαι πάντοτε ευτυχισμένη, ψιθύρισε.

– Είμαι πολύ ευτυχισμένη απόψε και αυτό το οφείλω σε εσένα, ανταπάντησε.

Στο δρόμο για το ξενοδοχείο την περιέργειά τους τράβηξε ένα συμπαθητικό μπαράκι που ξεχείλιζε από κόσμο. Μπήκανε μέσα χωρίς να συνεννοηθούν καν. Ίσως να τους τράβηξε και το περίεργο όνομά του. Bulldog, έγραφε η επιγραφή στην πόρτα του. Δεν ήτανε από τα γνωστά μπαράκια που συναντά κανείς σε όλα τα μέρη του κόσμου. Πνιγμένο στο μυρωδάτο καπνό, γεμάτο με πελάτες που «ταξίδευαν» σε δικούς τους κόσμους με ύφος αποξενωμένο από το περιβάλλον, άλλοι καπνίζοντας με πάθος και εισπνέοντας το καπνό όσο πιο βαθιά μπορούσαν, άλλοι ρουφώντας με ένα καλαμάκι από τη μύτη μία άσπρη σκόνη, κάποιοι με μια σύριγγα στο χέρι. Μερικοί μιλούσαν εύθυμα και ζωηρά, άλλοι τραγουδούσαν και γελούσαν παραληρητικά, ήτανε και κάποιοι που έμοιαζαν να κοιμούνται βυθισμένοι σε ένα βαθύ κώμα. Ο Αλέξανδρος ασυναίσθητα τράβηξε τη μικρή προς την έξοδο. Όμως με έκπληξή του είδε να αντιστέκεται.

– Όχι Αλέξανδρέ μου, σ’ αυτό το ταξίδι θέλω να τα δοκιμάσω όλα, θέλω να αποκτήσω όσο πιο πολλές εμπειρίες μπορώ από τη ζωή, είπε, ενώ έστριβε δύο τσιγάρα με τη μαριχουάνα που σε μηδέν χρόνο είχε προμηθευτεί από τον πρόθυμο μπάρμαν.

Για τον Αλέξανδρο δεν ήτανε η πρώτη φορά που δοκίμαζε. Ήξερε καλά το αποτέλεσμα. Κάποιο συναίσθημα ευεξίας, μία προσωρινή «αναχώρηση» από τα καθημερινά άγχη, ίσως κάποια σεξουαλική υπερδιέγερση και, στο τέλος, ένας βαθύς σαν το θάνατο, ύπνος. Δεν τού κακοφάνηκε η ιδέα. Όσο για τη μικρή, μία και τήν έβλεπε αποφασισμένη δεν εύρισκε το λόγο να τήν εμποδίσει. Στο κάτω – κάτω, δεν τον είχε διορίσει κανείς και κηδεμόνα της... Την παρέσυρε έξω από το μπαρ. Καθίσανε σε ένα παγκάκι στην όχθη του καναλιού και τραβήξανε μερικές δυνατές ρουφηξιές από τα τσιγάρα της Σόνιας. Εκείνη παρατηρούσε τώρα τα διάφορα φωτάκια στο κανάλι να τρεμοσβήνουνε, να πολλαπλασιάζονται, να χορεύουνε τρελά μπροστά στα ζαλισμένα μάτια της. Την έπνιξαν διάφορα συναισθήματα, ένας ασυγκράτητος πόθος για τον ώριμο σύντροφό της, μία αγάπη ανάμεικτη με στοργή, μία ακατανίκητη ανάγκη να τον κάνει δικό της, να γίνει δικιά του. Κινήσανε με γρήγορο βήμα προς το ξενοδοχείο. Δεν ζήτησε το κλειδί του δωματίου της, τον ακολούθησε στο δικό του. Δεν τηρήσανε κανένα πρόσχημα. Πετάξανε χωρίς κουβέντα, βιαστικά τα ρούχα από επάνω τους. Είχε έρθει η ώρα.

Ο Αλέξανδρος είχε γνωρίσει όλων των ειδών τους έρωτες. Τον ρουτινιάρικο συζυγικό με την ανούσια σύζυγό του, τον συγκαταβατικό με τις διάφορες βεντετούλες που νομίζανε ότι έτσι θα τον παρακινούσανε να τις προωθήσει στην καριέρα τους, το βίαιο και χωρίς ταμπού έρωτα με κάποιες ξελιγωμένες κυριούλες που κυνηγούσανε απελπισμένα την ηδονή βλέποντας ότι πλησιάζουν στο τέλος της σεξουαλικής τους ζωής. Όλα αυτά τα γνώριζε καλά. Είχε δοκιμάσει τα πάντα. Ή, τουλάχιστον, έτσι νόμιζε. Όμως, εκείνο το βράδυ η μικρή τον απογείωσε σε πρωτόγνωρες εμπειρίες. Είχε το έμφυτο ταλέντο να είναι την ίδια στιγμή τρυφερή και άγρια μαζί του, ένοιωθε το κάθε χάδι της να ξεχειλίσει από απαλότητα και αγάπη και συγχρόνως να του προξενεί έναν απίθανα ερεθιστικό πόνο. Το κάθε φιλί της ήτανε και μία ερωτική εξομολόγηση, ένα μήνυμα αγάπης.

– Ο έρωτας στην αληθινή του μορφή, συλλογίστηκε.

Ο έρωτας που κάνανε ξεπερνούσε τα όρια του απλού σεξ και συνδύαζε την αγάπη, τον πόθο, την εκδήλωση συναισθημάτων, τη βιαιότητα, και, τέλος, το σαδισμό που πηγάζει από την αμοιβαία διάθεση ικανοποίησης του ενστίκτου. Εκείνο το αλησμόνητο βράδυ ο Αλέξανδρος, έστω και αργά, ανακάλυψε τί είναι και πώς εκδηλώνεται ο πραγματικός έρωτας. Τον δίδαξε με το πηγαίο ερωτικό της ένστικτο η μικρή, η καινούργια – ίσως και τελευταία – κατάκτησή του.

Το πρωί, όταν ξύπνησε, ο Αλέξανδρος αισθανότανε να είναι δέκα χρόνια νεώτερος. Η γνωστή πρωινή κούραση, η ακεφιά και το βαρύ κεφάλι, τα «κομμένα» πόδια, όλα αυτά τα γνωστά πρωινά συμπτώματα που τον τυραννούσαν από καιρό είχανε εξαφανιστεί. Δίπλα του, το αγγελούδι, απολάμβανε ακόμα την αγκαλιά του Μορφέως.

Στο πρόσωπό της ήτανε αποτυπωμένη μία απόλυτη ηρεμία. Δεν υπήρχε η παραμικρή ρυτίδα να ταράξει τη θεία αρμονία των χαρακτηριστικών της. Τήν παρατηρούσε αμίλητος και πλημμυρισμένος από ανάμεικτα συναισθήματα πατρικής στοργής και αγάπης. Η έκτη αίσθηση την έφερε στην πραγματικότητα. ένα χαμόγελο χάραξε το πρόσωπό της.

— Καλημέρα, αγάπη μου, άκουσε την κελαριστή της φωνή και φιληθήκανε στοργικά.

Δεν άργησε να επανέλθει στη σκληρή πραγματικότητα. Σήμερα έπρεπε να τελειώνει και με το βραχνά της επίσκεψης στο γιατρό, να πάει να προμηθευτεί το πολύτιμο χάπι. Θα τελείωνε και με αυτή την τελευταία δυσάρεστη εκκρεμότητα της ζωής του και μετά θα άφηνε τον εαυτό του ελεύθερο να απολαύσει ό, τι του υπολειπότανε από τη ζωή. Πήρε μία βαθιά ανάσα, μάζεψε όλο το κουράγιο του και άρχισε να ντύνεται.

— Σήμερα, αγαπούλα, θα λείψω για μια επείγουσα δουλειά. Εσύ έχεις όλη τη μέρα στη διάθεσή σου να ανακαλύψεις αυτή τη μαγική πόλη και με το φως της μέρας. Ύστερα από αυτό, σού υπόσχομαι ότι θα είμαι συνέχεια μαζί σου. Τίποτα πια δεν θα μας χωρίσει τουλάχιστον για όσο καιρό θα θέλεις να είσαι κοντά μου, στο υπόσχομαι.

Τον κοίταξε παραξενεμένη. Κάτι μέσα της έλεγε ότι δεν έπρεπε να τού κάνει ερωτήσεις.

— Θα συναντηθούμε το απογευματάκι, ς είπε αποχαιρετώντας την και εισπράττοντας για άλλη μία φορά το μαγευτικό της χαμόγελο

— Μπορώ να εξετάσω τον ιατρικό σας φάκελο;

Η κυρία που τον είχε υποδεχθεί είχε ένα σοβαρό ύφος, αλλά και ένα ευχάριστο παρουσιαστικό. Τήν παρατηρούσε καθώς εξέταζε με προσοχή τις ακτινογραφίες του, την έκθεση των γιατρών, τις αναλύσεις του, όλα τα σχετικά έγγραφα. Τον κοίταξε σοβαρή.

– Είμαστε μία φιλανθρωπική οργάνωση που θέλουμε να βοηθήσουμε τους πάσχοντες συνανθρώπους μας, άκουσε να του λέει. Δεν εκμεταλλευόμαστε καταστάσεις ούτε θέλουμε να επηρεάσουμε τους συνανθρώπους μας που έχουν πάρει με ψυχραιμία τις αποφάσεις τους. Είστε σίγουρος ότι αυτή είναι η ανεπηρέαστη θέλησή σας, ότι δεν σάς έσπρωξε κάποιος να το αποφασίσετε; Φαίνεστε ώριμος άνθρωπος καταλαβαίνω ότι έχετε πλήρη επίγνωση αυτού που πάτε να κάνετε, πρόσθεσε.

– Και βέβαια έχω πάρει με πλήρη επίγνωση τις αποφάσεις μου. Δεν θέλω η ζωή μου να έχει μια τραγική κατάληξη, ούτε έχω τη διάθεση να γίνω πειραματόζωο. Θέλω να δώσω ένα αξιοπρεπές τέλος στη ζωή μου και για αυτό απευθύνθηκα σε εσάς. Ήρθα εδώ για να με βοηθήσετε και θα σας ευγνωμονώ εάν το κάνετε.

– Εφόσον αυτή είναι η επιθυμία σας, εμείς δεν έχουμε καμία αντίρρηση να σας βοηθήσουμε, είπε η κυρία χαμογελώντας και έβγαλε από το συρτάρι κάποια έγγραφα και τα έδωσε να τα διαβάσει.

– Υπογράψτε αυτά τα χαρτιά, αφού τα διαβάσετε προσεκτικά, είπε.

Ο Οδυσσέας πήρε τα χαρτιά με ελαφρά τρεμάμενο χέρι, τα διάβασε και άρχισε να τα συμπληρώνει.

– Λυπούμαι για τη δοκιμασία που σάς βάζω, αλλά καταλαβαίνετε..., πρόσθεσε.

Τον είχε πιάσει μια ανυπομονησία, ήθελε να τελειώσει μία ώρα αρχύτερα. Υπέγραψε βιαστικά και είδε την κυρία να τού παραδίδει σε ένα κουτάκι δύο χαπάκια.

– Το πράσινο θα το πάρετε, όταν αποφασίσετε ότι ήρθε η ώρα. Μόλις αντιληφθείτε ότι βυθίζεστε σε ύπνο, μπορείτε να καταπιείτε και το δεύτερο. Λυπούμαι που δεν βρίσκω τίποτα να σας ευχηθώ, είπε.

Σηκωθήκανε σχεδόν ταυτόχρονα από τις καρέκλες τους. Ο Αλέξανδρος την αποχαιρέτησε συγκινημένος.

– Θα σάς ευγνωμονώ για το υπόλοιπο της ζωής μου, είπε διαβαίνοντας την έξοδο.

Αισθάνθηκε την ανάγκη να περπατήσει για λίγο μόνος του. Έπαιρνε βαθιές ανάσες, ενώ συχνά πυκνά ψαχούλευε την τσέπη του να ψηλαφίσει τα πολύτιμα χάπια. Σύντομα αντέδρασε. Έστρεψε τη σκέψη του στη μικρή του αγάπη και αμέσως πλημμύρισε από χαρά. Ήθελε τώρα να τρέξει κοντά της, να μην χάσει λεπτό από τη ζωή του που ήξερε ότι τώρα πια είχε αρχίσει να παίρνει αντίστροφη μέτρηση. Κάθε λεπτό από εδώ και πέρα θα τον έφερνε και πιο κοντά στο τέλος. Βιαζότανε να απολαύσει όσο μπορούσε την κάθε στιγμή της ζωής του που θα περνούσε ανεπίστρεπτα. Δεν έμοιαζε να πολυνοιάζεται για το βέβαιο τέλος του. Κοίταζε τον κόσμο που τον προσπερνούσε αδιάφορος.

– Και εσείς θα πεθάνετε, έλεγε από μέσα του. Εγώ τουλάχιστον μπορώ να αποφασίσω μόνος μου για το «πότε», ενώ εσείς θα εξακολουθήσετε να ζείτε με ένα πελώριο ερωτηματικό. Δεν βλέπω γιατί είσαστε σε καλλίτερη μοίρα από εμένα, συλλογιζόταν, στην προσπάθειά του να παρηγορηθεί και να είναι έτοιμος να αντικρίσει την καλή του με καλή διάθεση, να μην προδοθεί!

Ξανασμίξανε χαρούμενοι και ανακουφισμένοι. Νοιώθανε να έχουνε τόση ανάγκη ο ένας για τον άλλον, ώστε και ο κάθε έστω και προσωρινός χωρισμός τους δημιουργούσε κάποιο άγχος, μήπως και το όνειρο που ζούσανε ήτανε μέσα στη φαντασία τους, μήπως και δεν ξαναβρισκόντουσαν πια. Τήν έσφιγγε πάλι τρισευτυχισμένος στην αγκαλιά του, τήν χαϊδολογούσε, της ψιθύριζε ερωτόλογα.

– Αγαπούλα μου, πάμε να φύγουμε από εδώ. Το Άμστερνταμ μάς έδωσε όσα μπορούσε να μας δώσει. Ήρθε η ώρα να σε πάω σε μία από τις ωραιότερες πόλεις του κόσμου, το Παρίσι. Θυμάμαι από τα φοιτητικά μου χρόνια μια συμπαθέστατη πανσιόν. Η ιδιοκτήτριά της, δεν μπορεί θα με θυμάται, θα μας περιποιηθεί και θα φροντίσει να περάσουμε καλά. Τι λες ξεκινάμε;

– Θα έρθω μαζί σου ως το τέλος του κόσμου, είπε αυθόρμητα, ενώ το πρόσωπό της φωτίστηκε για άλλη μία φορά με εκείνο το αφοπλιστικό της χαμόγελο.

*****

9

ΠΙΣΩ ΑΠΟ ΤΗΝ ΒΙΤΡΙΝΑ

*Α*κολούθησε η γοητευτική παρισινή περιπέτεια … Περάσανε ένα ήρεμο πρωινό ξεφυλλίζοντας παλιά βιβλία στα υπαίθρια βιβλιοπωλεία στις όχθες του Σηκουάνα. Χαζέψανε τους διάφορους μποέμ καλλιτέχνες, διανοούμενους και αιώνιους φοιτητές της αριστερής όχθης και κατέληξαν στην «Coupole» για στρείδια και ένα ελαφρύ γεύμα. Η όλη ατμόσφαιρα του κόσμου, που σουλατσάριζε, τα ατέλειωτα γέλια του φοιτηταριού που γευμάτιζε φλυαρώντας αμέριμνα δίπλα τους, ο ανοιξιάτικος ήλιος του Παρισιού, όλα αυτά μαζί άλλαξαν τη διάθεση και επανέκτησαν το παλιό τους κέφι. Τίποτα δεν πρόδιδε το δράμα που παιζότανε στα άθλια γκέτο της προσφυγιάς λίγο πιο έξω από τη λαμπερή βιτρίνα της πόλης. Οι εφημερίδες και οι τηλεοράσεις διαλαλούσαν τα δράματα και τις μάχες που εκτυλίσσονταν στα «προάστια», τις φτωχογειτονιές, όπου οι λαθρομετανάστες είχανε ξεσηκωθεί και πάλευαν με τους εφησυχασμένους πολίτες των «καλών» συνοικιών. Ο Αλέξανδρος ήθελε να δει με τα ίδια του τα μάτια το δράμα που παιζότανε εκεί. Ένας απαραίτητος μεσημβρινός υπνάκος και νάτοι πάλι ξεκούραστοι και πανέτοιμοι για τις πρώτες ανιχνεύσεις στις γειτονιές που έβραζαν. Η Jasmine, η νεαρή Ελληνογαλίδα υπάλληλος της πανσιόν, όπου είχε κρατήσει δωμάτια ο Αλέξανδρος, , υποδέχθηκε χαμογελαστή στο μικρό σαλόνι και προθυμοποιήθηκε να τους ξεναγήσει στα προάστια και να τους γνωρίσει με μερικούς γνωστούς τους που κατοικούσαν εκεί. Ήτανε ντυμένη απλά, κάπως χίπικα σαν ένα κοινό κοριτσόπουλο.

– Πάμε να δούμε την άλλη όψη του φεγγαριού, είπε. Απόψε θα πάρουμε το ταπεινό μου αυτοκινητάκι, δεν θα ήθελα να προκαλέσουμε τον «άλλο» κόσμο με το πολυτελές τζιπ που έχετε, οι άνθρωποι που θα συναντήσουμε τα μετράνε πολύ κάτι τέτοια. Είναι άνθρωποι ταλαιπωρημένοι και αδικημένοι από τη ζωή, αλλά από την άλλη είναι καλοί φίλοι με αγαθή ψυχή οι περισσότεροι. Δεν θα χάσετε τίποτα να τους γνωρίσετε, πρόσθεσε.

Στριμωχθήκανε στο παρδαλά και νεανικά βαμμένο Deu Cheveau αυτοκινητάκι και ξεκινήσανε για τα «προάστια» – ο Θεός να τα κάνει προάστια δηλαδή – έξω από το Παρίσι. Μισοέρημοι δρόμοι, λίγοι διαβάτες στην πλειοψηφία τους έγχρωμοι, κάποια παιδάκια χωρίς χαμόγελο να παίζουνε με τις λάσπες και τις πέτρες, γκρίζα πελώρια κτίρια που θύμιζαν σοβιετικές πόλεις, κατήφεια και αθλιότητα.

– Δεν πιστεύω στα μάτια μου, ψιθύρισε με απογοήτευση η Σόνια. Βρισκόμαστε λίγα μέτρα μακριά από το λαμπερό Παρίσι και όμως αντικρίζουμε τέτοια κατάντια, πρόσθεσε.

– Εδώ κατοικούν οι άνθρωποι ενός κατώτερου θεού, όπως τούς αποκαλούν. Αφού ληστέψανε και απομυζήσανε οι πολιτισμένοι Ευρωπαίοι το φυσικό πλούτο από τις πατρίδες τους, τους ενθαρρύνανε να έρθουν εδώ δίνοντάς τους την ελπίδα κάποιας αξιοπρεπούς ζωής, με μόνο σκοπό να επωφεληθούν από τα φτηνά τους μεροκάματα.

– Και από τότε συνεχίζουνε να τούς εκμεταλλεύονται με κάθε τρό-

πο, να τούς στέλνουνε να πολεμήσουν και να σκοτωθούν για λογαριασμό τους σε όποιες συρράξεις ανακατευότανε η Γαλλία. Συνήθι-
ζαν να τους αμείβουν για τις χαμαλοδουλειές που τους ανέθεταν με
μισθούς πείνας, να τούς αντιμετωπίζουν με περιφρόνηση, να τούς
έχουνε αποκλείσει σε αυτά τα άθλια γκέτο και να αδιαφορούνε για
την μοίρα τους.»

Προχωρούσανε βαθιά μέσα στις άθλιες γειτονιές. Το αυτοκινητάκι
σταμάτησε μπροστά σε ένα ερειπωμένο μισοκαμμένο κτίριο.

– Αυτό το κτίριο κάηκε πρόσφατα από πυρκαγιά παρασύροντας στο
θάνατο ανήμπορους γέρους και παιδάκια. Αδιάφορη η πολιτεία το
άφησε να καίγεται για ώρα πριν σπεύσει σε βοήθεια. Το αποτέλεσμα το βλέπετε μπροστά σας. Είναι ένα μνημείο της κρατικής αδι-
αφορίας και της κάθε έλλειψης κοινωνικής φροντίδας. Αυτή είναι η
άλλη όψη της λαμπρής μας πόλης, απολαύστε την.

– Έχω κανονίσει να περάσουμε τη βραδιά μας παρέα με κάποιους
από αυτούς τους γνωστούς μου τους, ανήγγειλε η Jasmine. Μην
ανησυχείτε, είναι ήρεμοι και ευγενέστατοι. Δεν πρόκειται να σάς
κάνουν κακό. Αντίθετα, νομίζω ότι έχετε να μάθετε πολλά από αυτούς και ελπίζω να τους κατανοήσετε, είπε.

– Αχμέτ, Κατρίν η γυναίκα του, Marie η κόρη τους, Ζοζέφ ο γα-
μπρός τους.

 Η Jasmine έκανε τις απαραίτητες συστάσεις. Ανταλλάξανε διερευ-
νητικά βλέμματα και αμήχανα χαμόγελα. Η Σόνια παρατηρούσε με
κάποια επιφυλακτικότητα το περιβάλλον που δεν ήτανε ό, τι το καλλίτερο.

Το φτωχικό μπιστρό, θολωμένο από τους καπνούς των κάθε είδους
και εθνικότητος φτηνών τσιγάρων αντηχούσε από τις θορυβώδεις
συζητήσεις. Έτσι που φάνταζε μισοσκότεινο και θλιβερό στην όψη,
δημιούργησε από την πρώτη στιγμή μια περίεργη ψυχολογική κατάσταση, μια τάση φυγής, ένα σφίξιμο μέσα της. Ο Αλέξανδρος από
τη μεριά του αντιμετώπιζε την όλη κατάσταση συλλογισμένος.

– Παντού τα ίδια χάλια. Τί να κάνεις μια τέτοια νιότη που προδικάζει μία άθλια και ταλαίπωρη ζωή και ένα ακόμα πιο άθλιο τέλος, συλλογιζόταν, παρατηρώντας μερικά εξαθλιωμένα γερόντια, βρόμικα και ξεδοντιασμένα να βρομάνε φτηνό οινόπνευμα καθώς μπεκροπίναναν σιωπηλά – τα περισσότερα ξεροσφύρι – στα διπλανά τραπεζάκια. Πού και πού τσάκιζε και κάποιος από το πιοτό και έγερνε το κεφάλι του στο τραπεζάκι.

Όταν το ροχαλητό τους επέμενε να ενοχλεί τους θαμώνες παρά τις παρατηρήσεις και τα σκουντήματα των γκαρσονιών, κάποιοι όμοιοί τους ανασήκωναν και τους έσερναν έξω από το μαγαζί. Εκεί συνερχόντουσαν προσωρινά χάρις στο σοκ από την παγωμένη βραδιά και τρικλίζοντας κινούσαν για το άθλιο δωμάτιό τους στο γκέτο που κατοικούσαν.

Στρωθήκανε στο τραπέζι. Το αρνάκι που σερβίρισαν, σκαρφαλωμένο πάνω σε ένα βουνό από κουσκούς ήτανε – σε αντίθεση με την εμφάνιση του μπιστρό – νοστιμότατο και άφθονο. Το αλγερινό κρασί που το συνόδευε, δυνατό και ελαφρά γλυκό, ζέστανε την ατμόσφαιρα και έλυσε τις γλώσσες. Δεν άργησε να δημιουργηθεί μία παράξενη οικειότητα ανάμεσα στις τόσο ανόμοιες παρέες καθώς φούντωνε η συζήτηση.

– Ευχαριστούμε για την τιμή που μας κάνατε να είσαστε οι προσκαλεσμένοι μας απόψε, είπε ο γηραλέος αρχηγός της οικογένειας που πήρε πρώτος τον λόγο. Οι φίλοι της Jasmine είναι και δικοί μας φίλοι, πρόσθεσε.

Σήκωσε το ποτήρι του να το τσουγκρίσει με τους ξένους του, να καλωσορίσει. Στο κουρασμένο του πρόσωπο, το πρόωρα ρυτιδιασμένο από τις ταλαιπωρίες μιας ζωής, έβλεπε κανείς να καθρεφτίζεται μια ταπεινότητα και συνάμα μια πραότητα και μια ευγένεια που σπάνια συναντούσε κανείς στην εποχή μας. Η φωνή του ήτανε σιγανή και ήρεμη, το ύφος του πρόδιδε έναν άνθρωπο συμβιβασμένο με τη μοίρα του και αποφασισμένο να συνεχίσει αυτή τη ζωή μέχρι το τέλος της χωρίς εξάρσεις και όρεξη για επαναστάσεις και αγώνες.

– Εμείς τελειώνουμε πια τη ζωή μας και δεν τρέφουμε ούτε ελπίδες ούτε ψευδαισθήσεις να ζήσουμε καλλίτερες μέρες, είπε. Γνωρίσαμε την αθλιότητα από παιδιά, μεγαλώσαμε μέσα στην πείνα και τη λάσπη στις πατρίδες μας, κάποτε ξεκινήσαμε για εδώ με ελπίδες και όνειρα, όμως γρήγορα προσγειωθήκαμε στη νέα πραγματικότητα, συμπλήρωσε. Ζούμε εδώ και χρόνια μέσα σε αυτά τα γκέτο, δουλεύουμε εξοντωτικά για να κερδίζουμε ένα κομμάτι ψωμί, βλέπουμε να περνά η ζωή χωρίς όνειρα και προοπτικές και το μόνο που μένει είναι να περιμένουμε το τέλος μας, ένα τέλος που παρηγοριόμαστε ότι θα μας φέρει πάλι στην ίδια μοίρα με τους υπόλοιπους, τους προνομιούχους, μία και όλοι καταλήγουμε μέσα σε δύο μέτρα χώμα. Τί κι αν οι άλλοι ζήσανε μέσα σε παλάτια, τί και αν εμείς περάσαμε τη ζωή μας στριμωγμένοι όλοι μαζί σε ένα άθλιο δωμάτιο, στο τέλος – και αυτό είναι το μεγαλείο της θεϊκής δικαιοσύνης – στο τέλος οι τάφοι όλων μας θα έχουνε το ίδιο μέγεθος. Άντε να διαφέρει η ποιότητα του κουτιού όπου βάζουνε μέσα, άντε και εκείνο των άλλων να γυαλίζει περισσότερο, ας το λιώσει πιο αργά το χώμα., ας το φάνε πιο αργά τα σκουλήκια. Κάνει κάποια διαφορά;», είπε ο γέροντας με χαμόγελο πικρό... Έτσι αντιμετωπίζουμε εμείς οι γεροντότεροι τη ζωή. Όμως οι νεότεροί μας, τα παιδιά που γεννήθηκαν εδώ τα βλέπουνε τα πράγματα με διαφορετικό μάτι, κατέληξε.

Οι γυναίκες παρακολουθούσαν σιωπηλές και, κατά πως ήτανε οι νόμοι σ' αυτές τις κοινωνίες, το λόγο είχανε μόνον οι άντρες. Μία μικρή σιωπή, δυο γουλιές κρασί και ακούστηκε η θεληματική φωνή του γιου του Ζοζέφ που πήρε το λόγο. Μιλούσε ζωηρά, το ύφος του έδειχνε άνθρωπο έτοιμο να παλέψει, να διεκδικήσει ακόμα και να θυσιαστεί για τα δικαιώματά του.

– Εμείς είμαστε η δεύτερη γενιά, αυτοί που γεννηθήκαμε και μεγαλώσαμε σ' αυτό τον τόπο, πρώτοι σε υποχρεώσεις και τελευταίοι σε δικαιώματα. Δεν ανεχόμαστε πια να είμαστε πολίτες δεύτερης κατηγορίας. Δουλεύουμε σκληρά πληρώνουμε τους φόρους μας, κάνουμε το καθήκον μας απέναντι σ' αυτό που θεωρούμε δεύτερη πατρίδα μας, απαιτούμε να έχουμε τα ίδια δικαιώματα σαν ισότιμοι πολίτες. Είναι φορές που μάς θεοποιούν για τις επιδόσεις μας στο ποδόσφαιρο και στον αθλητισμό, όταν κάποιοι από εμάς κάνουμε τη Γαλλία να θριαμβεύει. Σε αυτές τις περιπτώσει, όπως και σε καιρούς πολέμου, μάς δοξάζουν οι συμπατριώτες μας σαν ήρωες. Όταν, χάρη στους αγώνες μας και τις θυσίες μας η Γαλλία θριαμβεύει, τότε και μόνο μάς θεωρούν Γάλλους και λένε ότι είναι περήφανοι για μας. Κατόπιν, όταν τα φώτα της γιορτής σβήσουν, μάς τρώει η λησμονιά. Ξαναγινόμαστε οι άθλιοι εμιγκρέδες που τους παίρνουμε τις δουλειές, που μας φορτώνουν όλα τα εγκλήματα και τις παρανομίες. Δεν λέω ότι είμαστε άγγελοι. Φτωχοδιάβολοι είμαστε που οι άθλιες συνθήκες μάς σπρώχνουν συχνά στην παρανομία. Αν οι συνθήκες της ζωής μας ήτανε παρόμοιες με αυτές των γηγενών να είστε σίγουροι ότι και η συμπεριφορά μας θα ήτανε εντελώς διαφορετική. Η υπομονή μας όμως έχει τα όριά της. Δεν θα αντέξουμε για πολύ ακόμα την αλαζονική συμπεριφορά των συμπατριωτών μας. Θα έρθει η ώρα να παλέψουμε ενάντια στα φασιστικά κόμματα των ακροδεξιών που βαλθήκανε να μας εξοντώσουν, θα υπερασπιστούμε τη θρησκεία μας, τα ήθη και έθιμά μας, θα απαιτήσουμε το μερίδιό μας σε μία ισάξια ζωή. Η Γαλλία είναι πια και δική μας πατρίδα, δώσαμε πολλά, έχουμε τώρα και εμείς τις απαιτήσεις μας. Αν η κοινωνία δεν συνέλθει έγκαιρα από το εφησυχασμό της θα μάς βρει αντιμέτωπούς της. Θα παλέψουμε με ότι όπλα βρούμε μπροστά μας για να πετύχουμε τους σκοπούς μας. Τι και αν μας βαφτίσουν κομμουνιστές, εγκληματίες, παράνομους. Εμείς θα παλέψουμε. Θα σεβαστούμε τους νόμους, μόνον όταν οι νόμοι μας αναγνωρίσουν τα ίδια δικαιώματα με τους υπόλοιπους πολίτες. Μας περιμένουν σκληροί αγώνες, τιμωρίες, φυλακίσεις, βασανιστήρια. Θα αντιδράσουμε, θα έρθουν μέρες βίας και σκληρού αγώνα, αυτή η όμορφη πόλη που περικυκλώνεται από την ασκήμια και την εξαθλίωση, να με θυμηθείτε, θα μετατραπεί σε κόλαση των προνομιούχων. Θα αγωνιστούμε με όλα τα μέσα και στο τέλος είμαστε σίγουροι ότι θα νικήσουμε, όπως νικούν πάντοτε αυτοί που έχουν το δίκιο με το μέρος τους.

Άστραφτε και βρόνταγε ο Ζοζέφ, ενώ η γυναίκα του με μειλίχιο ύφος προσπαθούσε να τον συγκρατήσει. Η ατμόσφαιρα εξακολουθούσε να βαραίνει. Η Jasmine είχε τώρα σηκωθεί.

– Πάμε Ζοζέφ να γνωρίσουμε λίγο και τις στιγμές της χαλάρωσης, της διασκέδασής σας. Μη νομίσουν οι ξένοι μας ότι τούς έφερα σε κέντρο αιμοβόρων επαναστατών. Πάμε να ακούσουμε την καταπληκτική μουσική σας να γνωρίσουμε λίγο τον πολιτισμό σας.

Ο Ζοζέφ χαμογέλασε και πρόθυμος καβάλησε το μηχανάκι του μαζί με τη Marie και προηγήθηκε. Τους οδήγησε στο στέκι τους, εκεί που διασκεδάζανε τους καημούς τους. Φέρανε, χωρίς να το παραγγείλουνε στα αρσενικά της παρέας, από έναν ναργιλέ και μοσχοβόλησε ο τόπος από το μυρωδάτο καπνό. Η Σόνια, σκασμένη στα γέλια, παρακολουθούσε τον Αλέξανδρο που προσπαθούσε να μιμηθεί τη στάση και τις χειρονομίες των υπολοίπων. Ρουφούσε και φύσαγε στο ναργιλέ του χωρίς αποτέλεσμα. Το πρόσωπό του είχε γίνει κατακόκκινο από την προσπάθεια και είχε μία γκριμάτσα όλο απογοήτευση όσο δεν ένοιωθε τον καπνό να μπαίνει στα πνευμόνια του.

– Μοιάζεις τέλειος μουσουλμάνος, ένα σαρίκι σού λείπει και λίγη μπογιά στο πρόσωπο και δεν θα ξεχωρίζεις καθόλου, αστειεύτηκε η Jasmine.

Η παρέα ξέσπασε στα γέλια. Ξάφνου έπεσε σιωπή διέκοψε τα ενθουσιώδη χειροκροτήματα. Εμφανίστηκαν, σοβαροί οι μουσικοί και άρχισαν να ανεβαίνουν στη σκηνή. Ήρεμοι και με κάποια μεγαλοπρέπεια στις κινήσεις τους πήρανε τις θέσεις τους και η μυσταγωγία άρχισε. Μακρόσυρτες γεμάτες πάθος και παράπονο μουσικές κατέκλυσαν την αίθουσα. Το λαούτο, το τουμπελέκι, ο ζουρνάς ξύπνησαν στο ακροατήριο απωθημένες θύμησες από τις μακρινές του πατρίδες. Οι νεώτεροι ένιωσαν το αίμα τους να βράζει, οι παλιότεροι βυθίστηκαν στις αναμνήσεις τους, άλλοι άρχισαν να κουνιούνται στο ρυθμό της μουσικής να τη συνοδεύουν με παλαμάκια, να σιγοψιθυρίζουν τν σκοπό. Εμφανίστηκε και η τραγουδίστρια με το ντέφι της μέσα σε ενθουσιώδη χειροκροτήματα. Έπιασε να τραγουδάει τον αμανέ. Τα αισθησιακά τσακίσματα του λυγερού της κορμιού εναρμονίσθηκαν με την παραπονιάρικη φωνή της στα ανεβοκατεβάσματά της, δημιουργώντας ένα μεθυστικό σύνολο που συνέπαιρνε το ακροατήριο. Το μεθυσμένο ντέφι της ξεπεταγότανε ξέφρενο στριφογυρίζοντας μέχρι το ταβάνι και δεν αργούσε να προσγειωθεί με θαυμαστή ακρίβεια στο παχουλό της χεράκι που άρχιζε να το χτυπάει ρυθμικά. Πανδαισία! Το ρακί ανακατευότανε με τα ξαναμμένα αίματα, δημιουργώντας ένα σύνολο εκρηκτικό στο ακροατήριο. Πολλών παλικαριών τα μάτια γυαλίζανε παράξενα, οι χειρονομίες τους είχανε ζωηρέψει, ο χορός εκείνων που ξεσηκώθηκαν, μη αντέχοντας στην ακινησία, είχε κάτι το άγριο, το πρωτόγονο, το ζωώδες. Λυγίζανε τα πόδα μέχρι το πάτωμα. Το χτύπαγαν με πάθος με τις παλάμες τους και ύστερα σαν ελατήρια εκτινάσσονταν να φτάσουν το ταβάνι, να πλησιάσουνε το θεό τους. Η ατμόσφαιρα είχε τώρα κάτι το άγριο, ηλεκτρικά κύματα τη διαπερνούσαν, οι φυσιογνωμίες προδίνανε τα απωθημένα αισθήματα που ξυπνούσαν, μία σπίθα έλειπε για να ανάψουν τα μπουρλότα. Ο Αλέξανδρος αντάλλαξε ανήσυχες ματιές με την Jasmine. Εκείνη πήρε το μήνυμα. Έγνεψε στην παρέα ότι ήτανε καιρός να φύγουνε. Είχανε πια σηκωθεί και ανταλλάζανε τα ατελείωτα ανατολίτικα φιλιά , όταν ένας εκκωφαντικός θόρυβος τράνταξε συθέμελα την αίθουσα που σχεδόν ταυτόχρονα γέμισε από καπνούς. Πανικός. Δύο αυτοσχέδιες βόμβες μολότοφ είχανε σκάσει στην είσοδο του μαγαζιού. Ο κόσμος άρχισε να ποδοπατιέται προσπαθώντας να διαβεί τη στενή έξοδο του υπογείου προς τον καθαρό αέρα και την σωτηρία. Όμως η έξοδος ήτανε φρακαρισμένη από κορμιά σκορπισμένα στο πάτωμα που άλλα σφαδάζανε και βογκούσανε και άλλα είχανε μείνει ακίνητα και πλημμυρισμένα από αίματα. Ο Ζοζέφ προσπαθούσε να ανοίξει δρόμο με το ένα του χέρι ενώ με το άλλο κρατούσε το ματωμένο πλευρό του. Ύστερα ήρθαν οι πρώτες φλόγες να αποτελειώσουν το κακό. Ίσως από κάποιο θαύμα η παρέα βρέθηκε ξάφνου στον καθαρό αέρα. Ο δρόμος είχε μετατραπεί σε πεδίο μάχης. Οι φλεγόμενοι σκουπιδοτενεκέδες δημιουργούσαν ένα περίεργο, ένα μακάβριο ντεκόρ. Απέναντι από την έξοδο, σε απόσταση ασφαλείας, πίσω από αυτοσχέδια οδοφράγματα, διακρινόντουσαν «οι εχθροί», κάποια φασιστοειδή βδελυρά υποκείμενα με κουρεμένα κεφάλια, με πέτσινα μπουφάν και μπότες με σκουλαρίκια και χαλκάδες στη μύτη. Αλαλάζανε και πετάγανε τις προσφιλείς τους βόμβες «μολότοφ» στο πανικόβλητο πλήθος. Τα μάτια τους βγάζανε σπίθες από το μίσο. Οι βρισιές και οι βλαστήμιες πέφτανε βροχή.

– Βρωμοξένοι, ξεκουμπιστείτε πίσω στις πατρίδες σας, κραυγάζανε παθιασμένα.

Ο Ζοζέφ όρμησε εναντίον τους. Τον ακολούθησαν και άλλοι πολλοί που πήρανε φαλάγγι τους φασίστες. Κάποια μαχαίρια αστράψανε μέσα στη νύχτα. Κάποια ρόπαλα κάνανε την εμφάνισή τους. Η μάχη ανάμεσα στους γεμάτους μίσος εχθρούς φούντωσε. Καθυστερημένα, ως συνήθως, έφτασε και η αστυνομία. Άρχισε να χτυπά αδιακρίτως «επί δικαίων και αδίκων» προσπαθώντας να επιβάλει την ειρήνη. Ένα γκλομπ βρήκε τον Ζοζέφ στο κεφάλι. Το παλικάρι έπεσε για να μην ξανασηκωθεί πια. Πριν αφήσει την τελευταία του πνοή πάνω στην άσφαλτο, ακούστηκε να σαρκάζει με την ξενική του προφορά

"Liberte, egalite, frat..."

Η φωνή του έσβησε μαζί με τη ζωή του πριν προλάβει να αποτελειώσει τη φράση του. Οι φασίστες εξαφανίστηκαν στο λεπτό. Απέμειναν κάποια λίγα απομεινάρια από τους μετανάστες, που, αφού ξυλοφορτώθηκαν, οδηγήθηκαν στο κρατητήριο για ανακρίσεις και συμπληρωματικό ξύλο.

Κάποια λιγοστά νοσοκομειακά παραλάβανε τους τραυματίες για περίθαλψη. Κάποια οχήματα της πυροσβεστικής σβήσανε τις φωτιές σε αυτοκίνητα και σκουπιδοτενεκέδες, άλλα καθαρίσανε τον έρημο πια δρόμο από τα αίματα και τα καμένα σκουπίδια. Έτσι έληξε το επεισόδιο και αποκαταστάθηκε η τάξη...Οι ρεπόρτερ είχανε μαζέψει εγκαίρως τις κάμερές τους και συνηθισμένοι από τέτοιες καταστάσεις είχανε σπεύσει να εξαφανιστούν. Με φρίκη η Jasmine διάβασε την επομένη στις εφημερίδες την κυβερνητική ανακοίνωση.

– Επεισόδια σημειώθηκαν σε ένα κέντρο διασκεδάσεως μεταναστών στα Προάστια. Μεθυσμένοι μετανάστες παρέα με άλλα κακοποιά στοιχεία προκαλέσανε κάποιους πολίτες που πήγανε να διαμαρτυρηθούν για τα έκτροπα. Ακολούθησαν μικροσυμπλοκές μέχρι που επενέβη η αστυνομία. Ένας αρχηγός των μεταναστών βρέθηκε νεκρός, χτυπημένος στο κεφάλι από έναν σύντροφό του που πιθανόν να τον εξέλαβε για αντίπαλο μέσα στην παραζάλη της συμπλοκής. Μερικοί τραυματίες μεταφέρθηκαν στα νοσοκομεία με επιπόλαια τραύματα. Τα επεισόδια έληξαν αργά το βράδυ με τη σωτήρια παρέμβαση της αστυνομίας...

Έβρεχε το άλλο πρωί. Ήταν η γνωστή παριζιάνικη ψιλή και αθόρυβη βροχή που μούσκευε ως το κόκαλο τους αραιούς διαβάτες. Δεν έβλεπες ουρανό, στη θέση του κυριαρχούσε μία γκρίζα μάζα από σύννεφα που δίνανε τον τόνο τους στην γενική κατήφεια. Τα χτεσινοβραδινά επεισόδια δεν εντυπωσίασαν κανέναν στο κέντρο της λαμπρής πόλης. Μόνο στα προάστια της εξαθλίωσης οι φτωχομετανάστες συγκεντρωμένοι παρέες – παρέες συνωμοτούσαν απειλητικά. Ο σπόρος της διχόνοιας είχε γιγαντωθεί για καλά στις ψυχές τους. Η λέξη μίσος και εκδίκηση ήτανε στα στόματα όλων. Αλλά και οι φασίστες είχανε σύσκεψη και σχεδιάζανε καινούργιες κινητοποιήσεις. Η αστυνομία ήτανε σε επιφυλακή να παρέμβει και πάλι όπου χρειαζότανε. Η κυβέρνηση ανακοίνωσε κάποια χλιαρά μέτρα «ανθρωπιστικού» χαρακτήρα μπας και κατευναστούν κάπως τα πνεύματα. Πλησίαζαν άλλωστε εκλογές και οι μετανάστες είχαν αρχίσει να πληθαίνουν επικίνδυνα. Οι ψήφοι τους είχαν αρχίσει να γίνονται απαραίτητοι για την ισχνή κυβερνητική πλειοψηφία. Όλα αυτά την ώρα που οι εφησυχασμένοι πολίτες σπεύδανε μέσα στο γκρίζο πρωινό να πάνε στις δουλειές τους. Τίποτα δεν είχε αλλάξει, τα επεισόδια είχανε περάσει πια στα ψιλά των εφημερίδων. Οι διάφοροι σεφ σχεδιάζανε τα βραδινά μενού στα πολυτελή τους εστιατόρια. Περισσεύανε πάντα οι προνομιούχοι να επιδειχθούν με την παρουσία τους, να απολαύσουν τις εξεζητημένες γεύσεις στα χορτασμένα στομάχια τους. Οι disco εξαερίζονταν από τη βραδινή κάπνα και μπόχα, ενώ κάποιες κατσουφιασμένες έγχρωμες καθαρίστριες καθαρίζανε από τις βρομιές της χθεσινοβραδινής κραιπάλης. Η ζωή στο Παρίσι συνεχιζότανε...

– Πάμε να φύγουμε, αγαπούλα. Είπα. Ανυπομονώ να γνωρίσεις την πατρίδα μου την Ελλάδα. Ελπίζω εκεί τα πράγματα να είναι καλλίτερα, πιο ειρηνικά.

Και μόνο με αυτή την προοπτική, το κέφι τους έφτιαξε απότομα.

***

10

ΑΝΑΠΟΛΩΝΤΑΣ ΤΟΝ ΜΑΪΚ

– Ωστόσο παρ όλη την ευτυχία που μου χάριζε η φυγή μου και η συντροφικότητα του Αλέξανδρου, δεν έπαυα να έχω τις μεταπτώσεις μου, σκεφτόταν η Σόνια. Δεν ήτανε μπορετό να ξεγράψω τον Μάικ από το μυαλό μου, ιδίως τώρα που έχοντας φθάσει στην Ελλάδα είχα την προαίσθηση ότι βρισκόμασταν πολύ κοντά. Η σκέψη του έφερνε μελαγχολία. Ήτανε οι ώρες που με κυριαρχούσε μια βαθιά κατάθλιψη, συνέχισε. Κατάθλιψη! Τα είχα μελετήσει τα συμπτώματα και τα αναγνώριζα κάθε μέρα στον εαυτό μου. Πολλές φορές κυριαρχούσε μέσα μου μια διαπίστωση ανικανότητας για κάθε τι, ένα πάθος συχνά έντονο μια απελπισία που τη συνόδευε η βαθιά θλίψη. Κάτι τέτοιες ώρες δεν με ενδιέφερε τίποτα το δημιουργικό. Έπεφτα σε μία κατάσταση ολοκληρωτικής αδράνειας. Και οι στιγμές της κατάθλιψης κατέληγαν στην ανάμνηση της αναπάντεχης περιπέτειας που σε παρέσυρα καλέ μου Μάικ. Με κατακλύζουν οι τύψεις που σε εγκατέλειψα αμέσως μετά το κοινό μας «έγκλημα», σα να σε παρέσυρα στον πάτο ενός πηγαδιού και το σκέπασα με ένα καπάκι να μην ακούω τις κραυγές σου. Θύμωσες, το ένοιωσα αμέσως όταν σού πρότεινα να διακόψουμε. Κυριάρχησε μέσα σου το τρομαχτικό συναίσθημα της προδοσίας. Απαρνήθηκα ένα κοινό μέλλον μαζί σου. Ήτανε σε σένα ακατανόητο ότι δεν θα ήμουνα πια κοντά σου, όταν θα μελετούσες τον κόσμο, έναν κόσμο όπως τον ονειρεύτηκες με τις εξάρσεις της χαράς και της δυστυχίας του. Είναι αλήθεια ότι φαινομενικά είμαστε ένα ταιριαστό ζευγάρι που είχε τα ίδια γούστα, τις ίδιες αντιδράσεις γέλιου και συγκίνησης, τις ίδιες επιθυμίες. Πόσο όμως απατούν τα φαινόμενα... Καλέ μου Μάικ, ομολογώ ότι αποφάσισα να χωρίσουμε εκείνη τη νύχτα του πανικού, όχι τόσο λόγω της αποτρόπαιης πράξης που νομίζω ότι σε παρέσυρα – άλλωστε εγώ βρισκόμουνα εκείνες τις ώρες σε μία φάση πλήρους αναισθησίας – όσο γιατί ένοιωσα κοντά σου ένα είδος κορεσμού. Ξάφνου ένοιωσα να πλήττω δίπλα σου, να πνίγομαι από την επιπόλαιη αισιοδοξία σου που σε έκανε να βλέπεις τη ζωή μόνο από την καλή την εύθυμη πλευρά της. Δεν άντεχα πια τον τόσο ρομαντισμό σου και τις χίμαιρες ότι εμείς οι δύο θα διορθώσουμε όλα τα κακά του κόσμου. Ήμουν σίγουρη ότι δεν θα ένιωθες την ανάγκη μου για πολύ, ότι θα εύρισκες παρηγοριά στο διάβασμα, στην ποίηση που λάτρευες, στη συγγραφή βιβλίων που ήτανε ανέκαθεν το απωθημένο σου. Ύστερα, σιγά σιγά θα υποχωρούσες στις διάφορες προτάσεις που θα σου έκαναν τα θηλυκά του κόσμου, έτσι καλοστεκούμενος και φαινομενικά καλλιεργημένος που έδειχνες ότι είσαι. Χάρηκα που έμαθα ότι εδώ στον τόπο που σε παρέσυρα αφιερώθηκες στα νιάτα. Ήθελες, λέει, να τους διδάξεις λογοτεχνία και ποίηση, ψυχολογία και ανθρωπιά, ό,τι ευγενέστερο έβγαζες από μέσα σου.. Η ιδέα σε είχε ενθουσιάσει, την ημέρα δίδασκες και τη νύχτα προετοιμαζόσουνα μελετώντας το μάθημα της επομένης. Ξέχασες τον τεμπέλη εαυτό σου, ονειρεύτηκες ανώτερες σπουδές, πτυχία και διδακτορικά, έκανες καινούργια όνειρα. Αγαπούσες τους μαθητές σου και πολλοί σε αγάπησαν με τη σειρά τους. Τους συνόδευες συχνά στις καφετέριες και τα στέκια τους νοιώθοντας συνομήλικος τους. Τους ξάφνιαζες με τις ιστορίες σου προσπαθώντας να ψυχολογήσεις τις αντιδράσεις τους. Είχες πολλές κατακτήσεις και προτάσεις αρχικά από τις πρόωρα μεγαλωμένες μαθήτριές σου, αργότερα από πολλές από τις μητέρες τους που εύρισκαν πρόφαση την έννοια για τα παιδιά τους για να καταλήξουν να τραβήξουν το ενδιαφέρον σου για εκείνες. Όμως αυτά σε άφηναν αδιάφορο εσένα. Το ενδιαφέρον σου είχε στραφεί αποκλειστικά στην αφοσίωσή σου για τα παιδιά. Όχι ότι το λίμπιντό σου σε άφηνε αδιάφορο. Το ικανοποιούσες και με το παραπάνω χωρίς να καταβάλλεις καμία προσπάθεια. Βεβαίως, ήσουνα ανίκανος να δημιουργήσεις έναν πραγματικό δεσμό. Η κάθε σου κατάκτηση είχε αξία μόνο για όσο διάστημα σού προσέφερε κάποια σεξουαλική ικανοποίηση, μετά σε έπιανε ένα συναίσθημα φυγής, το οποίο συνόδευε η ανάγκη μιας καινούργιας κατάκτησης. Παρ όλα αυτά, όχι χωρίς κάποια τύψη, μάθαινα ότι εγώ σού είχα παραμείνει αναντικατάστατη. Στενοχωριόμουνα που δεν ένοιωθα την ίδια ανάγκη με εσένα, παρόλο που αυτή η σκέψη συχνά με κολάκευε. Ανυπομονούσα να ξανασυναντηθούμε, να σε γνωρίσω στον Αλέξανδρο. Ίσως αυτός να μπορούσε να σε βοηθήσει κάπως. Σε κάποια φάση της σεξουαλικής σου ζωής ένιωσες μια βαθιά μεταστροφή. Αποφάσισες ότι δεν ήθελες πια να προσφέρεις ηδονή στην όποια ευκαιριακή ερωτική σου σύντροφο. Σου αρκούσε να νιώθεις μόνον εσύ την ευχαρίστηση. Ήθελες μόνο να παίρνεις χωρίς να προσπαθείς να δώσεις. Καλέ μου εγωιστή, ρομαντικέ, αιθεροβάμονα Μαϊκ, δεν σου κρύβω ότι απόψε σέ έχω πολύ επιθυμήσει. Ελπίζω σύντομα να ξανασμίξουν οι δρόμοι μας, είπε η Σόνια, τελειώνοντας αυτό το μακρόσυρτο μονόλογο.

ΜΕΡΟΣ ΔΕΥΤΕΡΟ

ΛΑΟΥΡΑ

11

ΚΟΥΤΣΟΜΟΥΡΑ BLUES

Ήτανε μια παραξενιά της κυρά Μυρσινούλας, ένα «χούι», όπως το λένε στην πατρίδα της. Αναλογιζότανε ότι αυτό το δημιούργησε η έλλειψη ανθρώπινης επαφής από την οποία συχνά υπέφερε.

Όχι ότι έπασχε από μοναξιά. Διευθύντρια, μαγείρισσα, σερβιτόρα, λαντζιέρισα και λογίστρια ήτανε στο μικρό παραθαλάσσιο ταβερνάκι της. Μόνο που ο κόσμος που πήγαινε και ερχότανε και αποτελούσε την πελατεία της συνήθως θεωρούσε αρκετό να περιοριστεί σε ένα «Καλησπέρα σας» και ένα «καληνύχτα σας» πριν ρωτήσει τα στερεότυπα: «Τι καλά έχουμε απόψε» και πριν ζητήσει, τέλος, το λογαριασμό.

Άντε, και οι πιο συχνοί πελάτες, θέλοντας να δείξουν κάποια οικειότητα με την αφεντικίνα – πράγμα που νομίζανε ότι ανυψώνει κάπως το κύρος τους, κυρίως όταν «συνοδευόντουσαν» από κάποια τρυφερή ύπαρξη–, άντε να επεκτείνανε την κουβέντα τους και με καμιά ρητορική ερώτηση του τύπου «πώς πάνε οι δουλειές» ή «από υγεία καλά» πριν αρχίσουν να διαλέγουν τραπέζι και, φυσικά, χωρίς να περιμένουν κάποια απάντηση.

Έτσι η κυρά Μυρσινούλα υποδεχότανε και καληνύχτιζε τους πελάτες της χρόνια τώρα, ζώντας σε ένα περιβάλλον με αρκετό κόσμο χωρίς αυτό να περιορίζει το συναίσθημα της απόλυτης μοναξιάς και έλλειψης κάθε ανθρώπινης επαφής. Απέκτησε, λοιπόν, και εκείνη το χούι να ονομάζει τα πιστά της ζωάκια με ανθρώπινα ονόματα και να εξομολογείται σ' αυτά τους καημούς της, πιάνοντας μαζί τους κουβέντα, όταν αργά τα βράδια απέμενε ολομόναχη αυτή και ο γιος της ο «Αχμάκης», αυτή και το βουνό τα βρόμικα πιάτα, το βουνό τα αποφάγια και η γεμάτη υπολείμματα ψαριών αυλή της. Ο γιος της, δυστυχώς, γεννήθηκε «Αχμάκης», δηλαδή με ελαττωματικό το γεμάτο καλοσύνη μυαλό του, όταν ένα βράδυ μεθυσιού και απελπισίας τον φύτεψε στα σπλάχνα της ο μακαρίτης ο καπετάνιος άντρας της.

Ήτανε τότε που διαλύθηκε η κουρασμένη μηχανή του καϊκιού του, όταν διαπίστωσε ότι το φτωχικό του κομπόδεμα δεν έφτανε για την αγορά καινούργιου μοτοριού καταδικάζοντας τον πια σε μόνιμη αργία.

Να πάει παραγιός σε άλλο καΐκι, δεν το καταδεχότανε αυτός, καπετάνιος πράγμα. Τα γεράματα και τα αρθριτικά δεν άφηναν περιθώριο για καινούργια ξεκινήματα. Έτσι αφέθηκε έρμαιο του κισμέτ του, της κακής του μοίρας και ανέθεσε στην «κυρά» όλες τις ευθύνες του νοικοκυριού και του μαγαζιού.

Θα το θυμάται για πάντα εκείνο το βράδυ της απελπισίας η Μυρσινούλα, όταν εκείνος μεθυσμένος και απαρηγόρητος, έψαξε να βρει προσωρινή ανακούφιση στην αγκαλιά της, όταν φύτεψε μέσα της το μεθυσμένο και γεμάτο απογοήτευση, το αδυνατισμένο από την ηλικία σπέρμα του, όταν μέσα της συνέλαβε την ανήμπορη ύπαρξη του «Αχμάκη» της.

Λένε, και είναι συνήθως αλήθεια, ότι κάτι τέτοια παιδιά γεννάνε μέσα μας μια μεγάλη στοργή, ότι τα αγαπάμε περισσότερο και από τα «καλά» παιδιά μας, κι ας φέρνουν μαζί τους την απογοήτευση και την καταστροφή.

Ο καημένος ο Αχμάκης, παιδί καλοσυνάτο και εργατικό, με ένα μόνιμο αμφιλεγόμενο χαμόγελο αποτυπωμένο στο χαζό του πρόσωπο, προσπαθούσε όσο μπορούσε να παίξει ένα ρόλο στη ζωή της κι ας μην μιλούσε, ας έβγαζε ένα μικρό γρύλισμα για απάντηση, ένα γρύλισμα που η κυρά Μυρσινούλα είχε μάθει να το ερμηνεύει, να τού απαντά, να συνομιλεί κατά ένα τρόπο μαζί του.

Βοηθούσε την κατάσταση, όπως μπορούσε ο Αχμάκης. Σερβίριζε τους πελάτες, αδιαφορούσε για τα πρόστυχα πειράγματά τους, δεν έδιδε σημασία στις αθώα αδιάντροπες απορίες των μικρών παιδιών. Με άλλα λόγια ήτανε σιωπηλός και χαμογελαστός και με τις ίδιες πάντα, σαν καλοκουρδισμένου ρομπότ κινήσεις του, «έβλεπε τη δλιά του».

Ξυπνούσε αχάραγα κάθε αυγή και μπαρκάριζε παραγιός στον Καπτάν Στρατή. Η Ανατολή τον εύρισκε να σηκώνει με τα στιβαρά του μπράτσα τα δίχτυα αδιαφορώντας για τα κρύα και τις τρικυμίες, «πάντα γελαστός …και γελασμένος» όπως έλεγε και το αγαπημένο του τραγούδι.

Και θριάμβευε ο Αχμάκης, όταν αργά τα πρωινά γύριζε στη μάνα του με τις σακούλες γεμάτες σπαρταριστή κουτσομούρα, πληρωμή σε είδος για τους νυχτερινούς του κόπους. Αυτή η κουτσομούρα σε λίγες ώρες θα τσιτσίριζε στο τηγάνι ή στα κάρβουνα της Μυρσινούλας και θα εξασφάλιζε το φτωχικό μεροκάματο της οικογένειας γεμίζοντας τις κοιλιές των θαμώνων και αναγκάζοντάς τους να βάλουν το χέρι στην τσέπη.

Τέλος, ο Αχμάκης, παρ όλο που δεν μπορούσε να το εκδηλώσει, είχε ένα πλούσιο εσωτερικό κόσμο, μια ψυχούλα γεμάτη καλοσύνη και αγάπη, αγάπη για τους ανθρώπους, για τη φύση, για τα τραγούδια και τα πανηγύρια. Βέβαια, η κυρά Μυρσινούλα δεν τον πολυάφηνε να τρέχει σε πανηγύρια, μια και εκεί κάποιοι υπάνθρωποι δεν αργούσαν να τον μεθύσουν «για πλάκα» και να γελάνε με τα τρελά καμώματά του. Πίστευε ο καημένος ότι τα γέλια των διαφόρων, ήτανε γέλια θαυμασμού για τα αστεία καμώματα του μεθυσιού του και δώσ' του και γρύλιζε και έκανε αστείες χορευτικές φιγούρες.

Τέτοιες στιγμές η δόλια η μάνα του έσπευδε να τον συμμαζέψει και σχεδόν με το ζόρι να τον κλείσει στο δωμάτιό του.

Ήτανε μικρό αλλά συμπαθητικό το ταβερνάκι τους. Την αυλή του την έγλυφε το κύμα, τα καΐκια δένανε σχεδόν κολλητά στα τραπέζια, να χαζεύουνε οι θαμώνες τους ψαράδες που ξεψαρίζανε τα δίχτυα, να ξερογλείφεται και να διαμαρτύρεται το γατομάνι, όταν οι ψαράδες έδειχναν αδιαφορία στις επίμονες εκκλήσεις του, να σκοτώνονται οι γλάροι στα μακροβούτια μόλις κάποιο ψαράκι πεταγότανε στο πέλαγος.

Μοναδικό στολίδι του η ταμπέλα που φιγουράριζε κρεμασμένη κάθετα στο δρόμο να αναγγέλλει στους πελάτες ότι εδώ είναι, φτάσανε. Την ταμπέλα είχε φιλοτεχνήσει ο ντόπιος ζωγράφος. Στη μία πλευρά είχε ζωγραφίσει τον Αλέκο στην πιο νωχελική του πόζα, στη μέση υπήρχε η επιγραφή «Οικογενειακό κέντρο η Κουτσομούρα», ενώ στην άλλη άκρη έβλεπε κανείς ζωγραφισμένη μια λαχταριστή κουτσομούρα σε επιβεβαίωση του τίτλου του μαγαζιού. Χάρη σε αυτή την ταμπέλα, αλλά και χάρη στο πορτραίτο του μακαρίτη καπετάνιου, τον οποίο επίσης είχε φιλοτεχνήσει και φάνταζε στο καλλίτερο σημείο του μαγαζιού, ο ζωγράφος είχε εξασφαλίσει την επ' αόριστον δωρεάν διατροφή του στο ταβερνείο.

Μάλιστα το πορτραίτο του καπετάνιου ήτανε τόσο πετυχημένο,

ώστε – παρ όλα τα μυγοχέσματα και τα τηγανόλαδα που αιωρούνταν στην ατμόσφαιρα και είχανε δημιουργήσει μία πατίνα απάνω του,– φάνταζε σαν αντίκα και να τράβαγε τα βλέμματα κάποιων νεόπλουτων πρωτευουσιάνων.

Η Κυρά Μυρσινούλα βαρέθηκε στο τέλος να αρνείται τις συνεχείς εκκλήσεις για πώληση του μαγαζιού και, φοβούμενη και το «βάσκανο οφθαλμό», μετέφερε τον «καπετάνιο της» στο μικρό τους υπνοδωμάτιο να τού διηγείται τους καημούς της, όταν πεθαμένη από την κούραση έπεφτε επιτέλους να κοιμηθεί.

Τα ζωάκια με τα ανθρώπινα ονόματα, ήτανε, λοιπόν, η μόνη συντροφιά της Μυρσινούλας. Πρώτος και καλλίτερος ο πελώριος άσπρος γάτος της, ο Αλέκος, Γάτος με σχεδόν ανθρώπινο σε μέγεθος κεφάλι, με σχεδόν ανθρώπινη αντίληψη και προσωπικότητα. Άσπρος, κάτασπρος τις σπάνιες φορές που το τρίχωμά του δεν ήτανε λεκιασμένο από τηγανόλαδα, με μάτια παράταιρα – ένα πράσινο και ένα γαλάζιο – καταπώς ήτανε το γνώρισμα της μακρινής καταγωγής του από την Άγκυρα, βασίλευε και πρόσταζε όλο το μικρό ζωικό βασίλειο της ταβέρνας.

Όταν ο ήλιος έπιανε να δύει και να αποχαιρετά με εκείνα τα απίθανα χρώματα τη διέλευσή του από το νησί, όταν οι φωτιές στην ταβέρνα ανάβανε και οι πρώτες κουτσομούρες άρχιζαν να αποχαιρετάνε σιγοτραγουδώντας στο τηγάνι το μάταιο τούτο κόσμο, η Μυρσινούλα ένιωθε το πρώτο βελούδινο γαργάλισμα στα πρησμένα από την ορθοστασία και τα γεράματα πόδια της. Είχε έρθει η στιγμή να απαιτήσει και ο Αλέκος το μερδικό του από τη νυχτερινή ευωχία. Όταν τα χάδια του δεν εύρισκαν ανταπόκριση, όταν η κυρά του προσπαθούσε να τον διώξει με μικρές κλωτσιές να φύγει από την κουζίνα – μην πουν κάποιες μίζερες πελάτισσες ότι το μαγαζί ήτανε ακάθαρτο – το βελούδινο γαργάλημα εξελισσόταν σε απαιτητικό νιαούρισμα μέχρι που η Μυρσινούλα απαυδισμένη πέταγε προς την αυλή την πρώτη κουτσομούρα που εύρισκε μπροστά της να πείσει το απαιτητικό ζώο να απομακρυνθεί.

Κανένα από τα υπόλοιπα ζωάκια, η Μάρω η κολοβή, για άγνωστη αιτία αγριόγατα ,σύντροφος ερωτική και περιστασιακή του Αλέκου, ο Μανόλης, ο ψωραλέος από την ψαροφαγία κοπρόσκυλος, ο Παύλος, ο μοναχικός πελεκάνος, το Λενιώ, η Όλγα, η Κατίνγκω, οι αλανιάρες κότες που παχαίνανε το καλοκαίρι για να νοστιμίσουνε τη σούπα και το μερακλίδικο φθινοπωρινό πιλάφι, κανείς τους δεν τολμούσε να αγγίξει την πρώτη κουτσομούρα της βραδιάς, μια και δικαιωματικά ανήκε στον Αλέκο. Εκείνος πήγαινε να καταβροχθίσει την κουτσομούρα με αργά νωχελικά βήματα, σαν αριστοκράτης πελάτης που δεν καταδέχεται να δείξει λιμασμένος πέφτοντας με τα μούτρα στο φαΐ.

Ήξεραν τα ζωάκια ότι κάποτε ο Αλέκος θα χόρταινε και τότε θα ερχότανε η σειρά τους να γευθούνε τα αποφάγια που έριχναν από φιλοζωία τα παιδάκια των θαμώνων την ώρα που εκείνος ανέβαινε χορτάτος και μεγαλοπρεπής στα κεραμίδια να αρχίσει να ξερογλείφεται γουργουρίζοντας ηδονικά σαν να εξυμνούσε την αμέριμνη ζωή των γάτων, σα να ειρωνευότανε τη γεμάτη άγχη ζωή των ανθρώπων.

Υπαρχηγός στο βασίλειο των ζωντανών ήτανε ο Παύλος, ο πελεκάνος. Βρέθηκε μια μέρα να κροταλίζει στο μόλο, αυτός και η σύντροφός του, σα να είχαν έρθει από το πουθενά. Κάποιο γείτονες διηγήθηκαν, για να τους δώσουν κάποιο κύρος, ότι ήρθαν *πετώντας* από τη Μύκονο, ότι ήτανε νόθοι απόγονοι του φημισμένου Πέτρου.

Αλλά αυτά τα μυστήρια των πουλιών, κανείς δεν μπορεί να τα ξέρει. Εγκαταστάθηκε, χωρίς να ρωτήσει κανέναν, το ζεύγος των πελεκάνων εκεί στο μόλο, σένα καλυβάκι όπου έβαζαν οι ψαράδες τα δίχτυα τους, και όλη μέρη βαδίζανε με το κουτσό τους βήμα – σαν ξεγοφιασμένες κυράτσες – πάνω κάτω στη μικρή προκυμαία κροταλίζοντας τα πελώρια στόματά τους και σκοτώνοντας την ώρα τους – συχνά με κανένα συζυγικό καβγαδάκι– μέχρι να ακουστεί το μοτόρι από το καΐκι του καπτάν Στρατή που γύριζε από το ψάρεμα. Τρέχανε τότε στις δέστρες του καϊκιού και περιμένανε με χαρούμενη ανυπομονησία να πετάξει ο καπετάνιος κάβους.

Μόλις ο *παραγιός*, ο Αχμάκης, σιγουράριζε το καΐκι, πηδούσανε, πρώτος ο Παύλος, η σύντροφος του στη συνέχεια, να γευτούνε ένα μικρό μέρος από τα κόπια των ψαράδων. Άλλοτε πάλι, όταν την κυρία του έτρωγε η ρουτίνα της καθημερινότητας και άρχιζε τη γκρίνια, ο Παύλος την έπαιρνε και κάνανε μερικές μέρες διακοπών σε κάποιο διπλανό λιμανάκι να αλλάξουνε τον αέρα τους.

Ώσπου κάποια μέρα ο Παύλος γύρισε μόνος. Μερικοί παρεξηγήσανε στην αρχή το σοβαρό του ύφος, άλλοι τον εύρισκαν μελαγχολικό έτσι που ατένιζε με τις ώρες σιωπηλός τα πέλαγα και τους ουρανούς. Φοβήθηκαν ότι τον πείραξε η μοναξιά, φοβόντουσαν μήπως μαραζώσει από μελαγχολία.

Όμως τίποτα από αυτά δεν συνέβη. Μάλλον ο Παύλος απολάμβανε τις στιγμές της μοναξιάς του μακριά από πελαργίσιες μουρμούρες, γρίνιες και καβγάδες. Συνέχισε, λοιπόν, την αμέριμνη ζωή του ασυντρόφευτος και εφησυχασμένος και αυτός, κάνοντας παρέα με τα άλλα γεροντοπαλίκαρα, τον Αχμάκη, τον Αλέκο και τον Μανόλη.

Τρίτος στη ιεραρχία ο Μανόλης, ο σκύλος. Μυστήριο βέβαια τί μπορούσε να γύρευε ένας σκύλος στην ψαροταβέρνα. Το πολύ κάποιο κοψίδι κάθε Πάσχα και Χριστούγεννα, κάποιο υπόλειμμα από λαδωτήρι σαγανάκι, το χωνευτικό των θαμώνων, όταν αυτό δεν χώραγε άλλο στις πρησμένες από τα καλαμαράκια, τα χταποδάκια και ,κυρίως, τις κουτσομούρες κοιλιές τους.

Είχε ψωριάσει ο Μανόλης – φυσική συνέπεια της ψαροφαγίας των σκύλων – μια και η λαιμαργία του δεν τον άφηνε να αδιαφορήσει και για τα αποφάγια των ψαριών, αυτά που ο φίλος του ο Αλέκος τού παραχωρούσε με τη χουβαρδοσύνη του χορτασμένου. Το τρίχωμά του, τούφες– τούφες, δεν ήτανε βέβαια το μοναδικό στολίδι στο αδικημένο από τη φύση παρουσιαστικό του.

Το χοντρό του σώμα, που με το ζόρι στηριζότανε σε κάτι αδύναμα κοντά και λυμφατικά ποδαράκια, η τεράστια σε μήκος ουρά του, που αντίθετα σε κάθε φυσικό νόμο κατάφερνε και κουνιότανε ζωηρά και ρυθμικά μόλις το παράταιρο κεφάλι του με τα πεσμένα αφτιά αντιλαμβανότανε την ύπαρξη κάποιας τροφής που προοριζότανε για εκείνον, όλα θαρρείς και τα είχε διαλέξει η πλάση για να συμβολίσουν αυτό που λέμε «το τελευταίο καλούπι του θεού». Ευτυχώς ή δυστυχώς δεν υπήρχε εκεί κοντά καμία σκυλίτσα να γίνει αφορμή να φροντίσει ο Μανόλης την εμφάνισή του. Έτσι κι αυτός είχε περιορίσει τα ιδανικά της ζωής του στην καλοφαγία και – όταν δεν βρισκότανε εις άγραν τροφής – στον χωρίς τέλος ύπνο.

Όπως δεν υπήρχαν σκυλίτσες στην περιοχή, άλλο τόσο δεν υπήρχαν και νεαρά κορίτσια. Οι λίγες κοπέλες του χωριού, όπως και τα αγόρια, μόλις άνοιγαν τα φτερά τους, έτρεχαν στις πολιτείες να σπουδάσουν και να βρουν μια καλλίτερη τύχη. Έτσι και ο Αχμάκης, σαν τον Μανόλη κι αυτός, ζούσε ασυντρόφευτος προς μεγάλο καημό και στενοχώρια της μανούλας του. Σκεφτότανε η έρμη τί θα απογίνει ο Αχμάκης της όταν εκείνη έκλεινε μια μέρα τα μάτια.

Αποφάσισε, λοιπόν, πάνω στην απελπισία της να φροντίσει την υγεία της, να γιάνει τα ποδάρια της που όλο και πρηζόντουσαν, να κοιτάξει την πίεσή της που συχνά «ανέβαζε» και έφερνε ζαλάδα και βουητό στο κεφάλι της.

Πήγε σένα πελάτη της γιατρό να δώσει φάρμακα, να πει πόσα χρόνια απέμεναν ακόμα να περάσει πάνω στα τηγάνια της. Και, φυσικά, απάντηση στο ερώτημά της δεν πήρε. Μόνο συστάσεις έκανε ο γιατρός. Είπε να αδυνατίσει, να μην κουράζεται, να μην στενοχωριέται για τίποτα.

– Σάλια μπάλια δέκα τσβάλια, απεφάνθη η κυρά Μυρσινούλα, δείχνοντας ότι δεν καλάρεσαν οι συστάσεις του γιατρού. Αδιαφόρετα σπουδάζειν και δαύτοι μόνο η θιός ξέρ, συνεπέρανε και συνέχισε τη ζωή της όπως και πρώτα.

***

12

ΤΟ ΔΩΡΟ ΤΗΣ ΘΑΛΑΣΣΑΣ

Κάπως έτσι περνούσαν τα χρόνια στην ξεχασμένη– γι' αυτό και ειρηνική και αμέριμνη– αυτή γωνιά της γης με αποτέλεσμα να μεστώνουν οι μικρότεροι και να γερνούν όλοι οι μεγαλύτεροι, – άνθρωποι και ζωντανά – οι κάτοικοι της ψαροταβέρνας. Η υγεία της κυρά Μυρσινούλας πήγαινε προς το χειρότερο μια και τώρα στα παλιά συμπτώματα είχανε προστεθεί και οι γνωστοί γεροντόπονοι.

Ο Αχμάκης είχε πια μεστώσει και λύγιζε σίδερα, όταν τον βασάνιζαν τα βράδια οι ανεκπλήρωτες ερωτικές επιθυμίες του, ο Αλέκος παρατηρούσε πολύ ενοχλημένος το τρίχωμά του να χάνει τη γυαλάδα του και να αρχίζει να μαδάει, ο Παύλος είχε πάψει τα ατελείωτα σουλάτσα του και μόνο η θέα του καϊκιού του Καπτάν Στρατή τον έκανε να αποφασίσει να κάνει κάποια βήματα. Όσο για τον Μανόλη, τον ξεδοντιασμένο και με ξασπρισμένη μουσούδα Μανόλη, ας αφήσουμε καλλίτερα τις περιγραφές.

Κυρίως όμως το πρόβλημα της αποκατάστασης του Αχμάκη παρέμενε πρόβλημα και για εκείνον, αλλά φυσικά και για τη Μυρσινούλα. Μπορεί να το εξομολογιότανε κάθε βράδυ στο πορτραίτο του μακαρίτη, μπορεί και να παρακαλούσε όλο της το εικονοστάσι, όμως μάταια, λύση δεν φαινότανε πουθενά ώσπου...Εκείνη την αυγή ο μαΐστρος λυσσομανούσε και η Μυρσινούλα είχε τις αντιρρήσεις της για την ψαρευτική εξόρμηση του καϊκιού. Ο καπετάν Στρατής ξύπνησε μέσα στην νύχτα, βλαστημώντας όταν ένοιωσε την άγκυρα να ξεσέρνει, και αφού μάζεψε τα μπόσικα κοιτούσε μελαγχολικά τα στοιχειά της φύσης να παλεύουνε.

– Δεν είναι για να βγούμε απόψε, μονολογούσε. Φοβάμαι μην πάθουμε καμιά ζημιά. Ας περιμένουν οι κουτσομούρες. Μέχρι αύριο δεν θα αδειάσει δα η θάλασσα, σιγοψιθύριζε.

Ο Αχμάκης, πιστός στο καθήκον, καθότανε δίπλα του με την αμεριμνησία του ανθρώπου που δεν είχε καμιά ευθύνη για αποφάσεις. Καθότανε απλώς εκεί να φυσολογιέται από το μαΐστρο, έτοιμος να εκτελέσει κάθε εντολή του καπετάνιου.

Λύσσαγε ο μαΐστρος «καρεκλάτος», που λένε. Σήκωσε κάποιες καρέκλες του μαγαζιού και τις έστειλε να χορεύουν στο διπλανό χωράφι. Προσπαθούσε – και έμοιαζε να μπορεί να το πετύχει – να ξεκολλήσει τον τσίγκο που σκέπαζε την αποθηκούλα του ταβερνείου.

Κυριαρχούσε παντού με τη μανία του και αυτή η κυριαρχία του έμοιαζε να τον μεθά, να τού δίνει κουράγιο να φυσά όλο και δυνατότερα. Ξάφνου από μακριά φάνηκε το καταδιωκτικό του λιμεναρχείου. Είχε αναμμένα όλα του τα φώτα και με τον προβολέα του έμοιαζε να στέλνει κάποιο σήμα στο καΐκι. Πλησίασε αρκετά και ακούστηκε ο τηλεβόας του να απευθύνεται στον καπετάν Στρατή, νικώντας ακόμα και το ουρλιαχτό του μαΐστρου.

– Καληώρα καπετάν Στρατή. Έλα να βοηθήσεις, πήραμε σήμα SOS από ένα δουλεμπορικό που έμεινε ακυβέρνητο εδώ στο έμπα του κόλπου. Κινδυνεύουν άνθρωποι να πνιγούν, έλα να βοηθήσεις, κα-